Reunion
A NOVEL

by
TAMARA TILLEY

REUNION

By Tamara Tilley

Library of Congress Cataloging-in-Publication Data is on file at the Library of Congress, Washington, DC.

ISBN 10: 0692124276
ISBN 13: 978-0692124277

This book is a work of fiction. Names, characters, places, incidents, and dialogues are either products of the author's imagination or used fictitiously. Any resemblance to actual events or locales or persons, living or dead, is entirely coincidental.

Cover design: Design 7 Studio
Cover images: Shutterstock

ARCHER
PRESS

iii

Dedicated to Kathy Cornford

You encouraged me in my early years of writing
and convinced me I had something to offer.
Though you are no longer with us,
I know this story held a special place in your heart.
You are greatly missed.

♥

Acknowledgements

To Walter—my incredible husband—You encourage me every step of the way, even when it means time away from you.
I love you ♥

To my family, friends, and readers—Thank you for encouraging me and nudging me on. Your reassurance fuels me to tackle each new project.

To Michele Nordquist, Charlene Ponzio, and my amazing mom, Nancy Archer—Thank you for the many hours you spend polishing my stories. I could not do it without you.

To Scott—Your covers are the bow on the package.
Thank you

To my Savior—I pray others will see Your love, Your grace, and Your forgiveness in the stories You've given me.

ONE

"Wow! Is that who I think it is?"

Sarah Jenkins looked up from the reunion registration table and followed Melissa's gaze to the gorgeous woman exiting the elevator.

She watched as Ashley Trent glided across the polished tile floor. Her black halter-style dress outlined her trim figure, while her blond hair fell in soft waves across her exposed shoulders. Sarah scrutinized every detail of Ashley's appearance, looking for the slightest hint she'd been unable to defy the aging process. But as always, Ashley Trent looked as perfect now as she did back in high school twenty-five years ago. Her winning smile and golden tan looked natural, unlike some of the other women who showed up with Botox enhanced lips and sprayed on glows.

Sarah subconsciously pushed her vibrant red hair behind her shoulders and adjusted her I.D. tag identifying her as student body president class of '93. She and Melissa—the class vice-president—had the best seats in the house to critique the members of their graduating class, at least those brave enough to attend the reunion. They enjoyed dissecting everyone who stepped off the elevator, pointing out receding hairlines, facelifts, bad hair plugs, and expanding waistlines. The class of '93 was a walking billboard advertising the lengths people went to in order to stop the hands of time.

But then there was Ashley Trent, looking just like she did twenty-five years ago.

"She seems to have held together nicely," Melissa whispered as she and Sarah continued to watch Ashley walk the length of the banquet hall.

"Please," Sarah snapped, "who does she think she's kidding? I can spot a bottle blond a mile away. And where did she buy that dress? The junior prom section? I hate a woman who refuses to dress her age."

"Well, I think she looks great. If I had toned arms like hers and a figure to match, I certainly wouldn't hide it under long sleeves and camouflaging geometrics."

"Come on, Melissa, she's probably wearing Spanks from her armpits to her ankles."

"Even if she is, you have to admit she looks pretty amazing."

Sarah gave Melissa a darting look, then turned back to watch as Ashley approached the registration table.

Ashley tried to exude confidence while her insides twisted with uncertainty. She immediately recognized the two women staring at her from the registration table, and almost lost her nerve.

Sarah Cummings had been class president and one of the most popular girls in school. Of course, that was because she spent more time with the football team than they spent with their coaches. She and Ashley had never gotten along, mainly because Sarah was mean, vindictive, and always had to be the center of attention. Melissa Turner—the class vice-president and Sarah's loyal minion—wasn't much better. The quintessential airhead, Melissa did Sarah's bidding to stay on her good side and keep her "top girls to date" status.

Ashley slowed her steps as she focused in on Sarah, feeling a twinge of satisfaction to see that time had not been overly kind to her. Gravity had attacked the voluptuous figure she showcased in high school, and her wrinkle-free face was stretched so tight she had no choice but to smile.

"Ashley Trent," Ashley stated as she stood before the table.

"Well of course you are," Sarah said in a sugary sweet tone as she extended Ashley's name tag, complete with her senior year cheerleader picture on it. "I would recognize you anywhere. But . . . correct me if I'm wrong, I believe this is the first time you've attended a reunion. I don't remember seeing you at any of the others, and I most definitely would have remembered."

Ashley smiled, ignoring the coldness in her tone. "Sarah Cummings, right? How nice to see you again."

"Well, it's Sarah Jenkins now," she corrected Ashley with a raised brow.

"That's right. You married Jimmy Jenkins after graduation." Ashley remembered Jimmy all too well. He pursued her relentlessly their entire junior year. He was good-looking and the first-string quarterback, but his party antics and persistent flirting were major personality flaws.

"Well, it was nice seeing you again." Ashley turned, but before she could make her exit, Jimmy Jenkins plopped down in the chair next to his wife, a drink in his hand.

"Come on, Sarah, when is this shindig going to get—" When Jimmy looked up and saw Ashley, he stopped mid-sentence. After taking an indulgent look, he smiled. "Wow! I can't believe it. If it isn't Ashley Trent, the hottest girl in school."

Jimmy's obnoxious comment earned him a stabbing elbow from his red-faced wife.

"Ouch!" He turned to her and glared. "You can retract your claws, Sarah. I gave up *that* hunt years ago." He looked at Ashley with a lecherous grin. "You might have taken me off the market, but nothing says I can't enjoy the scenery."

Ashley watched Jimmy's drink slosh over the rim of his glass as his eyes traveled from her face to her breasts, then down the length of her dress. From the expression on Sarah's face, her husband's leering did not go unnoticed. Twenty-five years after high school and he hadn't changed a bit. Jimmy was still drinking and flirting. Marriage hadn't changed him in the least.

Ashley couldn't help but feel a twinge of pity for Sarah.

"Jimmy, why don't you make sure dinner is on schedule." Sarah said in a sharp, bitter tone.

"Oh, back off, Sarah, you know my bark is worse than my bite." Jimmy stood, a smirk on his lips. "See you around, Ashley. Maybe you can save a dance for me. You know . . . for old-times' sake." Jimmy walked away leaving an awkward silence in his wake.

Sarah cleared her throat as she shuffled papers in front of her. "Dinner starts in forty-five minutes. The number on your badge coincides with the table you will be dining at. Hope you enjoy your evening."

Ashley knew Sarah's good wishes were only out of courtesy and to save face in front of Melissa. She read Sarah's body language loud and clear. It said, 'back off.' A warning Ashley didn't need. She had no intention of spending time with Jimmy Jenkins. Not even one dance.

Walking into the crowded ballroom, Ashley immediately felt overwhelmed by the names and faces from her past. Her heart raced as panic set in.

What am I doing here?
This was a stupid idea!

She took a step back, feeling the need to slip out as easily as she had slipped in. But then she heard her name. She turned to the left and saw Julie Moore—one of her cheer teammates—frantically waving her arms in an effort to get her attention. Standing next to Julie was Christy Clark and Heather Jones. Her three closest friends in school.

Pasting a smile on her face, Ashley made her way across the room. After the squealing died down, and they all exchanged hugs, Ashley's friends introduced her to their significant others. Then, the assault of questions she had braced herself for began. Ashley avoided pointed questions and responded to others with vague, ambiguous answers. Ashley could tell Christy and Heather had already made quite a few trips to the bar, so it wasn't difficult to dodge their questions. Besides, she peppered them with plenty of questions of her own. When the band started playing the classic '90s tune "Jump", by Kriss Kross, Christy and Heather dragged their dates onto the dance floor, leaving only Julie for Ashley to contend with.

Julie leaned in close to Ashley with a mischievous smile on her face. "So, what do you think of Christy's date?"

"He seems nice," Ashley replied, not sure where Julie was going with her question.

"He's a hired escort. I bet he's not even thirty."

"What happened to Joe Marsh? I thought they were going to get married."

Julie laughed. "They did. Right after graduation but divorced less than a year later. Christy moved to New York to work on her acting career and became an informercial spokesperson. She's rolling in the dough and living the good life. She swore off marriage and instead dates guys looking to break into the business. They use her for her contacts, and she uses them for . . . well, you know." Julie turned to Ashley. "Hey . . . didn't you move to New York after high school?"

"Yeah, I was there for a brief time, but believe me, it wasn't as good to me as it was to Christy." Ashley laughed, trying to keep the mood light. When she saw another question forming on Julie's lips, she quickly cut her off. "How about Heather? She and her husband look happy."

"Oh, they are. It's true what they say, third times a charm." Julie chuckled.

"You mean—"

"Yep. Marriage number three and counting. But this one might actually last. Darren is good for Heather. He's willing to keep her in the lap of luxury and put up with her five kids. She'd be stupid to walk away from him."

Ashley didn't miss the cynicism in her friend's voice and assumed there was a reason behind it. "What about you, Julie? Are you married?"

Her friend shrugged and tossed her mousy brown hair over her shoulder. "I gave marriage a shot. Had two kids, a dog, a house in the 'burbs. It was good while it lasted. Then Tom told he didn't want to be married anymore. But what he really meant was, he didn't want to be married to *me* anymore. The week our divorce was final, he ran off to Bermuda and married his secretary."

"I'm sorry, Julie. That had to be rough."

Again, Julie shrugged as if it was no big deal. "It wasn't so bad. California law gave me half of everything. I took him to the cleaners and collected a tidy sum in child support. He got what he deserved, and I got everything else." She smiled and took a swig of her drink, but Ashley could tell her bitter tone was a coverup for the hurt she must've felt.

When the song ended, Ashley watched as Christy and Heather made their way back toward her and Julie.

"Look, I need to make a call," Ashley said quickly. "I'll be back in a minute."

"You better be. You still haven't told me why you went to New York."

"No problem, I'll catch up with the three of you when I get back."

Ashley hurried to the open doors on the far end of the ballroom. She walked across the expansive patio, clung to the wrought-iron rail, then let out the breath she was holding. A light breeze blew across her face, taking strands of her hair with it. Pushing them behind her ears, she looked out over the balcony. The view was spectacular, but it was lost on her.

What am I doing here? She lectured herself once again. *What did I think it would accomplish?* Ashley realized too late she'd made a monumental mistake. When she saw the Internet pop-up listing upcoming high school reunions, she thought it was a sign. *No, you were grasping at straws.*

She paced the length of the patio, milking her hands, knowing she would have to walk back through the ballroom in order to leave.

Hey . . . didn't you move to New York after high school? Julie's question taunted Ashley, stirring up memories she had suppressed long ago.

No! I'm not the same person I was back then. I'm stronger. Better. I survived, and I don't need to explain myself to these people.

She stopped her pacing and took a deep breath, once again holding onto the patio railing for support. Starring at the shimmering lights of the city, she gathered the strength she would need to walk back through the ballroom and leave the past behind.

She turned to leave but couldn't move.

There, in the doorway, stood Austin Taylor.

TWO

"Hello, Austin," Ashley whispered, even though the emotion welling inside her made it difficult to speak.

"I can't believe you're here!" Austin rushed to her side and pulled her into an embrace.

Ashley breathed in his signature cologne—familiar after all these years—then took a step back.

Austin quickly let her go. "I'm sorry. I shouldn't have done that. It's just . . ." he shook his head, "I looked everywhere for you when I got back to the states, but you just disappeared—vanished into thin air. What happened, Ashley? The last thing you told me was that you were going to New York on a business trip with your dad. The next thing I know, your house is up for sale, and no one knows where you are. What happened?"

"It's complicated." Ashley fiddled with the silver clasp on her evening bag, avoiding eye contact, not wanting to see the unanswered questions in his eyes.

"Well, maybe we could sit down and *un*-complicate things."

When Ashley dared to look into Austin's piercing hazel eyes, she was completely mesmerized. *He hasn't changed at all.* He still had the slight scruff on his neck she used to stroke, and his broad shoulders and sturdy chest exuded confidence. He radiated charisma the minute he walked into a room. Just as she remembered.

"What is it, Ashley?" He stepped forward, reaching for her hand. "Have I changed that much?"

His touch was like an electric shock, causing Ashley to drop her handbag. When Austin bent to retrieve it, it gave her a few seconds to compose herself.

I thought this was what I wanted. A chance to explain. But I can't. It's in the past. Where it should stay.

"Austin, I—"

"There you are." A beautiful blond glided across the patio to Austin's side and hooked her arm through his.

Ashley was speechless, the air surrounding them swallowed by an unseen vacuum.

"They're getting ready to serve dinner," the young woman said, casting a look in Ashley's direction.

"Okay, I'll be right there." Austin patted her hand where it rested on his forearm before she walked away.

He turned back to Ashley, but she averted her eyes. "I'd better find my seat. I'm sure we can talk more later." She quickly walked away, masking her disappointment with a smile.

How foolish she was to think Austin would have gone twenty-five years without finding himself the perfect wife. Perfect definitely described the blue-eyed blond who had attached herself to him like a string to a kite. *My gosh, Austin, she looks half your age. I never would've thought* . . . she shook her head. It didn't matter. She had no right to judge him.

Not stopping at the table that coincided with the number on her badge, Ashley kept walking . . . through the ballroom . . . into the elevator . . . and out into the parking lot.

Disorientated when she reached the sea of cars, Ashley pressed the button on her key fob and hurried down the aisle where the headlights flickered. When she reached for the door handle of the over-sized truck, a hand grasped her shoulder from behind. Startled, Ashley spun around to see Austin standing behind her.

"Ashley," Austin gasped, trying to catch his breath, "where are you going? I thought we were going to talk."

Unable to make eye contact, Ashley fidgeted with the keys in her hands. "Austin, I was wrong to come tonight. I don't know what I was thinking. It's obvious you have someone special in your life, and I have a very special man in mine. The past is the past, and I think it would be best to leave it there."

When Ashley chanced a glance at Austin, she saw hurt and betrayal in his eyes. But it didn't matter; she needed to leave. "I'm sorry, Austin."

She got into her extended cab truck, started the engine and roared out of the parking place. Ashley willed herself not to glance in the rear-view mirror. She didn't want the look of disappointment on Austin's face to be the last memory she would carry of him in her mind and heart forever.

Driving home, tears streaming down her face, memories of Austin played like a cinematic scrapbook in Ashley's mind. Her senior year had been magical because of him. Austin had made her feel special. Loved. He'd been her knight in shining armor, her chance at a happily ever after. But she had never told him about the ugliness in her life—the emotional and psychological abuse caused by her father. She had promised herself time and time again that she would tell Austin, explain to him the things she'd done, how she'd compromised herself for the sake of gaining her father's love. But she never did. It was too hard. And though Ashley knew Austin loved her, she was afraid the spell would be broken once he found out the things she had done. Unfortunately, her happily ever after came crashing down around her one night in New York City.

That night changed her life forever.

Her fairytale ending was not to be.

Ashley sobbed as she drove home, the road ahead of her a blur of cars and lights. "I only wanted to protect you, Austin. I couldn't stand to see you get hurt. That's why I left," she sobbed out loud. "Just like I am now."

What was I thinking going tonight? I can't go back. It will never be the same. She brushed the tears from her eyes, but it was no use. They continued to fall. "I never wanted to hurt you, Austin. I loved you. I've always loved you."

THREE

The second Ashley turned onto the long dirt driveway that led to her house, she took a deep calming breath. Wiping away the last of her tears, she sniffled. *This is where I belong. This is where my heart is.*

She walked into the darkened house and was met by an overwhelming silence. Glancing at her watch then at the clock on the wall, she realized it wasn't even nine o'clock yet. *You told C.J. you wouldn't be home until later. He has every right to be out with his friends.*

Ashley trusted C.J., that wasn't the problem. It was his friends she didn't like. His cowboy buddies liked to drink and carouse until they were falling-down drunk. Although C.J. assured her he knew his limitations, she still felt pangs of worry whenever he was out with them. After all she had been through, Ashley could not bear the thought of losing C.J., too.

Dragging herself upstairs, she decided to take her worries about C.J. and her confusing feelings for Austin, and soak them in a nice, long, hot bath. As she lay in the tub with her eyes closed, Ashley was transported back to her senior year.

Austin Taylor was an All-American running back as well as a pitcher on their championship baseball team. However, it wasn't his popularity that intrigued Ashley. And even though his gorgeous hazel eyes, rugged features, and athletic prowess made the other girls at school flip over him, it wasn't his good looks that attracted Ashley. It was the person inside.

Austin had been driven and intense when he participated in sports, but friendly to everyone when he wasn't competing. He was a great guy. Always polite. Always looking out for the other guy. He talked with her about subjects he knew she was interested in, and always made a point of crossing her path sometime during the day. But the afternoon he stopped to ask her out, she had been shocked. After all, he was the big man on campus, and she was just . . . well, she was a nobody.

Ashley had laughed many times remembering their first date.

A double date with Mark, one of Austin's teammates, had sounded safe enough. But when he and his date decided to get some beer and head for the peninsula to park, Ashley thought for sure it would be both their first and last date. It hadn't mattered how attracted she was to Austin, there was only one reason people went to the peninsula, and Ashley wasn't about to let that happen; not even with Austin Taylor.

Austin had apologized profusely—insisting he had no idea what Mark had planned—and promised he would fix it.

And he had.

Instead of going to the peninsula, Austin had Mark drop them off at Ashley's house. It had been the weirdest *non-date* she'd ever had. No dinner. No movie. Not even dancing. Instead, they had talked on her front porch for hours. It had been magical—until her father broke the spell and called her in for the evening.

Ashley could still remember standing at her front window and watching Austin walk down the driveway. She knew then and there, she was in love.

If only I had stood up to my father. If I hadn't been so determined to win his love, my life would've been so different.

Ashley's childhood was a train wreck.

A personal nightmare.

When she was only three-years-old, her mother died of cancer. Her father—a self-proclaimed workaholic—had no time for her, so he shipped her off to live with her aunt. Four years later, when her Aunt Janie died in a tragic auto accident, Ashley was once again without a home. Though her father considered sending her to boarding school, in the end, he decided to let her come back home. Ashley was so excited. For once, she felt loved by her dad. That is, until he introduced her to Miss Karen Ewing, her new nanny and housekeeper.

Karen would be the first of many.

By the time Ashley was ten, she realized the women hired to take care of her and the house were not really nannies. They were just the latest in a long line of women pursuing a relationship with her father. They always started out nice, thinking they had to win over Ashley in order to stay in her father's good graces, but they soon found out how little he cared about her. After that, they were all the same; harsh and manipulative. They would verbally abuse Ashley, expect her to do the housework, and threaten her into submission it she didn't. Eventually, they realized her father was only using them and would leave, or he would grow tired of them and let them go. Either way, he always had another woman waiting in the wings.

When Ashley was twelve and watched the latest *nanny* pack up and leave, she convinced her father she was old enough to take care of herself. She made her own meals, kept the house clean, and even did the laundry. It was tiring, but it was better than having just one more woman move into her house and treat her like trash. It was the last of the nannies but not the revolving door of women.

Ashley never told anyone what was going on at home, not even her closest friends. A few times they asked why she didn't have sleepovers, but she simply explained that her father worked long hours and expected a quiet house when he got home at night. They accepted her excuse without question. In fact, to the outside world, Ashley appeared to be growing up in the lap of luxury. Her father was all about appearances, so she always had new clothes representing the latest trends. And at Christmas and Easter, when school was on holiday, she traveled to places like Vail, New York City, Chicago, even Paris. But what her friends didn't know was she seldom saw anything more than the inside of a hotel suite. Her father would hire a hotel babysitter while he and his latest fling went out on the town. Ashley didn't care. The less time she spent with her father the better. He didn't love her or even care about her. She was nothing more than a failed acquisition he felt obligated to see through to completion.

But then things changed.

When Ashley turned sixteen, her father began to take an interest in her. She should have known he had ulterior motives, but her need to gain his affection clouded her thinking. When he arranged for her to intern at his company during summer break, she was over the moon. She finally felt like a person of value, someone worth his time. The weekend before she started work, he took her to an exclusive boutique and spent thousands of dollars on a new wardrobe for her. She wondered if some of the dresses were a bit short for a business office, but he assured her with a smile. *'You're young, and these are the latest styles. You'll look great.'* After hitting a shoe store and the beauty salon, Ashley went home feeling like she was on cloud nine. However, it only took a few weeks for her to realize she was being used as a pawn.

Thinking she would be in the secretarial pool or spending her day making coffee for the big-wigs, she was surprised when her father took her to corporate meetings and private lunches. He introduced her to some of his biggest clients and CEOs of new companies he was hoping to acquire. At first, it was all very flattering, until the V.P. from her father's latest acquisition put his hand around her waist and pulled her close. Too stunned to say anything, Ashley waited until everyone left before telling her father. He just laughed and told her not to worry about it. *'Older men like to think they still have what it takes to turn a young girl's head. It's harmless flirting. I assure you.'* But when it happened again the following week, she told her father it made her feel uncomfortable, and she'd prefer not to go to anymore special luncheons. He didn't smile at her or try to convince her it was harmless. Instead, he looked at her with a steely glare and explained how the tools of the trade worked. *'Eye candy and liquor have a way of distracting a man long enough to get the paperwork signed. Get used to it. It's how the world works. Just be thankful your assets work in your favor.'*

By August, Ashley couldn't wait to go back to school—anything to get away from her father's business practices and his handsy clients. He wanted her to continue to work through the fall, but after several conversations and just as many shouting matches, she convinced him that her senior year was very important to her. Academically, she had a shot at Valedictorian and needed every spare minute to study. He tried to guilt her into reconsidering by listing off the numerous things he had bought her because she was interning. He even called her spoiled and ungrateful. But in the end, she stood her ground, and in turn, he gave her the silent treatment for weeks.

Then, he called her one afternoon—when a major deal was on the brink of falling apart—and asked for her help. One dinner with a client; that was all. Because of her unexplainable desire to please her father and gain his love, she conceded. Once again, she was on his good side, but the favors did not stop there.

Every week it was something else.

And each time that she was roped into one of her father's ventures, it was harder for her to assimilate back into the normal life of a teenager. She pulled away from her friends and stopped dating, terrified someone would find out about her less than appropriate personal life. Guys thought she was playing hard to get, and the girls in her class still held to the opinion she was a rich snob; but she didn't care. As long as they didn't find out the truth, they could think what they wanted. All she had to do was make it through her senior year, graduate, pick a college far from home, and put the past behind her.

Then she met Austin, and everything changed.

FOUR

Ashley heard a noise downstairs, jolting her from her memories. *C.J. must be home.* She stepped from the bathtub—the water now tepid—then slipped into her robe. Walking down the hallway, she heard sounds coming from the kitchen. Though thoughts of Austin filled her mind as she descended the steps, overwhelming guilt tugged at her consciousness for lying to C. J. She had kept the reunion a secret, afraid he'd ask too many questions. But now that she knew her past was just a distant memory, she would come clean with him.

When she rounded the corner, C.J. had his head stuck inside the refrigerator. The clinking of glass was a dead giveaway he was looking for something to drink. When he stood to his full 6'2" height, he saw her leaning against the wall.

"Hey, you're home early." He closed the refrigerator and unscrewed the lid from the bottle he was holding.

Ashley moved closer to give him a hug. Her embrace was full, the guilt of her actions gnawing at her.

"Wow! What was that for? When I give a hug like that, it usually means I've done something wrong. So, what gives?" His silly grin and raised eyebrow made Ashley chuckle. He always had a way of bringing a smile to her face. But when she remembered what she had to say, her smile quickly faded.

"I lied to you tonight, C.J. I didn't go to an auction."

C.J. took a swig from the bottle in his hand, then leaned back against the granite countertop. Setting the bottle down, he crossed his muscular arms against his chest. "I know."

His calm tone surprised her, compounding her guilt. "How did you know?"

"Well, there were no auctions that I knew of," C.J. paused as he crossed the kitchen. "and you left this on top of the mantle." Dangling between his fingers was the reunion invitation. Ashley had misplaced it several days ago and assumed she had thrown it away.

"I'm sorry. I shouldn't have lied to you. I guess I—"

"Was he there?" C.J. interrupted.

Ashley tried to pretend she didn't know who he was talking about. "Was who there?"

"Come on," C.J. scoffed, "you know exactly who I'm talking about. Austin Taylor. Was he there?"

"Yes . . . he was there."

"Did you speak to him?"

She nodded.

"And . . ."

"And nothing. He was there with a beautiful blond who was probably half my age. We exchanged pleasantries, then I left. End of story."

C.J. stepped forward and pulled Ashley into a hug. "I'm sorry, Mom. I was actually hoping that . . . well, I'm not sure what I was hoping, but I know he meant a lot to you at one time. I guess I was thinking maybe you two could strike something up again." C.J. leaned back against the counter. "Are you okay?"

"Sure. I'm fine." She smiled, hoping it looked convincing. "I guess I needed closure. Now I have it."

After walking upstairs together and saying their good nights, Ashley lay on her bed convincing herself C.J. was all she needed. She didn't need a man to complete her, especially not a ghost from her past. Her reason for going to the reunion had been a long-shot, and now she knew it had been a waste of time. She would just put the whole thing behind her and allow the past to remain just that.

~Ⓡ~

"She was an old girlfriend, wasn't she?" Jenna asked Austin as they drove home.

"What?"

"That woman on the balcony, the one you ran after in the parking lot, was she an old girlfriend?"

"You saw that, huh? I thought you were in the powder room."

"Yes, I saw. And it's been driving me crazy all night."

"Then why didn't you just ask?"

"Because you looked so sad. I didn't want to make you feel worse."

He smiled at Jenna's perception.

"You loved her, didn't you?"

Austin glanced at Jenna. Seeing the look in her eyes, he realized there was no use lying. "Yes."

"Is she why you never got married?"

"Well, let's just say I never found anyone who could take her place."

"Wow," Jenna whispered. "You must have had it bad, Uncle Austin."

"What?"

"You know. Fallen hard. Head over heels. All this time you've been lost on her, hoping for one last chance to see her. Finally, you see her across the room. You speak with her . . . and then she's gone, like a vapor caught in the wind."

Austin rolled his eyes at his niece's dramatics but had to admit she was right.

Jenna continued her theatrical monologue all the way home. By the time Austin pulled into the circular driveway, her story had warped into a Romeo and Juliet tragedy. She rattled on as they walked up the cobblestone entryway and through the front door. When she finally came up for a breath, Austin set the house alarm and wished her good night. Jenna put her hands on his shoulders and looked him straight in the eye.

"I hope you find your mystery woman, Uncle Austin. You deserve to be happy." Jenna kissed him on the cheek, thanked him for taking her along, and disappeared into the room set up just for her.

"Me too, Jenna. Me too." Austin's words were barely audible, certainly nothing Jenna could hear. He walked to his room, threw his jacket on the bench at the foot of his bed, stretched out on top of the comforter, and turned on the TV. He flipped through channels long into the night.

The noise from the television began to lull him to sleep, but his subconscious replayed his chance encounter with Ashley Trent over and over again into the wee hours of the morning.

FIVE

Austin stared at the ceiling of his bedroom unable to fall back to sleep. Since before dawn, his mind played a continuous loop of what ifs. Seeing Ashley at the reunion blew his mind; then watching her drive away broke his heart.

When she had vanished after high school, he'd nearly gone crazy. He'd made several attempts to find her but was stonewalled at every turn. The police were no help, and her father refused to take his calls. He even flew to New York when he found out Ashley's father had relocated his offices there, only to be thrown off the property with the threat of an arrest if he came back. After months of dead-ends and pressure from his parents, Austin finally come to the realization Ashley did not want to be found. It crushed him at the time, but he finally grew to accept her disappearance.

Until now.

Ashley had finally resurfaced.

Austin closed his eyes, reliving the chain of events from the night before. Seeing Ashley talking with Julie Moore. Following her out onto the patio. He had stopped in the doorway—momentarily stunned—afraid his imagination was playing tricks on him.

But it *was* her.

It was Ashley.

He had watched as she leaned against the railing. Took a deep breath. Brushed her hair away from her face. He was struck with how beautiful she was—more beautiful than he had remembered. If that was even possible.

He walked toward her, but before he could take more than a few steps, she turned and saw him. It was the moment he had prayed for with every reunion he attended.

And then he watched as she drove away, disappearing once again without any explanation.

"Not this time," Austin said out loud, snapping back to reality.

He stared at his phone, looking at the picture he had taken as she drove away. Using his thumb and index finger, he enlarged the picture until the license plate on the Dodge truck was legible. *I'm going to get my answers, Ashley, one way or another.*

He glanced at his watch. *Six o'clock.* Simon would not appreciate a wakeup call this early on his day off. Figuring he could kill some time in the pool, Austin decided to burn off some nervous energy before calling his business partner for a favor.

By seven o'clock, Austin was showered, dressed, and pouring himself a glass of orange juice, when Jenna staggered into the kitchen.

"Well, good morning sleepyhead. Did I keep you out too late last night?" Austin ruffled Jenna's hair as she yawned.

"Right," she said in a huffy tone, "like my nightlife usually ends at eleven o'clock. Get real, Uncle Austin. I could've easily outlasted you if you hadn't dragged me home so early."

He just laughed.

It was Jenna who had convinced him to go to the reunion. When she saw the invitation on the kitchen table, she begged Austin to go and let her come along as his date. She was on the planning committee for her high school prom and wanted to get some ideas.

After Ashley's abrupt departure, Austin had wanted to leave. But he stayed. He refused to disappoint his niece. She got all dressed up for a night on the town, and that's what she was going to get. Of course, if he had known then that Jenna had watched him go after Ashley, maybe he would have said something. Done something.

It's water under the bridge now. Hopefully, Simon will be able to give me a lead.

"Hello? Uncle Austin? You haven't heard a word I said, have you?"

Austin snapped out of it, scrambling for something to say. "Sure. Shopping. Nail appointment. The mall. I heard every word." *What else did teenage girls talk about.*

"You're so cool. Let's say nine o'clock?"

"For what?"

"See, I knew you weren't listening."

"I'm sorry, Jenna. I'm just a little preoccupied this morning."

"The mystery woman?" she asked, her whole face lighting up.

"Would you stop calling her that? Her name is Ashley Trent. Well, at least that's what it was when we were in high school."

"You're not going to let her little disappearing act discourage you, right?"

"No, that happened once before. This time she at least owes me an explanation."

"Well look, heaven forbid I get in the way of a life-long search. I'll call Sarah; she can pick me up and take me to the mall."

"Are you sure, Jenna? I know this is supposed to be our weekend together."

"Are you kidding, I think it's cool. This is better than some of the stuff I watch on TV."

Jenna changed her voice to the low baritone of a radio announcer. "Dashing young executive, Austin Taylor chases the woman he left behind. Ashley Trent, the beautiful woman from his past holds the answers he's searching for. Will these two ever find true love? Tune in next time . . ."

"Okay, okay, I know it sounds like a soap opera, but she at least owes me an explanation."

"Hey, I'm all for it, but on one condition. If I give up my day with you, you have to promise to let me know what happens. Good, bad, or indifferent."

"Deal."

~®~

Ashley headed out early for her morning jog. It was barely light, but it was when she did her best thinking. She realized what a mistake last night had been. For twenty-five years, she had allowed the past to stay in the past. And now, because of one impulsive act, she had opened a Pandora's box of memories and regrets.

As she trudged along the wooded trail, she tried convincing herself she could put last night behind her, but the image of Austin in his tailored suit, crisp white shirt, and silk tie, kept working its way into her thoughts.

Time had been kind to him. Sure, she saw the small creases at the corner of his eyes, and a few gray hairs mixed in with the brown. But he still had his winning smile and penetrating hazel eyes that could see straight through to her soul.

Having followed his career for years, she knew he had made a name for himself in the financial world. Touted as a boy genius since the day he graduated college, his success story had been well documented in *Forbes*, *Fortune,* and other prestigious periodicals.

Picturing again how Austin looked as he approached her on the balcony made Ashley's heart race. Then, without permission, the gorgeous blond who had so easily slipped in beside Austin at the reunion popped into Ashley's thoughts. Marriage or a wife had never been mentioned in any of the articles she had read on Austin. Somehow, she just assumed he was still single. *Single maybe, but that didn't mean he was unattached.*

Ashley chided herself for the impulsiveness that had led her to attend the reunion. She attributed it to the introspective mood she'd been in lately, not because she was unhappy. She loved her life, truly she did. God had blessed her beyond her imagination and helped her carve out a lifestyle she was comfortable with. The ranch kept her busy, and C. J. was a wonderful son and business partner. Even so, she knew life didn't always go according to your plans. That's what had started her down this road; longing for the way things might have been. She was looking for closure and had gotten it. Even if it wasn't what she expected.

It's that stupid list. When are you going to learn you can't go back?

A few weeks ago, she had started working on a list of things she wanted to accomplish or put to rest. Austin Taylor was at the top of that list. The way she left him without any warning—without any explanation—it hadn't been fair. Then again, neither was what happened to her.

But the reunion seemed like a sign. The perfect way to . . .

To what? Rehash the low point of your life? Bleed old wounds? She realized now that she hadn't been thinking straight. She was letting her emotions run wild, and it had to stop.

Ashley jogged toward the stables where C.J. was loading equipment into the trailer. "I'm going to grab a quick shower, then I'll be right down."

Ashley tried to drown her turbulent emotions in the cold water washing over her. *I know you have a plan, Lord, even if I can't see it. Help me to know what's important and what I need to leave behind. Be with me as I sort out my thoughts and feelings. I know your plan is perfect, and that will have to be my comfort.*

Ashley got dressed and hurried downstairs, determined to put last night behind her.

"Are you sure you don't want me going with you?" C. J. asked as he tossed the last of the equipment she would need into the back of the truck.

"No, I think this will be a good distraction for me." Ashley put her personal duffel bag in the back seat of the extended cab before walking to the rink to get the three mares needed for the shoot. She loved the work she did with the movie industry and always enjoyed being on location. Though this shoot could prove to be challenging, she was looking forward to the down time to sort through her feelings.

"But I could go with you," C.J. said. "Billy and Willow can handle things around here for the next few days."

"C.J., I'll be fine. This is only a preliminary shoot to see if this is the look the director is going for. I'll be home by Tuesday morning."

"Tuesday! I thought this was a one-day thing?"

"Well, by the time I get out there and set up, there won't be time for day shots. We'll have to wait until tomorrow, and it could take a while. If it gets to be too late, I toyed with the idea of staying another night and coming back Tuesday morning." Ashley could tell by C.J.'s expression, he was not happy with her plans. "What's got you so agitated?" she asked.

"I just don't like the thought of you being out there by yourself. What if something goes wrong and you get in over your head?"

Ashley had to hold back a smile. She had done numerous movie shoots over the years, but now, all of a sudden, he was afraid she couldn't handle it? "C.J., I will hardly be by myself. With all the techies, stand-ins, producers, and direct—"

"That's exactly what I'm afraid of!" C.J. raised his voice as he leaned against the doorframe of the barn. He looked at her with his deep blue eyes, then gentled his tone. "Mom, I'm worried about you. I don't like this director. What are you going to do if he comes at you again?"

Now she understood what was bothering C.J. Ashley had thought he was afraid the horses were going to be too much for her to handle, but it was the director he was worried about. It was true. The last time she worked for this director, he had a hard time understanding the meaning of the word "no." He was so used to starlets throwing themselves at him, he didn't think Ashley would really refuse his advances. But she did, and that made him mad. So mad, he refused to use the Circle-R Ranch for any of his productions. Until now.

"I'm not worried about him, C.J. I figure he must have gotten over himself by now. The high price he was paying to shoot films out-of-state probably put too big of a dent in his budgets. I'll be fine." Ashley placed a reassuring hand on C.J.'s forearm. "Now, help me with the horses so I can get out of here."

After everything was loaded, C. J. was still wearing a scowl, but

Ashley refused to coddle him. She drove away, leaving a laundry list of repairs behind. Hopefully, it would be a big enough distraction to keep C.J. occupied so he wouldn't worry about her.

SIX

"It was registered to a man," Simon said as Austin cradled the phone next to his ear.

Austin was momentarily stunned. He had just assumed Ashley was single since she had come to the reunion solo and wasn't wearing a ring. *But that didn't mean she wasn't dating someone.* Simon continued as Austin switched the phone to speaker and set it on his desk.

"It's registered to a Christopher John Summers."

"What's the address?"

"Topanga Canyon."

Austin could believe it. He paced his home office as a barrage of questions sifted through his thoughts. *Has Ashley really been in California this whole time? How can that be? It doesn't make sense. I looked everywhere, I even—*

"Austin . . . you there?" Simon asked.

"Yeah. I'm still here. Just processing." Austin plopped down in his desk chair. "Go ahead and text me the address. I'll get back to you if I need anything else."

"Sure thing."

After ending the call, Austin reclined in his black leather chair, trying to absorb the idea that Ashley had been right under his nose all this time. When he heard his phone chime, he stared at the address in Simon's text. *I wondered what would happen if I showed up unannounced and asked to speak to Ashley?* He didn't want to get her in trouble with whoever this Christopher guy was, but he needed answers. He stood and slipped his cell phone into his pocket. *I'll never know if I don't try.*

When Austin slid into his car, he noticed a heart-shaped piece of paper sitting on the passenger seat. It was a note from Jenna. It simply read, 'I hope you find her.'

He smiled. "Me too, Jenna."

Jenna, his sister's only child, was an amazing girl. Austin loved spoiling her because she seemed so unaffected by it. She gave her parents heart failure on a regular basis because of her combined beauty and zeal for life. Jenna trusted everyone and chose to see the bright side in everything. Some would call it naivety, but Austin chose to look at it as part of Jenna's charm.

He tucked the note by the gear shift of his prized possession, his Alpha Romeo Spider, a gift from his father on his sixteenth birthday. Austin held onto the car for nostalgic reasons and kept it in excellent condition, making him the original owner of a true classic. He had a Lincoln Navigator for when he needed more room, but the Spider was his ride of choice.

Deciding fresh air would help him clear his head, Austin headed for the coastal route of Highway 1.

After he had been driving for close to an hour, he still didn't know what he would say if Ashley was home. Worse yet, what would her reaction be when she found out he traced her license plate number? Would she be upset he pursued her? Would she even give him a chance to talk?

Austin analyzed his feelings after all these years. He wasn't sure if it was his love for Ashley that had kept him thinking about her, or the fact that she had left him without explanation.

Well, I guess I'm about to find out.

Turning off Pacific Coast Highway and onto Topanga Canyon, he traversed the winding road for a little over thirty minutes then slowed. Paying close attention to the few addresses posted at the end of secluded driveways, he was beginning to wonder if this was a good idea. Confronting someone in the middle of nowhere wasn't exactly the smartest thing to do. Especially if this Christopher guy was her boyfriend.

After a few more turns, he saw a beautifully carved sign in a meticulously landscaped flowerbed with the address he'd been looking for. But it wasn't a residence, at least it didn't appear to be.

Circle-R Ranch
Boarding·Riding Lessons·Movie Productions

I guess this Summers guy is doing pretty well for himself.

Austin pulled through the high-arching entrance—branded with a circled R—and parked his car alongside trucks and trailers. His sports car looked completely out of place in both size and design.

Getting out of the car, he saw two main buildings off the

driveway. Obviously, one was a residence, while the other looked like a small office building. As he approached the office, he noticed a path leading around to the back of the building.

He decided to take a look.

Instantly, he was impressed by the size of the operation. Three large barns served as a backdrop, while three arenas—one complete with risers—were spaced throughout the property. An assembly of horses and riders crisscrossed the yard, some looking like elite equestrians with their snug white pants tucked in their expensive riding boots, while others looked like extras from a western movie set. He watched as people went about their business. Riders. Instructors. Spectators.

Pretty. Darn. Good.

"May I help you?"

Austin turned around and smiled at the young cowboy. "I'm looking for a Christopher Summers."

"Then I guess you found him, but you can call me C.J. Everyone does."

Austin was surprised to say the least. Though Christopher Summers stood as tall as he did, and had a similar build, it was obvious he was quite a bit younger. *Maybe he's not her boyfriend after all. They could just work together, and she borrowed his truck the night of the reunion.*

"Did we have an appointment?" he asked, a puzzled look on his face.

Austin stuttered. "Ahh, no, no, I didn't have an appointment. However, I am interested in boarding some horses." *Where did that come from?* He had never been on a horse, let alone have one of his own.

"I'm sorry, but we're at our max right now. Would you like to leave your name and number? I could have Ashley call you when an opening becomes available."

At least he knew he had the right place and the right Christopher, but hearing the young man speak Ashley's name with such familiarity irritated him. "Well, maybe I could talk to Ashley myself? To let her know what my needs are."

"Actually, she's out on a movie shoot right now and won't be back until Tuesday."

There was something in guy's stare that caught Austin's attention. He couldn't put his finger on it, but he definitely saw something in his eyes.

"Well, maybe I'll come back then. Thanks for your help." Austin walked away, knowing he had to get out of there before he made anymore stupid comments about his nonexistent horse.

Pulling out of the driveway, he took off toward the coast.

C.J. watched from the front office window as the man in the fancy sports car pulled away. Something about the guy was familiar, but he couldn't quite put his finger on it. He was glad the guy had left though, and that they didn't have a vacancy to offer him. Something about him didn't seem right. And if he was trouble, he didn't want any part of him.

SEVEN

Ashley arrived at the movie location and was set up before the infamous Hamilton Gentry arrived with his entourage. The technicians already had things in place and had been waiting around for some time. It didn't seem as if these men appreciated Hamilton any more than she did.

Staying with the horses at her makeshift campsite, Ashley waited. She didn't mind the rustic living arrangements when she was on location. It only added to the charm of working on a movie set.

Soon enough, Hamilton Gentry arrived and made his way to her campsite. She was brushing one of the mares and didn't bother to stop when he spoke to her.

"Hello, Ms. Summers. It's been a long time."

Ashley ignored the glare Hamilton gave her.

"I see you've brought me four fine specimens to work with."

"I'm sorry, Mr. Gentry, there must be some mistake." Ashley turned to address him. "I was told you needed only two horses. I brought one extra, in case there was a problem, but no one told me you needed four."

"Oh no, I'm correct in saying that I am looking at four very beautiful creatures."

Hamilton Gentry was slime personified. Ashley ignored his remark and the way he stood back and studied every inch of her.

"You know, Ms. Summers, I think there was a little confusion the last time we worked together."

"No, Mr. Gentry, there was no confusion. However, in case you need a refresher, let me tell you the guidelines I'm willing to work under. You tell me where, when, and how you would like the horses, and I'll handle it. That's what I do. I handle horses, not directors. I'm getting paid quite well for this job and have no desire to walk off your set, but if you decide to use your power to put me in an awkward position again, I will have no recourse but to leave.

So, Mr. Gentry, do you think that clears up any *confusion* we might have?"

"Perfectly!" Gentry's eyes turned steely as he walked even closer to where Ashley was standing. "You know, Ms. Summers, most women will do anything to get into my bed. I don't need to waste my time on you." He took one more long exaggerated look at Ashley, then turned and left.

Ashley was shaken. She wasn't normally so abrupt, but she wanted Hamilton Gentry to know up front she wouldn't be putting up with any of his unwelcome advances, even if it did cost her the job. Money and fame spoke volumes in Hollywood but meant nothing to her.

Austin was doing laps in the pool when he felt something hit him in the head. When he broke the surface, he saw Jenna laughing poolside, her feet dangling in the water, a volleyball bobbing in the swallow end.

"Hey, what was that for?" he asked while treading water in the middle of the pool. "I thought you had a nail appointment?"

"And I thought you were going to look for your mystery woman, but here you are still swimming. Really, Uncle Austin, you disappoint me."

Austin couldn't help but laugh. Jenna was never one to hide her feelings. She always said exactly what was on her mind. "For your information, smarty pants, I made a few calls and got an address."

"Really? Did you go check it out?" Jenna leaned forward, almost falling into the water as she hung on to Austin's every word.

"As a matter of fact, I did 'go check it out.' "

"And?"

"She works on a horse ranch in Topanga Canyon. Ashley wasn't there, but I talked to the guy the truck was registered to. He could be her boyfriend, for all I know."

"No way! What did you say?"

"I told him I was looking for a place to board my horse." Austin watched Jenna's expression turn from happy to confused.

"You lied?" She looked at him like he had just killed the family dog.

"I didn't mean to, but he kind of put me on the spot. I was afraid if I asked for Ashley, and he was her boyfriend; he could be the jealous type. I didn't want to say anything that would get Ashley in trouble. Sorry to disappoint you."

Jenna smiled. "I'm not disappointed, I guess I'm just a little surprised. You've always told me nothing good comes from lying. I know nobody's perfect, but to me, you're the closest thing to it."

"Well, I don't think I can take that kind of pressure. I mean, I remember not too long ago you thought Bob, from VeggieTales, was the greatest thing since ice cream." Austin positioned his hand to splash Jenna as she jumped to her feet in protest.

"Don't you dare, Uncle Austin! You know I don't like getting splashed. I would hate for you to fall off your pedestal twice in one day."

~⑧~

The movie shoot was a bust.

Even though Hamilton kept his distance and the horses behaved perfectly, nature chose not to cooperate. A pesky breeze kept churning up dust, and the unexpected cloud cover wreaked havoc with shadows and lighting. Ashley knew it was Hamilton Gentry's attention to detail that made him a much sought-after director, but it only served to put him in a foul mood. In a tirade, he called it quits mid-morning on Monday.

Even so, Ashley's time wasn't a total loss. Ironically, the actor she had dated years ago was the leading man in the film and just happened to be on set. She was surprised to see him at a preliminary shoot, but even more surprised when he told her she was the real reason he was there. He went on to explain that when he found out she was working on the movie, he couldn't help but remember all the good times they'd had together and wanted to see if there was something more for them to explore.

As flattering as that was, Ashley politely told him nothing had really changed since they had gone their separate ways. His schedule was just as demanding as ever, and the ranch was thriving, not leaving her much time to nurture a romantic relationship. He took it well, and they enjoyed a great afternoon catching up. Even so, Ashley knew there was more to her refusal than scheduling conflicts. The challenges that lay ahead of her were both physical and emotional and would require all the strength she could muster.

After packing up her campsite and trailer, Ashley was on the road by four o'clock. She was excited to be heading home at a decent hour, knowing she would have enough time to unpack and put everything away before dark. That would leave her all of

Tuesday to work on the bookkeeping and payroll.

She smiled as she drove home, reminiscing about her time at the Circle-R, how she had gone from office girl to ownership. The ranch was her pride and joy, and her greatest achievement beside C.J. She was so thankful for the way it had flourished under her management, literally doubling in size. With a staff that included four trainers, eight stablemen, a secretary, and Billy the handyman/groundskeeper, Ashley felt blessed beyond measure. She knew the Anderson's—the original owners—would be proud their legacy lived on, and Ashley prayed the Circle-R would continue to thrive with C.J. at the helm after she was gone.

After pulling into the yard and stretching her legs, Ashley realized how tired she felt. Roughing it on location probably wasn't the smartest thing to do in her condition. Her bones were not as forgiving as they used to be, and her body not as strong as it once was.

"Hey, Mom, you're back early," C.J. shouted from atop Knight. "I'll be right there to help you unload."

Ashley watched as C.J. dismounted Knight and gave the reins to Charlie, one of the stablemen. As he walked across the yard, she wondered when her little boy had turned into a man. He was tall, blond, extremely handsome, and the work on the ranch had sculpted his physique better than any gym membership could have. However, it was the smile on his face that melted her heart. C.J. was passionate—and at times it got the better of him—but he was also caring and considerate and loved her fiercely. These were the traits she treasured in her son and the very attributes that would make him a wonderful husband someday.

He swallowed her up in a bear hug and asked, "So, how was the shoot?" He took a step back, a stern expression on his face.

"We will be doing it again. Things weren't perfect for his royal highness, so we're going to try again in three weeks."

"And did his royal highness behave himself?"

"He was his rude, ill-tempered self, but he kept his distance. He had some bimbo hanging off his arm the whole time. She seemed all too willing to be his playmate for the day." Ashley looked around the ranch. "How about here? Everything okay?"

"Pretty much. I did have an interesting conversation with Mr. Peterson. He's thinking about buying Jessica a new mount for her English riding competitions. I told him we wouldn't have the room, but that didn't seem to faze him."

"Does he think Jessica will give up Sugar that easy? She's had that horse since she was six."

"I don't think he cares much about Jessica's feelings. He just wants her to keep winning." C. J. led the mares across the yard and handed them off to Charlie, then walked back to the trailer. "And then there's Russell."

"What happened with Russell?" Ashley asked, even though she already knew what C.J. was going to say. Russell Richards was a belligerent kid who thought nothing of taking his anger out on his horse. Jarrod, Russell's trainer, had warned her of his outburst once before, and from the set of C.J.'s shoulders she could tell what he had to say wasn't good.

"Jarrod found more cuts on Champ yesterday. I think we need to get rid of Russell. His behavior is bordering on inhumane."

"Did you talk to him?"

"No, I was too angry. I didn't trust myself to handle the situation without blowing up."

"Okay, I'll give his parents a call tomorrow. Anything else?"

"Oh yeah, some guy came by looking to board some horses. I told him we were full, but it sounded like he would be back tomorrow to talk to you. I told him he could leave his name and number, but he said he would just come back."

Ashley nodded, as she continued to unload the tack. Her pace was slow, and her body ached. She felt zapped of her strength and could barely lift the saddles from the back of the truck.

"Mom, you look wiped out. Why don't you go on in; I'll take care of this."

She sighed. "I'm not even going to argue with you, C.J. I'm too worn out." Walking toward the house, Ashley turned around and asked, "What would you like for dinner?"

"How about pizza? The kind that comes in a box and rings the doorbell."

"Sounds great to me. I'll order it when I'm done with my bath. Right now, I just want to soak."

Ashley headed toward the house, angry at herself for feeling so weak. She was used to a demanding schedule, and hated the limitations her body was putting on her. She liked working with the horses and around the property, much more than dealing with people. She would choose an ornery mare over egotistical parents any day, but lately, she didn't have the strength for either.

As Ashley ran her bath water and undressed, she formulated a to-do list in her mind. *I'll talk to Mr. Richards tomorrow regarding Russell. He's not going to like what I have to say, but I'm not going to put up with it anymore. And I need to work on the books before the end of the month. At least, get halfway caught up.*

She sank into the tub and closed her eyes. When she did, she no longer thought about Mr. Richards, Russell, or the books. Instead, she saw Austin. Designer suit. Hazel eyes. Smile.

Don't go there, Ashley. This time it was your choice to walk away. You can't blame it on anyone else. The past is the past. The sooner you realize that the better off you will be.

EIGHT

Austin glanced at his watch for the hundredth time.

This is ridiculous. I'm not getting anything done.

Turning off his computer, he stood and walked around his desk. When he exited his office, Victoria, his personal assistant, looked up and smiled.

"Going out for lunch?" she asked.

"Actually, I'll be gone the rest of the day."

"Should I hold your calls or forward them to your cell phone?"

"Hold them. There's nothing pressing that can't wait."

Inching his way through mid-day traffic, Austin used the time to formulate what he was going to say when he saw Ashley. He tried to anticipate what her reaction would be—and practiced what he would say—but nothing sounded right.

I could always take Jenna's advice and sweep Ashley off her feet—tell her I won't let her go until she proclaims her love for me. He smiled at the idea, then cringed. *What if she told her boyfriend or business partner, or whoever that Christopher guy is about us? He might coldcock me before I even get the chance to say anything.*

With one outrageous scenario after another playing through his head, Austin pulled into the Circle-R drive, still not sure what he was going to say.

Even if she never wants to see me again, I need answers. She owes me that much. At least then I'll finally have some closure.

He stepped into the office and approached the young girl sitting at the desk. Her head was down, deep in thought, her bronze curls falling around her face. When she finally looked up, she smiled and introduced herself as Willow.

"How can I help you?"

"I'm here to see Ashley."

The girl moved some papers aside and looked at her desktop calendar. "Do you have an appointment?"

"No. I . . . I don't."

"Well, Ashley's not here right now. She's running some errands. But she'll be back soon."

"Then, if it's okay, I'll just wait outside."

"Sure."

He stepped outside and waited for Ashley.

Just like he'd done for the past twenty-five years.

When Ashley drove through the gate of the Circle-R, her stomach knotted. There, wedged between a pickup and an SUV, was a sports car identical to the one Austin drove in high school. She parked her truck and slowly walked back to the little black convertible, her heart racing. What were the chances she would see Austin and a car identical to the one he drove in high school, within a few days of each other? It was a coincidence. It had to be. Ashley allowed her hand to slide down the length of the car, memories flooding her mind. Pulling her thoughts from the past, she turned, only to find Austin standing there watching her.

"Hello, Ashley."

She was stunned. Shocked. It was one thing to see Austin at the reunion—a neutral location—but here, on her land, she felt stripped of her privacy. It took a moment to find her tongue and when she did, she found her anger as well. "What are you doing here?" she snapped.

"We need to talk."

"We talked at the reunion."

"No, we didn't. You said we would, right before you took off. Just like you did twenty-five years ago." Austin's tone was sharp, his words laced with resentment.

What have I done? Why did I go to that stupid reunion? Why couldn't I leave the past in the past?

"Come on, Ashley, is it too much to ask—"

"Wait a minute," she interrupted. "How did you find me?"

"Your license plate number. I had a friend run it for me."

"You had me checked out? How dare you! You have no right to . . . to . . ." Ashley took a deep breath and lowered her tone. "You need to leave," she said calmly, then walked past Austin on her way to the house. She had only taken a few steps when he grabbed her arm.

"Ashley, please, why are you being like this? I just want to know what happened. Is that too much to ask?"

"It's none of your business." She jerked her arm free, throwing herself off balance. Stumbling backwards, she landed in the soft gravel of the driveway. Austin extended his hand to her, but she slapped it away. "Leave me alone."

"Ashley, I'm only trying to help." He took hold of her arm and pulled her to her feet. She tried yanking her arm away from him, but this time he had a firm grip.

"Leave me alone and get off my property."

"No. Not until—"

In a blur of motion, C.J. stepped in front of her and connected a left hook to Austin's chin.

"C.J.!" Ashley gasped.

Austin stumbled backwards—clearly shocked—but quickly shook off the blow.

Ashley watched as C.J. charged him again, but Austin was ready for him this time and blocked his punch.

"C.J. stop!"

Ashley watched in horror as her son raged out of control. Austin did his best to deflect C.J.'s punches without throwing any of his own—for which she was grateful—but it only seemed to anger C.J. more.

"Stop it! Stop it both of you!" she yelled, but to no avail.

She watched as the two men stumbled and fell on the ground, a jumble of arms and legs. When Austin got the upper hand, he straddled C.J. and pinned him face down in the dirt.

"Leave him alone!" Ashley yelled, pulling on Austin's shirt collar, trying to drag him off her son.

When Austin got to his feet, he rested his hands on his hips, panting from the exertion. C.J. scrambled to his feet and rushed Austin once again, but Ashley quickly stepped between the two men and pushed her son back. "That's enough, C.J.!"

"But he—"

"C.J., please," she pushed him back a few more steps, "just walk away." Then she turned to Austin and watched as he spit blood on the gravel drive. "You need to leave."

"But, Ashley," he looked at her, his eyes pleading, "we need to talk."

"No. I think it would be best if you just left."

"Not until you promise we can talk. I'm not leaving until you—"

"That's it!" C.J. yelled as he pulled his cell phone from his pocket. "I'm calling the cops!"

"Don't C.J. That won't be necessary." Ashley turned around. "Austin, why don't you come back around six o'clock? We can talk then."

"Austin?" A dumbstruck expression twisted C.J.'s face. "You're Austin Taylor?"

Neither Ashley nor Austin acknowledged him.

"Will six o'clock work for you?" she asked him for a second time.

"Six o'clock is fine, but just the two of us, okay?"

Ignoring Austin's question, Ashley turned to leave, but grabbed C.J.'s arm to make sure he didn't have any parting shots for Austin, physically or verbally. "I'll see you at six," she said over her shoulder as she walked with C.J. toward the house.

Ashley barely had the door closed before C.J.'s questions started to fly. "What did he think he was doing? Are you all right? Did he hurt you? Why did you invite him back?"

"Okay, okay, just calm down. I can't answer any of your questions if you keep firing off more at me." Ashley took a deep breath, needing a few seconds to regroup. "No, he didn't hurt me. He just wanted to talk. I agreed to meet him later because now that he knows where I live, I know he won't give up. He's as stubborn as you are. So, I might as well talk to him and get it over with."

"He's the guy I told you about, the one who asked to talk to you yesterday. I knew he looked familiar, but I couldn't place him. So, I guess it wasn't just a coincidence he ended up here?"

"No. He traced the truck's license plate number. That's how he got our address."

"What are you going to tell him?"

Ashley had to ask herself the same question. What was she going to tell him? They had been strangers for twenty-five years. Did she really feel it necessary to give him details about her past after all this time? It wasn't like anything she was going to say would change the past or the present. She had her life, and it was obvious he had his.

She watched as C.J. paced like a caged animal, waiting for an answer. "Well?" he finally said, stopping right in front of her.

"I guess I'll have to figure that out when he gets here."

"He better not try anything, or he's going to find himself in worse shape than he already is."

"You won't be here, C.J.; I want to talk to him alone."

"No way! I'm not leaving you alone with him."

"I'll be fine, really."

"He was assaulting you. I saw it with my own eyes."

Now she understood why he'd gone ballistic. "He wasn't assaulting me. He just wanted to talk. I got defensive and stumbled backwards. He was only trying to help me up."

"Help you up, my eye. He had his hands all over you. The guy has a lot of nerve showing up after all this time and manhandling you the way he did." C.J. crossed his arms against his chest and shook his head. "He certainly isn't the person I expected."

She chuckled, "What were you expecting?"

"I don't know, but he's sure not it."

Ashley decided to change the subject. "Look, C.J., you have work to get done, and so do I. My files are not going to update themselves, and I'm still expecting to go a few rounds with Mr. Richards. He's not going to be happy when I tell him he needs to find a new place to board Champ."

C.J. stepped closer, his demeanor no longer confrontational, but soft and filled with concern. "Are you sure you're okay, Mom?"

"To tell you the truth, no, I'm not okay. Even so, I still have things I need to get done before the day is through. Life goes on, C.J., and that's exactly what I'm going to tell Austin."

Austin drove with no destination in mind. He was too agitated to go back to the office, but he didn't want to drive all the way home. Ending up at a turnout overlooking the ocean, he leaned against the hood of his car and inhaled the salty sea air. He thought about Ashley and how good she looked, even if she was mad at him. Then realized she never clarified if it would be just the two of them meeting later. He groaned, not looking forward to going another round with Christopher Summers. Nevertheless, it didn't look like he would have a choice. If he wanted the chance to talk to Ashley, he would have to play by her rules.

Austin thought again how good Ashley looked. *She's an equestrian now. That's interesting.* She had never shown an interest in horses while in high school. But he had to admit, the lifestyle certainly seemed to fit her as well as her slim fit jeans. She looked wonderful, as if time had stood still.

Austin's cell phone rang, interrupting his thoughts. "Taylor. Oh hi, Jenna; what's up? No, not yet . . . I will tonight . . . No, it's far from a date. In fact, I'm not even sure if we'll be alone. Yeah, he was there, too . . . I promise . . . you'll be the first to know . . . okay, Jenna, bye."

Austin slid his cell phone into his pocket and smiled. Jenna was hoping for a fairytale ending. So was Austin. The only difference was Austin knew things didn't always end the way you dreamed they would. Otherwise, Ashley never would have left him twenty-five years ago.

NINE

Ashley glanced at the clock, frustrated. She had spent the last forty-five minutes waiting for Mr. Richards, and of course, he was a no show. *Great! Time I could have used to prepare myself for talking to Austin. Instead, I waste it on a customer I should have let go months ago. Oh well, at least I won't have to play referee between Austin and C.J.*

Begrudgingly, C.J. went out with some friends. He had wanted to be home when she talked to Austin, but Ashley insisted she would be okay. Besides, this was something she needed to do on her own.

She debated what approach to use. Keep it simple or give Austin the expanded version. It would be difficult to relive the past she had tried so hard to put behind her. Memories of her teen years were painful and emotional. Then again, maybe she wouldn't tell him at all. *What right does he have to search me out and expect an explanation after all these years?*

Still not knowing what she was going to do, Ashley shut down her computer and put the reports she was working on in a nice neat stack. She was ready to leave when Mr. Richards walked in.

"Did you want to speak to me, Ms. Summers?"

Ashley was annoyed he thought he could waltz into her office almost an hour late, and still expect to speak with her. But she wasn't going to do it. She was not going to adjust her schedule to accommodate him. Standing behind the front office desk, Ashley smiled politely. "Mr. Richards, I was expecting you earlier. Unfortunately, I have another appointment to get ready for, so we will have to reschedule for tomorrow."

"Well, tomorrow won't work for me. I have a business meeting in Denver, and I fly out first thing in the morning. In fact, now isn't convenient either, but C.J. made it sound important. So, can we just get on with this?"

He was sharp, his tone condescending. Ashley decided to get

right to the point and clear the matter up as quickly as possible.

"Russell is abusing Champ. We've had several conversations with him regarding his actions, but he doesn't seem to care. We can no longer offer our services to Russell. You will need to board Champ elsewhere."

"I don't understand. Why wasn't I told about this earlier?" Mr. Richards' voice was controlled but strained.

"Your wife was told on several occasions."

"My wife is a self-centered imbecile," he snapped. "She only cares about herself and her allowance. You should have spoken to me."

"Mr. Richards, Russell is sixteen years old. He's smart enough to know he was hurting his horse and intelligent enough to know we were serious about withdrawing your membership. His lack of concern for the well-being of his horse is something we can no longer tolerate. I'm sorry for the inconvenience, but I will not reconsider my position."

Ashley tried to sound firm, but inside, she was not so self-assured. It was obvious from Mr. Richards demeanor, he was unimpressed as well. He placed his hands firmly in the center of the desk she stood behind and leaned his towering frame over until he was just inches from her face.

"I'm sure there is something I could say or do that would make you reconsider. Perhaps a substantial donation to the Circle-R Ranch, or maybe you'd prefer a healthy check made out directly to you? Name your price, Ms. Summers."

"Mr. Richards, I believe this conversation is over. You have until the end of the week to remove Champ, but as of today Russell is no longer welcome on my property." Ashley didn't move from her position behind the desk but let out a quiet sigh of relief when Mr. Richards walked toward the office door.

Until he closed it and turned back around.

"This is what you call a closed-door session," Mr. Richards said as he walked toward her. "In the business world, that means no one leaves until both parties are satisfied. And quite frankly, Ms. Summers, I am far from satisfied."

Ashley was shaken.

She kept her demeanor calm, but inside her mind was racing. "Mr. Richards, the Circle-R Ranch has done quite well for itself, and I'm insulted you feel this matter could be resolved with money. Russell needs to learn how to control his aggression. Right now, he's taking it out on an animal. What would happen if he turned that anger toward a person? I don't think the issue is Champ. It's your son. I would suggest you take the money you so graciously offered me and invest it in some anger management classes for Russell. He's not a bad kid; he just needs some direction."

Mr. Richards slammed his hand down on the desk, making Ashley jump. "I don't need some self-righteous broad telling me how to raise my son." He walked around to Ashley's side of the desk and cornered her against a filing cabinet. "My son is just fine. He doesn't have anger issues. I've just taught him not to take anyone's crap. I'll speak to him about Champ, but I'm not going to remove my membership."

Ashley tried to move away from Mr. Richards, but he stopped her by slamming his hand up against the wall. "I don't believe we're done here, Ms. Summers."

"We are more than done Mr. Richards, and if you don't remove your arm, I'll have no choice but to call the police."

"And how are you going to do that?" he asked arrogantly, moving even closer.

Ashley brought her knee straight up into his groan and watched as he lurched backwards in pain. Scrambling for the bottom drawer of the desk, she grabbed the tranquilizer gun and aimed it directly at him.

Mr. Richards backed away slowly, his hands up in surrender.

"Get out of here, right now," she yelled. "If I ever see you on my property again, I'll take it as a personal threat and press charges. Now get out!"

Austin stepped out of his car and took a deep breath. He could not believe he was going to talk to Ashley after all these years. Raising his hand to knock on the office door, he was shocked to hear Ashley yelling at someone to get out.

When he flung the door open, he was stunned to see a man backing away from Ashley, a gun in her hand.

Instinct took over.

He put himself between Ashley and the man, then slammed him against the wall, pinning the man with his forearm against his throat. "What's going on here?" Austin asked as the man struggled.

"It's okay, Austin. He was just leaving," Ashley said, as her arms remained outstretched, the gun clamped between her hands, her stare, as well as the weapon, still trained on the man.

Austin released his hold, then walked backwards until he was standing alongside Ashley.

The man coughed and sputtered, nearly collapsing, but quickly gathered his composure. He stood up straight, his face covered in perspiration and a livid shade of red. Looking from Austin to Ashley, he tugged on the hem of his jacket, then straightened his tie. "I'll send someone to pick up Champ in the morning. You, Ms. Summers, are lucky I'm not pressing charges of my own." He left, slamming the office door behind him.

Ashley placed the gun on top of the desk and sank into the chair. She was shaking, her eyes filled with tears.

"Are you all right?" Austin squatted in front of her. "What happened? Who was that guy?"

"Just a disgruntled parent. I was withdrawing his membership because his son is abusive. I guess he didn't like my advice." Ashley chuckled, trying to look unaffected, but Austin saw her hands were shaking.

He didn't know what to do. He wanted to draw Ashley into his arms and comfort her, but it wasn't his place.

"Maybe I should come back later?" Austin broke the silence. "We need to talk, but obviously now is not the time."

"No, I'll be fine. I just need a few minutes to clear my head."

Austin watched as Ashley pushed the rolling desk chair away from him and stood. With her hands still noticeably shaking, she put the gun back in the drawer, grabbed a set of keys from the desktop, and walked around the desk. Austin moved toward the door, and held it open for her. After she locked up, he trailed her to the house.

"I'll be just a minute," she said after they walked into the living room.

She disappeared down the hall while he took a seat on the couch.

Calmly, Ashley walked to the downstairs bathroom, closed the door, then sunk to the rim of the tub and cried. She pulled a towel from the rack and buried her face in it, not wanting Austin to hear her fall apart. An entire spectrum of emotions boomeranged around inside her. Fear. Anger. Desperation. Regret. How was she supposed to talk to Austin now? She was shaking like a leaf. *Help me, Lord. Why is it when I try to do the right thing, things just seem to get worse?*

A faint knock on the bathroom door, startled her.

"Ashley, are you going to be okay?" Austin's tone was soft. Soothing.

"Just a minute." Wiping her cheeks with the towel, she reached for the door knob. "I'll be right out," she said, then took a couple of deep breaths before opening the bathroom door.

Austin was at the end of the hall—his hands tucked in his front pockets—leaning against the wall. He stood up straight as soon as he saw her.

"Sorry about that." She plastered on a fake smile. "I . . . I needed to . . . I mean . . . I just needed a couple minutes to . . . Uhh . . .

"Ashley . . ."

She stopped her mumbling and looked at him.

"I think it would be best if I came back another day. We have a lot to talk about, and I don't think you're in the right frame of mind to do that."

"I'm sorry, Austin. I don't mean to prolong this, but . . ."

"It's not your fault. I understand. Can I call you tomorrow?"

"Sure. Here, let me give you my business card." Ashley walked into the kitchen and came back with her card. Austin was already standing by the front door when she handed it to him and watched as he slipped it into his pocket.

"Austin, I'm really sorry about this. I guess timing has never been my strong suit."

"Don't be sorry. That was a pretty intense situation. You're still shaking."

She looked down at her hands, unable to control the trembling.

"When will Christopher be home?" he asked.

"C.J.? He should be home around eight o'clock. I asked him to give us some space for a few hours, but he'll be home soon."

"Okay then, I guess I'll call you tomorrow." Austin descended the front steps, then turned back around. "Are you sure you're going to be okay? I could sit with you until Christopher gets home? We wouldn't have to talk. We wouldn't even have to be in the same room. I just don't think you should be alone right now."

Ashley realized Austin kept using Christopher's given name, but no one ever called him that. He had always gone by C.J., so she asked, "How did you know his name was Christopher?"

Austin cleared his throat. "Car registration."

"That's right." Ashley had forgotten about his sleuthing. Though she wanted to be mad at him all over again for violating her privacy, she didn't have the energy. "Look, Austin, I'll be fine. Thank you for your concern and for your help earlier."

He muffled a laugh. "Well, you looked like you were handling the situation all on your own, but I'm glad I was there anyway." He stared at her for a second, then smiled. "Good night, Ash."

Closing the front door, she leaned against it to steady herself. Taking a deep breath, she wondered if Austin had felt it to.

The electricity between them.

It was still there.

Austin still didn't feel good about leaving Ashley alone. Knowing that jerk could come back and cause more trouble, he decided he would stay put until Summers came home.

Walking to his car, he put the top up and settled in for who knew how long. Reaching into his pocket, he pulled out Ashley's business card. It was embossed with the ranch's logo and the services it provided. The raised lettering listed Ashley Summers and C.J. Summers as proprietors.

His heart sunk.

They're married.

It was like a punch to the gut and sent his mind reeling. The kid was so young, it never even occurred to Austin that they could be married. *He doesn't even look old enough to drink. And why isn't she wearing a ring?*

Judgmental and condescending thoughts instantly polluted his mind. He was disappointed in Ashley and questioned what Summers' angle was. *Why would a good-looking guy like Summers want to be with a woman twice his age? Because she's beautiful, that's why, you idiot. Any guy would be lucky to be with a woman like Ashley.*

He laughed at the irony. "What am I saying, I don't even know what kind of woman Ashley has become." *Obviously, she's changed.* He turned the business card end over end in his hand, his thoughts shifting from disbelief to disappointment.

Somehow, over the last few days, he'd allowed himself to fantasize about the possibility of having a future with Ashley.

They would reconnect.

Strike up a friendship.

Old feelings would resurface.

They would have that aha moment and realize they were meant

to be together.

Just now, I felt it. That same electricity. It was there.

But he was only fooling himself, thinking something was there when it wasn't.

Ashley was married.

End of story.

There would be no happily ever after.

He sat in his car, chastising himself for losing his grip on reality, for conjuring up a make-believe future that would never exist.

Eventually, he would have a conversation with Ashley—get answers to his questions—but there would be no going back. He would get closure but nothing more.

Defeated, Austin waited for Summers to get home.

In less than an hour, the same red truck Ashley drove away from the reunion pulled into the driveway.

~®~

C.J.'s tires popped gravel as he pulled into the driveway. He saw Austin Taylor sitting in his car, and immediately his hackles were up. He backed up to block him in, got out of his truck, and came around to the driver side of the little sports car. Glaring at Austin, he waited for him to roll down the window.

"Is there a reason you're sitting in my driveway?" C.J. did nothing to mask his belligerence.

"Some man came by earlier causing trouble. He left, but I didn't feel comfortable leaving Ashley alone in case he came back. I knew you'd be home soon, so I waited. I'll leave now, if you'll just move your truck."

C.J. didn't know what to say, so he didn't. He just got back into his truck, pulled forward, and watched as Austin's taillights disappeared from his rearview mirror.

Now to find out who was causing trouble.

He put the truck in park and scaled the front steps two at a time. "Mom?" C.J. yelled, as he hurried through the door. "Mom, where are you?"

"I'm in here."

C.J. hurried to the great room. Walking through the kitchen, he saw his mom curled up on the couch, staring through the large bay window that overlooked the ranch.

"What happened tonight?" C.J. pushed some pillows aside so he could sit by her.

"Nothing, really. Austin and I didn't get a chance to talk because I got into an argument with Mr. Richards."

"Austin made it sound like it was more than just an argument. He thought—"

"What? Wait a minute," Ashley interrupted, "when did you talk to Austin?"

C.J. wasn't sure if she was surprised or irritated. "Uhh . . . he was in the driveway when I got home. He said a man was causing trouble, and he didn't feel comfortable leaving you alone. He just left."

"Really?"

"Yeah. So, are you going to tell me happened?"

His mom explained her *disagreement* with Mr. Richards, but he could tell she was trying to downplay it. The fact that she pulled a gun let him know the situation must have gotten out of hand.

"Are you sure you're okay? He didn't hurt you, did he?"

"No," she smiled. "In fact, he'll be feeling the effects of our altercation longer than I will."

"What about Champ?"

"He said he would send someone to pick him up tomorrow. I told him if he ever came on the property, I would press charges. So, I don't think we have to worry about him coming back anytime soon."

Ashley spent over an hour explaining to C.J. her argument with Mr. Richards, and how Austin showed up at just the right time. She also emphasized how considerate Austin had been to realize she was too upset to talk, and how he agreed to come back another day.

And then he sat in the driveway to make sure I was okay.

Sinking into the soothing bath water, Ashley pictured Austin standing between her and Mr. Richards, his shoulders taut with anger; the look on his face equal parts bewilderment and compassion. *And then he left, voluntarily, even though he had waited twenty-five years for answers to his questions.*

Ashley closed her eyes.

Lord, thank you for Your protection tonight—for sending Austin at just the right time. She smiled to herself. *He's still the same Austin. Always putting others before himself. I know he deserves answers, so please, give me the words to explain. Allow him closure. And help me put my past to rest and navigate my future with strength only You can give. Amen.*

Ashley had not always been a praying woman. In fact, she struggled with the Lord for some time before surrendering her heart to him.

That was when her new life began.

TEN

Austin woke in a daze.

Stretching his arms over his head, he realized he was on the couch in the living room not his bed.

He quickly replayed the previous day's events. Going to Ashley's. A scrimmage with that Summers guy. Returning to Ashley's later. Coming between her and a whacked-out customer. Finding out she was married. Waiting in his car for her husband to come home. Lying on the couch too amped to sleep.

He'd had three tense encounters with Ashley in the last few days, but still had no answers. And now that he knew she was married, any future he thought they might have together was just wishful thinking.

As he pulled her business card from his pocket, he glanced at the clock, wondering if it was too early to call. *She works on a ranch. She's probably been up for hours.*

Deciding to stick to his normal routine, Austin swam his morning laps, showered, then drove to the office. He was earlier than usual, wanting to make up for the time he lost yesterday. *Once I'm caught up, I'll give Ashley a call.*

When it hit ten o'clock, Austin could wait no longer. He pulled Ashley's business card from his pocket and placed it on his desk. It was only a formality since he had already memorized her number.

"Circle-R Ranch, Willow speaking."

"Ashley Summers, please."

"I'm sorry, Ashley isn't available at the moment. Can I take a message?"

"Well, she was expecting my call. When would be a good time to call her back?"

"I'm sorry, Ashley is in and out all day. I can take your name and number and have her call you when she comes in?"

Frustrated, Austin gave the girl his name and number before hanging up.

Once again, the ball was in Ashley's court, and Austin had no choice but to wait.

~®~

Ashley spent the better part of the morning walking the ranch, writing down repairs that needed to get done and the supplies that were necessary to fix them. She stopped to watch April, one of the trainers, instruct her student on the proper seat and leg placement for dressage. The little girl bobbed her head with understanding. It made Ashley smile. She loved watching kids as they learned how to handle such enormous animals. Their wide-eyed enthusiasm reminded Ashley of how she felt when she was first introduced to the ranch. She had been a lot older than this student but had still felt the wonder of it all.

It was almost one o'clock before Ashley returned from her maintenance walk. Willow was still on her lunch break, so Ashley went straight to her office. She had a stack of papers on her desk, but she was only looking for one thing. She picked up the slip with Austin's name on it and saw that he called almost three hours ago. Taking a breath, Ashley dialed the number on the pink message paper.

"Taylor."

"Austin . . . it's Ashley."

"Hi, Ashley. You must've had a full schedule today. I was going to invite you to lunch, but I guess it's a little late for that."

"I'm sorry. I just now got to my office and saw your message. But if it's all right with you, I would prefer not meeting in a public place. We have a lot to talk about, and I think I would feel more comfortable not doing it where other people could overhear us."

"No, no, you're right. Where would you like to meet?"

"You're welcome to come here. I promise no angry men. No stray punches. No guns." Ashley giggled, trying to mask her nervousness.

"What time would be good for you?"

"Anytime would be as busy as the next, so just come when it's convenient for you. I'll make myself available."

"Okay, I'll be there shortly."

Ashley walked toward the stables but slowed when she saw C.J. in the practice rink with Gallant Knight, his prized American Quarter Horse. It was always exciting watching the two of them work together. The line they cut was incredible, and their gate so smooth, it was hard to see where rider ended, and horse began. Ashley couldn't help but hold her breath whenever she watched C.J. race around the barrels. Though his motion was flawless, his speed always caused her to wince with worry.

Looking at her watch, she hurried toward the stables. She wanted to get inventory done before Austin showed up, so she could fax over her order first thing tomorrow morning, and she needed to spend some quality time with Dominus. Between the reunion and the movie shoot, she felt like she'd neglected the only other man in her life.

Silently, Austin watched as Ashley brushed a horse, but it wasn't her work he was admiring. It was the woman. She was captivating. Everything about her. Her petite figure. Her long blond hair. The way she moved with confidence around a horse twice her size. She looked just as good in a pair of faded jeans tucked in riding boots, as she did a black evening dress and heels. With her silky hair pulled back in a single braid, she reminded him of the girl he once knew. The only thing different was the beat-up straw hat perched on her head . . . and the passing of time.

He cleared his throat. "Your secretary said I would find you here."

Ashley spun around. "Austin, hi," she smiled. "Just give me a minute while I finish up." She set the brush in a bucket, lovingly stroked the horse a few more times, then exited the stall and closed the door behind her.

"I don't know anything about horses, but he's beautiful."

"I think so, and unfortunately, so does he," she laughed as she put the bucket on a shelf and walked further away. "How long since you've been on a horse?" she asked over her shoulder.

"How about never."

She turned around. "You've never ridden a horse?"

"Not unless you count a pony that walks in circles at the fair or the kind that takes quarters in front of the supermarket."

She laughed. "Well, it's your loss."

"No, I think the only horse power I'm interested in comes from a turbo engine under the hood of a car."

Ashley walked back with a bucket of oats. "Okay, have it your way, but you're the one missing out." Opening the stall door, she walked in and hung the bucket on a loop on the wall. Immediately, the horse dipped his head toward the food. She stroked his neck a few times, then exited, latching the stall. She smiled nervously. "We can talk in the house."

Austin fell into step alongside Ashley and followed her to the back porch of the house. Entering the kitchen, she asked, "Can I get you something to drink?"

"Sure, water would be fine."

He walked to the couch in front of a large picture-window and took a seat. He watched Ashley pull two tumblers from the cupboard and pour them each a glass of cold water. She sat in the loveseat across from him after handing him his drink. They both sat for a few moments without speaking.

Ashley looked at him. "I guess I don't know where to start. Maybe you could help me out here."

"Well, besides the fact that you refused to go to prom with me and missed the last few weeks of school, I guess I want to know why you disappeared without telling me?"

~®~

Ashley swallowed hard and prepared herself for the most difficult conversation she would ever have.

"Austin, I don't think there is an easy way to say this, so I'm just going to say it. When I moved to New York . . . with my father . . . I was pregnant."

The shock on Austin's face was exactly what she expected.

"Pregnant?" He looked at her unbelieving. "I don't understand. I thought you and I were dating exclusively? We never . . ." Tears welled in his eyes.

Ashley hated this. She was betraying him all over again. She stood and paced to the far side of the room, wishing she could run away, but knowing she couldn't run away from herself.

If she hoped to get through this, she would have to disassociate from her own story. Twisting her hands together, she blurted out, "I worked for my father . . . entertaining his clients."

Austin refused to look at her. He kept his head down, his elbows digging into his knees.

"I went with my father to New York that April. I was the carrot he dangled in front of important clients in order to seal the deal. He promised me there would never be anything . . . sexual. Unfortunately, he forgot to tell that to his client.

"My father apologized and promised it would never happen again, but it was too late. I felt ashamed, and I think I might have been in shock. When I got home, I was a basket case; I couldn't even look at myself in the mirror, let alone look at you."

Austin sat up straighter. "I remember when you got home from New York, I was so excited to see you, but you told me not to come over, even though I was leaving the next day for a month. You said you were contagious and didn't want me to get sick before my big trip. We even argued about it."

She nodded in agreement. "You were so excited to spend that time with your dad. He had pulled so many strings, so you could take your finals early and get the time off to preview business colleges abroad. Barcelona. Berlin. Grenoble. It was all you talked about for months. I didn't want to ruin it for you. I just figured, if I could avoid seeing you that one last night, I would have time to deal with what happened—try to put it behind me."

"But we talked on the phone almost every other night. Why didn't you tell me then?"

"I just couldn't. I was spiraling. It took all the energy I had to talk with you without falling apart. That's why so many of our calls were *interrupted* by static. Whenever I thought I was going to lose it, I would blame it on a bad connection and hang up."

Austin's shoulders slumped as he shook his head in disbelief.

"I fell into a state of depression, which led to me getting really sick. Then I realized it wasn't depression that was making me ill; I was pregnant." Ashley stared out the window, unable to look at Austin. "I was either too depressed or too sick to go to class. I missed weeks of school, and my grades plummeted. When my father realized there was a strong possibility I might not graduate, he stepped in and made arrangements for me to take my finals early. When I was done, he flew us to New York."

She stopped so Austin could take it all in. She waited for him to say something, but he just sat there, never once looking at her, so she continued.

"Once we got to New York, I approached my father's client about my condition. He informed me he was married and had no intentions of jeopardizing his personal life because of me. He told me to get an abortion and never bother him again, but I couldn't do it. I felt horrible and blamed myself for the situation I was in, but I wasn't going to make matters worse by getting an abortion. Deep down, I knew I wasn't to blame. I was a victim. But I refused to make my baby a victim, too."

"What about your father?"

"He told me I would ruin my life if I continued with the pregnancy and gave me an ultimatum. He was unbelievable," she shook her head and wiped away a tear, "it was his fault I was in the situation I was in, but he was ready to throw me out on my ear if I decided to keep the baby. When I couldn't take it any longer, I ran. I located my mother's parents here in the San Fernando Valley and came back to California. I took on my mother's maiden name, moved in with my grandparents, and had Christopher seven months later."

Austin's head snapped up, stunned. He looked at her with red-rimmed eyes. "Christopher is your son?"

"Of course he's my son. Who did you think he was?"

"I just thought . . . well, I guess . . . It doesn't matter." Austin shook his head. "You mean you've been here in the valley all these years?"

"Yes."

"And you never once thought about contacting me?"

Ashley felt the sting of his words.

Austin stood and moved to within inches of her, making it impossible for her to ignore the hurt on his face. "Just tell me this, did you or did you not ever love me?"

"Please don't ask me that, Austin. That was a long time ago, and we can't go back."

"But you never even gave me a chance to accept your situation or try to help you through it."

"How could I? Even if I thought you could handle it, I knew your parents wouldn't have. They never liked me to begin with, and they were right. I was never good enough for you."

"But I loved you, Ashley!" Austin's voice boomed. "How could you ignore my feelings like that? You're right. I deserved better. Not because of what happened, but because of the way you handled it."

"Put yourself in my shoes, Austin. I felt like a whore and was pregnant to prove it. I had a father who used me rather than love me and a man who was threatening me into getting an abortion. Now, imagine what would've happened if I had dropped that bombshell in your lap. How would you have handled it?" Ashley paced back and forth. When she tried to continue, Austin cut her off.

"You never even gave me a chance to handle it!"

"That's just it, Austin, you wouldn't have handled it. Your parents would have handled it for you. They would've made sure I never came near you again. You wouldn't have had any say in the matter. Just like me."

They both stood silent for quite some time before Ashley continued in a softer tone.

"If I had it to do over again, I don't know what I would change. I can't imagine my life without Christopher. We had a rocky start, but God has seen fit to give us each other and a comfortable lifestyle. I would have loved to have had you be a part of it, Austin, but you know as well as I do that it never would've worked. I couldn't come between you and your parents. It wouldn't have been fair to them or to you. I'm sorry for the way things ended for us, but I can't say that I'm sorry for the way things have turned out for me. This is my life. I know nothing else."

Austin sat back down on the couch. Ashley could tell he was trying to digest everything. Just then, C.J. walked into the room, looked at Austin, then at her.

"I heard some loud voices; I was just making sure you were okay." C.J. looked at her intently. She assured him with a small smile. "We're fine, C.J. I think Austin was just about to leave."

"Leave!" Austin shot up from the couch. "I'm not leaving. You can't just drop this on me and expect me to keep my questions to myself."

C.J. stepped forward. "Look, if my mom wants you to leave, then that's what you're going to do."

"C.J., it's all right." Ashley stood alongside her son trying to reassure him that she was in control. "I just assumed we were done."

"We're far from done, Ashley. Don't you understand? I never got over you! All these years I wondered, I worried, I imagined what it would be like to see you again. This might not be what I expected, but I'm certainly not going to give up that easy."

Ashley turned to C.J. "Would you have Willow reschedule my appointments for another day?"

"Sure, Mom, but call me if you need me." C.J. glared at Austin before leaving the room.

Austin paced but Ashley needed to sit down. She was both mentally and physically exhausted.

"Look, Austin, I'll answer whatever questions you have, but I don't see what good it will do."

"Why did you go to the reunion after all these years? If you didn't want to be found, why come out of hiding now?"

It was a fair question, and one Ashley could easily answer, but should she open yet another can of worms? It took her a moment to compose herself and decided to be honest. Something she should have been twenty-five years ago.

"Austin, I have cancer."

ELEVEN

Austin's complexion turned an ashen gray. He sunk to the edge of the couch and just looked at her.

"I've only known for about a month. No one else knows. I haven't even told C.J., yet. The doctors are hopeful they caught it in time, but I guess I panicked. I don't know what I thought I would accomplish by finding you, but I was feeling pretty desperate. I wasn't acting very logical."

"Wait. You went to the reunion to find me? Ashley, I don't understand."

"I was being irrational, Austin. I don't know how to explain it."

"Yes, you do, Ash. Why were you looking for me?"

Tears rolled down her cheeks, her resilience weakening.

"Ashley?"

Wiping her tears away, she tried to explain. "I'm all C.J. has. The only family he's ever known is gone. I was fearful of leaving him alone if I found out my condition is . . . bad. I guess in my desperation, I thought maybe . . . I mean you're the only other person, but not that I assumed you'd be available . . . I mean—"

Ashley was frustrated she couldn't put her thoughts into words. Finally, exasperated with herself, she just blurted out what she'd been trying to say. "I wanted to make sure C.J. had somebody to turn to after I was gone. You were the only person I thought was good enough for him. I didn't want to leave him alone in the world. There . . . I said it. Are you happy? I know it was a totally preposterous idea, but I guess dealing with life and death issues makes a person do crazy things. I'm sorry I opened past wounds. I'm sorry that I hurt you. And I'm sorry I'm dumping all this on you now."

Ashley stood, putting some distance between them. But then she broke. "I'm scared, Austin. I have no one to talk to and—" She looked out over the ranch she loved, knowing she would trade it all to secure a good life for C.J.

"I'm so sorry, Ash. I'll help any way I can."

She felt Austin's hands on her shoulders. He turned her around, pressed her to his chest, and held her tight. She sank into the warmth of his embrace, knowing she was no longer strong enough to carry this burden on her own. She knew God was with her, and that He had a plan. But right now, she needed a tangible strength she could lean on.

A strength she found in Austin's arms.

It took a few minutes to compose herself; all the while, Austin held her close, stroking her hair. When she finally pulled away, she saw tears had traveled down his face and reddened his eyes.

"I've made a terrible mess of things," Ashley said as she stepped out of his embrace and sat on the couch.

Austin sat down next to her and squeezed her knee. She turned to the man she had never stopped loving.

"You haven't created a mess, Ashley. It took courage on your part. You've protected yourself all these years, but you were willing to put that aside, so you could provide something for your son. That's not a mess, that's admirable."

The room was silent again until Austin cleared his throat. "Look, Ash, I want to be here for you, and for Christopher, but if you haven't told him about your . . . your condition, maybe we should talk somewhere else."

Ashley noticed Austin couldn't bring himself to say the dreaded "C" word. "You're right. I know I need to tell C.J., but I haven't quite figured out how yet. I would hate for him to overhear us without having a chance to explain."

"Would you feel comfortable at my place?" Austin asked.

"I guess, but what about your . . . girlfriend, or is she your wife?"

Austin looked puzzled.

"The woman you were with at the reunion?"

He laughed. "That wasn't my wife or my girlfriend. Jenna is my niece." He looked at her dumbfounded. "I can't believe you thought I would be with someone young enough to be my daughter."

"Well, it can't be too outrageous; you thought the same thing about C.J."

"Touché!" Austin raked his fingers through his hair. "So, how about my house tomorrow? We could—Oh shoot! I can't tomorrow. I have a huge meeting, and it involves too many people to reschedule. How about Friday?"

"How about this weekend? I have an open calendar on

64

Saturday."

"Sure, I can do Saturday, but should you wait that long to talk to your son? He has a right to know."

"I know. I'll do it soon. I have a test next week that requires anesthetic, and I'll need C.J. to drive me home." She looked at Austin. "You've waited twenty-five years to talk. Are you sure you can wait another few days?"

"I can wait."

They walked to the living room side-by-side. Ashley opened the door for Austin, but he stopped and turned to her. "Can I ask when the test is?" His tone was somber.

"Tuesday."

He leaned forward and placed a light kiss on her forehead. "You have my cell phone number. Call me if you need anything."

Ashley watched Austin as he walked down the driveway, the feel of his lips against her forehead still lingered. He was hardly out the front door before C.J. came in the back.

"So, how did it go?"

"Fine." Ashley looked at C.J. and knew it was time to tell him the truth.

"Are you done for the day, C.J.?"

"I can be, why?"

"We need to talk."

TWELVE

Ashley barely got past the word *cancer* before C.J. started ranting.

"There has to be a mistake. This isn't fair. You've been through so much already."

"C.J.—"

"God wouldn't allow this to happen to you. Someone made a mistake."

"C.J.—"

"A technician, or the lab. Maybe the doctor got the files mixed up."

"C.J.! Stop it!" she shouted, then lowered her voice before continuing. "It's not a mistake. I've already had preliminary tests. Knowing my mother died from cancer, I should've gone in for screening earlier."

He stopped his pacing and looked at her, tears streaming down his face. "What are you telling me, Mom? Are you telling me you're going to die?" Not waiting for an answer, C.J. swallowed her up in an embrace that allowed them both to shed their tears together.

It took a while before either one of them could speak. Ashley proceeded to answer C.J.'s questions about uterine cancer, then explained what tests she had already taken. She knew it was a lot for him to absorb, but it felt good to finally have it out in the open.

"How long have you known?"

"I've been having tests for the last few weeks. I wanted to be sure before I told you—just in case there was a mistake. I have a colonoscopy on Tuesday, and I'll need you to drive me to the hospital."

"Why a colonoscopy?"

"They're making sure it hasn't spread further."

"What if it has?"

"Why don't we take one step at a time, C.J., and pray for the best."

"Pray? You think I should pray? Why? Obviously, God's going to do what He wants to, regardless if we pray or not. You go ahead, but as for me and God, I think this is where I call it quits."

Ashley watched as he stormed out of the room, her worst fear becoming a reality. C.J. was choosing to turn away from God instead of leaning on Him.

She waited the rest of the night for him to come out of his room, but he didn't. Ashley knew she had to give C.J. time to digest all she had told him, so she allowed him his solitude. When she prayed that night, she didn't pray for God to remove the cancer from her body. She prayed C.J. would find peace with God instead of running from Him.

Death she could handle.

But losing her son for eternity—she could not.

THIRTEEN

Ashley and C.J. went about their business the next few days like normal, but she knew he was watching her closely. The minute she looked fatigued or took on a laborious project, C.J. was right there by her side. He didn't mention the cancer, but she knew he would ask when he was ready. Until then, she would just give him his space.

She was surprised when Austin called Thursday evening to see how she was doing. She assured him she was fine, and told him she had spoken with C.J. When Austin asked how he took the news, she explained that he was angry, but didn't go into detail. The important thing was he knew, and now there was no reason they couldn't talk at her place. Austin sounded disappointed but agreed.

It was Friday evening before *her condition* came up again. C.J. picked up takeout for dinner, then straightened the kitchen after they were finished. He sat in the great room reading a hot-rod magazine while Ashley sat at the desk going over bills. After a long silence, C.J. finally breached the subject.

"Are you afraid?"

"A little, but not so much for myself. More so for you."

"Why me?"

"Because I'm afraid your anger and emotions are going to get the better of you."

"But I'm not angry at you, Mom. I just don't understand why God would put you through this when you've been through so much already." He tossed his magazine on the end table and stared at her sitting across the room. "Can you honestly tell me you aren't angry with God?"

"I was when I first found out. I felt like you do now. But I decided if I couldn't do anything about it, I wasn't going to waste what energy I had being angry or living in self-pity. I don't want you to be angry either, C.J. I mean, I know you need time to adjust, but I worry you're going to storm out of here one day and not be around when I need you most."

"Mom, I don't want to make this any harder on you than it already is. I'll try to improve my attitude, but I'm not going to make any promises." He went to the kitchen, grabbed a soda from the refrigerator and headed for the stairs.

"Austin will be stopping by tomorrow," she raised her voice, so he could hear. "I just thought you should know."

C.J. walked back into the room. "Why is he coming here? Hasn't he made enough trouble?"

"If I remember correctly, you were the one throwing punches."

"What does he want?" C.J. asked, clearly annoyed.

"He just wants to talk."

"And you . . . what do you want?"

"I'm not really sure."

She glanced out the window, asking herself the same question. *What do I want?* She had to admit, finding out Austin wasn't attached had given her a certain sense of relief—not that anything would happen between them after all these years. Even so, at least she felt more comfortable meeting with him, knowing she wouldn't cause problems in his personal life.

"I guess I just want . . ." Ashley turned to answer C.J. but he was already gone, leaving her with her jumbled thoughts and feelings.

FOURTEEN

Ashley watched from the window as Austin pulled into the driveway. Ten o'clock sharp. Just watching him step out of the car he drove in high school brought back a flood of memories.

She didn't want to seem anxious, so even though she knew he stood on the other side of the door, she waited for him to knock before opening it.

"Hi, Austin. Punctual as always." Ashley stepped back to allow him in, but he stayed on the doorstep.

"I know you said we could talk here, but do you think we could still go to my place? I thought the drive would be nice, and I'm not so sure I'm welcome here."

"Of course, you're welcome. I invited you."

When he removed his sunglasses, Ashley saw the uncertainty in his eyes.

"But I don't think your son would—"

"Mom . . ." As if on cue, C.J. hollered from the other room.

"I'm in here," she answered, waiting for him to make an appearance.

Walking into the living room, C.J. gave Austin a once over. "Oh, you're here."

The moment was awkward, and Ashley realized Austin was right. It would be easier to talk without C.J. hovering nearby.

"Ah, C.J., we've decided to go for a drive, so I won't be home for a while."

Ashley saw the look of relief on Austin's face before he slipped his sunglasses back on.

C.J. on the other hand, stood up straighter, pushed his ragged cowboy hat back from his brow, and planted his hands on his hips. "I thought you were going to talk here?" He directed his question at her but trained his penetrating stare on Austin.

"Austin thought it would be nice to go for a drive."

"So, you think you're going to take my mom for a little test

70

drive, is that it?"

"C.J., don't start!" Ashley snapped.

He looked at her, then back at Austin. "Don't think I don't know what you're doing. I know how guys like you operate. What starts off as an afternoon drive ends up as an evening back at your place. But just so you know, Mom doesn't drink so you might have a hard time loosening her up."

"Well, since you have me all figured out, don't wait up. Your mom and I have a lot of catching up to do."

"Why you—" C.J. lunged at Austin, but Ashley stepped in front of him.

"Stop it!"

He backed off, but his eyes never left Austin's.

Ashley didn't know who she was more upset with, C.J. for overreacting, or Austin for provoking him even further.

"Austin, why don't you go wait in the car. I'll be out in a minute."

"Sure. No problem." He glanced at C.J. then walked out the door.

Ashely spun around, furious at her son. "What's gotten into you?"

He crossed his arms against his chest. "I just don't like the guy. I think he's going to take advantage of your situation. You're not in the right state of mind to make rational decisions."

"Oh, and your behavior is rational?"

"You heard him, Mom. He insulted you, and you don't even know it."

"Actually, you insulted me more by calling me irrational."

C.J.'s ridged expression softened. "That's not what I meant."

"Then you have to trust me, C.J. I'm not going to do anything foolish or careless with Austin. Besides, I don't expect him to be around much longer. I'm sure once he gets the explanation he's looking for, he'll be ready to move on. We're both just looking for closure. So, could you cut your old mom a little slack, and let me handle this?"

C.J. pulled her into a hug. "You'll call if things get out of hand or if the situation gets too uncomfortable?"

Ashley laughed. "So, who's the parent now?" She pulled back and looked into his eyes. "I'll be okay, C.J., really."

Walking down the front steps, Ashley took a deep breath, trying to control her anger. She was ticked at Austin for inciting C.J. and wasn't going to let him get away with it. However, when she saw him leaning against the passenger door of his classic convertible, she nearly melted. With his ankles crossed and his large forearms stretched against his chest, he was the epitome of casual. His slightly frayed jeans and expensive leather loafers—with no socks—were such a contradiction. And the oxford shirt that fit tight around his muscular arms made him look way too good.

It was like stepping back in time. Ashley had butterflies just like she had whenever Austin picked her up for a date. She might be over forty on the outside, but inside, she felt like a seventeen-year-old girl again.

As she approached, Austin opened the passenger door for her, but she just stood there.

"Look Austin, I don't appreciate what you had to say back there. I know C.J. is acting a little overprotective, but that doesn't give you the right to bait him with offhanded comments."

"Well, it's obvious he already thinks the worst of me. So, I told him what he wanted to hear."

"You know what, I can't do this." Ashley turned to leave, but Austin tugged on her arm before she could walk away.

"Okay, I'm sorry. I don't know what got into me. I guess I've never had anyone take such an instant dislike to me, and it put me a little on the defensive."

"Then a word of warning," Ashley looked him in the eyes, "don't put me in the middle again. Because if you do, you will lose. Understand?"

"Understood," he replied sheepishly.

Ashley slid into the front seat of his car. Austin waited for her to put her seatbelt on before closing the door, then hurried around to the driver side. Once in, he latched his belt, started the engine, and pulled out onto the highway.

They wound their way through Topanga Canyon without saying a word. Ashley closed her eyes and rested her head back, enjoying the feel of the wind on her face, but after twenty minutes, she decided to break the silence.

"So . . . how's your family?"

"Pretty good. Dad's retired, and he and Mom are spending a lot of time traveling. In fact, they're in Scotland right now. Jessica is on her second marriage and self-absorbed as always. Jenna spends every other weekend with me since she doesn't get along with Jessica's new husband. She's such a great girl. I don't understand why all the friction at home. But I don't mind having her around, so I try not to interfere."

It was silent again, and another ten minutes went by before Austin blurted out, "So, why doesn't C.J. approve of me?"

She smiled. "It's not that he doesn't approve. You two just got off on the wrong foot. He really is a good kid, Austin, but he's a little headstrong."

"Gee, I wonder where he got that from?" He grinned while keeping his attention on the curving road.

"I'm not headstrong!"

"Liar!" Austin laughed. "How can you sit there and say that? You own a ranch, have what appears to be a very lucrative business, and thought nothing of pulling a gun on a man. Those aren't exactly the character traits you would associate with a timid woman."

"Well, I guess I've grown a tough exterior over the years," she answered, feeling defensive.

"Ashley, I wasn't criticizing you. I was just pointing out that you're not . . . I mean . . . you're differ . . ." He sighed. "Okay, now that I've stuck my foot in my mouth, how about you back up and tell me about the Circle-R. I never knew you were such an equestrian."

"Well, I wasn't back in high school. Like I said before, I moved in with my grandparents before C.J. was born. They lived in a small mobile home park down the hill from the ranch. C.J. and I used to walk there every day to pet the horses. The owners doted on C.J. and struck up a friendship with me. When the expenses of raising a child began to add up, they gave me a job on the ranch."

"So, how did you go from worker to owner?"

"The Andersons didn't have any kids of their own, so they kind of adopted C.J. and me, like surrogate parents. When my grandparents died, they offered me the cottage on the property. Over the years, I learned a lot about running a ranch. Ann taught me the business side like bookkeeping and payroll, while Lee taught me everything about horses. He was your typical crusty old cowboy, but inside, he had a heart of gold. Lee was very patient with C.J., always taking the time to answer his questions or show him the right way to do something. C.J. was Lee's little shadow and followed him everywhere. He grew up every bit a cowboy in the middle of a bustling city."

A flash, like a snapshot filled Ashley mind. C.J. and Lee, walking side by side, Lee carrying a saddle, C.J. stumbling over the lasso in his hand. She smiled; the memory sweet.

"Anyway, I didn't realize they were grooming me to take over the ranch. I just thought I was helping Ann wherever I could. Then, when they died in an auto accident, I found out they had transferred the ranch, the house, everything, into my name, with the stipulation that everything be split with C.J. when he turned twenty-one."

"That must've come as quite a shock?"

"It did. At first, I freaked out, not thinking I could handle it all. Raising a child, a horse ranch, boarders, bills, payroll. But I just took it one day at a time, and before I knew it, it was my new normal."

"How did your grandparents die?"

"Grandpa's health was failing when I first came to live with them. He lived long enough to see C.J. turn one but passed away that March. I know having C.J. around helped Grandma deal with her loss, but she began to slow down and died a year and a half later. That's when we moved to the Circle-R."

"And became Ashley Summers." Austin concluded as he turned south and drove along the coast.

Ashley nodded and continued. "When I moved back to California, I changed my name so that—"

"I couldn't find you?" Austin interrupted as he stole a glance her way.

"No. So my father wouldn't be able to find me." Ashley turned and watched as the coast sped by. The thought of her last confrontation with her father made her shudder.

"Are you cold? I can put up the top."

"No, I'm fine. The fresh air feels good."

When she closed her eyes, memories she had locked away for years, played in her mind. Some good, some bad.

"So, why didn't you—"

"Austin, I realize you have a hundred questions, but let's wait until we get to your place, so we can enjoy the drive."

He glanced at her, while trying to keep an eye on the traffic. "Are you okay?"

"Yeah. Just processing. Some of this stuff I haven't thought about for years."

He squeezed her hand where it rested next to the gearshift. "That's fine. Enjoy the drive. We can talk later."

When Austin drove through the entrance of the exclusive gated community, Ashley watched—mesmerized by the size of the houses as they zipped by. She had read about the level of Austin's success, but seeing it first hand was something altogether different. When they pulled into the circular driveway of a sprawling ranch-style house, Ashley smiled.

It suits him.

After helping her out the car, Austin guided her up the brick walkway with a lightly placed hand on the small of her back. His simple touch transported her to a time she had locked away in her memories.

God, if we could just go back.

They had just stepped into the entryway, when a phone rang in the distance. Austin closed the door behind her and said, "I'd better get that, but go ahead and look around." He hurried through the living room and disappeared down the hall.

Ashley allowed her eyes to wander, to take in the spacious room. *Inviting. Rugged. Just like Austin.*

A rock fireplace filled one corner of the living room, and next to it was a huge bay window that overlooked the front drive. Crossing to the other side of the room, Ashley instinctively stroked the back of the couch, wanting to see if it felt as luxurious as it looked. Though the furniture was massive, with a distinct masculine flair, the creamy shades of chocolate and tan made it feel warm and cozy.

However, it was the back of the house that had Ashley standing with her jaw hanging open. The far wall was nothing but glass and stretched the length of the enormous room complete with an indoor pool, chalet fireplace, a beautifully tiled bar, and a pool table.

This is incredible.

Ashley stepped down to the first level where the pool table sat. Sliding glass doors led to a rock patio that jutted out from the house and boasted an amazing view of the canyon, but it was the pool that captured her attention. She had never seen anything like it . . . well, at least not indoors. She watched her fair share of home improvement shows that showcased backyard oases, but this was truly spectacular.

The pool was massive and looked as if it had been carved from the earth hundreds of years ago. The rocks encasing the pool were gray, marbled with veins of black and white, and served as large planters for the rich foliage and exotic flowers overflowing their borders. In the far corner, a twelve-foot high waterfall trickled over stair-stepped rocks and flowed into the pool. A smooth-topped boulder that towered over the others served as a diving platform.

To say it was impressive would be an understatement. Then again, everything in Austin's home seemed to make an architectural statement.

The circular chalet-style fireplace with its candy-apple red hood was unique and obviously held a dual purpose. Though it had grates for grilling—and the distinct aroma of mesquite was present—the sitting area had over-sized cushions that semi-circled around it and spoke of the warmth the fire would provide on a chilly winter day.

The bar area with its high-gloss tile to match the chalet hood boasted eight high-back barstools with a modern flair. However, the polished brass rails that trimmed the bar and served as a footrest, made it look like a restored antique. *Eclectic.*

Turning back to the pool table, Ashley was admiring the workmanship of the intricately carved legs, and woven leather pockets, when the memorabilia on the built-in bookshelves to the left caught her eye. She studied the numerous awards and accolades that filled the shelves, along with photos that spoke of Austin's extensive travels: standing in front of the Eiffel Tower, atop a camel with the Sphinx as a backdrop, in safari gear, leaning against a jeep in the middle of nowhere. But it was the picture to the far right that drew her closer.

She gasped.

It was a picture of Austin and her when they were named Homecoming King and Queen.

I can't believe he kept it after all these years and placed it with his prized possessions.

"Do you remember that night?"

Ashley spun around to find Austin watching her.

"Of course I do." She walked back to the living room.

"What happened, Ashley?"

She sat on one of the overstuffed loveseats while Austin took a seat opposite her. Taking a deep breath, she stepped back twenty-five years and tried to explain as best she could.

"It started when I was sixteen, before I even knew you. I was an intern at my father's work, or more specifically, a social hostess. At first, I didn't realize what I was doing was wrong. I was so naive. All I knew was, for the first time in my entire life, my father actually wanted me around. So, I did whatever I could to please him. One day, I was pulled into the lap of one of my father's most important clients, and my father did nothing to help me. I realized then that I was being used as a pawn instead of an intern."

Ashley waited for Austin to voice his disgust.

He was silent, so she continued.

"After that year, I threw myself into all kinds of school activities and clubs. I figured the less free time I had on my hands, the better off I'd be. I tried to make myself too busy to be used by my father, but it didn't stop. He still put certain demands on me. I learned really well how to dissociate myself from the person I wanted to be and the person he used for his own financial gain."

"Were you . . ." Austin cleared his throat. "When we were dating?"

"No, Austin, I swear." Ashley got up, her anxiousness no longer allowing her to remain still. "I cared too much for you. I never would've done that to you. I thought it was over with my father and his business practices. Then I ended up in New York. I went because my father said he was surprising me with a Broadway show. I should have known better. Never once had he ever done anything for me, but I so wanted to have a relationship with him, I didn't realize how he was manipulating me. Once we got to New York, we ended up having dinner with a client of his. After we finished eating, my father handed the tickets to the man and left. I was furious but knew if I embarrassed my father by causing a scene, it would only make matters worse. All night, I rehearsed what I was going to say to my father when I got back to the hotel, but I never got the chance."

Ashley glanced at Austin, then turned away.

"I remember getting into the man's limo after the show. We exchanged polite conversation, critiqued the stage performance, and shared a bottle of sparkling water. I remember stepping into the elevator at the hotel, and suddenly feeling exhausted, lightheaded even. Jerr—the client wrapped his arm around my waist and mumbled something in my ear."

Ashley stood in front of the bay window staring into the face of her past, whisking the tears from her face.

"The next thing I remember is waking up in my hotel room. It was morning. I was in bed, undressed, and with no recollection of how I got there, but from the way I felt, I knew what had happened."

"He raped you," Austin whispered.

She nodded.

"Does C.J. know?"

"Yes. It was difficult to tell him, and I actually thought about lying, but I realized he deserved the truth." Ashley turned to Austin. "But you need to understand, my love for C.J. could not be stronger, no matter how he was conceived. I'm sure that's hard for you to understand, but no matter what, C.J. is still my child."

Austin moved closer, but she looked away, realizing how defensive she sounded. He turned her to face him, gently tipped her chin up, and looked deep into her tear-blurred eyes.

"I know all about love, regardless of circumstance, Ashley. I've never stopped loving you, and I was convinced of those feelings the moment I saw you at the reunion."

"But Austin—"

Placing his finger over Ashley's lips, he silenced her rebuttal. "Nothing you've said has changed my mind. There are no 'buts' about it. I love you."

Moving his finger, Austin pressed a kiss to her lips, a kiss Ashley accepted and returned with feelings of her own. She allowed herself to bask in the moment—a moment she had dreamed about for years. But it only took a split second for her to realize what she was doing was selfish. She stepped away from Austin and spoke what she knew he did not want to hear.

"I can't do this, Austin. It's not fair to you or to me." She walked across the room to the floor-to-ceiling windows and stared at nothing in particular. She could see Austin's reflection in the glass. He was leaning against the pool table waiting for an explanation. He wasn't going to like what it was she had to say.

"Austin, I can't start something with you I may not be able to finish."

She refused to cry; he was tired of the way it made her feel so vulnerable. When Austin didn't speak, she turned around. "Do you understand what I mean?"

"Yes, I understand." Austin waited a moment and then extended his hand to her. "How about we take a walk? Maybe the fresh air will help us both."

Austin didn't wait for Ashley to answer. He just took her hand in his and led her outside onto the walking path that twisted along the hillside.

FIFTEEN

Austin could feel his emotions getting the better of him every time he thought about what it was he wanted to ask Ashley. He waited until he felt strong enough, then asked, "What have the doctors told you so far?"

"I have uterine cancer, like my mom."

"How advanced?"

"They're not sure. Stage III, possibly stage IV."

"What does that mean?"

"Stage IV would mean it has spread beyond the pelvic cavity into other organs. They did an MRI and noticed some spots on my colon, so I have a colonoscopy scheduled for Tuesday to see if it has spread there or not."

"Then what?"

"It depends on what they find."

Austin cleared his throat of the emotional knot lodged in it. "Could it be terminal?" *Please, God, no. I can't lose her again.*

"If it has spread . . . possibly."

They walked hand in hand without speaking, Austin's mind spinning. He thought about the doctors and surgeons who had crossed his path in a professional capacity. *What if her insurance doesn't afford her access to the best physicians?* "Ashley, maybe you should get a second opinion or—"

"Austin, I trust my doctor. He's one of the best in his field. Even so, I've already decided not to have any kind of surgery or treatments if it has spread. What time I have left I don't want to spend in a hospital hooked to machines. I also don't want to be too sick or exhausted to enjoy life."

"And if it hasn't spread?"

"Then I'll need to have a hysterectomy, possibly radiation."

Austin let out a slow, even breath when what he wanted to do was scream at the injustice of it all. He glanced at Ashley, not understanding how she spoke with such calm. A monster had invaded her body, intent on destruction, yet she seemed at peace. Or was it just a facade she hid behind?

"Are you—"

"This is—"

They both stopped and laughed.

"You first," Austin said.

"I was just going to say how beautiful this is." She looked from side-to-side and up into the treetops. "I thought the ranch was therapeutic, but this is pretty incredible. What a luxury to have this right out your backdoor."

"Uh huh." He took in their surroundings afresh through her eyes. Rich foliage, rugged rock walls, leafy trees shading their path, the moist scent and feel of earth beneath their feet.

"Your turn."

"What?"

"What were you going to say?"

"Oh. Right." He didn't want to plant ideas in her head but needed to know. "Are you afraid?"

Ashley chuckled. "You know, C.J. asked me the same question."

"And?"

"I'm more afraid for C.J. than for myself." Ashley stopped walking and stood to face him. "Austin, I'm a Christian now, and I know I'll be in heaven the minute I die. As for C.J., he'll have to go on without me, and I think that scares me more than ever." Ashley started walking again. "C.J. is a good kid. When he was a little boy he loved the Lord, and talked as if Jesus was his friend, but now he's pretty bitter. To him, God has taken away everyone he's ever loved. His grandparents. The Andersons. He's struggling, and it breaks my heart." Ashley's voice cracked.

Austin squeezed her hand a little tighter. "I get the struggle, Ashley. I became a believer a little over three years ago. It hasn't always been easy, and I know I don't have all the answers, but I do know God doesn't choose random people to punish. Maybe He's using your illness to get C.J.'s attention?"

Ashley stopped. "Why didn't you tell me you were a Christian?"

"I just did."

"I mean sooner."

"Sooner? What, you mean I should have said, hi Ashley, where have you been all these years? I never stopped loving you. Oh, by the way, while you were gone, I became a Christian."

She laughed.

Austin smiled. "I've missed your laugh, Ashley."

"Well, I haven't had much to laugh about these past few weeks." She and Austin walked in silence until they were all the way down the hillside and standing beside the crashing waves of the ocean. Removing their shoes, they walked along the moist path the receding water left behind.

"I want to marry you, Ashley."

"Stop it, Austin." Her tone was clipped as she walked away, but he grabbed her arm and pulled her close. "Austin, don't!"

He did not loosen his hold but waited until she looked him in the eyes.

"Ashley, I'm serious. I've never been so sure of anything in my life. If your time is limited, I want to be there with you through it all. I don't want to waste any more time. We've already wasted enough as it is."

Austin proceeded to get down on one knee in the soaked sand. Ashley looked at him with astonishment.

"Ashley Anne Trent Summers, will you marry me? Promise me I will always get the last kiss at night, the first kiss each morning, and every dance in between, for as long as we have together?"

"Austin—"

"I don't need an answer right now. I know—"

"But Austin—"

"Please, Ashley, I know this has caught you by surprise, and you'll need to discuss it with C.J. But will you at least promise me you'll think about it and pray about it before you give me your answer?"

"I'll think about it, but—"

Before Ashley could say anything more, a wave crashed into Austin, knocking him forward, taking her down with him. They lay in a heap, shock giving way to laughter.

"I tried to warn you," Ashley said, pushing her hair back from her face.

"I thought you were going to decline my proposal. I didn't want to hear you say no."

They were wet from head to toe, sand in their hair, as they lay side-by-side, still laughing.

"I'll think about it," Ashley whispered.

Austin stopped laughing and perched himself up on one elbow, so he could see Ashley's face. She pressed her hand to her forehead blocking out the sharp rays of the sun, her beautiful smile evident.

"Did you just say what I think you said?"

She nodded. "Austin, I won't promise I'll marry you. There are too many unknowns at the moment, and I'm still processing the fact that you're really here. You have to admit it is a little surreal."

"I know. It's crazy if you think about it."

"But I promise I'll pray about it. That's the best I can give you right now."

Austin leaned closer to Ashley and pressed a passionate kiss to her lips. He was living a scene that had played out in his mind a hundred times over. He had actually proposed to Ashley after all these years, and she didn't disappear in a puff of smoke or down some darkened alley like she had done in all his dreams.

Austin got to his feet and offered Ashley a hand. She stood next to him for just a moment before another wave sent them running up the beach and back to the hillside path.

Ashley plucked at her sun dress as it clung to her body. Austin took one look at her and realized that the gauzy material of the dress was not only clingy but transparent. He quickly looked away out of respect for Ashley, but it took all the willpower he had to keep his eyes on the path in front of them and not on her.

When they got back to the house, Austin led her down the hall and motioned to one of the guest rooms. "There's a robe in the closet so you can get out of your wet clothes; the bathroom is right through there. I'll put your things in the dryer while we eat lunch. Take your time."

As soon as Austin shut the door, Ashley collapsed onto the rattan chair in the corner. Sitting on the edge, she rocked back and forth. *This can't be happening. This can't be real.*

Closing her eyes, she relived what just happened. Lying on the beach in Austin's arms. His kiss, passionate and possessive. The sand. The sun. A proposal. It was like a scene from a movie. *A fiction movie.*

Leaning back against the chair cushion, she struggled with her thoughts. She knew she was fooling herself and Austin by telling him what he wanted to hear. *I can pretend for today. Live in a dream world for a couple more hours.* However, the reality of her situation would be waiting for her tomorrow. And she knew from past experiences, real life always had a way of dashing her dreams.

She stroked the tears from her cheeks and opened her eyes.

Looking around the room, she enjoyed the simplistic mixture of whites and grays. It was tranquil, soothing. Slipping off her sandals, she loved the feel of the plush gray carpet under her feet. Crossing to the bed, she ran her hand across the chevron patterned linens and white chenille bedspread folded at the foot of the bed. The charcoal sketches of sand dollars and sea shells that hung on the wall were the perfect complements to the minimalist design, and the drape-less french doors bathed the room in sunlight. *Beautiful.*

When Ashley's stomach growled, it reminded her the day was moving too fast. *I don't want it to end, Lord. Just let me enjoy today.*

Grabbing the thick terry robe from the closet, she hurried to the bathroom, and quickly removed her soaked dress. Too self-conscience to discard *all* her clothing, she left her lingerie on, hoping it would dry well enough on its own.

With the robe wrapped snugly around her, she walked back to the living room. Not seeing Austin, she decided to go in search of the laundry room, so she could dry her wet clothes. She didn't get far before the pool stole her attention. *To think someone would have such a beautiful pool right inside their house.* When Ashley walked along the upper walkway past the red tiled bar, she noticed a whole other wing to the house.

She ducked her head into the first room and saw that it was a shower/changing room; perfect for guests using the pool. Thinking the laundry room must be close by, she walked further, but stopped when she reached a large sliding glass door. Peering inside, she saw a massive bed, leather chair, and a huge flat screen TV on the wall. *Another bedroom. The master suite. Austin's bedroom.* Before she could turn away, Austin walked into the room, ruffling a towel through his hair, another wrapped around his mid-section. She took a step back, but not before Austin saw her. Flustered, she hurried into the living room.

Twisting her dress in her hands, she realized she was dripping on the carpet. *What am I doing?* She hurried back to the guest room and wrapped her dress in a towel. When she returned, Austin was standing in the living room wearing black sweat pants and a charcoal colored V-neck shirt. His hair was still damp and in disarray, but even disheveled, he looked absolutely incredible.

Ashley was embarrassed and knew her heated complexion gave her away. "I wasn't trying to spy on you. I was looking for the dryer."

His playful eyebrows danced as he stepped closer.

"I guess we're even then."

"Even . . . what do you mean, even?"

Austin tugged at the towel in her hand. "Let's just say I'll never forget the way you looked in this dress."

"Austin!" Ashley shoved the balled-up towel at him as he laughed.

He held the towel and pulled her close. "Come on, you can keep me company while I make lunch, after I put these in the dryer."

Austin was still laughing as he led them to the kitchen. "I'll be back in a second."

The kitchen was beautiful. Like everything else in Austin's house, every detail and décor choice were perfect, right down to the quartz countertops, red tile backsplash, and stainless-steel appliances. Ashley was admiring the built-in pizza oven when Austin walked in behind her.

"So, what do you think?" he asked as he pulled a few items from the refrigerator.

"It's beautiful. Pizza oven. Indoor grill. Convection oven. You've thought of everything."

"I can't take credit for much. Most of this was here when I bought the place. I just updated a couple of things."

Ashley stood back and watched as Austin prepared their lunch. He definitely knew his way around the kitchen and even seemed to enjoy the process. As she watched, her mind drifted from lunch to Austin's proposal. The thought of it terrified her on so many levels.

C.J. is going to have a fit.

Not only did he and Austin get off on the wrong foot, but C.J. was now having to deal with her health issues too. Was it fair of her to pile on more? And what if the cancer *is* terminal? It doesn't seem right to involve Austin. Even though he said he wanted to share what time she had left, how could she expect him to stand by while she deteriorated?

"Earth to Ashley."

Her head snapped up to see Austin staring at her. "Sorry, what did you say?"

"I asked if you like grapes in your chicken salad?"

"Sure. That sounds great."

He pulled a bag of red grapes from the refrigerator, rinsed them, then began to dice them. "What were you thinking about?" he asked, glancing over his shoulder at her.

"What I'm going to tell C.J. when I get home."

"I'd like to talk with him, if that's all right with you. I think we got off to a bad start, and I would like to rectify that, if possible. I don't want him to see me as a threat or an intrusion. It's obvious you two have a special bond, and I want him to know I'm not trying to take his place in your life."

Ashley nodded in agreement but didn't say anything.

"So, how receptive do you think he'll be?" Austin continued as he pulled a plate of fruit and cheese from the refrigerator.

"I'm not sure. I mean . . . he's been pushing me for years to date and go out and meet people. But now that the time is here, I'm not sure he's all that thrilled about it."

"Had you spoken to him about me before this week?" Austin asked as he walked past her and into the dining area that overlooked the bar and pool. Ashley followed but didn't answer his question. She watched as he placed two plates of croissant sandwiches on the dining room table then returned to the kitchen. After making two more trips for the fruit plate and drinks, he joined her at the table where she had already taken a seat. He reached his hand across the table and waited for her to put her hand in his. "Do you mind if I pray?" he asked.

"Please do."

"Dear Lord, where to start is hard to say. Thank You for bringing Ashley back into my life, and that she is allowing me to stay. Work on C.J.'s heart, so he doesn't turn away from You during this challenging time. I pray C.J. will not be resistant to Ashley's and my relationship, and that he will consider his mother's happiness above his own protectiveness. Lord, I petition You now for a miracle in Ashley's body. We know You're the Great Physician and can heal her completely, but if that is not Your will for her life, help us to celebrate every day we have together. Bless this food to our bodies and thank You for the wonderful day You have given us so far. In Jesus name we pray, Amen."

Austin's prayer was so eloquent and heartfelt, it left Ashley speechless. She just smiled at him before taking a bite of her sandwich.

"You never answered me," he said before he took a large swallow of soda.

"I'm sorry, what was the question?"

"Had you told C.J. about me, or about us? I seem to remember him using my full name right after he punched me."

"Oh, Austin, I'm so sorry about that." Ashley was genuinely sorry but could not help but laugh as she remembered their little scrimmage.

"Laugh all you want, but is this what I can expect the next time I talk with him?" Austin's tone wasn't as jovial as hers.

"No, I think he'll show a little more self-control next time. And yes, he knows who you are. When I told him you showed up at the reunion with somebody else, he was actually disappointed."

Ashley took a sip from her soda before she explained further.

"When C.J. was a boy, he would always pull out my old scrapbooks from high school. Since there were so many pictures of you and I together, he figured you were special to me back then. As he got older, I explained why I left New York and changed my name. I told him I had left you without saying goodbye. Funny, back then he always seemed to feel sorry for you."

Ashley popped a grape into her mouth before continuing.

"When C.J. saw the write up of you in *Fortune Magazine*, he started tracking your career. He even threatened me a few times, saying he was going to go to your office in the financial district and tell you where I was. He was only teasing though. He respects the choices I've had to make in life and understands why I made them. But at times, I think he felt I had given up a lot because of him, and he wanted to do something to make it right."

"Did you ever speak to your father after leaving New York?"

"No. When I left, I took money that technically belonged to him. When I contacted him after C.J. was born, it seemed like the money was the only thing he was interested in getting back. I took out a loan, wired him the money, and never heard from him again. He knew he could get a hold of me at my grandparents, but I never told him I had changed my last name. So, I guess it's probably my fault we lost contact, but frankly, I don't think he ever tried."

Austin shook his head in disbelief.

"So, what about C.J.'s father, did he ever try to make things right?"

Ashley swallowed her bite of sandwich while she rolled a grape around on her plate. "I really don't think of C.J. as having a father. As far as he was concerned, I had an abortion, and he doesn't know any different."

"Do you think your father would've told him?"

"He had every opportunity to since I'm sure his social circles haven't changed much. But no, I don't think Dad would've told him. He wouldn't want to lose his edge or association with someone who could further his career."

"What about C.J.? Has he ever wanted to contact his father or grandfather?"

"No. At least I don't think so."

"If he wanted—"

"Could we not talk about my father anymore? You put a lot of work into this lunch, and I would really like to enjoy it."

As they silently finished their lunch, Ashley felt responsible for the mood turning so somber, but did not know what to do about it. Austin finally broke the silence when he asked, "Would you like to see the rest of the house?"

"I'd love to," she said, thankful for the change in subject.

They both stood, and with his hand on the small of her back, Austin led her to the far end of the hall. "This is Jenna's room when she is here. As you can see, pink is her favorite color."

Ashley looked around the room admiring the little details; the Battenberg lace curtains, the antique dresser, and the display of tea cups that seemed to cover every surface.

"Jenna collects tea cups."

"Yeah. It kind of became our thing. I brought her that little tea set sitting on her dresser from England when I was there on business. Well, every time I went somewhere after that, she would ask me to bring her home a tea cup."

"Wow, you've obviously done a lot of traveling."

"More miles than I can count," he said before moving on to the next room. "This is the room my friends usually stay in when they crash with me. As you can see, there's no lace, pink, or tea cups."

The masculine design was not lost on Ashley. Cherry wood bedroom set. Large sturdy pieces. Deep olive and brown accent colors.

"Then, there's the room you changed in."

"It's beautiful. Definitely feminine. Did you have someone specific in mind when you designed that room?" Ashley teased.

"I didn't decorate it, Jessica did. And no, I didn't have anyone in mind at the time."

For some reason, that pleased Ashley.

"You've already seen the pool area and billiard table, and maybe a nanosecond of my room, but would you like to see the rest of it?"

"Sure."

Austin led her down the hall to his home office. The room was what she expected from a man's office. Big desk. Leather chair. Lots of bookshelves. A flat screen TV mounted on the wall.

"Do you do a lot of work from home?"

"I try not to, but sometimes it can't be helped."

Attached to his office was a sitting area with a large leather couch, another big-screen TV and wet bar. Ashley could picture Austin sitting, watching a football game, drinking in his success.

"And this is my bedroom," he opened the door for her.

Again, Ashley was awed by the attention to detail and Austin's sense of style. Iron accents decorated the room while rich textures in deep reds and gorgeous greens brought the space to life. Though the room was quite manly, it still had a refined elegance to it. Ashley stepped forward and touched the intricately carved woodwork on the massive bed, clearly the focal point of the room.

"This is beautiful," she said.

"I got it while I was traveling through Transylvania. Isn't it incredible?"

Ashley nodded in agreement.

"Legend has it this bed was built for a king hundreds of years ago. He had taken a wife by arrangement, but she didn't love him, and swore she never would. So, the king had a sorcerer put a spell on the bed. If two people lay down together, they would fall madly in love and only have eyes for each other."

Ashley was getting rather uncomfortable with where this story was going but tried not to let it show.

"Unfortunately," Austin continued, "the bed arrived while the King was away on business. When he returned home, he found out his queen was very much in love with the gatekeeper. When he realized what had transpired in his bed, he had it taken away before he slept a single night in it. His queen and the gatekeeper were tried for treason and hung. Shortly after that, in utter despair, the king killed himself because he longed for his queen. I don't know if the legend is true or not, but it makes for an interesting story."

"Interesting, but sad." Ashley slipped back into the hallway, then in the direction Austin had gone with her dripping dress. Finding the dryer, she removed her dress, even though it was still a little damp. Walking back down the hall, she saw Austin clearing their lunch dishes.

"I'm just going to go get dressed."

"I had no ulterior motives by telling you that story, Ashley."

"I know," she said before disappearing down the hall.

When she walked back into the living room, Austin was standing in front of the bay window.

"I should go home now, Austin. I'm kind of overwhelmed at the moment, and I think I need some time to digest everything that's happened today. And I need to talk with C.J."

Austin pulled her close. "I didn't mean to overwhelm you, Ashley. It's just that I've been waiting for this day for the past twenty-five years."

"I don't understand, Austin," she said, feeling frustrated and confused. "Are you telling me you've never had a relationship with someone because you've been waiting for me? Why? Why didn't you just forget about us, put it behind you and start over?"

"Because I loved you."

"But that's ridiculous!" Ashley did nothing to hide her agitation. "We were just kids. You're an adult. A successful, attractive man. What happened between us was complicated. You should have just let it go."

"Isn't that basically what your father told you to do with C.J.?"

Austin's insensitivity crushed Ashley. "I need to go." She turned and walked out the front door.

"Ashley," Austin called after her, "I didn't mean to compare you to your father. I'm sorry."

She stopped in the driveway and waited for him to catch up.

"Ashley, look at me."

She turned around.

"I'm just trying to show you that I feel as protective about my love for you, as you do about your love for C.J."

"And I would like nothing better than to marry you and live happily ever after, but we both know that might not be possible. For the last twenty-five years, C.J. has been my life. It wouldn't be fair to complicate things now with a relationship. If I find out I only have—" She quickly coughed back her emotion. "If I only have a limited amount of time left, I need to spend it with him, not on a relationship with no future. You might have thought about this moment for the past twenty-five years, but I had to move on for the sake of my son. I just think it would be selfish of me to think only of my happiness right now, and not think about how this is going to affect him."

Ashley noticed the defeat on Austin's face as he reached for the car door handle and opened it for her. She wanted to say something, to apologize for being so blunt, but it was true, and he had to come to terms with it. Even with all his hoping and praying, reality might not work in their favor.

The ride home was uncomfortable and painfully quiet. Ashley was confused, frustrated, happy, but incredibly scared. Her life was in turmoil once again. She wanted to say something to Austin, but felt he really needed to think about what she had already said. She was aching inside but was trying not to let it show. She knew she would have to have a serious conversation with C.J. when she got home. His future was her top priority, and she had no idea how he would react to this drastic change in her life. She would never do anything to push him away, especially not now.

Austin pulled into her driveway and stopped by the front porch. The sun was just beginning to set and was casting a shadow on Austin's face. Ashley couldn't read his emotions, but heard it in his voice when he asked, "Can I call you?"

"Why don't you give me a few days. I need to spend this time with C.J. right now."

"Can I see you before your test on Tuesday, so we can at least have prayer together?" The sunglasses shading his eyes worked well to mask his feelings.

"Why don't you come over on Monday? We'll go for a ride, and we can pray then."

"Remember, you promised to think about it." Austin forced a smile, but it wasn't his trademark million-dollar smile that could melt hearts and change minds. It was an anxious smile and did little to hide his fear.

"I promise," she assured him, swallowing hard to control the emotion in her voice. Then she watched as Austin pulled from the driveway and drove away with her heart.

C.J. was not waiting for Ashley when she got home, but it didn't surprise her. Saturdays were busy at the ranch. Those boarding their horses showed up for their weekly ride. It was therapeutic for city dwellers, a way to refresh their minds and ready themselves for another busy week.

Knowing she would see C.J soon enough, Ashley dragged herself upstairs and changed out of her dress and slightly damp lingerie. Pulling on her favorite sweat pants and her Ariat sweatshirt that was two sizes too big, Ashley decided to use her time to process and pray. She was actually afraid to tell C.J. about Austin's proposal, knowing he would not understand. It was difficult enough for her to wrap her mind around it, how could she expect him to understand?

"Okay, God, where do I go from here?" she asked out loud.

Knowing that sitting quietly, bowed in prayer would not help her sort out her feelings, she began to pace. She had gotten in the habit of carrying on conversations with God as if He sat in the chair in the corner. A best friend to bounce ideas off of. Pacing and processing, that is how she worked through her problems with God—her ultimate sounding board.

"I know everything happens for a reason. But does it all have to happen at the same time? I also know it's my fault. I brought this on by going to the reunion. But if it was such a bad idea, why didn't you stop me?"

Sure, blame God, Ashley. That will make it better.

"I'm sorry. That wasn't fair. It's just I don't know what to do. I'm not afraid to die, Lord, really, I'm not. But the thought of C.J. growing up without any family, that's almost more than I can bear. I'm not asking You to remove this cancer from me. I'm just asking You to give C.J. more time to digest it. Work on his heart, Lord. He's angry and blames You. Be real to him, God. Show him You are here, and that You care."

She sat on the cushion of her window seat and looked out over her corner of the world. She thought of Austin's proposal—her heart skipping a beat. "Help me, God. I didn't plan for this to happen. I know I prayed I would see Austin at the reunion, but I was doing it for C.J."

At least I thought I was.

Having followed Austin's career, Ashley knew he was the same upstanding guy she'd fallen in love with in high school, and that he would be a positive influence in C.J.'s life. She wanted her son to have someone he could talk with, look up to, and be there for him when things got tough. Then, after finding out Austin was a Christian, Ashley was convinced he was exactly the kind of role model she wanted for C.J.

But now things were so much more complicated.

"I'm begging you, God. Show me what to do. It doesn't seem fair to accept Austin's proposal when my future is so uncertain. I know what he said about being there for me regardless of how much time I might have, but how can I do that to him? How can I ask him to put his life on hold? It would be like walking away from him all over again. I just don't think I can do that."

Ashley walked over to her bed, exhausted. Lying down with her head propped against the headboard, she closed her eyes. Just as she was beginning to drift off to sleep, she heard a quiet knock at the door.

"Come in."

She felt tired, which was becoming a normal occurrence. Her body was trying to fight off the enemy inside it, causing her to become easily fatigued.

"Well?"

Ashley did not miss the belligerence in C.J.'s tone. "Well what?"

"How'd it go?"

"Do you really want to know?"

"Yes."

She waved him over to sit with her. He plopped down on the antique trunk at the foot of the bed.

"Austin asked me to marry him." Ashley had not intended to blurt it out like that, but now that it was out, she waited for C.J. to respond.

He looked at her dumbfounded. "You're kidding, right?"

"No, I'm not kidding. He said he's loved me all this time and nothing I told him today changed his mind."

"You told him about the cancer, didn't you?"

"Well, yeah; I mean, how could I not?"

C.J. got up, stuffed his hands in his pockets, and walked toward the window. Shaking his head, he turned back around. "You know what, Mom? I always thought you were smarter than this. How can you be so naive?"

Ashley was speechless. C.J. had never spoken to her with such disrespect.

"Don't you know pity when you see it? I mean, look at this from his point of view. His high school sweetheart comes back into his life, battling a serious disease. He gets to play the part of a hero. Do you honestly think he has been waiting for you for the past twenty-five years? Do you really think he hasn't had other relationships?"

Ashley remembered asking Austin that same question, but he never answered her.

"Look at him, Mom. He's good-looking, extremely rich, well-respected. You don't think women have thrown themselves at him? He might be a gentleman, but all men have a little alley cat in them. You can bet after all these years, he hasn't ignored every offer."

Ashley did not want to believe C.J., even though it sounded painstakingly obvious. Maybe she wanted a relationship with Austin so bad, she was willing to believe whatever he said?

No. Austin wouldn't lie to me.

"C.J., you're wrong. Austin accepted the Lord three years ago. He's a Christian, now."

"Great, what accounts for the other twenty-two?"

With a sinking heart, Ashley realized what he was saying made sense. "Maybe you're right, C.J. Maybe I'm too vulnerable to make rational decisions right now. I thought I was dealing with all of this in a logical manner, but I guess I've let my emotions cloud my judgment."

C.J. sat with her, sympathy in his eyes. "Mom, I'm not saying he's not attracted to you." He spoke with gentleness, not with the bravado of just a few seconds ago. "You're a beautiful woman and very successful. I just don't want you disillusioned when you find a chink in his armor. He'll leave when the pressures get to be too much, but I'm here for you, Mom. I'll always be here for you. Haven't we always been enough for each other?"

Ashley nodded in agreement and pulled C.J. into an embrace. This is exactly what she did not want to happen. She would not let him feel pushed aside by a relationship with Austin. She might not agree with his character assassination of Austin, but that wasn't what mattered. She would not be selfish where her son was concerned. He needed to be her focus right now.

One hundred percent.

SIXTEEN

Ashley rolled over and looked at her bedside clock. *Ten o'clock?* "You're kidding me!" She quickly sat up and threw back the comforter, only to see she was still wearing her sweatpants and sweatshirt from the previous night. Playing catch up in her mind, she pieced together the events of yesterday, then leaned back against the headboard.

Saturday had been a day filled with highs and lows, excitement and uncertainty. She had debated long into the night about what she would do next. She had a proposal to contemplate, but she also had a son to consider.

Glancing at the clock again, she realized she was going to miss church because she did not have the emotional energy it would take to get up and ready in time.

But you can't lie around in bed all day either.

Dragging herself to the bathroom, she turned on the shower and began to undress. Catching a glimpse of her reflection in the vanity mirror, she leaned on the sink and stared at herself . . . wondering.

Twenty minutes later, she walked into the kitchen and saw C.J. working at the stove. "Good morning," she said, taking a seat at the bar.

"Is it?" he looked up at her, then back to the plate he was loading up with food. "You were beginning to worry me. I can't remember the last time you slept this late."

He smiled when he set a plate of eggs, hash browns, and toast in front of her, but Ashley could read the concern on his face. "I guess the last few weeks have caught up with me—but I'm fine. Really." She forced a smile to put him at ease.

C.J. made small talk over breakfast, and Ashley did her best to hold up her end of the conversation, but her heart wasn't in it; it was still back on the beach with Austin.

After breakfast she sat down on the couch that overlooked the ranch. Pulling her knees up to her chest, she laid her head down on the overstuffed pillow, and stared out at the sloping hills.

C.J. tried to ignore the sadness evident on his mom's face, but knowing he was partially responsible for her melancholy mood made it difficult to shake off.

He knew his remarks the previous night had bordered on extreme. Admittedly, he might have exaggerated his appraisal of Austin, but he did so for good reason.

I'm only looking out for mom's best interest. He tried to convince himself, but his conscience would not let it rest. *If you did the right thing, why do you feel so horrible?*

Wrestling with his feelings as he cleaned up the breakfast dishes, he questioned why he had been so negative regarding Austin. For the past few years, he'd encouraged his mom to find someone who could make her happy, but now he wasn't so sure. Especially with Austin's fast-forward approach.

No. I need to look after her, protect her from Austin's smooth talking. She doesn't realize how vulnerable she is right now, and Mr. Taylor sounds just a little too good to be true.

The silence between his mom and he extended into the early afternoon. He checked in on her a few times between chores—every time finding her still on the couch. She just sat there, staring out the window at the hills in the distance, but he could tell her thoughts traveled further than that.

Knowing he needed to say something to clear the air, he sat down across from her and sighed. "Mom, I'm—"

Before he could say three words, the phone rang.

"Just let the machine get it," she said. "I don't feel like talking to anyone right now."

He assumed *anyone* meant Austin.

Glancing at the phone, C.J. saw five other calls had gone straight to voice mail. When he played back the messages, his suspicions were confirmed.

They were all from Austin.

SEVENTEEN

Ashley was up earlier than usual for her morning jog.

Running usually energized her, but the tests she'd be taking tomorrow were monopolizing her thoughts, bringing her down. She had put up with C.J.'s doting yesterday, knowing he was trying to prove he could handle caring for her and the ranch, but she wasn't ready to be treated like an invalid.

And then there was Austin . . .

By the time Ashley made it back to the house and showered, her thoughts had spiraled. Her emotions were pulling her in a dozen different directions making her feel agitated and out of control. Needing to eliminate at least one of the complications weighing her down, she decided to call Austin.

"Taylor."

Hearing Austin's voice made Ashley hesitate, knowing he wasn't going to like what she had to say. But she had to. "Hi, Austin, it's Ashley."

"Hey, I'm glad you called. I tried getting a hold of you yesterday, but all I got was voicemail. I know you're a busy woman, but I was a little worried when you didn't call me back. Is everything all right? Are we still on for today?"

The relief she heard in his voice was going to make it twice as hard, so she took a deep breath to strengthen her nerves. "Austin, I think it would be best if we didn't see each other right now. I have some things I need to take care of before the test."

"But Ashley . . ."

Hearing the dejection in Austin's voice broke her heart, making her glad he couldn't see the tears rolling down her cheeks.

"It's C.J., isn't it? He doesn't approve."

"This is my decision, Austin."

"But he's why the change of plans, right?"

"Please, try to understand." Her voice faltered. "I know when you look at him, you see a man, but when I look at him, I see my son. He's struggling, Austin. He's angry and confused and doesn't need to be dealing with outsiders right now."

"Oh, I understand, Ashley; I understand completely. He's being selfish and only thinking about himself. But if you're asking me to stay away, I will. Not because of him, but because I don't want to make this more difficult on you."

"I just think it would be for the best."

"Can you at least tell me where you're having your procedure?"

"Memorial."

The long silence between them was deafening. Ashley was ready to hang up when Austin finally asked, "If I can't see you before tomorrow, can I pray with you now?"

"I'd like that," she said, her voice thick with emotion. "Because right now, I'm having a hard time doing it myself."

There was another long stretch of silence before Austin prayed. When he was done, Ashley said a quick goodbye and hung up the phone before she completely fell apart.

After spending most of the day in the house, Ashley went upstairs and took the concoction that would clear her colon. The remainder of the day she spent resting in bed, in-between sprints to the bathroom.

EIGHTEEN

It was six in the morning when C.J. arrived at the hospital with his mom. When she introduced him to her doctor, the older gentleman quickly extended his hand.

"Hi. I'm Dr. Allen. Your mom talks about you all the time. It's nice to meet you."

"I wish I could say the same," C.J. said, feeling like he was going to throw up.

Dr. Allen smiled in understanding. "I know this has to be hard on you C.J., but let me assure you, your mom is getting the best care possible. The colonoscopy is just a precaution. Although I'm confident the cancer hasn't spread further, I just want to be sure."

"And if it has?" C.J. blurted out.

"We'll cross that bridge if we have to," he said softly.

"Will we know today?"

"No. But I'll know before the end of the week. Do you have any questions about the procedure itself?"

He shrugged. "I read about it online."

"Well, it's pretty straight forward and completely painless. Your mom will be out during the procedure, so she won't feel a thing. The entire colon will be examined, and if any polyps are found, they'll be removed and biopsied. Ashley will stay in recovery until the sedative wears off—usually an hour or two—then she'll be released so she can recuperate at home. I recommend people spend the remainder of the day resting, which most likely is what she's going to want to do anyway. She might feel slight discomfort because of the extra gas in her system, but that won't last long. She can eat whenever she feels hungry, and there are no real restrictions. She just needs to listen to her body. That's about it," he said assuredly. "Do you have any questions?"

"Will you be doing the procedure?" C.J. asked, trying to keep it together for his mom's sake even though he felt like he was going to lose it.

"No. A gastroenterologist will. I'm just here for moral support."

C.J. nodded in understanding.

"Okay, then . . ." The doctor smiled at C.J. then turned to his mom. ". . . Ashley, if you'll come with me."

She hugged C.J. and whispered in his ear. "Everything is going to be fine. Don't worry."

Don't worry? How was he supposed to do that?

Once his mom disappeared down the hallway, he began to pace. *Confident. Precaution. Painless.* C.J. tried wrapping his mind around the words the doctor had spoken, but somehow words like cancer, terminal, and advanced, kept edging them out. Feeling exhausted, he glanced at the clock on the wall. Only ten minutes had passed. Groaning, he sat down in the waiting area. Leaning forward, with his head in his hands and his eyes closed, his thoughts started to spiral again. The doctor sounded so optimistic, but C.J.'s fears were winning the battle in his brain. When he sat back up, he was shocked to see Austin sitting across from him.

"What are you doing here?" C.J. snapped.

"I knew your mom would be in no condition to call me after the procedure, and I doubted you would, so I decided to wait here until it was over. Don't worry, I'm not here to bother you or make things more difficult. I just want to hear for myself that everything went okay."

C.J. watched as Austin got up from where he was sitting and took a seat on the other side of the waiting area, then bowed his head.

An hour had passed when C.J. heard the compressed air of the automatic doors. He looked up to see Dr. Allen approaching him, and out of the side of his vision, he saw Austin stand.

C.J. listened to the doctor, shook his hand, then turned and walked over to where Austin was waiting.

"They found some polyps," he volunteered. "The doctor doesn't believe they are cancerous, but they were removed and will be biopsied to be sure. He should have results in a few days."

"And Ashley?"

"She's fine. She'll be ready to leave in about an hour."

"Thank you, C.J. I know this must be hard for you, and I promise I won't bother you further. Even so, here's my business card, in case something comes up, and you need to get a hold of me. If you don't mind, I'd like to know how things progress. I don't want to burden

Ashley, so if she doesn't want to talk to me, I'll respect her privacy. Just know I'll be praying for you both." Austin turned around and disappeared into the elevator.

C.J. just stood there with Austin's business card in his hand. He felt like such a jerk. Unless this guy was an incredible actor, he had just volunteered to step out of the picture, and he did it without a confrontation. C.J. could see the emotional exhaustion on Austin's face and knew that wasn't something he could just conjure up.

Maybe this guy is for real?

He had just looked at his watch for the hundredth time, when a young nurse dressed in a floral smock wheeled Ashley down the corridor. C.J. hurried to his feet. His mom smiled—a sleepy smile—and reached for his hand, then gave it a weak squeeze.

C.J. walked alongside his mother as the nurse pushed the wheelchair to the patient loading area—part of the private hospital's strict procedure. The nurse repeated some of the instructions Dr. Allen had already told him. Discomfort from gas. Can eat when she feels like. Groggy. She then waited while he pulled the truck around and helped his mom into the cab.

Once Ashley got home, C.J. helped her upstairs to her room and into bed, then sat in the chair by the window and stared at her. He could not imagine what life would be like without her. Even now, seeing her in such a fragile state was such a new experience for him. He had never seen his mother incapacitated, and it scared him.

Leaning his head back against the chair, he tried to rest, but every time he closed his eyes, all he could see was Austin Taylor praying for his mom.

~®~

Ashley stirred.

When she opened her eyes, C.J. got up from the chair in the corner and sat on the edge of her bed.

"How do you feel?"

"Not as bad as I expected. I think rushing to the bathroom all yesterday was more uncomfortable than this."

"So, do you feel like eating something?"

"Not yet. Maybe in a little bit." Ashley looked at C.J.'s pale complexion. "Are *you* all right?"

"Yeah. It just hurts to see you so . . . I don't know . . . so . . . not like yourself."

"You mean bossy and mean?" Ashley joked.

"Right now, bossy and grumpy sounds a whole lot better than sick and fragile."

"Hey, who said anything about grumpy?" Ashley jabbed C.J. in fun, then shifted her head on the stack of pillows so she could sit up. "You know, chicken soup sounds pretty good."

"Chicken soup coming right up." He leaned over and gave her a quick kiss on the forehead before reaching for her phone. "I'm taking your cordless with me. If you need anything while I'm downstairs, just hit the pager button."

NINETEEN

Ashley's mind wandered while waiting for C.J. to bring her lunch.

The ranch.

C.J.

Cancer.

Austin.

She knew she should call him, but she didn't know any more now than she did on Sunday, and the doctor didn't expect to have her results back until the end of the week. *I'll call him when I have a little more energy. Physically and emotionally.*

C.J. returned with a tray full of goodies. Along with the soup, he brought crackers, soda, juice, and Ashley's favorite sugar cookies. He looked so proud of himself when he set the tray in front of her.

"Looks great, C.J. Are you going to join me?"

"Nah, I had some leftover pizza. I didn't want to make you feel bad by eating it in front of you."

C.J. sat and visited with her as she sipped on her soup and nibbled some crackers. When she finished, she set the cookies on the nightstand, so she could snack on them later.

"Is there anything else I can get you?" he asked as he stood and picked up the tray.

"No. I'm fine."

"Okay . . . well . . . I'm expecting a feed delivery, and I want to be there when it arrives. I'm tired of getting stale bales hidden on the bottom of the stack. You sure there's nothing you need before I go?"

"No. I'm fine. I'm just going to rest. But I really should call Austin; at least let him know everything went okay today."

C.J. removed his hat and raked his fingers through his hair. "Well . . . just so you know . . . Austin was at the hospital this morning. He left as soon as he found out everything went okay, and you were in recovery."

"What? Why didn't you tell me sooner?"

C.J. shrugged.

"Did you two talk?"

"Briefly. He told me he wasn't there to interfere; he just wanted to make sure you were okay."

Ashley wanted to ask more but sensed the belligerence in C.J.'s tone. Not having the energy to get in to it with him, she decided to change the subject. "Is Willow in the office?"

"Yeah, are you feeling up for visitors?"

"Well, I know she was expecting to hear from the veterinary school she applied to. I just wanted to ask if she knew anything yet."

"I'll tell her to come up before she leaves." Standing in the doorway, he turned. "Last chance. You sure you don't need anything else?"

"No. Thanks for lunch, though. It was just what I needed. I'm lucky to have such a doting son."

C.J. left his mother's room feeling like dirt. He saw the way her eyes brightened when she found out Austin had been at the hospital, but all it did was frustrate him. He didn't want to see his mom get hurt. He was sure Austin would disappear the minute things got tough, and that kind of disappointment was just one more thing she should not have to deal with.

C.J. tried convincing himself he was only looking out for his mom's best interest, but was he really?

TWENTY

"Ashley, I hear you've been bumming around since Tuesday."

She quickly looked at C.J. and whispered, "Did you call Dr. Allen?"

"I was concerned. You haven't left the house. That's not normal. Well, not for you."

"Ashley?" Dr. Allen interrupted.

"I'm just feeling a little out of sorts."

"How would you feel if I told you that your test results came back negative?"

Tears immediately filled her eyes. "Are you sure?" she whispered as she reached out for C.J.'s hand and clenched it— smiling to let him know it was good news. "So, where do we go from here?"

She listened intently while the doctor spoke. C.J. stood by, concern furrowing his brow.

"What did he say?" he asked the second she hung up.

"The tests were negative. The cancer hasn't spread."

He took a deep breath. "So, what's next?"

"I'll still need a hysterectomy and possibly radiation. Dr. Allen's going to schedule surgery for next week."

C.J. pulled her close and held her tight. "That's great, Mom. I don't mean that you still need surgery, but that the results were good."

She knew what he meant, because she felt the same way. A sense of relief swept over her, knowing her prognosis appeared to be a little more positive. And though she felt a heavy burden lifted from her body, she still felt an emptiness in her heart.

An emptiness that required a different kind of healing.

"C.J., I think I'm going to go for a ride."

"Great, I'll go with you."

"No, I'd like to go alone."

"Mom, you haven't even been strong enough to leave the house.

I don't think you should go riding alone."

"I haven't left the house because I didn't *feel* like it, not because I couldn't. It was emotional fatigue, not physical. I'll be fine."

C.J. was relieved to see his mom's burst of energy, so he didn't push the idea of going along with her, but he watched as she climbed the stairs and realized, even though his reaction to the doctor's report was pure excitement, his mother was still weighed down with heavy thoughts.

He was being selfish, and his selfishness was getting in the way of his mother's happiness. She had sacrificed so much for him over the years. Even now, while she struggled with one of the biggest battles of her life, she was putting her happiness aside because of him.

C.J. decided his self-centered thinking had gone on long enough.

It was time to give back to the woman who had given so much to him.

It took longer than usual for Ashley to saddle Dominus. His excitement in seeing her—knowing he was going for a ride—fueled his rambunctiousness. The prized white stallion lived up to his name in both size and strength. He was well aware of the power he possessed and flaunted it whenever he got the chance.

After exerting much of her strength, Ashley was finally on her way. Tipping her head back, she was thankful for the sun that warmed her face and the gentle breeze that helped diffuse the heat of the day. Though she felt gloomy on the inside, being outdoors was doing wonders for her disposition.

Dominus' gate was slow and smooth, almost hypnotic. Ashley took her time riding her favorite trail as it rose to the rim of the canyon. When she reached the top, she dismounted and looked out over the vast ocean. Taking a seat on a massive rock that flanked the trail—Dominus' reins hanging over her shoulder—she reflected on the things of the Lord, once again, speaking out loud to her counselor.

"Lord, sometimes I feel so insignificant in this creation of Yours, and then You surprise me with such an amazing show of Your mercy. I look at these rugged hills and the endless coastline, and I'm in awe of You. It amazes me that the Creator of all this just touched my body and ceased the smallest of deadly specks from spreading. You did that just for me, and I feel embarrassed that I'm not jumping up and down for joy. It's because I'm selfish, I know. I want it all, good health, my son's affection, a successful career, and someone who will crawl into bed with me at night. I've worked with some amazing men in the film industry over the years, but not one of them stirred these feelings in my soul. But now, after seeing Austin, I realize I long for the man I never stopped loving."

Dominus nuzzled her shoulder, making her laugh. "I love you, too, boy." She stroked the blaze that streaked his muzzle before turning back to the rolling sea.

"I know it sounds pretty ungrateful to say, thank you for touching my body, God . . . oh, and by the way, yeah, I want a love beyond what You've given me. I know without a doubt You have provided all my needs. I came to You angry and hurt twenty-five years ago, and You put up with me until I let the barriers down that separated us. You saved me and called me your own. Now, I am asking that You help me with my heart once again. Prepare me for a life of singleness or give me some type of sign that it's okay to pursue a relationship with Austin. I know You'll need to work on C.J.'s heart in order for that to happen. I guess that's what I'm asking for. If this is too selfish, please make it abundantly clear, so I don't lead Austin on or put an obstacle between C.J. and me. He is still my first priority, God, because he truly is a gift from You. Thanks for letting me ramble on when You already know my thoughts and desires. And please help me in the days ahead physically. Amen."

Ashley stayed on the mountaintop a while longer, taking in the scenery and enjoying the breeze against her face. She felt a new energy after spending time with God. It had forced her to verbalize her feelings instead of keeping them all stifled inside, and she felt stronger for it.

When she and Dominus finished their outing, Ashley went through their usual routine. Exchanging bridle for halter. Taking care of her tack. Hosing him down. With no breeze in the stable, she felt the full force of the heat and took off her button-down shirt and tied it around her hips. Though she was tired, she continued Dominus' rubdown, spoiling him as best as she could, making up for their uneventful ride. She knew he wasn't satisfied. The most she'd allowed was a canter, when he had wanted to run.

"Thank you for being patient with me, boy. I promise, once this is all over, we will tear up the trail like nobody's business."

Heading for the house, Ashley bellowed the red tank top that clung to her chest. Her bare arms glistened with perspiration, and her jeans stuck to her like a second skin. A shower was definitely the next order of the day.

Entering the house through the backdoor, Ashley called out to see if C.J. was around.

"In here, Mom," he answered from the living room.

Ashley poured herself a glass of water, drank half of it and then placed the tall, cold glass against her forehead. C.J. finally appeared in the doorway between the living room and kitchen.

"How was your ride?"

"Just what I needed. Now, I'm going to go take a nice long shower, and then I'll be in my office."

As she stepped around C.J., he said, "There's someone here to see you."

When she walked into the living room, movement by the fireplace caught her attention.

"Hi, Ashley."

"Austin?" She was thrilled to see him, but irritated, too. "What are you doing here? I thought you understood I needed—"

"It's okay, Mom, I invited him."

Ashley turned to C.J. who stood with his arms crossed against his chest.

"Look, I can't say I'm thrilled with the idea of having Austin around, but I realize I've been acting like a jerk. Besides, I can't stand to see you moping around the house any longer."

Thank you, Ashley mouthed for C.J.'s eyes only.

He smiled at her, but when he turned his attention back to Austin his smile disappeared. "If you hurt her, you'll have to answer to me."

Austin put up his hands in mock surrender. "Understood." Then, moved forward and extended his hand. "I appreciate you giving me a chance."

C.J. looked reluctant, but accepted Austin's handshake.

"And, if you're not opposed to it, C.J., I'd like to spend some time getting to know you, too."

"I appreciate that." He gave Austin a slight nod before heading for the door. "But right now, I have some fence posts that need my attention, and Mom has some things to discuss with you. Maybe you can stick around for dinner. We can talk then; just the two of us."

"I'd like that very much."

"Then I guess I'll see ya later. And Mom," he turned to her, "don't overdo it."

C.J. walked away, leaving Ashley speechless.

Once he was gone, Austin pulled her close and pressed a welcoming kiss to her lips. Ashley closed her eyes and enjoyed the moment. His hands on her hips. His lips against hers. Then she pulled back. "I had no idea he was going to call you."

"It surprised me, too. When I heard C.J.'s voice on the line instead of yours, I panicked, thinking something was wrong. Then, when he said he was going to back off, so we could spend time together, I was dumbstruck. But . . . now that we have the green light . . ." Austin smiled, pulling her close once again and stroking her back, reminding Ashley how badly she needed a shower.

"Look, Austin, why don't you make yourself comfortable while I take a quick shower. Then we can talk."

"Your tests? Can you at least tell me how they went?"

She smiled. "They were negative. The cancer is contained, and I'll have surgery sometime next week."

Austin squeezed her so tight Ashley almost felt faint. Then she realized it wasn't just Austin's embrace that had her feeling light-headed. It was the realization that God had answered her prayer. He was paving the way for her and Austin to be together.

Thank you, God. Thank you, Thank you!

After she took her shower, Ashley still felt faint. Although her excitement level was sky high, she had to acknowledge her lack of food and the exertion from her ride had her feeling a little unsteady. Taking it slow, she shuffled through her closet for the perfect outfit.

Unfortunately, the wardrobe she had acquired over the last few years consisted mostly of jeans and just a few dresses for church. Wanting to feel comfortable, she settled on a crisp white blouse and her nicest Levi's. Pulling her hair up off her neck, she clasped a barrette, then applied a little blush to her cheeks to camouflage her pale complexion. Standing back and taking in her reflection, she realized she looked the same as she always did. *Oh well, this is as good as it gets.* Slipping on a pair of leather clogs, she headed downstairs.

Ashley found Austin sitting in the living room leafing through the scrapbook on the coffee table. When he heard her enter the room, he scooted over, making room for her on the couch.

"This is really fascinating. You really worked on all these

films?"

"In one way or another."

"Some of these were huge box office hits with some pretty famous actors. Did you get to meet all of them?" Austin was obviously impressed with the clientele of the Circle-R.

"Most of them. Some shoots were just opening shots and prairie footage, but sometimes we worked on the full-length films."

Austin continued to thumb through the book, pointing out the stars he recognized as Ashley explained what she did on each shoot.

"Wow! Is that who I think it is?" Austin scrutinized a photo, interrupting Ashley's discourse. "He sure seems to be holding you pretty close."

"Oh, he was just thanking me for getting him a Benton saddle."

Austin's look was quizzical.

"It's a special type of saddle, and it's pretty pricey. He was just thanking me for making him more comfortable. It was a long shoot and he was appreciative."

"Yeah, well, he looks *very appreciative*," Austin said as he continued to flip through the book. After seeing several more shots of her with the same celebrity, he finally asked, "Were you two an item or something? That doesn't look like he's just thanking you for a saddle." Austin pointed to a picture of her dressed up for a special event, the man close to her side.

"Actually, we did date a few times. We had worked on several films together, and I went with him to a few premieres. I knew he was attracted to me, and I enjoyed his company a lot, but I wasn't interested in anything serious. I told him so at the end of that evening. He was very gracious about the whole thing."

"You're telling me you dated a movie star and gave him the brush-off?" Austin's tone was playful and serious at the same time.

"No, I wouldn't say it was like that. I just wasn't interested."

He looked at her with a raised brow. "I'm impressed."

Ashley gave him a gentle shove. "Stop it, Austin, you're embarrassing me."

Austin continued to flip through the pages, occasionally shaking his head in unbelief. Ashley found it amusing that he was so impressed with the work she had done. It made her realize how proud she was of her accomplishments. When Austin was done with the book, he closed it up and sat back on the couch. Edging his way closer to Ashley, he casually draped his arm around her shoulders.

"Do you feel well enough to go out for a bite to eat?"

"No, I better not. My ride kind of wore me out. Besides, you have an open invitation to stay for dinner. Why don't we order takeout? That way you and C.J. can get to know each other a little better."

"I'd like that, but would he? I know he invited me for dinner and all, but I don't want to push it. I mean, I have no qualms being around C.J., and I appreciate his change of heart, but I'm not so sure he wants me invading his territory. At least not just yet."

Ashley shrugged her shoulders. "He said he wanted to get to know you. Why not tonight?"

"Okay. As long as you think it's a good idea."

"I do. And, in the meantime, I can give you a mini-tour of the ranch."

He looked into her eyes. "I don't want you over doing it. You just said how tired you were."

"I'll be okay. Besides," she smiled. "I'll use you as a cane."

Ashley led Austin around the yard, explaining the setup of the Circle-R. They walked all three stables, and then watched April correct the technique of her young student. Ashley was feeling tired and knew she should head back to the house, but C.J. was practicing his barrel riding in the far arena, and she wanted to see how he was doing. Walking up to the metal fence, she rested her arms on the top rail and hooked her heel on the bottom.

Austin stood alongside Ashley and watched as C.J. whipped around the barrels. "I'm not sure what I'm watching, but he seems pretty good to me."

"He's the district champion and is practicing for the state finals." Ashley smiled, filled with a sense of pride.

Billy—the ranch fix-it man—stood by, stopwatch in hand. Clicking the timer as C.J. raced past him out of the arena, the older man hollered with excitement. "You're doing it, boy! That was your best time yet. You're within three one-hundredths of the state record."

C.J. slowed Knight, circled back, and rode over to where Austin and she were standing. "That was great C.J.!" Ashley shouted with excitement. "You're going to blow away the competition at finals."

He looked at them from where he sat high in the saddle, sweat running down his face. He pulled off his hat and wiped the perspiration on his forehead with the sleeve of his shirt then placed his hat back on his head. "Are you going to be there, Mom?"

"You bet I will. I wouldn't miss it for the world." Ashley

mentally did the math. Finals were in eight weeks. If her surgery was next week, she would have seven weeks to recover before the championships. But if she needed radiation, it would be cutting it close. *If nothing else, they can prop me up in the stands.*

After watching C.J. and Knight perform some stunt riding, she and Austin walked back to the house, Ashley holding on to his arm for balance. Once indoors, she collapsed with a heavy sigh on the couch in the great room.

"How about something to drink?" he asked as he walked around the kitchen island.

"Sure. I'll take some orange juice. Glasses are in the cupboard to the left of the refrigerator."

She studied Austin as he poured her a glass of juice. He looked up and caught her staring.

"What?" Austin said with a grin as he handed her a glass and sat beside her on the couch.

"I just can't believe you're here," Ashley said, feeling a sense of wonderment.

"Well, I am. And this time you're not going to be able to get rid of me."

Without even thinking, Ashley leaned into Austin until her nose brushed against his. She kissed him with the love she had tried to deny for so many years. Austin returned her affection with an indulgent kiss. Wrapping her in his arms, their spontaneous moment turned into a passionate embrace. *This is real. He's really here.* As quickly as they fell into the moment, Austin pulled away from her and paced across the room. Running his hands through his hair, he turned to her, mischief in his stare. "That's why I want us to get married."

She laughed. "So we can kiss?"

"Because I don't want to stop at kissing," Austin said with blunt honesty. "I have no self-control when I'm around you, and I'm afraid we will wind up in a position that challenges my celibacy."

Ashley glanced away—embarrassed—knowing she was the one who initiated the kiss. "I'm sorry Austin. Not that I kissed you, but that I let us get carried away. I guess I just wanted . . . wanted to know I wasn't imagining you. I keep thinking—at any moment— I'm going to wake up and realize all of this has been a dream."

"It's not your fault. I didn't want to stop any more than you did. I'm just admitting I don't think I can be trusted to be strong in this area."

"Is that based on past experiences?" Ashley asked, candidly.

"No. Not at all. God has done a tremendous job protecting me from empty relationships. I'm an admitted workaholic; everyone knows that about me. I don't know if it's good or bad—exchanging one vice for another—but I'm thankful I don't have a string of regrets weighing me down."

"But you *have* had intimate relationships before, right?" Ashley decided to be bold, knowing there was no use wasting time dancing around sensitive subjects.

"No, Ashley, I haven't." He squatted in front of her, took her hands in his, and brought them up to his lips. Pressing a kiss to her fingers, he looked into her eyes. "And I want to make sure when we're together, its right, not something we've rushed into or done outside of marriage. I don't want us to blow it physically, then feel guilty. I don't want our intimate moments to be anything but perfect."

"Austin, I don't think you're being realistic. This situation is far from perfect." Ashley pulled her hands away and sank further back into the couch cushions, putting some distance between them.

"How can you say that?"

"Because . . . this isn't a fairytale where everyone lives happily ever after. I have cancer, Austin. And right now, we have no idea what that means. But I do know, no matter the prognosis, I won't be having any more children. Have you even thought of that? If we get married, you will never have a child of your own."

"I'm over forty, Ashley. I've already come to terms with the idea of not having kids of my own." He reached forward and brushed a strand of hair out of her eyes, then looped it behind her ear. "Why do I get the feeling you're trying to pick a fight?"

"I'm not. I'm just being realistic."

"No. You're being negative. There's a difference."

Before she could offer a rebuttal, he leaned forward, kissed her, then pushed to his feet. "I don't know about you, but I'm starving." With a playful smile, he walked to the kitchen. "Why don't you let me fix you and C.J. dinner? I don't want to brag or anything, but I do know my way around a kitchen pretty well. I bet there is a feast in these cupboards just waiting to get out."

Ashley watched as he explored cupboards, then looked inside the freezer. "Okay, but only if I help." She uncrossed her legs and stood.

"No. You stay put and rest. I'll ask if I can't find something."

Austin continued to look in the freezer, bobbing and weaving, moving things around.

"Are you sure?"

"Positive."

"Okay. Far be it from me to stand in the way of your creative process." Ashley sat back down, punched at a stray pillow and placed it under her head. "I'll just rest my eyes here. But call if you need something." She curled up on the sofa, not caring if she was dreaming, only hoping she would never wake up.

TWENTY-ONE

C.J. pulled off his boots at the backdoor before making his way into the kitchen; the smell of garlic permeating the air. He saw Austin working at the stove with a hand towel over his shoulder. When Austin saw him, he signaled with a finger against his lips to be quiet. C.J. turned and saw his mother, asleep on the couch, with a peaceful look on her face that he had not seen in quite some time. He knew it was because of Austin, but instead of letting jealousy rear its ugly head again, he decided to head upstairs and remove himself from the situation.

"Hey C.J., where does your mother keep the cheese grater?" Austin asked as C.J. rounded the corner.

"Here, I'll get it. It usually disappears behind the mixing bowls." He got the grater out for Austin, then looked at the casserole dish on the counter. "Chicken Parmesan?"

"Yeah, do you like Italian?"

"I'm not really hungry," he lied, not trusting himself to carry on a civil conversation with Austin. Even so, he stood and watched as Austin grated cheese across the top of the dish, put it in the oven, and set the timer. Realizing he was just standing there, he turned to go.

"C.J. wait."

He turned back around.

"Thank you for having me here, and for caring for your mother the way you do. I know if it wasn't for that, you never would've called me."

"You're right. I won't say I'm thrilled you're here. I just know my mother never stopped loving you, and she's already sacrificed so much for me. I wasn't going to be the person who stood between her and the happiness she deserves."

"I'm not going to force a relationship between you and me, but I do hope over time, we can learn to appreciate each other."

"I don't hate you, Austin. I guess I'm just wondering what your angle is. Asking my mother to marry you after twenty-five years and two brief encounters seems a little extreme. Are you sure her cancer has nothing to do with your decision?"

"Actually, it does."

"See, I knew it!" C.J. raised his voice, knowing his mother was being duped. She stirred on the couch, so he muffled his anger as he continued. "I told her that was why you were here. She doesn't need your pity, Austin, or your sympathy. She's not some play thing for you to enjoy then leave when you can't handle the hard stuff. We don't need you around. We've done fine all these years, just the two of us."

"You didn't let me finish." Austin spoke in hushed tones. "Yes, the cancer might have made me move a little quicker, but not out of pity. I want to let Ashley know I'm not just interested in her for some fairytale ending to make my life complete. I want her to know I'm serious about us and always have been. Regardless of the circumstances, good, bad, or indifferent, I want to be there for her and for you. I want to give her some security in the face of uncertainty. I want her to know if she has fifty more years or just a few months, I want to spend every moment I can with her."

C.J. rolled his eyes.

"I'm sorry you find that so hard to believe. Maybe it's time you come to the realization that someone besides you can love your mother without ulterior motives."

"Look, you might be able to snow my mom, but you can save the lecture for somebody else." He stalked out the backdoor, slamming it as he left.

Ashley startled awake. When she sat up, she glimpsed C.J. stomping down the back steps. Concerned, she watched him walk across the yard while she headed toward the kitchen and took a seat on a barstool. "What just happened?"

Austin leaned against the counter, clearly frustrated. "I guess he's still having a hard time believing I'm not in this relationship just to get you into the sack. He thinks I'll leave when the pressure gets to be too much."

"Maybe I should go talk to him." She slipped off the barstool and started toward the backdoor.

"Come on, Ash, you can't run after him every time he explodes. He's not a kid. He needs to man up and realize he can't always have it his way."

"But I don't like seeing him so upset, especially right now. I'm just going to make sure he's okay." She saw the disappointment in Austin's eyes, but it didn't stop her. C.J. was her son, and now was not the time to debate parenting styles.

Knowing exactly where he would go, Ashley walked to the barn. She felt her arms shake as she climbed the ladder to the hay loft, but sure enough, C.J. was lying on his back, head in his hands, with a piece of hay between his teeth. Just like he'd done since he was a little boy.

"I'm not hungry, Mom," he said as she approached.

"It smelled awfully good, and I know Italian is your favorite." When C.J. didn't answer, Ashley lay down on the hay next to him and stared at the holes in the roof.

"Why invite him over if you're going to act like this?"

"Because I was tired of seeing you mope around. Look, Mom, I don't care if you keep seeing him, but don't expect me to be there."

"But how do you think I'm going to feel if every time Austin comes in the front door, you go storming out the back?"

"At least you won't have to worry about a fight breaking out."

"C.J.!" Ashley sat up and pulled the piece of hay from his mouth. "I won't sacrifice our relationship just so I can have one with Austin. Say the word and I'll ask him to leave."

C.J. sat up and looked her straight in the eye. "I don't get it Mom, why is it so important to you that I like him?"

"Because I love him!"

C.J. groaned as he fell back into the pile of hay. "All right, all right. I'll try to act civil around him. No more yelling matches, okay?"

"But that's just it, C.J., I don't want you to *act* around him. I want you to give him a chance."

He lay in the hay, not saying a word.

Ashley knew she was getting the silent treatment, so she got up to leave, but before she walked out of the barn, C.J. jumped down from the last few rungs of the loft ladder and lay his muscular arm across her shoulders. "Only for you, Mom . . . only for you."

When they walked into the house, the delicious aroma of marinara and cheese met them at the door.

But no Austin.

Ashley picked up the note lying on the counter.

Ashley,

Dinner should be ready by six o'clock. I hope you enjoy it. I would've stayed, but I seem to have lost my appetite. Call me.

Love, Austin

Ashley dropped the note on the counter and rubbed her forehead. C.J. read the note, then chuckled. "Great. More food for me."

"Well, I hope you enjoy it, because you can have it all."

Ashley stormed upstairs to her room and slammed the door. Snatching her old duffel bag from the closet floor, she tossed it on the bed, then turned to her dresser. She pulled out a few pieces of lingerie, something to sleep in, a couple pairs of jeans, and a few shirts. From the bathroom, she grabbed her toothbrush, toothpaste, hairbrush, and a scrunchy and shoved them into an old makeup bag, then tossed it into her duffel and zipped it up. Reaching for her purse and car keys, she headed downstairs, her hand shaking as she grasped the banister. She saw C.J. out of the corner of her eye but didn't stop. She stormed out the front door and hurried straight to the pickup. C.J. caught up with her by the time she threw her bag on the passenger seat and shoved the key into the ignition.

"Mom, where are you going?" C.J. asked, clearly confused.

"I can't take this, C.J. I will not be put in the middle. I know you care and I know Austin cares, but both of you are forcing me to choose. Well, you know what . . . I choose me. The one who's had her body poked and prodded and analyzed for the last month. I can't do this right now, C.J. I have to take care of myself, not play referee. I have no right forcing Austin on you, and I have no right pulling him into my screwed-up life. I just need some time to myself. I'll call you later tonight."

Ashley didn't give C.J. a chance to answer her. She just drove off and headed for the coast.

TWENTY-TWO

After driving for over an hour, Ashley realized she should not be driving at all. She felt shaky and light-headed and was having a tough time keeping her mind on the road. When she saw a sign—Oxnard next five exits—she thought of the oceanfront hotel she once admired while doing a commercial shoot on the beach and decided that would be her destination.

Stepping out of her truck, she inhaled the ocean breeze.

Perfect!

When she walked into the decadent lobby with its high ceiling and beautiful floor-to-ceiling windows, Ashley couldn't think of a better place to stay. Unfortunately, by the glare the desk clerk gave her as she approached the front desk, Ashley was certain the service wasn't going to be as pleasant as the accommodations.

"Can I help you?" The woman asked, through pinched lips with an expression to match.

"Yes. I need a room for a few nights, preferably with an ocean view."

The woman cleared her throat. "All of our ocean view rooms are suites. I'm very sorry."

"A suite sounds lovely."

The woman glanced at the tattered duffel bag slung over Ashley's shoulder and smiled smugly. "If you're interested in something more economical, there's a quaint motor lodge closer to the freeway."

Pulling her gold card from her wallet and laying it on the counter, Ashley smiled. "A suite will do just fine."

Making her way to room ten-twenty-four, Ashley let herself in, then leaned against the closed door. The room was lovely but did little to raise her spirits. She crossed to the draperies covering the sliding glass door and pulled them back to expose a magnificent view. As she watched the ebb and flow of the churning waves, it felt symbolic of her life. Rising, cresting, crashing, then slowly rolling back to be swallowed up by the sea.

Ashley collapsed across the bed and zoned out for a few minutes. She knew she needed to call C.J. so he wouldn't worry, but after that, she would turn off her cell phone, so she could have the quiet she needed to make some very important decisions.

Digging her phone out of her purse, she dialed. "Hi, C.J., I just wanted to let you know I've checked into a hotel."

"Where are you?"

Ashley ignored his question and gave him further instructions. "I'll be back by Saturday, so don't worry if you don't hear from me tomorrow. I just need some time to myself."

"But what if something comes up? What if I need to get a hold of you?"

"Leave a voicemail. I'm going to turn off my phone, but I'll check for messages."

"Mom, this isn't like you. You're worrying me."

"Maybe that's the problem, C.J.; I've always done everything for everyone else. First my father, then Grandma and Grandpa, then the Anderson's, and now you. I've been so busy pleasing everyone else, Ashley never existed. At least not to me. Well, now I have to take care of myself if I'm going to make it through this cancer thing. So, the next few days are for me. I'm not mad at you or at Austin, but your little tug-of-war helped me see something very important. I can't please everyone, so I'm going to concentrate on taking care of myself. The only problem is, I don't know who that is anymore. Do you understand what I'm saying?" Ashley knew she was rambling but hoped C.J. was listening.

"I'm sorry, Mom. I never meant to take you for granted."

"I don't want an apology. I just want you to think about what I'm saying and tell me you understand."

"I understand, Mom." He hesitated before continuing. "Just remember I love you, okay?"

Ashley could hear the emotion in his voice. "I know, C.J., and I love you, too. Very much. I'll talk to you by Saturday, okay?"

"Okay." C.J. agreed.

Ashley hung up the phone and relaxed on the bed. Still feeling light-headed, she called room service and ordered a light dinner. After she ate, she took a long hot bath, crawled into bed with her Bible and enjoyed the silence.

Austin stared out over the canyon as he made his way home. He knew leaving the note for Ashley had been extreme. He should have stayed for dinner and ignored C.J.'s behavior, but he hated watching her be manipulated. Of course, Ashley didn't see it that way; she saw herself as an attentive parent. Austin knew C.J. wasn't a bad kid; he was just use to having his mom all to himself, which gave him an unhealthy hold over her.

Austin argued with himself for critiquing Ashley's parenting skills, especially since he had no real experience of his own. He knew whenever Jenna was with him, he had a tendency to spoil her, but that was what extended family was for, right? He thought about the way he would rearrange his calendar at the drop of a hat to accommodate last minute plans with Jenna. There was the time she begged him to let her have a pool party at his house. He bought three hundred dollars' worth of food and snacks, only to find out Jenna had decided to go to the beach instead. If he wanted to admit it or not, Jenna had him wrapped around her little finger. But he loved her like a daughter, so it had never bothered him.

Like Ashley loves C.J.

He groaned.

Boy, did I blow it.

Austin pulled into his driveway, knowing he needed to call Ashley the minute he got inside, but first he had to answer the phone that was ringing in his pocket.

"Taylor."

"Uncle Austin, you sound uptight. Did I get you in the middle of something?"

"Kind of. What's up, Jenna?"

"You haven't talked to me all week. What have you found out about your mystery woman? Have you talked to her yet?"

"Yes."

"And . . . come on Uncle Austin, details . . . details."

"How much time do you have?"

"Oh, this sounds good. I've got all the time you need."

Austin walked through the house to his private sitting area, slumped onto the couch, and brought Jenna up to speed on all that had transpired in the last week. By the time Austin was done telling her everything, and had answered a thousand questions, he was exhausted. It was all so unbelievable. If it wasn't for the fact it had happened to him, he would have thought it was the storyline for a Lifetime movie.

"What are you going to do now, Uncle Austin?"

"Call Ashley and apologize for my behavior. In fact, I was going to do that when you called."

"Well, don't let me keep you. Hey, when do I get to meet her?"

"Let me make sure she's still willing to see me, then we'll work on an introduction for you, okay?" Austin hung up the phone, smiling. Jenna always had a way of cheering him up.

Austin dialed Ashley's cell number; it immediately went to voicemail. "Hey, Ash, I'm sorry. I screwed up. Please call me when you get this message."

He disconnected and dialed her home number. When the phone stopped ringing, he smiled. It disappeared the minute he heard C.J.'s voice.

"C.J., it's Austin. May I speak to your mom, please?"

"She's not here," he said coolly.

"Will you have her call me when she gets in?"

"Okay, but it might not be for a few days."

"Come on, C.J.," Austin snapped. "Enough with the games. The least you can do—"

"I'm not playing games," C.J. shouted back. "Mom's ticked. She took off and said she wouldn't be back until Saturday."

"What do you mean she took off?"

"She got in the truck and left. She called about an hour ago to let me know she had checked into a hotel somewhere, and not to expect her back until Saturday."

"I shouldn't have left the way I did," Austin said, regretting his actions for the hundredth time.

"Well, I didn't help matters much by storming out of the house."

"How did Ashley sound when she called?"

"Okay, but I'm still worried. She didn't look so good before she left. What if something happens to her while she's gone?"

"Don't worry, C.J., your mom's a smart woman. She's not going to do anything stupid while she's gone. We forced her into this little disappearing act, so I think we need to give her some space. She has her cell phone with her, right?"

"Yeah, but she said she was going to turn it off. She said she would check for messages but didn't want to talk to anyone right now."

"Okay, C.J., then this is what you should do. Call her phone and leave her a message. Tell her you're sorry and you'll be waiting for her when she gets home."

"What are you going to do?" C.J. asked, defensively.

"I'll do the same. I'll tell her I'm going to give her some space, and that I didn't mean to put so much pressure on her. Her well-being is what's important right now. I'll support whatever she decides, even if that means I have to take a step back."

C.J. exhaled, sounding like he had something more he wanted to say.

"What is it? Is there something you're not telling me?"

"No. It's just that . . ."

"It's just what?"

"I guess you're not that bad after all. If you were the jerk I thought you were, you wouldn't be so willing to back off. I'm sorry I accused you of using my mom."

Austin let out the breath he was holding. "And I'm sorry for thinking you were manipulating her. I can only imagine how you must feel. It's been just you and your mom for so long. I'm sure any guy would seem like an intrusion to you. But believe me when I tell you, I love your mom. I always have, and I would never do anything to hurt her. And if me staying away is what she needs right now, then I'll do it."

They talked for a few minutes longer and actually carried on a civil conversation. Before they hung up, they agreed to check in with each other if either of them heard from Ashley.

TWENTY-THREE

Ashley awoke the next morning feeling rested. She was surprised she had slept so well, with her thoughts in such turmoil. But after a long conversation with the Lord, she had come to the conclusion that doubt and worry were only exhausting her and tearing her down emotionally. The peace she was feeling could only be attributed to her time spent with God.

After getting dressed, she decided to take a walk on the beach. Still feeling a little fatigued, she laid out a towel, sat down, and let the warm sand sift through her toes. Tilting her head back, she allowed the sun to soothe her tired body. With her journal and Bible in her lap, she listened to the gentle roar of the ocean, before expressing in words what she felt in her soul.

The waves are different now. I no longer see them as being crushed against the rocks, having to yield to their surroundings. Now, I see their power and strength and how they roll back out into the sea to try once again to conquer the jagged coast. I too, am ready to try again to conquer the obstacles in my life. I'll explain to C.J. how I feel about Austin. And as long as my relationship with Austin does not compromise my relationship with You, I will continue to see him. I know You made this reunion possible, and I choose to see it as a gift, not as a complication.

She thought a moment about the other obstacle in her life, then put pen to paper.

I am ready to face my surgery with strength and determination. I allowed myself to be a victim for too many years, but I refuse to take a step back now and allow my fear to have the victory. I know that I am not defenseless against the disease trying to destroy my body. I have You—the Master Physician—on my side and resolve in my soul.

Closing her journal, Ashley lay back on the warm sand and after a whispered prayer, drifted into a light sleep. When she awoke, she felt a little disoriented until she realized where she was. She sat on the beach a while longer enjoying the sounds and the scenery, then walked back to the hotel where a jazz band played poolside. Pulling up a chair, she listened to the soothing music while having a late lunch. When she returned to her room, she stood on the balcony, closed her eyes and listened to the rhythm of the waves. With the sun warm on her face and the breeze playing with her hair, she felt energized. Rejuvenated. She'd gotten what she came for.

Rest.

Answers.

Time alone with God.

Realizing she didn't need another day of solitude, Ashley took a shower, gathered the few things she had brought with her, and headed for home.

Austin called the ranch around noon and talked to Willow. Unfortunately, no one had heard from Ashley yet. He tried to keep busy the rest of the afternoon but could not concentrate long enough to get any work done. At four o'clock, he decided to call it quits and drive out to the ranch and see if C.J. had heard anything. When he arrived, he walked around to the back and saw C.J. talking to someone near the stables. When C.J. saw him, he waved him over.

"Did you hear from Mom, yet?" C.J. asked as Austin followed him up the backstairs and into the great room.

"No, I was hoping maybe you did."

C.J. just shook his head as he walked to the kitchen sink and washed his hands. After drying them, he extended his right hand to Austin. "Truce?" he asked, with a sincere smile.

Austin smiled back and accepted his handshake. "Truce."

Opening the refrigerator, C.J. took out a plastic container. "Would you like something to eat? It's only leftovers, but I hear it's a great recipe for Chicken Parmesan."

Austin laughed as he took a seat at the kitchen island. "It just so happens to be one of my favorites."

C.J. placed the container in the microwave, pushed some buttons, then took two plates from the side cupboard.

"You know, I don't know much about horses," Austin said, "but you looked pretty good out there the other day. Your mom said you were a state champion."

"*District* champion," C.J. corrected. "I'm practicing for state finals."

"You look like you really enjoy what you do."

"Probably as much as you enjoy what you do." C.J. said as the microwave beeped.

"How do you know I enjoy what I do?"

"Because you're successful," he said as he dished the leftovers onto two plates. "When I found out you and mom were an item in high school, I started following your career. What you've accomplished is pretty impressive."

Austin shrugged. "It's just business."

C.J. shook his head in disagreement as he handed him a plate and some silverware. "No, if it was just business, you would be like every other schmuck out there. Putting in your eight, then calling it a day. I believe 'passionate,' 'brilliant,' and 'ahead of his time,' are the words *Fortune* magazine used to describe you. You really know your stuff, Austin."

"Well, it's no different than you and horses. I'm sure you've learned it takes a lot of discipline, hard work, and positive reinforcement to get horses to do what you want them to, and once they learn, you work as a team. It's the same in business. People are a lot more willing to work with a person that treats them like an equal, than someone who wants to walk all over them to get to the top. You have a gift with horses. I like to think I have a gift with people and business."

"Did you know investing was what you wanted to do when you were dating Mom?"

Austin thought back to his senior year, knowing the only thing he really cared about then was spending time with Ashley. Sure, he had been accepted to seven top universities before he graduated, but school had always come easy to him. He was intuitive and good with numbers. Besides, the aerospace industry his father had always touted was on shaky ground, and he didn't see a future there. "Yeah. I knew I wanted to work with investments. It's rewarding to help young businesses get off the ground—see that something special others miss. That's where I began, with small start-ups. After a few years with several success stories, larger companies began approaching me, wanting to partner with me as well. I don't know about the moniker 'brilliant,' but I do enjoy what I do."

C.J. nodded, then took a seat at the far end of the island. When he picked up his fork and pierced a piece of chicken, Austin asked, "Mind if I pray?"

"Go ahead," C.J. replied, but didn't choose to join him. They ate for a few minutes in silence before C.J. asked. "What was mom like in high school?"

The very thought of Ashley made Austin smile. "Did she ever tell you why she became a cheerleader?"

C.J. shrugged his shoulders. "No, I just assumed she liked that kind of thing."

Austin laughed, remembering how Ashley felt stuck with the title *Head Cheerleader.*

"Are you going to share," C.J. asked, "or is it a private joke?"

"Okay . . . so there was this girl named MaryAnn Meyers." Austin shook his head. "She always had a way of getting under your mom's skin. They turned everything they did into a competition. Class President. Club chairman. Highest test score if they were in the same class. SAT's. Everything. Senior year they were both vying for Valedictorian."

"So, Mom was a nerd?"

"No. Not exactly. She was just competitive."

"So, why'd she become head cheerleader?"

"Because MaryAnn Meyers threw down the gauntlet."

"The gauntlet?" C.J. peaked his brows as he continued to eat.

"Yep. She told your mom she could be Valedictorian."

"How is that throwing down the gauntlet?"

"Because MaryAnn said she would rather be head cheerleader, something Ashley would never be. Well, that was like pouring gasoline on a fire. Ashley didn't care about being head cheerleader one bit, but the opportunity of beating MaryAnn Meyers, that was something Ashley just could not walk away from."

C.J. laughed. "Wow, I never knew mom was so competitive."

"Really?" Austin said, a little shocked. "Maybe she's mellowed with age."

C.J. took a few more bites, then asked, "When did you and Mom start dating?"

"That's hard to say. We spent a lot of time together because we were in the same clubs and activities. So, we were always doing something together. In fact, everyone just assumed we were already dating."

"But do you remember when you officially asked her out on a date?"

"Actually, it was pretty embarrassing. Since it was our first date, I thought a double date with one of my teammates would be a good icebreaker. All I wanted to do was show Ashley a nice evening.

Since the other couple was also on their first date, I thought it would be good. Wrong! They went from zero to sixty in less than an hour. We barely got past the introductions before they were all over each other. They didn't even care that Ashley and I were right there, and I mean *right . . . there*. Now, don't get me wrong, I knew my buddies weren't all Boy Scouts. It's just that the jerk was treating the girl like a piece of trash. And since he was one of the popular guys, she let him."

"Yeah, I know the type. When my friends and I go to a club, it takes them all of five minutes to find the girls who are willing to put out. They aren't interested in girlfriend material, they just want to use them for sex."

"What about you, C.J.? Is there anyone you're serious about?"

C.J.'s smile quickly disappeared. "Not anymore." He got up from where he was sitting and took his plate to the kitchen sink, his mood quickly downshifting.

Austin knew he was treading on shaky ground but continued. "What happened? If you don't mind me asking."

"I dumped her when I found out she had done it with another guy."

"While you two were seeing each other?" Austin asked.

"No, but she lied to me about her past. We were getting pretty serious and had already had *the talk*. You know, former boyfriends. Girlfriends. Past experiences. She told me she was still a virgin, and I had no reason to doubt her. We had gotten pretty close a few times, but knowing she was a virgin . . . somehow, I was always able to stop before we went too far. I wasn't completely sure yet if our relationship was going to last, and . . . I don't know . . . I just didn't want to cross that line."

"So, how did you find out?"

"I was at a competition. At the end of the day, while I was loading up my tack, this guy comes up to me and congratulates me for 'taming' Heather. I thought he was insulting her, so I nailed him. He hustled to his feet and threw up his hands saying he didn't mean anything by it. He went on to explain that while he was dating Heather, she told him they would never be exclusive; that no one guy was going to tell her what she could or could not do." C.J.'s face was red, and his hands were clenched, but he continued. "That's when I found out she'd been quite the party girl in college."

"Did she admit to it?" Austin asked.

"Oh, yeah, she admitted to it, cried, and said she was sorry.

127

Then, she tried to seduce her way out of it. I took her home, and that was that."

"Is that why you don't trust me?"

"I just don't get it, Austin." C.J. turned a questioning look on him. "I mean, I'm only in my twenties, and even though my mom raised me with conservative values, I've still come really close to screwing up. You're over forty, and I'm supposed to believe you've never done it? I mean, come on, Austin, you're rich. Good-looking. Successful. You can't tell me attractive women don't make themselves available to you. But I'm supposed to believe you never got in over your head?"

Austin debated how much he should say. *Just be honest.* His inner voice reminded him.

"Okay, C.J., I'll be straight with you. There was a time when I was trying to forget about your mom. It was seven years after high school, and I realized I was never going to find her. So, I started dating. And yes, I've dated very attractive women. But I've got to tell you, when women just assume they'll end up in your bed at the end of a date, it's a real turnoff. I have gone out with a senator's daughter, the niece of a billionaire, and a woman who was chief counsel for a corporation I was working with at the time. But it didn't matter that they were wealthy or came from a prestigious family. I no longer considered them attractive the minute they served themselves up like a cheap piece of meat."

Austin paused as he thought back to a certain night, several years ago. "There was this one night, when I was struggling with depression. I had just turned thirty, and I still hadn't gotten over your mom. One of my friends set me up on a blind date, and I decided to go. I met this gorgeous woman in the lobby of a really swank hotel. We had dinner, then got a room and proceeded to get drunk. It didn't take much since I'm not a drinker."

Austin stopped for a minute, embarrassed he was telling C.J. about the lowest point in his life after losing Ashley, but continued anyway.

"The woman I was with had already . . . how should I say . . . disposed of her clothing and was working on mine. I was hesitant, even though I was plastered, so she took the lead, and we got pretty physical. She knew I wasn't looking for a relationship, but that didn't seem to deter her. My friend had told her I was trying to get over someone, so she said she'd pretend to be whoever I wanted her to be, that she didn't mind role playing—said I could call her

Ashley, if it would help. Just hearing her speak your mother's name was like a knife in the gut. I was disgusted with her and myself. It was enough to bring me to my senses. I got dressed, hailed a cab, and never saw her again. That was the closest I came to screwing up."

It was obvious C.J. was shocked with Austin's honesty.

"Look, C.J., I'm not proud of what I did. I wasn't a Christian at the time, but I still knew it was wrong. I swore to myself, I would never let my personal life get that out of hand again. I know that probably makes me sound like a real choirboy, but it was an issue of self-respect. I wasn't going to be used by anyone."

Austin could tell C.J. was thinking. About what, he wasn't sure.

"You know C.J., I would never encourage you to keep things from your mother, but if you ever need someone to talk to . . . about relationships, I'm available."

"Thanks. I appreciate that. Mom's great and all, but some things are hard to talk about without her overreacting."

Silenced settled between them, then C.J. completely changed subjects.

"It must've been something for you to see Mom at your reunion. I mean, to have waited this long, and then, bam! There she is."

"It was incredible!" Austin beamed, reliving that very moment.

C.J. shook his head and laughed. "Man, you've got it bad!"

"Hey, what can I say? Your mother is unlike anyone I've ever known."

After dinner, Austin and C.J. sat in the great room, where Austin told him story after story about his mom's high school days.

C.J. sat in awe as their conversation jumped back and forth from pranks and predicaments his mom got herself in to, and Austin's willingness to be transparent about things in his own life.

Somehow, it was comforting for C.J. to hear that his mom's entire childhood wasn't a train wreck, and that she'd had some fun before she got pregnant with him. It made his mom seem more human, knowing she had flaws of her own.

C.J. also realized Austin was a pretty decent guy. He was extremely candid about his personal life and didn't try to sugarcoat his shortcomings. He also didn't pull any punches when offering advice. C.J. asked some pretty pointed questions about sex that he would never have asked his mom, and Austin was very straightforward with his answers. C.J. finally felt he and Austin had some common ground. His friends harassed him because of the limitations he put on himself, but Austin seemed to understand something his friends didn't.

"Come on, Austin," C.J. laughed. "You can't expect me to believe that Mom single-handedly scaled a twelve-foot fence, picked a lock, and somehow carried a baby bobcat back over the fence?"

"I'm telling you, C.J.," Austin said between peals of laughter, "your mom could not walk away from a challenge. She was gutsy, and it always got her into trouble. When everyone said it couldn't be done, she broke into our crosstown rival school and stole their mascot." He laughed some more. "And she had the scratches to prove it."

~®~

"What's this?" Ashley couldn't believe what she was seeing. Austin and C.J. laughing together.

"Ashley!" Austin jumped to his feet and hurried across the room to embrace her. She returned his embrace and allowed him to give her a well-meaning kiss.

Ashley looked at C.J., then back to Austin. "What did I interrupt? If I'm not mistaken, it sounded like you two were actually having a good time."

C.J. crossed the room to where she was standing and gave her a quick hug. "Austin and I were just getting to know each other. It's amazing how much information he has on you."

Ashley turned to Austin, her brow raised. "And what have you been telling my son?" Austin looked ten shades of guilty. She pointed a disciplinary finger at him, trying not to laugh. "Look, I've tried very hard to be the voice of reason and common sense to C.J. over the years. I sure hope you haven't undermined everything I've worked so hard to portray."

"Me?" Austin pressed a hand to his chest with a grin. "Undermine your authority? Never. But if you hope to silence me in the future, it's going to take a little bribery."

"Bribery? You want me to bribe you?"

"No . . . I want to bribe *you*." Austin got down on one knee and reached for her hand. "Ashley, agree to be my wife, and I promise I won't incriminate you with your high school antics."

Ashley pulled her hand away. She knew Austin was only

kidding, but his mocking marriage proposal bothered her. "That's blackmail not a proposal. Ask me again when you're serious." She turned to walk away, but Austin reached for her hand again and turned her to face him.

"Okay, then," he looked at her with nothing but seriousness in his eyes, "marry me, Ashley. Let's not waste another moment . . . another second."

Ashley looked at C.J. He casually chuckled. "Hey . . . don't look at me. This is your deal. But if you're asking for my opinion, you could do worse."

Ashley began to cry. She could not believe after all these years, this was really happening. Austin proposing, and C.J. kind of, sort of, giving his blessing

Taking a deep breath—and throwing common sense and caution to the wind—she turned to Austin, tears running down her cheeks. "Yes, Austin. I'll marry you. And I pray we have many years together to make up for the one's we've lost."

Austin stood to his full height, framed Ashley's face in the palms of his hands, and kissed her passionately.

C.J. applauded in a slow, well-what-do-you-know fashion. Ashley moved from Austin's embrace to that of her son's. C.J.'s arms swallowed her up and held her tight. "Are you really okay with this, C.J.?" she whispered.

"Yeah, Mom, I really am. It seems too fast for me, but I know you've both been waiting a long time. I just didn't want to admit to myself that someone else could love you the way I do, but I can see Austin cares a lot. I still don't think it's as much as me, but I'm sure he would debate me on that."

Tears streamed down her face. She held tight to the six-foot-two man in front of her whom she would forever see as her little boy.

Once she felt she had control of her emotions, Ashley placed a kiss to his cheek. "I don't know what makes me happier, Austin's proposal or knowing I have your support to accept it." She smiled up at C.J. before stepping back to where Austin stood. Ashley couldn't help but beam as she looked into the eyes of the man she would finally be able to call her husband. "So, do you have any idea how much planning goes into a wedding?" she asked Austin.

"I think we're going to have to skip all that because we only have one day," he said with a firm smile.

"One day! Austin, are you crazy?" Ashley couldn't read his expression. Surely, he was kidding.

Reaching out for her, Austin pulled her close, a serious expression creasing his face. "Ashley, you're going to have surgery next week. I don't want to wait another day to be able to hold you and wake up with you in my arms. We can have a small ceremony on Saturday. Then, on our first anniversary, we can recite our vows for all our friends and family and have the celebration of a lifetime."

Ashley took a step back. "You're serious, aren't you?"

"Come on, Ashley, what is there to stop us? You can have C.J. as your best man and I can have Jenna as my maid of honor. I'll talk to Pastor Stan and explain to him the situation; I'm sure he'll be willing to officiate. What else do we need?" The sparkle in Austin's eyes was mesmerizing and contagious. How could Ashley do anything but agree?

"Could I at least have until Sunday? I'd liked to be able to shop for a nice dress."

"Is that a yes?"

"Yes."

Austin picked her up and twirled her around until she begged him to stop. He placed her back on her feet and held her steady. Laughing, Ashley turned to C.J. "So, what do you say? Are you available on Sunday to walk your mom down the aisle?"

C.J. shrugged, then smiled. "I think I can work it into my schedule."

Ashley's mind was spinning. She looked at Austin, unable to suppress a giggle of amazement. "Okay then, I guess we're going to do this thing." She grabbed a note pad and pen from the kitchen counter and started rambling while she wrote. "Okay, I need a dress, shoes, need to get my nails done . . ." Ashley's words turned into mumbling as she paced and wrote at the same time.

"I guess there are a few things I need to do, too." Austin pulled out his phone and started his own list. "Uh-oh."

Ashley looked at Austin, looking at his watch. "What do you mean, uh-oh?"

"Ashley we've got to get down to the hall of records right now. We can't do anything without a marriage license."

"Oh my gosh, you're right. They won't be open tomorrow."

"We'd better hurry; we only have about half an hour before they close."

Ashley scooped up her purse and headed out the door with Austin. They raced to the car and quickly got in. Before Austin pulled from the driveway, he leaned over and gave Ashley a deep, indulgent kiss.

"Do you know how much I love you?" he asked.

"I think so, but are you willing to break the law for me?"

Austin looked puzzled.

"Well, that kiss just cost you about five seconds. You're going to have to do some major driving to get us downtown in time."

"A speeding ticket would be a small price to pay, but don't worry, I've got my connections."

TWENTY-FOUR

Ashley held on as Austin sped from the driveway and voice activated his phone. "Call Victoria."

Ashley swiveled toward him. "Who's Victoria?"

"Just a minute." He put in his Bluetooth earpiece. "Victoria, I need you to get Simon on the phone for me, quick." Austin was silent as he maneuvered down the road into the dense residential section at the foothills of Topanga Canyon.

"Simon, I need a favor. Go to the hall of records and stall for me. Talk, flirt, fill out some sort of application. I don't care what you do, just make sure they don't close before I get there." Austin pulled onto the freeway and quickly merged into the fast lane. "A marriage license. Yeah, yeah . . . I'll explain when I get there. In fact, start filling out my portion of the application." Austin ended the call while switching lanes and dodging in and out of traffic.

"So, Victoria is your secretary?"

"Well, yes, but the politically correct term would be business assistant."

Ashley rolled her eyes. "And Simon?"

"My business associate."

"Well, I guess he's in for a surprise."

"Yes and no. He and I have been together for a while. He knows all about you, and that you were at the reunion."

"Yes, but does he know you proposed?"

"I told him I proposed to you last week, and that I was going to propose to you every week for the rest of my life until you said yes."

Ashley stared at Austin's profile, amazed. "You were going to propose to me every week until I said yes? Wow, I guess I gave in easier than you expected."

"I knew you wouldn't be able to make a commitment without C.J.'s approval. I was willing to respect that, but I wasn't going to let it stop me."

Austin was concentrating on his driving when Ashley realized something. "So, why were you at the house?"

"C.J. told me that you took off Thursday after I left, so I came over to see if he'd heard anything. We just got talking. He asked me to be gut-level honest about my feelings for you, so I was. He opened up about some personal things, and I gave him my opinion. I think we actually broke through some barriers. I answered his questions honestly, but he had a hard time believing I am still a virgin at my age."

Ashley's jaw dropped as she gasped. "He asked you that?"

"Yeah. So, I told him I messed up a few times but never allowed myself to lose complete control."

Ashley did not know what to say. She wasn't sure what surprised her more, finding out Austin was still a . . . hadn't had . . . or that C.J. was forward enough to ask.

"What are you thinking, Ashley?"

"I'm just sorry I interrupted you two. I knew C.J. was struggling with . . . those types of situations. I'm just surprised he opened up to you. I try all the time to talk to him about serious issues: drinking, drugs, sex, but he always changes the subject."

"I think he just needed to know—from an outside source—that sexual purity is important, and not a thing of the past. I mean, you're his mom. Of course you want him to stay pure. But I got the impression he wasn't getting much support from his friends."

"The guys C.J. hangs around with are all his cowboy buddies, and he has slowly pulled away from the church group he used to spend time with. The older he's gotten, the more distance he's put between himself and God. I've tried not to push him, and he still attends church with me out of respect. But I know he's allowed his heart to be hardened to the things of God. His friends are tough guys who drink and talk about their sexual exploits. I know C.J. doesn't really respect their behavior, but it's not helping the situation. They're all having what looks like the time of their lives while C.J.'s been miserable since he broke up with Heather, his ex-girlfriend."

"C.J. talked about her. It's obvious he felt betrayed, duped, angry even. Maybe I can show C.J. that a relationship with God is not considered a crutch but a support system. Again, I'm not his mom. I'm an outsider. A male. And it wasn't just a coincidence that we were reunited after all this time. God did that. That should speak volumes to him."

"I hope so. I try not to ignore the fact that he's a man now, not a boy. But I can't help but mother him. I just wonder how much time I have before he decides what his friends say is more important than how he's been raised."

Ashley was quiet while Austin navigated through downtown traffic. He glanced at his watch several times before pulling into a parking structure. "Are we going to make it?" she asked as they hurried up the front steps and into the elevator.

He smiled. "Simon is very persuasive."

Ashley held Austin's hand as they rushed into the massive building and down a hallway. She was glad he knew where he was going, because if they would have had to stop and read every directional sign, they never would have made it. When Austin pushed open a glass door, a man spun around and looked at him.

"Nothing like cutting it close." The man was Austin's age with a demeanor that was all business.

"Simon, this is Ashley, Ashley this is Simon, my business associate and close friend."

"So, this is the notorious Ashley Trent. I just thought you were a figment of Austin's imagination." Simon reached out his hand to Ashley and smiled. "It's nice to know he isn't crazy after all."

"Well, proposing to a woman he hasn't seen in twenty-five years isn't exactly rational."

"Look," Austin laughed, "we have plenty of time to discuss my sanity later. Right now we've got to get our license before the place closes." He stepped up to the transparent partition and asked for a marriage license application. The portly woman behind the counter pointed to Simon. "He already started filling it out, but you need to hurry, sir. Your friend explained your situation, but I can only stall for so long."

Austin looked down at her name tag and gave her a smile. "Thank you, Harriet, we'll be right back."

Austin and Ashley walked over to a high counter where the form lay. Austin filled in what Simon couldn't, then Ashley quickly filled in her section. Austin handed the completed form to the waiting clerk along with the filing fee. Harriet verified the information against their identification, then disappeared behind the glass partition, returning a few minutes later.

"Okay, Miss Summers," the clerk said with a wink, "there's no backing out now." She handed the official document to Austin. "Good luck you two." She smiled as she shut her window.

With a sigh of relief, Austin kissed Ashley, then pulled her to his side as the three of them headed for the elevator at the end of the hall. Ashley was in a daze thinking about everything she needed to accomplish in a twenty-four-hour period, while Austin talked to Simon regarding his schedule.

"I need to push back everything for about two weeks. You can handle the Hawkins portfolio and the Henderson file. We'll be gone for a few days, then Ashley will be having surgery. I'll check in with you after that and let you know when I expect to be back in the office."

When they stepped out of the massive office building, Ashley felt the balminess of the late-afternoon sun reflecting off the towering glass buildings. She turned her face up to enjoy its warmth while Austin continued to square things away with Simon.

"Can you relay all this to Victoria for me?"

"Oh no!" Simon argued. "You know as well as I do no one tells Victoria anything. She'll want to hear it straight from you."

"Okay, I'll call her tonight, but you'll keep things going until I get back, right?"

"You bet." Simon extended a hand to Austin. "I can't believe this is happening for you, man. I mean, it's pretty crazy if you think about it. So, when is the big day?"

Austin turned and smiled at her. "Sunday. I've got a lot of calls to make, but unless something cataclysmic happens, it will be Sunday."

"So, am I invited, or do I have to crash the party?"

"Of course you're invited."

"You know, I don't mean to brag, but I'm a pretty decent photographer. I could take some pictures for you, or did you already make arrangements for that?"

"We haven't had a chance to make any arrangements yet, but that would be great if you could take a few pictures, right, Ashley?"

Austin looked at her for approval. She nodded. "Sure, that would be great!" Ashley hadn't even thought about pictures. *What else haven't I thought of?* Maybe Sunday was too soon after all? Maybe she should tell Austin they needed to rethink this crazy idea?

"Well, it was nice to finally meet you after all these years, Ashley. I guess I'll see you on Sunday."

Ashley extended her hand to Simon, but he pulled her into a quick embrace before walking away. It caught Ashley off guard, and it must've shown on his face.

Austin chuckled. "He's a pretty friendly guy. I hope he didn't offend you."

"No. Just surprised is all."

Austin reached out for Ashley's hand as they walked through the parking structure.

"Austin, maybe we need to rethink this. I don't know if I can get my act together in time."

She didn't know if it was the thought of getting married or nerves in general, but she suddenly felt lightheaded. When her body swayed, she reached out a shaky hand to the nearest car to steady herself.

"You okay, Ash?" Austin wrapped his arms around her waist, offering her support.

"Yeah, with everything that's going on, I guess I got a little light-headed."

"Have you eaten anything today?"

"I had a little something at the hotel."

"Okay, but we need to get you something to eat."

Slowly, they walked to the car. When he opened the door, he waited until she was seated before closing it. Then, he hurried around to the driver's side and slid into place. "Where do you want to eat?" Austin asked as he backed out of the parking stall and slowly slid into traffic.

"Home. Austin, I need to get home. I have a thousand things to do, and only one day to do it in. I don't have time to eat."

"Well, you'd better make time. I don't want my bride fainting during the 'I do's', and a certainly don't want you sleeping through our honeymoon."

She turned to him. "Honeymoon! Austin, I'm having major surgery next week. We can't go away on a honeymoon."

"Well, maybe we can't go away, but we can still have a honeymoon." He reached for her hand. "Your surgery date isn't set yet, right?"

She nodded.

"I would never do anything to endanger your health, but do you think having your surgery at the end of the week would be a problem?"

"I don't see how a day or two would be detrimental, but I won't hear from my doctor until Monday. By then, he could've already set the surgery date."

"If he doesn't plan on calling until Monday, he certainly can't have you scheduled any earlier than Wednesday. We can leave right after the ceremony, even if it's only for a few days. When your doctor calls, we'll go from there."

Ashley closed her eyes, feeling overwhelmed. She wanted nothing more than to run away with Austin and pretend the disease spiraling through her body didn't exist. When Austin squeezed her hand, she looked up. His profile was rigid, and she could see tears in his eyes. "Ashley, you're sure you can trust your doctor, right?" His voice was strained with emotion. "I know I've already asked you this once, but I just want to make sure. Because if you have even the slightest doubt about him or your diagnosis, I can refer you to my doctor. Even if it's just to get a second opinion."

She held his hand tight. "No, Austin. I have a great doctor, and I trust his opinion completely. We'll just have to wait and see what he says." She smiled to reassure him, or was it to reassure herself?

They were both quiet as Austin pulled off the freeway and wound his way through the foothills.

Ashley continued with her mental check lists, trying to ignore the somberness of the mood. *I trust you, God, to give us time. Please don't let me down.*

It was dark by the time they made it home. When Austin walked around to her side of the vehicle and helped her out, he took a moment and pulled her close. When he bent down to kiss her, Ashley leaned against him and wrapped her arms around his neck. The intimate moment, quickly escalated to passion, then passion gave way to desire. She wanted to offer him what she never had before, but once again, it was Austin who stepped back and put some distance between them.

"I think I'd better go," he said as he twisted a strand of her hair around his finger. "I have plans to make, and so do you. Besides, I don't think I trust myself tonight."

Ashley felt flush, and her heart was racing. Inwardly, she chastised herself for acting like a hormonal teenager. *A few more days.* Waiting was the honorable thing to do not only out of respect for each other but out of respect to God—the same God who so wonderfully orchestrated their paths to cross at this exact moment in time.

"Will you promise me you'll get yourself something to eat, or do I have to talk to C.J. and have him keep an eye on you?"

"I promise. I'll make myself some toast and start working on my list for tomorrow." Ashley climbed the steps of the front walk, then turned around. "Austin, where are we going to get married? We could do it here if you want to. There are some beautiful vistas up the canyon."

Austin took Ashley's hand and brought it up to his lips, gently pressing a kiss against her fingers. "I thought we could get married on the beach, where I first proposed."

She smiled. "Then I guess it's a good thing I asked before going shopping. I'd look pretty silly on the beach with a silk train dragging on the sand."

Austin's charming smile quickly turned into a worried frown. "Is that okay with you, Ash? I mean, if you wanted a formal wedding, I'm sure we could use the church. I would just have to—"

"No," she quickly assured him. "I think the beach is perfect. Really, I do. What time where you thinking?"

"Sunset or close to it, if that's okay?"

"It sounds wonderful." She shook her head, feeling dumbfounded.

"What is it?" he asked, pulling her close once again.

"I can't believe I'm talking about my wedding day. I can't believe this is actually happening."

"But it's a good thing, right?"

"It's perfect." Ashley smiled from ear to ear. "I'd better go if I'm going to get anything done tonight."

"Yeah, me too. I'll call you tomorrow, Ash." He gave her a short but passionate kiss before walking back to his car and pulling out of the driveway.

Ashley went inside the house, leaned against the doorframe and felt her heart fluttering. She was marrying Austin Taylor after all these years. "God, you are so good to me," she said aloud as she walked to the kitchen.

There on the refrigerator, was a note in C.J.'s handwriting.

Doctor called. Surgery set for Friday.

Call for more information.

Ashley teared up, relieved. *We'll have almost a week before I have to worry about my . . . no . . . I'm not going to think about it. Not my surgery, the ranch, the photo shoot, nothing. The only thing that matters right now, is in less than forty-eight hours, I'm going to become Mrs. Austin Taylor.*

Opening the refrigerator door, she took out a bottle of water, grabbed a pen and paper from the kitchen counter, and plopped down on the sofa. Immediately, her mind started spinning with details she needed to leave for C.J., instructions on what to do if . . . *I'm doing it again. Worrying instead of planning.* Then, as if God whispered in her ear, she remembered the Bible verse that warned not to borrow trouble from tomorrow.

Okay, God, I'll try not to worry, but I'm going to need Your help.

Tucking her legs up under her, she jotted down the many things she would have to do tomorrow, buying a dress being foremost on her list; and she knew exact where she would go. Though she wasn't one to dress up much, she had stumbled across a little offbeat boutique while shopping for the reunion. It was eclectic, with an old Hollywood kind of flair to it. While there, she had admired a dress that was completely wrong for the reunion, but so beautiful she had tried it on anyway.

It will be perfect.

Ventura Boulevard here I come.

TWENTY-FIVE

Austin called Jenna as he drove home. He would've rather told her in person just to see the expression on her face, but he knew he didn't have time for that. He had to tell her right away, or she would never forgive him.

"Hey, Uncle Austin, so what's the news?"

"What's your schedule look like for Sunday?"

"I had plans to go to the beach with my friends. Why?"

"How would you like to go to a wedding with me instead?"

"Who's wedding?"

"Mine." Austin said with a smile, even if no one could see him.

"What?" Jenna screamed.

Austin heard a loud clattering noise and then silence.

"Jenna?"

"Don't hang up!"

He heard her, but she sounded distant and distorted.

"Uncle Austin, are you still there? Hello?"

"I'm here."

"Oh, good," she exhaled. "I accidentally dropped my phone."

"Did you hear what I said?"

"Of course I heard what you said. Why do you think I dropped my phone?" she laughed. "Are you serious? You're getting married on Sunday? How did this happen so fast? I mean, the last I heard, you had to apologize for insulting her son or something like that. How did you go from an insult to a proposal? How did you do it? What did she say? I can't believe she agreed. Oh my gosh, you're actually getting married. I can't believe it."

Jenna was giddy with excitement, so Austin could not get a word in edge wise. He decided to wait until she came up for air.

"Uncle Austin, are you still there? Hello?"

"I'm here. I was just waiting for you to take a breath. Now, do you want some answers to your questions, or are you going to continue to ask more?" Austin was only teasing. He loved Jenna's

142

zeal and enthusiasm. He would never do anything to dim the fire and passion Jenna brought in his life.

"Answers, answers. I want answers. First, how did you propose? No, no, no, you told me that. When did she say yes? I thought you said she needed to think about it? How did—"

"Jenna, you're doing it again."

"Okay, okay. I'm listening."

"Ashley did some soul searching these last few days, and I had a heart-to-heart with her son. Having C.J.'s blessing made it that she could commit to me. Now, back to the question at hand. Do you want to be my maid of honor?"

"You're kidding me, right?"

"No, I'm completely serious. Since this wedding is anything but traditional, we're not going to stand on ceremony. C.J.'s going to be Ashley's best man, and I couldn't think of anyone else I would rather have stand up with me. So, will you?"

Austin could hear sniffling over the phone and knew Jenna was crying. He gave her a moment to compose herself and then repeated the question.

"I would love to, but are you talking about Sunday? Like day after tomorrow, Sunday? Why the rush? I mean, I know you've waited an eternity already, but you deserve the wedding of the century."

"I know it seems incredibly fast, but what I didn't tell you is that Ashley has been diagnosed with cancer." Austin heard Jenna gasp. "She has to have surgery next week, and I want to be able to spend these few days with her before she goes into the hospital."

In a tone barely above a whisper Jenna asked, "Is she dying, Uncle Austin?"

"No, Jenna, no. Her doctor is optimistic that after surgery and maybe some radiation therapy, she'll be fine."

"She must be scared to death."

"More scared than she lets on. That's why I want to be there for her."

Jenna continued to sniffle, causing Austin's eyes to water. "Jenna, you're going to have to control your emotions, or I'm going to start crying, and then I won't be able to drive."

"It's just so tragic. You lost her once, but now you've found her. She can't have a terminal illness; she just can't. It's not fair, Uncle Austin."

"Maybe not, but we're together now, and we're going to fight this. Ashley's strong. She's going to be okay." Austin quickly swiped the tears from his cheeks. "Look Jenna, I have a lot to figure out by Sunday, so I'd better go. I'll call you tomorrow."

Austin disconnected the call as he pulled into his driveway. Once in the house, he grabbed a soda from the refrigerator, sat on the couch, and scrolled through his contacts.

"Pastor Stan, it's Austin. What does your schedule look like for Sunday, after evening services?"

~⑧~

Ashley made herself some toast—like she promised Austin—then went upstairs to her room so she could continue listing her game plan for tomorrow. When she heard a light tap on the door, she looked up.

C.J. stuck his head in. "Can I come in?"

"Sure." Ashley sat up straighter and leaned back against the pillows on her bed while C.J. took a seat near the foot board. Ashley waited for him to say something, but he didn't. He just kept looking at her.

"What?" Ashley leaned forward and playfully slapped his knee.

"I don't think I've ever seen you this happy."

"That's because you didn't see me the day you were born."

"Come on, Mom." He looked pensive.

"C.J., I'm serious. The day you were born was the happiest moment in my life. Nothing is ever going to change that."

"So, are you going to move into his place and give up the ranch?"

Now Ashley understood his serious tone. He was afraid he was losing her all together.

"C.J., I'm getting married, not running away from home. Austin and I haven't had time to talk about everything yet, but I know I want to be here after my surgery. I want to recover where I feel comfortable. As for the ranch, you'll be in charge." C.J. was ready to balk when she stopped him with a raised hand. "You were going to have to take over for a while anyway; you knew that. You also know how important the ranch is to me. As soon as I'm feeling well again, I'll be barking orders and right back in the thick of things. I'll drive you crazy as usual."

"Does Austin know this ranch means everything to you?"

"Not *everything*, but yes, he knows how important you and this ranch are to me. But if for whatever reason things don't go the way

144

we expect them to, you have to—"

"Mom, don't talk like that. You're going to be fine. The doctor said so."

"I know, but I have to be realistic, too. I have to make sure things are taken care of just in case I—"

"Hey, I came to talk to you about your wedding, and you're turning all morbid on me."

"C.J., are you going to be all right with this? I mean, what if I *do* decide to move into Austin's house, and only work the ranch. Will you be okay with that?"

"I guess I'll have to be."

"C.J.," Ashley looked at him, remembering what she had decided on her little sabbatical. He was an adult. She needed to start treating him like one. She couldn't soothe away all his worries or continue to make sacrifices in order to make his life easier. She loved him to death. That would never change. Even so, change was definitely coming, and he needed to learn how to adapt.

"Look," she decided to change the subject. "I'm going shopping tomorrow for a dress. Do you want me to pick up something for you to wear as my best man?"

He chuckled. "C'mon, Mom, why don't you ask Willow instead? I mean, I promise to be there. I just think you should be able to have a friend stand up with you."

"I know. That's why I chose you." Ashley leaned over and placed a kiss on his cheek.

C.J. stood. "Okay, but nothing too fancy."

"You mean no ruffles and silk?"

"Exactly! Hey, why don't we have the wedding here?" he said as he walked toward the door. "We can have it in the pasture where I can wear my boots and jeans and a string tie. After all, this is a special occasion." C.J. pretended to straighten an imaginary tie.

"Austin wants to get married on the beach, where he originally proposed." Ashley closed her eyes, remembering how he looked that day. Down on one knee. The wave crashing into him. The two of them tangled together, laughing.

Ashley didn't realize C.J. had walked away until she heard the bedroom door close. She opened her eyes, still lost in thought, imagining what her life would be like with the man of her dreams at her side.

TWENTY-SIX

Ashley was up early the next morning. A brisk walk, a shower, and a cup of yogurt with granola. Then, she went to the office to check in on Willow.

Willow was a godsend. Though she was only twenty years old, she ran the office with the efficiency of a seasoned professional. What started out as a couple of hours in the afternoon—so Ashley's time could be freed up to do other things—had quickly evolved into a full-time schedule. Along with answering phones and basic office work, Willow was now in charge of keeping the files on boarders up-to-date, along with billing statements, and ordering supplies. Ashley knew Willow's natural abilities could get her a high paying job elsewhere, but Willow appreciated the flexible schedule Ashley allowed. Since her heart's desire was the veterinary field, a vocation she hoped to pursue further the first of the year, she liked the idea of working close to animals instead of a cubicle in a stuffy office building.

Secretly, Ashley had hoped something might develop between C.J. and Willow. She was a beautiful young woman with such potential, and a love for animals that mirrored C.J.'s. Unfortunately, Willow already had a boyfriend, and regarded her relationship with C.J. as strictly employer/employee. They were good friends, but nothing more.

"Hi, Willow."

"Hey, how are you doing? I saw you come in from your walk; you must be feeling a little better." Willow shuffled some papers around on her desk before giving Ashley her full attention.

"Willow, let's talk for a minute. I have some things I need to bring you up to speed on."

"Does it have anything to do with that handsome guy who's been around the last few days?"

A slight smile pulled at the corners of Ashley's lips. "Yes, among other things."

Willow and Ashley walked into her office. Ashley closed the door and sat in the chair next to Willow instead of behind her desk.

"Willow, did you find out about your application yet?"

"No, not yet, but I should know by the end of September or the beginning of October. I'm trying not to worry about it, but I'm getting more and more anxious every day."

"And if you are accepted, you won't leave until January, right?"

Willow looked puzzled. "That's okay, right? I mean, I did tell you about it when you hired me. I know I've had some delays, but it's still what I want to do."

"No, no, no. I'm fine with it. I mean, I'm going to hate losing you, but I want this for you as much as you do. I just needed to know the earliest you'll be leaving."

Willow relaxed her shoulders and leaned back into the chair. "If I'm accepted, I won't start until January 15th. Why?"

Ashley squirmed a little in her chair before she spoke. She hadn't told Willow anything regarding her health or Austin, so she knew this was going to hit her like a ton of bricks.

"Willow, I have to have surgery next Friday, and I'll be out of the office for three to four weeks after that."

"Surgery? What kind of surgery?" Willow sat forward and grabbed Ashley's hands.

"I have cancer." Ashley didn't know how else to say it. She knew the word carried a stigma, but there wasn't time to ease into this. She saw the look of horror come over Willow, so she needed to quickly explain things in a very casual, everything-is-going-to-be-all-right tone.

"I'll be fine after the surgery, at least that's what my doctor is saying. I have to have a hysterectomy and possibly some radiation. I'm not sure how long it will be before I'm able to come back and handle the business side of the ranch. I was hoping I could count on you to keep the day-to-day office responsibilities going for me."

"Sure, Ashley, anything." Willow looked stunned and was quiet for a few seconds, then asked, "How is C.J. taking it? He has to be devastated." The amount of concern in Willow's tone caused a lump to form in Ashley's throat.

"He's handling it as well as can be expected. I know he's probably more scared than I am, but he's doing okay."

Willow got up and started to pace. "I feel like such an idiot. I thought you were going to tell me you finally met someone and share all the juicy details. I didn't even notice you were sick until just the other day. I was so preoccupied with my own . . ."

Ashley reached out for Willow's hand and pulled her down into the chair across from her. "Willow, you didn't know. There was no way you could have. I didn't want anyone to know until I had some answers."

"What can I do? I'm sure there is more I can take off your plate. What about payroll? You could teach me that. I could also do the bills and the—"

Ashley squeezed Willow's fingers to stop her from rattling on. "That's what I was hoping for because I'm going to need all the help I can get."

"Okay." Willow stood, brushing tears from her face as she walked around Ashley's desk and sat in front of her computer. "I can learn payroll today and maybe billing tomorrow. I'm a fast read. Just show me what to do, and I'll do it."

"There's more, Willow."

"More?" She swallowed hard.

"I'm getting married."

Willow slouched further into the chair and stared at Ashley in utter disbelief. "Have I been living under a rock? It's that guy, right? But I've only seen him a couple of times. How did I not know about him sooner? I mean, I know you're my boss, and I'm your employee, but I thought our relationship had shifted into the friend zone."

Ashley could tell by the emotion in Willow's tone, she was hurt. "Willow, please don't be upset with me. I didn't hide my relationship from you. It just kind of happened. C.J.'s only a little less shocked than you are."

"How long have you two been an item?"

"Apparently for twenty-five years." Ashley answered with a chuckle and a toss of her hair. "Okay, let me try to give you the Reader's Digest version of all of this."

They laughed and cried as Ashley explained, one amazing detail after another.

"There you have it, in a nutshell. Now I have to go shopping for my wedding dress. Can you believe it? *My wedding.* It doesn't even sound right coming from my lips."

Willow had tears in her eyes as she and Ashley walked out of her office and into the main room. "I can't believe all this is happening." Willow said as she gave her a hug.

"Me neither. And it's happening to me!"

"Can I come to the wedding?"

"Of course you can. As soon as I know the where and when, I'll fill you in. In fact, I was going to see if you could stick around until I got home tonight, so we could go over the payroll and billing. I'll have heard from Austin by then and should have more details about the ceremony."

"I'll be right here when you get back." Willow slipped behind her own desk. "Regardless of what time it is."

Ashley smiled, then turned to walk away.

"Ashley?"

She turned back around, her hand on the doorknob.

"Are you sure C.J.'s all right with this? I mean, it's only been the two of you for so long. This has to be hard on him. I don't mean hard, but you know . . . difficult."

"He's adjusting. He wants me to be happy but is not so sure about my timing. It's been a little difficult for him to digest, but he's being very supportive."

"Good. Okay, well, you'd better get going. Call if you need anything."

"I will, and thanks."

With one more thing on her to-do list before heading out for the day, Ashley walked back to the house to make a call. She grabbed Dr. Allen's business card from the refrigerator, the one he gave her when she'd been diagnosed, and flipped it over. He'd written his cell phone number on it and said she could call him anytime. She really didn't want to bother him, but she did have some questions that needed answered.

"This is Kent."

"Dr. Allen, it's Ashley . . . Ashley Summers."

"Ashley, are you okay?" His voice immediately slipped into doctor tone.

"Yes, I'm fine. I know this is your day off, and I'm sorry to bother you, but I needed to ask some rather personal questions, and I don't have time to wait until next week."

"Can you hold for just a moment?"

"Sure." Ashley waited for a minute before she heard Dr. Allen come back on the line.

"Sorry, Ashley, I just needed to step into my office for confidentially reasons."

"Oh, are you at your office?"

"No, I'm at home, but I have an office here, as well. Now, what is it you needed to ask me?"

"Remember when you asked about my *physical* activity?" Ashley paused slightly. "Well, that's going to change, and I need to know if there are any health risks I need to consider."

"Ashley, what do you mean? Are you planning on climbing Mt. Everest in the next few days?" Dr. Allen chuckled. "What could be so physically demanding that you would think your health is at risk?"

Okay, this is awkward. Even though he is my doctor.

Ashley took a deep breath realizing she needed to be more specific. "Maybe *physical* activity isn't the right term. What I meant to say is *sexual* activity."

"Oh!"

The surprise in his tone made her cringe. *Can this be anymore humiliating?* She cleared her throat. "Dr. Allen, I just need to know if I shouldn't have sex." She closed her eyes, feeling her complexion heat up. *I'm so glad I'm not having this conversation in person.*

"Ashley, there are no restrictions regarding sexual activity," he said in a professional tone. "There might be a level of discomfort, especially because of your . . . ahh . . . inactivity, but you can't endanger your health, if that's what you're asking."

"Thank you, Dr. Allen. That was what I needed to know. Also, what will my restrictions be preceding the surgery?"

"Well, your surgery is set for eight o'clock Friday morning. You'll need to be there by six o'clock for prep work. You won't be able to eat anything past lunch on Thursday. You can have water and clear broth after that, but then nothing solid or liquid past ten o'clock at night."

"Will I meet you at the same location?"

"Yes. Just go to admissions, and they will take it from there."

"Thank you, Dr. Allen. Sorry I bothered you on your day off. I just—"

"Ashley," he interrupted, "this is off the record, and I don't mean to pry," he hesitated before continuing, "but as a friend, can I ask why you're considering a physical relationship now? I know many women are afraid of reduced sexual pleasure and stimulation after a hysterectomy. I understand that, but is that really any reason to . . . to indulge in . . . I mean, I know your faith is important to you, and this isn't . . . you know what, Ashley, forget I said anything. I have no right questioning your decisions. I'll see you on Friday."

At first, Ashley was upset Dr. Allen would assume she would be so cavalier regarding sex. She too, had felt they had established a rapport in these last few months. They attended the same church, and he had been more than a physician to her; he'd become a friend. She then realized he was speaking out of concern for her well-being. He wasn't passing judgment; he was just being a friend.

"Actually, Dr. Allen, I'm getting married tomorrow. I know I told you I wasn't involved with anyone, but it's kind of hard to explain."

"You've told him about your condition, though, right?"

"Oh yes, he's completely aware of what to expect in the next few weeks."

Ashley could still sense a tone of concern in Dr. Allen's voice, so she took a few minutes to explain the turn of events that had transpired in the last two weeks.

"Ashley, that's incredible, and I couldn't be happier for you."

"Thank you. I know it's a lot to absorb, even for me."

"Does your fiancé have any questions or concerns? I would be more than happy to meet with you both."

"No. I told him I have complete confidence in you. That's good enough for him."

"I'm glad to hear it. Then I guess I will meet him on Friday."

Ashley glanced at her watch, knowing she was already behind schedule for all she had to accomplish. She hadn't planned on going into such detail with Willow or Dr. Allen, but she could hardly blame them for asking so many questions. They cared. They only wanted what was best for her. It made Ashley feel even more confident that she would be in the best of hands with Dr. Allen.

Ashley was re-prioritizing her mental to-do list as she pulled into the parking lot of the dress shop. She was just getting out of the truck when she heard the muffled ringtone she assigned to Austin. Digging out her phone, she quickly answered, "Hi."

"Good Morning, Ashley. Only thirty-three hours to go."

Her pulse quickened, and her heart skipped a beat. "Does that mean everything is set with your pastor?"

"Yep. I talked to him last night. He wishes he could've met you before the ceremony, but since you come with such a high recommendation, he's willing to forgo the formalities."

"Thirty-three hours. That means about seven o'clock in the evening?"

"Give or take. I didn't want it to be too late. The sun won't quite be setting, but it should be beautiful just the same. Besides this will give us time to get back to the house before dark." Austin paused, then asked, "Are you nervous?"

"No, not nervous . . . well, not really." Ashley thought about all she had discussed with her doctor and knew she was blushing. "I'm just trying to think if there is anything else I need to be doing. Oh Austin, it's okay that I invited Willow, isn't it?"

"Of course. You can invite anyone you want. Give them my address. I figured we would walk to the point from my house and then have a little gathering afterward. Jenna's going to be my maid of honor, and Simon's going to take some pictures. Pastor Stan and his wife will be there, and I invited Victoria. My parents are still out of the country, but my sister and her husband will probably come. Jerry—he's my brother-in-law—wasn't sure if he could postpone his foursome for golf. He let me know how difficult it is to get a reservation at the Night-lite Golf Course, but said he would try to work me in."

"You don't seem too upset at the thought of him not showing up?"

"I'm not. I really don't like the guy. He and Jenna have their differences, and I tend to side with Jenna. Hey, but I didn't call to talk about Jerry. What are you doing?"

"Hopefully, buying a dress."

"Good, because that's all you have to worry about. I've taken care of everything else. The flowers, the cake, the pictures, the . . . honeymoon."

His sexy tone sent shivers through her.

"Austin, I heard from the doctor. He called while I was out and left a message with C.J. My surgery is set for Friday."

"Perfect! That means we have all week."

"Well, maybe not all week. I won't be able to eat on Thursday, and I have to be at the hospital by six o'clock Friday morning."

"But still, we'll have at least four days and four full nights together before we have to come back to reality. I want to take those four days and make you forget about everything else."

Ashley could feel the tears rise inside her. She too wanted to forget, but would she be able to?

"Ashley, are you there?"

"I'm here. Look, Austin, if I'm going to show up at this shindig properly dressed, I've got to get off the phone. Oh . . . when you said you took care of everything, what about the rings?"

"I'm going to pick them up at two o'clock. Why? Did you have a preference on the cut? Setting? How many carats?" Austin asked, sounding absolutely charming.

"No. I trust your judgment, but I want to get your ring, okay? I mean, I want it to be from me to you. Do you still wear a size ten?"

"Yeah, but Ashley, you don't have to do that."

"I want to, Austin. I want it to be special."

"Sure, Ash, whatever you want. For the rest of your life. Just whisper your heart's desire, and it's yours."

"You, Austin. All I want is you."

After Ashley hung up, she entered the boutique and immediately walked over to the rack where she had first seen the dress, but it wasn't there.

Her heart sank.

She looked through the other racks searching for it. *It has to be here. It just has to be.*

"Can I help you find something?" a young sales clerk asked.

"I hope so. I tried on a dress a couple of weeks ago, but I don't see it."

"Can you describe it to me?"

"It's an ivory sheath dress in silk with a crochet overlay. The sheath has spaghetti straps and is about knee length, but the crochet overlay is almost floor length with beautiful fluted sleeves."

The clerk smiled. "I know exactly the one you're talking about. I think it's in the backroom."

"It is?"

"I think so. Let me go look."

Ashley waited anxiously, praying the clerk was right. When she reappeared with the dress draped over her arm, Ashley nearly burst into tears.

"Is this the one?"

Ashley cleared the knot of emotion in her throat. "Yes, that's it. Is it still for sale?"

"Yes. It was on hold, but the person never came back. I just didn't return it to the sales floor yet. Did you want to try it on again?"

"No. That won't be necessary."

"Okay. I'll put it in a garment bag for you, and then I'll ring it up."

"Thank you so much."

Five minutes later, Ashley exited the shop, dress in hand. She carefully hung the garment bag from the hook in the backseat, climbed into the truck, and scanned her to-do list. Shoes. Nails. Something for C.J. to wear. Austin's ring.

Next stop, the mall.

~Ⓡ~

Austin was sitting in his office, trying to get his work done. However, Victoria was making it near impossible with all her interruptions, pumping him for information about Ashley.

Then his sister called.

"Carrie, I'm really busy right—"

"Too busy to tell me the time of the ceremony?"

Austin dialed it back, needing to give her the benefit of the doubt.

"Seven o'clock. We'll meet at the house, then walk to the beach together."

"Sounds beautiful."

"That's the idea."

Carrie was silent. Never a good thing.

"You're making a mistake, Austin. A stupid, stupid mistake."

"And there it is, the *real* reason you called. You know what, Carrie, if you can't be happy for me—"

"I care about you, Austin. I just don't want to see you get hurt."

"I'm hanging up now."

"Ashley is nothing but a gold-digging opportunist. She left you high and dry your senior year, never even bothering to keep in touch. But now that she knows how successful you are, she simply waltzes back into your life, wanting to pick up where you two left off."

"You're wrong, Carrie. She's known about my success all along. And for your information, I'm the one who's been pursuing her. I'm the one who proposed. Twice. Finally convincing her we were meant to be together."

"Because you're crazy enough to think you can recapture what you shared in high school. That was over twenty years ago, Austin. People change. You've changed. She's changed. Better yet, maybe she hasn't changed at all. Ashley had you believing you two were exclusive when you were together, yet she had a child with someone else. I did the math, Austin. She got pregnant her senior year. And, since she never went after you for child support, it proves she was sleeping with someone else while pretending to be madly in love with you. She's not good enough for you, Austin. She never was and never will be. Ashley is nothing but a two-bit—"

"Stop, Carrie!" Austin shouted. "Right now! Before you say something you can't take back!" He took a deep breath, then lowered his voice to be civil. "I'm not naïve, and Ashley most certainly is not a gold digger. She's a very successful businesswoman. She doesn't need my money. As for C.J., I know all I need to about him. I'm not making a mistake. I've never been so sure of something in my life."

"But Austin, you're not—"

"Carrie, this is my decision, not yours. So, just back off. I've never tried to tell you what to do with your life or ridiculed the choices you've made. If you can't be happy for me, I'd rather you not come to the ceremony. I will not subject Ashley to your name calling or vindictive attitude on her wedding day."

Austin didn't give Carrie a chance to answer him back, he just hung up the phone. He then depressed the call button that rang Victoria's desk.

"Victoria, if my sister calls back, I'm not available."

TWENTY-SEVEN

Ashley walked the mall trying to focus on just a few things at a time. First, find a pair of shoes that would complement her dress, then something for C.J. to wear. She wandered from storefront to storefront, looking for something simple, yet nice. C.J. was a jeans and T-shirt kind of guy. When he did dress up, he usually wore a loud button-down shirt he'd ordered out of the Sheplers' catalog. So, the challenge for Ashley was to find something comfortable enough he wouldn't balk at it, yet nice enough for the occasion.

She slipped into the trendy store with the cabana façade and found what she was looking for. On the mannequin—casually posed with its hand in the pockets—was a white linen shirt untucked, sleeves rolled up, over a pair of casual khaki pants. It had beachy written all over it. Imagining how it would look with C.J.'s blond hair and crystal blue eyes, Ashley smiled. *Perfect*.

With C.J. taken care of, she crossed the mall to a swanky shoe store she walked by all the time, but never had a reason to go in. The front window display was filled with an array of sandals in every color and style imaginable. Some flats, some with heels. Some simple, some that laced all the way up the calf. When she walked inside the store, she was immediately drawn to a pair of white slip-ons. They were flats, the straps thin and delicate, but it was the small silver charms decorating the straps that grabbed her attention. The little daisy-shaped charms gave the sandals a whimsical yet elegant flare that added something special. After trying on a few sizes, Ashley made her purchase.

With two things off her list, and her nail appointment still an hour away, she decided to check out a few of the jewelry stores. Ashley wasn't sure what she was looking for but knew she would recognize it when she saw it. She looked in several glass cases, starting with the wedding sets, then moving on to the men's section, but nothing caught her eye. She was ready to give up when she saw a ring in a display case of mismatched items.

156

The ring was made of three individual bands. The outer bands were platinum, and the center band was channel set diamonds. Ashley craned her neck, trying to count how many diamonds made up the center band when a salesman approached her.

"Can I show you something, Miss?"

"Yes, the man's wedding band there in the black box."

"Excellent choice."

Ashley could tell by the man's excitement he probably worked on commission. She would have to be shrewd and keep her emotions in check or else he might decide to hike up the price.

He took the band from the box and handed it to Ashley. He was telling her the weight and clarity of the diamonds, but Ashley was more intent on the number. She smiled to herself when she realized there were twenty-five perfectly set diamonds in the ring. Exactly what she wanted. She contained her excitement, knowing she would buy the ring, regardless of price. However, the salesman *did not* need to know that.

"I'm sorry, what were you saying?" Ashley interrupted his spiel, trying not to sound overly impressed.

"This ring is platinum and gold with twenty-five channel set diamonds totaling three carats. The quality and the clarity are exceptional."

Ashley studied the ring as he spoke. She slid it onto her index finger, and it fit just like she thought it should. She dared to ask, "What size is it?"

He fumbled with the title card he had been reading from. "It's a ten."

Ashley almost lost it but stayed composed. "How much?"

"Well, it is on sale. This ring normally sells for $5,500, but it is on sale for $3,500."

"Why is it on sale? Is there a flaw or something?" Ashley looked closely like she was inspecting the ring.

"No. No flaw, but whenever our wedding sets get broken up, we sell the remaining ring at a drastically reduced price. To keep inventory down. That's why we have this whole case of mismatched items. But I assure you, there is nothing wrong with the quality."

"Could you discount it further if I wanted to pay cash?"

"Well, it's already on sale. I'm not sure if I can do anything to lower the price further."

It seemed as if the salesman didn't want to budge, so Ashley handed him the ring, thanked him for his time, then walked away, praying he would call her back.

"Miss . . . Miss . . ."

Ashley turned with a nonchalant look on her face. "Yes?"

"If you can wait a moment, I'll ask my manager if we might be able to negotiate a cash price for you."

"Okay, but I have a nail appointment in fifteen minutes, so I can't wait too long."

The salesman turned and hurried back to the glass office space at the rear of the store.

Ashley put on her game face, trying not to look too interested. Lee had taught her the art of negotiating where horses were concerned. Rule one—do not show too much emotion. Rule two—the price is never set in stone. Rule three—if you can't agree on a price in the first fifteen minutes, the deal most likely is not going to happen. She hoped the same rules applied to jewelry.

Standing at the end of the aisle, her arms crossed against her chest, Ashley glanced at her watch a few times for good measure. Finally, the salesman, along with an older gentleman emerged from the office and headed her way. The senior salesman twirled *Austin's* ring on his finger while looking directly at her.

"You are prepared to pay cash?"

"Yes."

"And what did you have in mind?"

"Three thousand, with a warranty."

"You'll still have to pay the sales tax."

"Fine."

"Write it up, Dennis. Twenty-seven hundred dollars for the ring, three hundred for the warranty." The manager turned to Ashley and shook her hand. "You got yourself a beautiful ring there, young lady. He must be pretty special."

"Very special," Ashley said, picturing the moment she would slide it onto Austin's finger.

The sales clerk brought the receipt over for Ashley to sign along with the warranty. Ashley pulled out the large bills from her wallet and carefully counted them out. She watched as he put the black velvet box into a little black gift bag with a gold corded handle. Ashley gently lifted the bag from the counter and walked away smiling from ear to ear.

Ashley arrived at her nail appointment with a few minutes to spare, then made two more stops for personal items. She was just pulling into the driveway at seven o'clock, when Austin's ringtone chimed.

"Hi," she said as she gathered her packages.

"Twenty-four hours until we say, "I do.""

Ashley could hear the smile in his words and was sure it matched the one on her face. "I know, I can hardly believe it. I've done so much today. The time has just flown by." Ashley struggled to reach one of her packages that had fallen onto the floorboard.

"Ashley, are you okay? You sound out of breath."

"I'm fine, Austin. One of my bags fell, and I was having a hard time reaching it."

"You're sure you didn't over do it today?"

Ashley could hear the worry in his tone. "I'm fine, Austin, really I am. You worry too much. How could I be anything but perfect? Word has it I'm getting married tomorrow. Is that amazing or what?"

He laughed. "It's amazing all right. The kind of amazing that miracles are made of. Hey, the reason I called was to see if I could swing by tonight after work? I don't think I can wait until tomorrow."

"Sure." Ashley lit up, wanting to see Austin after such a long day. It was just a shame she wouldn't be able to show him all her purchases. At least not yet.

"I'm almost finished here," Austin said. "So, I'll probably be there sometime around eight."

"Have you eaten?" Ashley asked as she juggled the garment bag that held her dress, bags from a half dozen stores, and fiddled with her door key.

"Not since lunch. You want me to pick something up?"

"No, I'll have something for you when you get here." Movement to her right caught Ashley's attention. When she saw C.J. and Willow walking her way, she tried to wave, but was bogged down with packages. "Okay, I'll see you in a little bit." Ashley disconnected the call as C.J. took some of the bags from her hands.

"Austin will be here around eight for dinner."

"So, do some of these bags have groceries in them?"

"No. They're for the wedding."

"How many weddings are you planning on having?"

Ashley gave C.J.'s arm a nudge. "Very funny. Besides, one of these is for you." Still holding the garment bag, Ashley picked through the bags C.J. had taken until she singled out his. "This one is for you; the rest are mine."

"Here, I'll take them," Willow offered, taking the bags from C.J. "Did you find a dress?"

"The exact one I wanted. Do you want to see it?"

"Sure." Willow's face lit up, stirring the excitement Ashley already felt.

"Follow me to my room, and I'll show you what I got. Oh, but before Austin gets here, let me show you the ring I bought him." Ashley handed the garment bag to C.J. to hold and took the little black bag with the gold insignia from Willow's hand.

"Wow! Truman Gems," Willow commented. "You didn't spare any expense, did you?"

"What do you mean by that?" C.J. asked.

"Only that everyone knows it's one of the most prestigious jewelry stores in Southern California. They even have a store on Rodeo Drive. Truman Gems started here in the valley many, many years ago. That's why they've kept this store. Nostalgia."

"Wow, I didn't realize you were such a jewelry connoisseur, Willow. I just heard they were known for their quality." Ashley pulled the black box from the bag and snapped it open. At the sight of Austin's ring, her heart fluttered.

"Oh my gosh, it's gorgeous!" Willow exclaimed.

"Wow, Mom, that's pretty impressive." C.J. took the ring from the box and inspected it closer. "That had to set you back a small fortune."

"Well, yes and no. It was fairly expensive, but I got a great deal. I knew I wanted something with three bands—a reminder our marriage is to have Christ at the center—then when I counted the diamonds and there were twenty-five, I knew it was perfect."

C.J. gave a shrug and handed the ring to Willow, who couldn't wait to see it.

"So, what do you think, C.J.?"

"You're right, Mom. It's perfect." He sounded a little choked up as he leaned over and gave her a kiss on the forehead, then cleared his throat and said, "I thought I would barbecue steaks. Does that sound okay for dinner?"

"Sure." Ashley looked at C.J., knowing his change of subject was his way of dealing with his emotions.

Willow was still ogling Austin's ring. "So, why was it on sale?"

"They said the set had been broken up, so they discounted it. I really didn't care what the reason was. I just knew I had to have it."

Willow handed it to Ashley, who gently put it back in the box.

Ashley took the garment bag from C.J., and together she and Willow went upstairs to her room. They put all the bags on Ashley's bed and then closed the door. Ashley unzipped the garment bag and pulled out her beautiful crocheted dress and laid it against her chest. "So, what do you think?"

"Oh, Ashley, it's exquisite." Willow touched the delicate silk and fingered the crocheted sleeves. "Go put it on."

"Oh, come on, Willow. I don't have time for that. We have all kinds of paperwork to go over. Plus, I have to pack and . . ." Willow stared at her with a dreamy look in her eyes, like she wouldn't take no for an answer. "Oh, o-kay." Ashley scooped up the dress and grabbed the bag that had her shoes in it. She stepped into her bathroom and put the dress on for the second time. She loved it then, and she loved it now. It fit her perfectly. It hugged her body in all the right places before the skirt flared and swirled around her ankles. The silk shell stopped at the knees, her tanned legs visible through the crochet. The sweetheart neckline lay against Ashley's chest, and the long, fluted sleeves rested on the back of Ashley's hands. She slipped on the delicate white sandals with the pretty silver charms, then stepped from the bathroom. "Ta-da."

Willow didn't say a thing, she just started crying. Ashley glided across the room, then looked at her reflection in the mirror over her dresser. She had a hundred other things she needed to get done, but she stood transfixed. *I can't believe that's really me.*

"It's perfect, Ashley."

"I think so, too."

After changing her clothes, Ashley carefully draped the dress across the chair in the corner, then showed Willow the other things she bought. While Willow was admiring her purchases, Ashley casually slipped the pink bag of lingerie off the side of the bed. Those were things only Austin would see. The mere thought of it made her heart skip a beat.

After Willow gave her vote of approval on the things Ashley bought, they walked downstairs, just as Austin pulled into the driveway. Ashley met him on the front porch with a welcoming kiss. Then, he turned around as if he was going to leave, but Ashley stopped him. "Where are you going?"

"I'm going out, so I can come back in again. I want to get a little more of that."

"Austin!" Ashley laughed.

He grabbed her around the waist and pulled her close. They

shared a long, lingering kiss. Willow slipped passed them and out the front door. "I'll give you two a little privacy. Ashley, I'll be in the office when you're ready."

Ashley felt heat race to her cheeks.

"It was just a kiss, Ashley. You don't need to be embarrassed," Austin teased.

"I'm not embarrassed!"

"Really?" he laughed. "You look like you have a pretty serious sunburn."

Ashley touched her hands to her face. "I guess this is going to take some getting used to."

"Well, then, I guess I'll have to keep kissing you to help you overcome your shyness. Think of it as therapy." Austin leaned in to kiss her again, but Ashley pressed her hands to his chest, laughing, trying to keep him at arm's length.

"Austin, I need to show Willow how to handle the payroll. Why don't you see if C.J. needs help with dinner? He's around back at the barbecue."

"Are you going to be long?"

"Hopefully not too long. Go ahead and visit with C.J. We'll be there as soon as we can." Austin took a step toward the kitchen but spun back around to steal another kiss. "Austin!"

"Just helping with your therapy."

~Ⓡ~

The feel of Ashley next to him was still on Austin's mind when he saw C.J. working at the grill. "How's it going?"

"Good, but what happened to you? You look like you were out in the sun too long."

Austin couldn't help but laugh. He brushed it off and tried making small talk, but C.J. never looked up from the barbecue. He just turned the steaks and repositioned the corn. His quietness concerned Austin.

"You're sure you're okay with this? Us getting married and all?"

C.J. stacked the corn on a plate, then climbed the porch steps.

"C.J.?" Austin asked again, following him into the kitchen.

"Yeah, I'm cool with it. But can I fill you in on something? Just because I don't think my mom will?"

"Shoot." Austin sat on the arm of the sofa while C.J. checked on the potatoes in the oven. He closed the oven and turned to Austin.

"Regardless of what Mom says, this ranch means a lot to her. I just don't want to see her have to give it up to fit into your world."

Austin was puzzled. "My world? Why do you make it sound like I live on the other side of the planet?"

"Well, you've got to admit, the contrasts are pretty big. Let's see, Black tie versus wranglers, pickup car versus pickup truck, fancy dinner parties versus rodeos. Come on Austin, Mom is used to working hard and enjoying simple pleasures. To her, a night out on the town is dinner and a movie."

"I think you underestimate your Mom, C.J. She knows what a night on the town is. I saw the pictures in her scrapbook."

C.J. looked confused, but Austin knew the minute he made the connection. "Oh, that! That was a onetime date. She did it as a favor to a friend, but it's nothing she would want to do on a regular basis."

"I'm not sure what you think I do every night, C.J., but I go to maybe a dozen dinner parties a year—mostly work related. My evenings are spent swimming laps or playing pool alone, but now I'll have someone to share my life with. I'm looking forward to being able to curl up with your mom at the end of a busy day and watch an old movie on TV."

"So, what about working? Do you mind if she still works the ranch?"

"Not at all; once the doctor gives her a clean bill of health. Look, C.J., I don't expect her to change everything about her life. We haven't even discussed where we're going to live after we get married. I just assumed Ashley would move to my place, but maybe she won't want to. Who knows, we might end up living here. Which I'm fine with. Change doesn't bother me, as long as that change includes Ashley by my side."

C.J. glanced his way before heading back to the barbecue. Austin didn't follow him, figuring he needed some time to process. Instead, he wandered around the house looking at mementos and memorabilia. Glimpses of the life Ashley led for the last twenty-five years. After he finished looking through another of Ashley's scrapbooks, he glanced at his watch and realized it was getting late. He decided to head over to the office to see how much longer she and Willow would be. Knocking before entering, Austin stuck his head in the office door.

"You two almost through? It's close to nine o'clock."

Ashley looked at the clock on the wall. "I'm sorry, Austin, I didn't realize how late it was getting. I just have one more thing to show Willow, then we'll be done. Give us fifteen minutes."

"Okay, but those steaks of C.J.'s smell pretty good. I'd hate to see them get ruined because they were over cooked."

Ashley was already showing Willow something on the computer, oblivious to his comment. Austin saw his way out and walked back to the house, but every time he thought about what he would be doing tomorrow, his heart raced out of control.

C.J. had everything on the table and ready to go when Austin returned to the dining room. The two men went ahead and dished up their food. Austin offered to pray, and C.J. shrugged with a noncommittal attitude. The women finally joined them, and together they ate and discussed the next day's event.

Ashley listened as Willow peppered Austin with questions. She asked for a short recap of their reunion and swooned and sighed as if she was hearing a fairytale.

"That has to be the most romantic thing I've ever heard," Willow said. "And if it wasn't for the fact that I know Ashley, I don't think I would believe it."

Ashley laughed. "Well, I am Ashley, and I still don't think I believe it."

Everyone seemed to be having a good time. Ashley enjoyed sitting back and listening as Willow grilled Austin and scolded C.J. for his sarcastic eye rolling. Ashley also noticed C.J. seemed to be a little more animated around Willow. Playful even. Something Ashley hadn't seen before. *Hmmm . . . maybe there could be something there.*

Ashley had always thought Willow and C.J. would make a good couple. Willow was a beautiful, smart, motivated worker, and she loved animals as much as C.J. did. But Willow also had a boyfriend—a boyfriend who had caused Willow to pull away from her and C.J. Willow no longer hung around the ranch after business hours, talking and chatting like she used to. Now, the minute she was done with work, she left. She had also stopped attending church with her and C.J., something that had really concerned Ashley. When she asked Willow why, she explained that she and Steven were visiting other churches together, trying to find a place with a younger congregation.

It made perfect sense. Of course Willow would want to spend her spare time with her boyfriend and find a church where they both felt comfortable. It had eased Ashley's concern, but the mom in her still thought Willow would be perfect for C.J. *Maybe if things go south with her boyfriend . . .*

Ashley shook off her matchmaking, knowing she had her own life to worry about. She didn't need to be meddling in Willow's. Standing, she started to clear the table, when Willow interrupted her.

"C.J. and I can get this. I'm sure you and Austin have things to discuss." Willow started stacking the plates, and C.J. stood to help her.

"Are you sure? I hate to keep you too late."

"It's no problem. Steven had some kind of business event to go to anyway."

"Well, if you're sure . . ."

Ashley and Austin left the dining room hand in hand. Walking out the backdoor to the porch, they sat on the hanging swing and looked out over the ranch.

"You know, Ashley, we haven't talked about our living arrangements yet."

"I know. In fact, there's a lot we haven't had time to talk about." Ashley paused for a moment before turning to him. "Austin, I want to be able to come home after my surgery. I want to recuperate where I feel comfortable. Not to say your house isn't comfortable, but it's not what I'm used to. I mean, here I know where everything is, and—"

"That's fine, Ashley."

"Are you sure? I mean I think your house is lovely, but—"

"It's fine. Really. I knew you would want to be close to home, to make sure the ranch was running smoothly and be available in case C.J. or Willow had questions."

"And what about you, Austin, what do you want? I don't want you to feel like you're third or fourth in line."

"What do I want?" Austin snatched up Ashley's hands, brought them to his chest and stared into her eyes. "I want to be able to hold you close every night. I want to wake up with you in my arms and see your face as I fall asleep at the end of the day. I want to take you to faraway places and give you everything you ever wanted. I want to love you the way I imagined all these years. I want to make you Mrs. Austin Carrington Taylor. That's enough for me."

Ashley was in tears by the time Austin finished his declaration. He lightly brushed the wetness from her cheeks with his thumb and kissed her with a fervor that spoke of his commitment to her. She wanted to remind him of her uncertain future but didn't want to ruin the mood. Leaning into Austin's shoulder, she snuggled close, enjoying the warmth of his body next to hers. With his outstretched foot, he pushed off from the porch, the swing rocking in a steady rhythm. Ashley closed her eyes against the silence, perfectly happy to stay this way forever. But after a few minutes, she asked, "So, what's the plan for tomorrow?"

"I'm sending a car for you at six o'clock. C.J. can ride with you or separately, whatever he prefers. Then we will all walk to the bluff overlooking the beach, have the ceremony, and walk back to the house. I've arranged for a small cake and some refreshments, and then we're off on our honeymoon."

"And who have you invited again? Besides Simon and Jenna."

"My secretary, Victoria, and possibly my sister and her husband."

"That's right; he had a golf game or something?"

"Well, yes, but I had a little falling out with Carrie, too, so I wouldn't be offended if she didn't show up either."

"I guess she's not too thrilled about your spontaneous plans?"

"Not exactly, but Jenna will be there to represent the family, and that's just fine with me. I do wish my parents were home. I tried calling them, but they are on a pilgrimage to my mother's grandmother's thatch house in the hill country of Scotland. I didn't leave a message, because I was afraid it might alarm them."

"What do you think they will say when they get home and find out you're married?"

"Mom will be disappointed but thrilled. She knew I never stopped loving you. She'll just be upset we didn't have a big, formal wedding where she could show us off to all of her friends."

"But your mother never acted like she approved of me."

"Mom has changed a lot over the years. When she saw my sister's first marriage crumble, she realized things don't always turn out the way you plan. Paul was from the right family, with the right career, and the right circle of friends, and he ended up having an affair and publicly embarrassing my sister. It's done a lot to change my mom's outlook on life."

"And your father?"

"Dad . . . he'll be his own skeptical self. Spontaneity to him is planning a vacation three months in advance, instead of a year. This trip they're on now . . . three years in the making. He wanted to make sure everything was mapped out precisely. To him, good planning means no room for disappointment."

"What do you think they're going to say when they find out I have a son?"

Austin pulled her even closer. "You know what, Ashley, I don't know what they'll say, but it doesn't matter. I'm an adult. I have prayed extensively about this, and the best part is, you've already said yes. I'm not going to let you back out now."

Ashley looked up at Austin, seeing love in his eyes as he placed a tender kiss to her forehead. "Like it or not Ashley Trent Summers, by this time tomorrow, you'll be my wife, and the rest of the world will just have to deal with it."

TWENTY-EIGHT

Ashley woke the next morning with an unspeakable peace. She prayed before getting out of bed, then showered and dressed for church. She sat quietly as C.J. drove.

"You don't even seem nervous," C.J. said.

"Why should I be nervous? It's only church," Ashley teased.

"You know what I mean."

"I know, but you're right. I don't feel the least bit nervous. I've spent a lot of time in prayer these last few days, and the Lord has given me peace about this."

"What about later this week? Are you at peace with that, too?"

Ashley knew C.J. was referring to her surgery and could hear the bitterness in his tone. She thought a moment before answering.

"Yes, C.J., I am. I know God is in control, and He made sure I saw a doctor before my condition was deemed inoperable. I am choosing to rest in the thought of God's healing, and that after surgery, my body will be fine."

"Well, you'll excuse me if I don't share your optimism. If God really wanted to prove Himself, He would have healed your body without surgery. He would have made sure you didn't have to go through any of this."

"Let me ask you this. Have you been praying about it, C.J.?"

"Well, maybe not praying, more like pleading. I just keep asking God why? Why would He allow this to happen to you after all you've already been through?"

"What was your prayer life like before I told you I had cancer?"

"I don't know. I guess I've kind of gotten out of the habit of praying." C.J. pulled the truck into the church parking lot and maneuvered into a space, then turned to look at her. "So, what's your point?"

"Maybe God is trying to get a line of communication open with you again. Maybe He's using this as common ground."

C.J. lapped his arms over the steering wheel and laid a sideways glance on her. "Are you saying this is my fault? That the only way God could get my attention was by making you sick?"

C.J. didn't give Ashley time to rebut his remark. He got out of the truck, slammed the door, paced angrily, then leaned back against the fender with his arms folded against his chest.

Ashley walked around to the driver's side and stood in front of him. "God doesn't punish one person to get the affection or respect of another. I'm just saying that everything works in God's time. Maybe your lack of commitment to God and my total dependency on God has overlapped for a reason. I'm trusting in God, and I'm the one going through this illness. You should be able to trust in God to meet your needs and give you the comfort I can't while I'm recovering. I'm just saying, C.J., you've come to rely on me to be your everything, which I love. But I'm only human. I'm going to let you down and possibly not be here some day when you need guidance or help. If you don't have God, who will you turn to then?"

Ashley could see the agitation in her son's demeanor, and she didn't want to frustrate him further. "Look, C.J., I don't want to argue with you today. It's my wedding day for heaven's sake. Just think about what I said, okay?" Ashley reached for his hand and gave it a squeeze. "Church is starting . . . shall we?" Ashley tucked her arm into the crook of his elbow, and together they went into morning services.

Jenna waved to Austin as she circled the church parking lot. He smiled and waited for her to find a space, not understanding why he felt so nervous. He paced the front steps, feeling like he was going to jump out of his skin.

"Good morning, Uncle Austin," Jenna said as she climbed the steps giggling.

"What's so funny?" he asked as he leaned forward and gave her a peck on the cheek.

"You. I've never seen you so nervous before. You look like you're freaking out. In the time it took me to cross the parking lot, you must have put your hands in and out of your pockets a half dozen times."

"I don't understand why I'm feeling this way. Everything is set; everything is in order. I just wish it was here already. This waiting is going to be the death of me."

"What? Are you telling me successful, confident, business genius, Austin Taylor, is a pile of nerves? Then it most definitely is love."

Just then Pastor Stan came up to Austin and put a firm hand on his shoulder. "Well, Austin, this is the big day. How are you feeling?"

Austin gave him a nervous smirk. "Numb. I lost feeling about an hour ago."

Both Jenna and Pastor Stan laughed.

"Where is the bride to be? I thought I would at least get a chance to meet her before the actual service."

"We decided not to see each other until this evening. She went to church with her son."

"Well, I sure hope I don't lose you as a parishioner when the two of you get married. I want to be able to sit back and watch this relationship grow."

"No worries there, Pastor. Ashley and I already decided we will come here after we're married. She's not that comfortable attending a church the size of a small city. She never really got plugged in at Wayside."

The music began to play in the sanctuary.

"Well, that's my cue," the pastor said. "I guess I'll see you both tonight. Is seven o'clock okay?"

"That's fine, and thanks again for everything."

Jenna and Austin made their way to the third pew from the back, their standard spot on Sunday mornings. Strains of "Shout to the Lord" filled the sanctuary, but Jenna was uncharacteristically silent.

Austin leaned over and whispered. "Are you okay? You seem quiet all of a sudden?"

"I just realized I'll no longer be your girlfriend." Jenna gave him a teary smile. "I've been your girlfriend since I was seven-years-old, when you took me to see my first Disney movie. I told you then, that I wanted to be your girlfriend, and you said you'd be honored. I guess I'm being replaced."

Austin reached his arm around the back of the pew and pulled Jenna close in an affectionate hug.

"No one could ever replace you, Jenna. I think Ashley will be glad to know you held my heart until I was ready to give it back to her."

They sat quietly through the rest of the service. The theme of the message—*The Faithfulness of God.*

Willow showed up early, so she could help Ashley with her hair.

"I don't know if I should wear it up or not?" Ashley said.

"Oh, I think you should. It's going to be pretty warm, and the neckline on your dress is so beautiful. If you wear your hair down, it will cover up all the detailing across the back."

Ashley agreed, so they worked together piling her long blond tendrils on top of her head.

"Now we just need something to hold it in place."

"I've got something that will work." Ashley walked over to her jewelry box and pulled out an antique hair comb. "What if we use this?"

"Oh my gosh, this is gorgeous," Willow said while turning the sterling and crystal leaf pattern over in her hand.

"It was my grandmother's. I forgot I had it. I've never had a use for something so fancy."

"Well, you do now."

Willow worked on Ashley's hair, sweeping it up and to one side, rolling it into itself, and securing it with the comb and a few well-placed bobby pins. Allowing a few wisps to frame her face and touch the bridge of her shoulders, the ethereal look was the perfect complement to her exquisite dress.

Willow took a few steps back and stared at Ashley through the mirror. "You look stunning."

"Thank you." Ashley got up from the stool she was sitting on and carefully removed her dress from the hanger. "Oh shoot, I should have at least put the slip on before we did my hair."

"That's okay; I'll help. Put your arms up." Willow lifted the satin slip over Ashley's head and carefully allowed it to glide down her frame. Then, she gathered the crocheted dress. Ashley slipped her arms into the sleeves and stood very still while Willow maneuvered the dress over her head. When Willow took a step back, tears glistened in her eyes.

"Ashley, you look amazing. You look like you just stepped off the cover of a romance novel."

Ashley admired her reflection in the full-length mirror. She loved the way the dress fit in all the right places and was glad her long hair didn't cover up the low-cut scalloped back. She liked that it was a bit daring, romantic, but not scandalous. And, with her bronzed skin peeking through the intricate needle work, it couldn't have been more perfect. She closed her eyes. *God, I can't believe this is happening.*

A tap on the door stole her attention. "Is it okay if I come in?" C.J.'s muffled voice filtered through the door.

"Come on in," Ashley replied.

When he opened the door, he looked stunned. "Wow!"

"I guess for an old ranch hand, I clean up pretty well."

C.J. didn't say anything; he just gave her a hug. Ashley could feel the depth of his emotion in the way he clutched her tight, like he never wanted to let her go. It brought tears to her eyes. Even Willow began to tear up again.

"C.J., don't get all emotional on me, or you're going to make me cry." Ashley stepped back from his embrace and took in his tall stature and deep blue eyes. "That shirt looks perfect on you. Just how I imagined it."

"Uh huh," Willow said.

Both C.J. and Ashley turned to Willow.

Willow looked surprised. Clearly, she hadn't mean to speak out loud. She instantly turned bright red and started fiddling with all the hair products that were on the dresser. "I'll just get these things cleaned up." She started knocking the bottles over and grasping at them as they fell, then stopped abruptly. "Better yet, why don't I step outside for a moment so you two can have some privacy."

Willow quickly made her way toward the door, but not before Ashley saw her steal one more glance at C.J., attraction evident in her eyes.

"What was that all about? I thought it was the bride who was supposed to be nervous. You would think it was Willow getting married."

Ashley smiled to herself and said, "Maybe she was surprised how well *you* clean up?"

"Why?"

"Because you're a very attractive young man."

"Whatever."

Ashley sighed. C.J. was an intelligent guy, but completely ignorant about his good looks. He had no idea how attractive he was to the opposite sex.

She turned back to the mirror and studied her reflection, and that of her son's. The look on his face was stoic, causing Ashley to wonder what he was thinking, but before she could ask, he volunteered his thoughts.

"Are you sure you're ready for this, Mom?"

She turned to face him. "Of course I am. I've thought of this moment for the last twenty-five years, except then it was just a dream, but now it's coming true."

"That's just it, Mom. You've dreamt about this moment, the fairytale part of it. The knight in shining armor, the beautiful gown, being swept off your feet, but are you ready for the reality of it? This is a lifelong commitment you're making, not just an antidote to get you through hard times."

Ashley was hurt C.J. still did not understand the depth of emotion she felt for Austin, but she couldn't blame him for voicing his concern. She was glad their relationship was open enough he could pose such a hard question at the last moment. She was also grateful he understood the magnitude of marriage. Ashley took C.J. by the hand and led him to the foot of her bed. She sat next to him, her hand still clutching his.

"C.J., thank you for loving me so much that you'd be willing to ask such an important question. I'm glad you realize the importance of marriage, and that you understand it is an unending decision. Let me assure you, this is the third most important decision I have ever made. And I'm just as sure now as I was then."

"What do you mean?"

"When I accepted the Lord into my life, I never looked back. From that moment on, I have felt God's presence and have experienced His peace. Even in the hard times, He's been there for me, offering His strength when I had nothing left to give. My commitment to the Lord means everything to me. It's the most important decision I have ever made."

C.J. shifted on the bed. Ashley knew this wasn't the time for a lecture, so she didn't say anything more about her relationship with Christ.

"Then what was number two?" C.J. asked.

"The day I decided to have you." Their eyes locked. "Those two decisions have changed my life forever, and I'm as sure now as I was then, that this is the right decision, and the life God has held for me. I don't know why the cancer. I don't know why I had to wait so long to find Austin again, but I do know that it's right, and that God will be with me every step of the way."

"I love you, Mom," C.J. said. "I hope someday I can make you as proud of me as I am of you." Their embrace lasted for only a moment. C.J. stood up abruptly and struck a pose in front of the full-length mirror. "I don't know, I hope Austin has his stuff together. I would hate to show him up at his own wedding."

Ashley laughed at C.J.'s wit—his attempt to lighten the mood. Willow stuck her head back in the door, looking more composed than when she left.

"I don't mean to rush your time together, but the car should be here any minute."

Ashley quickly glanced at the clock on the bedside table. It was almost six o'clock. In two hours, she would be married.

"Do you need help with anything, Mom?"

"Actually, I have a few more things to pack; then I could use a hand with my suitcase."

"Did Austin give you any idea where you would be going on your honeymoon?" Willow asked as she gathered a few of her own things.

"No. He just said to pack casual."

After C.J. and Willow left her to herself, Ashley placed the last few items in her suitcase. She carefully laid the white lace nightie she had bought especially for tonight on the top of the pile. Her heart skipped, and her stomach tightened. She wasn't afraid, but she wasn't at ease either.

She knew she was putting undue pressure on herself. Even so, she wanted to make the next few nights with Austin as romantic and fulfilling as possible. After Friday, she wasn't sure where the road would take them, so the next few days needed to be perfect.

"You ready?" C.J. was standing at the door.

"Yep. How about you?"

"Sure."

"Are you going to ride with me?"

"Nah, I'd prefer to drive myself, so I can leave when I want to."

"Are you sure?"

"Yeah. Willow's doesn't know the area, so I told her she could follow me."

C.J. carried her bags downstairs, still discussing travel arrangements with her, when they heard a car honk out front.

Willow looked out the window. "Your ride is here."

Ashley peered over C.J.'s shoulder as he opened the front door. There, in the driveway, was a white stretch limo. A man in a dark suit quickly came to the front door and removed the bags from C.J.'s hands. He pressed some buttons on a remote and both the trunk and the backdoor opened wide. It wasn't the limo that impressed Ashley. She'd seen them on movie sets all the time; she'd even rode in them on occasion. It was what was inside that took her breath away. As C.J. did the honors of helping her into the backseat, she was immediately surrounded by dozens of yellow tulips, covering every surface inside the limousine. Ashley started to cry.

"Mom, you okay?"

She nodded. "He remembered my favorite flower."

The driver came around to close Ashley's door, but C.J. waved him off. "I've got it," he said, then squatted down next to the car. Ashley smiled at C.J., trying to regain her composure.

"Are you ready, ma'am?" the driver asked once he got behind the wheel.

"Yes, I'm ready. Oh, C.J., you have the ring, right?"

"Yes, Mom, it's right here." He patted his deep pants pocket, and sure enough, Ashley saw the impression of the little velvet box. "I'll see you there, Mom. We'll be right behind you." C.J. leaned in and kissed her cheek, then carefully closed the door.

TWENTY-NINE

C.J. watched the limo slowly pull out of the driveway. Once it was out of view, he turned to Willow and asked, "Are you ready?"

"Sure, just let me grab my purse and stuff from inside."

C.J. walked to his truck and waited for Willow to get into her car. He wasn't really paying attention—his thoughts were on his mom and on how everything was changing so drastically—so when he finally looked in his rearview mirror, he was surprised to see Willow lifting the hood of her car. He jumped out of his truck and walked to where she was standing with her hands on her hips. She glanced his way and then back to her car.

"I told Steven something was wrong, but oh no, he said it was just my imagination." Frustration was evident in her voice.

"What happened when you tried to start it?"

"Nothing. At least before there would be a low moan before it finally turned over, but this time it didn't even do that."

"Look, we really don't have a lot of time before the wedding. Just drive with me. You can call for a tow truck to take your car back to your place or to a shop."

Willow twisted her hands and scrunched her brow. "Steven doesn't like surprises. Maybe I should call him and let him decide what he wants me to do."

"Well, either way, we need to get going. You can decide what to do on the way."

"Okay. Just let me get my purse."

C.J. slammed the hood of the car while Willow grabbed her purse from the front seat.

"Thanks, C.J.," Willow said as she hopped in the passenger seat. "It would have been horrible if I had missed the wedding."

"No problem." While navigating his way to the freeway, C.J. couldn't help but notice the way Willow fidgeted with her phone, as if she was stalling or afraid to make the call.

"It's no big deal, Willow. Cars break down all the time. He

176

should know that; especially if you already told him you suspected something was wrong. Things like this happen."

"Yeah, but why always to me," she mumbled then dialed, her foot tapping nervously.

"Hi, Steven, it's me." Willow's voice was bright and cheery. Too cheery.

C.J. looked at her, wondering why she sounded so peculiar. It bothered him.

"I've had a bit of car trouble . . . no, I didn't smash the car. It won't start. Remember, I told you I heard a funny noise, well, I guess it was something after all. No, I'm not blaming—No, I didn't say—"

C.J. could actually hear the guy yelling over the phone, and with every angry response, Willow seemed to shrink against the seat.

". . . I'm sorry, Steven . . . I didn't do it on purpose; it's just an old car. Where am I?" Willow hesitated, like she wasn't sure what to say. "I got a ride from someone else going to the wedding. The car is at the ranch in the driveway. No, I didn't want to miss the wedding when there was nothing I could—Steven, I'm sorry I bothered you. I know, I know, this ruins your day. I should have handled it myself. I'll just call a tow truck. Well, I've got to get it to the mechanic some—"

Willow turned closer to the window and lowered her voice barely above a whisper, but C.J. could still hear. "Don't worry Steven, I'll pay for it. It won't cost you a dime."

C.J. could hear anger begin to creep into Willow's tone, but just as quick, she lowered her voice and began to apologize. C.J. couldn't believe someone would be so upset about a car breaking down. It's not like Willow was in a careless accident or got a speeding ticket. She even warned him something was wrong with her car. His hands tightened on the steering wheel. *This guy sounds like a grade-A jerk. Why is Willow with him?*

"Okay, Steven, okay. Look, if you want to go take a look at it, go ahead. The spare key is under the front fender, by the license plate. I'm not sure how late I'll be, but I'll be home as soon as I can."

Willow hung up the phone and slipped it back into her purse. She looked at C.J. but quickly turned away before he could say anything. She was on the verge of tears so C.J. thought it was best to keep his comments to himself.

~®~

The limo ride was a unique time for Ashley. Alone with her thoughts, she watched as the traffic sped by, and memories flooded her thoughts. Feeling anxious once again, she decided to pray. She prayed for the perfect day. She prayed for God's blessing and praised Him for His endless mercies. She prayed for her future, her new husband, and her loving son. As she prayed, her father came to her mind. It stung. She didn't want thoughts of him to ruin her day. Prompted by God, she prayed for him, as well, that he would discover the love of God, before it was too late.

When she finished praying, music began to play. She looked up to see a small DVD screen flip down from the ceiling. To her surprise, pictures of Austin and her began to fill the screen, one after another. Ashley was mesmerized. Austin and her at a pep rally. The two of them at an ice cream social fundraiser. Sitting on the quad eating lunch. Dressed for the Sadie Hawkins' dance.

She watched completely captivated by the snapshots from her past and listened as the words from "Time in a Bottle" spoke of spending the rest of eternity together. When the pictures stopped, and the music softened, words play across the screen.

For I know the plans I have for you, says the Lord, plans for good and not for evil, plans to give you a hope and a future. Jer. 29:11
With all my love and prayers,
your husband to be, Austin

Stunned, Ashley sat as tears rolled down her face. Lost in thought, she hadn't even noticed the limo had come to a stop. The door swung open, and the driver extended his hand to help her step into her dreams.

"Just a moment, please." Ashley grabbed the tissues she'd stuffed into her purse, and dabbed at her cheeks, thankful for waterproof mascara. She quickly got herself together, then stepped from the limo.

The driver circled to the rear of the car and took her bags from the trunk. Feeling short of breath, she took a second to inhale and exhale slowly, then walked the cobblestone path to the front door. She knocked, not feeling comfortable enough to walk right in. Austin met her there.

Ashley was breathless. Austin stood in the entryway in linen dress pants that were the same shade as her dress, and a tuxedo shirt untucked and unbuttoned at the neck. He looked so incredibly handsome; Ashley felt dumbstruck.

Austin didn't say a word. He just stepped forward, wrapped his hand around her neck and pulled her into a passionate kiss. Ashley accepted it without hesitation. When Austin came up for air, he rested his forehead against hers and whispered, "I know I should have waited until the ceremony, but I've waited far too long already."

Ashley smiled, looking into his eyes. "I love you, Austin," she spoke in a hushed tone.

Austin wiped away a tear from her cheek with the back of his hand and smiled. "You have never looked more beautiful in your life."

"I guess you bring out the best qualities in me."

"Are you ready to do this?"

"Absolutely."

"Are you going to introduce me to my new aunt, Uncle Austin?"

Ashley turned to see the girl from the reunion standing in the hallway.

"Jenna, this is Ashley, Ashley this is my niece, Jenna."

Before Ashley could extend her hand, Jenna quickly stepped forward and pulled her into a hug, then took a step back.

"I can't believe I finally get to meet you. I've heard so much about you, but not nearly enough. You look even more beautiful than you did at the reunion. Where did you get your dress? It's perfect for today. Don't you think so, Uncle Austin? We'll have to go shopping together. I bet you know all kinds of crazy things about Uncle Austin. I can't wait to hear what he was like as a teenager. I mean, my mom has told me some, but I bet you know all the juicy stuff."

Austin laughed, and Ashley hid her smile behind her hand.

Jenna's shoulders sunk, and a frown creased her forehead. "What's so funny?"

"You, Jenna," Austin said, with a chuckle. "You're talking a mile a minute. However, your questions are going to have to wait. Today is Ashley's wedding day, not her inquisition."

Jenna put her hands to her hips and stood up straight. "Well, Uncle Austin, I do believe if you had brought Ashley around sooner, I would've had a better chance to get to know her."

Ashley grinned, remembering how she felt when she saw Jenna

on Austin's arm at the reunion, thinking Jenna was his date or possibly his wife. Now, she stood back and enjoyed watching the playful interaction between the two of them. It was obvious they had a special connection, and loved each other deeply

"You're absolutely right, Jenna," Austin said with dramatic flair. "I should have postponed the wedding until after you two had met, gone out to lunch, and become fast friends. How selfish of me not to consider your feelings."

"That's not what I meant, and you know it."

He laughed again. "I know." He pulled her into a side hug. "And believe me, you and Ashley will have plenty of time to get to know each other later."

"Excuse me, sir, where should I put these?" The limo driver asked, Ashley's suitcases in hand.

"First door on the right," Austin said, then pulled Ashley close. "Come on, I want you to see everything else before we head to the beach."

Walking into the living room, Ashley was astonished by the transformation. The pool table was no longer a pool table. Instead, it hosted an elaborate buffet, complete with china, silver, candles and at least five different entrees. A smaller table was set up in front of the bay window where their wedding cake was on display. Ashley went to get a closer look.

"Do you like it?"

"It's beautiful." The petite cakes couldn't be more than twelve inches around, but each of the three layers had an exquisite basket weave pattern decorating it, and the top of the cake was covered with delicate yellow tulips sculpted out of fondant.

"Austin," Ashley spun around, "I didn't thank you yet for the amazing video and the limo full of tulips. I can't believe you remembered my favorite flower."

"Of course I did. I never forgot."

"And the video? How on earth did you get that video done so quickly?"

"Actually, that was Jenna's doing. She's sort of a media buff."

"Jenna," Ashley turned to see the young girl smiling. "It was incredible. I felt transported back in time. It must have taken hours to do."

"Not really. It went together fairly easy. I just took the pictures Uncle Austin had, and some from his yearbook."

"Well, it was truly amazing!"

"I'm glad you liked it."

"Everything . . ." Ashley glanced around. "Everything looks so beautiful." As she stole one more glance at the cake, she looked out the front window and saw C.J. pull into the driveway. When he parked, Willow jumped out from the passenger side, and the two of them hurried up the walkway together.

Ashley thought again what a great couple they would make if Willow wasn't already involved with someone else.

Austin met them at the front door and ushered them into the living room. "Jenna, this is Ashley's son, C.J., and her assistant, Willow. C.J., Willow, this is my niece, Jenna. She'll be my maid of honor today."

After everyone said their hellos, shook hands, and stepped into the living room, Ashley watched as C.J. and Willow walked around Austin's home. Willow was admiring it, while C.J. was scrutinizing it. When he came back to stand next to her and Austin, he shrugged. "Nice digs, Austin."

"Thanks, C.J., I'm glad you approve. But like I told you before, if your mom and I decide to stay on the ranch, I'm fine with that, but if not, I hope you can see that she'll be comfortable here."

Before much more could be said, three more people arrived. Austin quickly introduced Ashley to his secretary, Victoria, and then to Pastor Stan and his wife, Connie.

Pastor Stan was quick to step forward and shake her hand. "It is a pleasure to meet you, Ashley. I must say, you and Austin have quite the story. When I told Connie, she was in tears."

Ashley smiled at the older woman.

"It's a beautiful story, dear. I dare say, almost as beautiful as you look tonight."

"Thank you," Ashley whispered, feeling a little nervous.

"Although we don't have a lot of time," Pastor Stan said, "I would like to talk with the two of you privately, if I may?"

"Of course," Austin spoke up, then slipped his arm around her and led them down the hall to his office.

"I don't really have much to say, but I would be remiss in my duties if I didn't speak with Ashley before the ceremony." Pastor Stan sat in one of the leather chairs, while Ashley occupied the other. Austin sat on the arm of the chair and gently laid his hand on her shoulder.

"Ashley, Austin tells me you accepted the Lord some time ago. Can you tell me about it?"

"Well, when I went to live with my grandparents as a teenager, I was having a hard time of it. Out of respect, I started going to church with them but continued going when I realized I needed a partner in life. Someone who wouldn't fail me. I gave my life to the Lord before Christopher was born and brought him up with a respect and love for Jesus. We've had our ups and downs, but I can see how God has worked in my life—many times in spite of myself."

Austin squeezed her shoulder. When she looked up at him, he mouthed, *You're incredible*.

The pastor smiled at her and then looked at Austin. "Well, I would like to have prayer with the both of you before we head out this evening." Pastor Stan leaned forward to link hands with her and Austin, then led them in a prayer for their future.

When Austin and Ashley walked back into the living room, Ashley noticed Jenna pacing in front of the large picture-window. Austin noticed, too. "Jenna, what's wrong?" he asked.

"Nothing, nothing at all." She smiled a little too brightly.

"Jenna . . ."

She wilted. "Mom and Jerry aren't here yet. I can't believe she would do this. I mean, I know you two don't always see eye-to-eye. Even so, you are her brother, and this is your wedding."

Austin looked around the room. "Well, Simon isn't here yet either. We can wait a few more minutes."

Austin spoke with Victoria while Ashley talked with C.J. and Willow. When they told her why they had arrived together, Ashley was slightly disappointed. Her heart had told her it was kismet. Perfect timing. Fate. Car trouble had never entered her thinking.

Fifteen minutes had passed when Austin slipped behind her and whispered in her ear, "You ready to do this thing?"

She smiled then turned around. "Austin, we can wait. Maybe they got held up in traffic?" Even though he said he didn't care if his sister or brother-in-law showed up, Ashley knew Simon was important to him.

"No. I don't want to miss the sunset. Simon will understand." He handed her a beautiful bouquet of yellow tulips and kissed her cheek. "Shall we?"

THIRTY

The walk to the bluff was surreal. Ashley felt like she was walking through pathways in her life. She thought back to the time when C.J. was little and would follow behind Lee on the ranch. She remembered the way her grandmother would pray for her every night. She thought about all the times she laid awake at night praying for God to provide for her and C.J., and how she desperately wanted a happily ever after. And now that day was here.

When they reached the bluff, everyone took their places. Jenna stood next to Austin and C.J. next to her.

"If everyone is ready, I'll—"

All of a sudden, someone hollered from up the walkway. The wedding party turned to see Simon running up the path with his cameras in hand. When he reached the bluff, he was gasping for breath.

"I'm sorry, Austin . . . I got a flat . . . tire. It took forever . . . for AAA . . . but I'm ready now."

Simon was still panting as he steadied the camera in front of him and started clicking off pictures.

"Okay, if everyone is ready, let's begin."

Just as the sun was lowering over the Pacific Ocean—casting a bronze glow on everyone—Pastor Stan started the service.

"Austin, take Ashley's hands."

Ashley handed her bouquet to C.J. He didn't even flinch. He was being the perfect maid of honor.

"Austin and Ashley would like to say something before they recite their vows. Austin." Pastor Stan turned to him and smiled.

Austin cleared his throat.

"I've waited twenty-five years for this day, and I can't believe it's finally here. If I could've planned for the grandest wedding of all, it could not have been more special than today. I feel honored to have those here who really love us as we pledge our tomorrows to each other. I know God had this day appointed for us from the beginning of time. I'm just glad it's finally here."

Austin squeezed her hands as Pastor Stan nodded to her to speak.

"This is a dream I dared not dream. It amazes me how God has continued to show Himself throughout my life. He has blessed me with a wonderful son . . ." Ashley stopped for a moment to still the emotion in her voice ". . . and now He's blessing me with an amazing husband. I know sometimes I feel the uncertainty of life, but I am certain this is the road God has chosen for me. I pray I can walk it with strength, courage, and peace, but whatever I do, I know I'll be walking it with the man God chose for me."

The pastor paused and looked over the small ensemble; so did Ashley. Jenna and Willow were pushing tears from their eyes, but C.J. stood tall and stoic, refusing to let them fall. When she looked at Austin, he did nothing to hide his tears as he brushed hers from her cheek. Through it all, Simon continued to click away.

"Austin, do you take Ashley to be your lawfully wedded wife, to cherish her always, for richer, for poorer, in sickness and in health, forsaking all other as long as you both shall live?"

Austin squeezed her hand. "I do."

"Ashley, do you take Austin to be your lawfully wedded husband, to cherish him always, for richer, for poorer, in sickness and in health, forsaking all other as long as you both shall live?"

With tears rolling down her cheeks, she smiled. "I do."

"Austin do you have something as a symbol of your love for Ashley?"

"Yes. A ring." Austin turned to Jenna, who then slipped the ring into Austin's hand. He turned back to Ashley and began to speak.

"I wanted to buy you the biggest diamond I could find but when I saw this ring, I knew it was meant for you." He raised the ring up to Ashley's hand. When Ashley saw the ring perched on her fingertip, she could do nothing to confine another onslaught of tears. "This ring is made up of three bands. I believe this represents how very present God is in this union and will be in our marriage. The center band is made up of twenty-five diamonds, one for every year we've waited for this day. I love you, Ashley. I always have and always will."

Austin, repeat after me. "With this ring . . . I thee wed . . . in the name of the Father, the Son, and the Holy Ghost."

Her hand was shaking so much, Austin had to brace her fingers before he could slip the ring into place.

"Ashley do you have something to give Austin as a symbol of

your love?" the pastor continued.

Ashley couldn't even speak; she just turned to C.J. who handed her the ring with a kiss. When she turned back to Austin and he saw the identical ring, he could not keep silent.

"Ashley, how did you know what ring I bought you?"

"I didn't. When I went looking for your ring, this is the one I knew was meant for you. It had to be, because of the three bands and the twenty-five diamonds."

Austin leaned down to steal a kiss from Ashley, but with a clicking tongue, Pastor Stan stopped him and whispered, "Patience, patience." Everyone laughed as Ashley slid Austin's ring into place and repeated her vow.

"With this ring . . . I thee wed . . . in the name of the Father, the Son, and the Holy Ghost."

"With the powers vested in me by the State of California, and as a minister of the Gospel of the Lord Jesus Christ, I now pronounce you man and wife. What God has joined together, let no man put asunder." Pastor Stan looked at both Ashley and Austin before he addressed the small gathering.

"Allow me to introduce to you for the very first time, Mr. and Mrs. Austin Carrington Taylor. Nooow, you may kiss your bride." Pastor Stan smiled and stepped to the side while Simon stood poised and ready. Austin drew Ashley closer, and lightly cradled her face in the palms of his hands. He placed a gentle kiss to her lips, paused before giving her a deeper kiss, then completely enfolded her in an embrace and continued kissing her and kissing her, until she began to giggle.

"Austin, I think we can stop now."

"I was just making sure Simon got a good picture." He placed one more kiss on the tip of Ashley's nose and then reached across to shake C.J.'s hand while everyone else applauded.

"Thank you, C.J., for allowing me into your family. I promise I'll make her happy."

Ashley reached over and gave Willow a hug, exchanging words of disbelief regarding the perfect ceremony, then she hugged Jenna. "I can't wait to get a chance to know you better." Jenna agreed with a nod and a tissue pressed to her eyelid.

Ashley turned to C.J., who was red-eyed but the picture of composure. She kissed him on the cheek and rested her head against his chest as they hugged. His pounding heart gave away his strong, but controlled emotions.

"Congratulations, Mom."

"Thank you, C.J. Thank you for everything."

"Hey, everybody, let me get some pictures before we lose the light."

Simon was in full photographer mode—positioning everyone in various groupings, until every imaginable combination was had.

"Now I'd like to get a few shots of just the two of you, while the sun is setting," Simon said, "but everyone else can head back to the house."

"Okay," Austin agreed. "Everyone," he addressed the gathering, "there is a feast back at the house. Go ahead without us; we'll join you in just a few minutes."

Simon took a few more pictures, then said, "Ashley, the back of your dress is gorgeous. I would like a shot that shows it off. Do you mind if I get a little daring?" Simon's question was posed to Ashley, but she wasn't quite sure how to respond. She looked to Austin for some help.

"He's not going to make me undress in public, is he?" she whispered.

"No," Austin laughed, then asked, "Simon, what did you have in mind?"

"Austin, you just stand there. Ashley, stand facing Austin with your back to the camera. Now, put your right hand on Austin's shoulder, and look toward your left shoulder. Good; perfect. Now, Austin, place you left arm around Ashley's waist and slip the crochet part of her dress off her shoulder. Now, kiss her shoulder."

Austin did what he was asked, and with every kiss, Ashley's pulse intensified. When their eyes met, she saw passion and fire like she'd never seen before.

In a sensual tone, Austin whispered in her ear, "You are so beautiful, Ashley. I can't wait to start the next chapter of our lives together, but if we don't call it quits right now, I can't be held responsible for my actions."

She whispered back, "Neither can I."

"Okay, I think I'm done here," Simon said, as he put the lens cap on his camera. "We can head back now."

Oblivious to the passion he had ignited in them, Simon trudged up the hill, Ashley and Austin hand in hand behind him.

When they reached the house, they were greeted by a round of applause, and another hug-fest of congratulations.

Everyone visited and mingled as they ate, except for Ashley.

Afraid she was going to spill something on her dress, she decided she would eat later. She even opted to drink only water as a safety precaution.

She talked with C.J. and Willow—discussing last minute details—but her eyes remained trained on Austin. He stood on the other side of the room, talking to Victoria, looking so incredibly gorgeous in his tuxedo shirt and linen pants; she couldn't take her eyes off him.

After a few minutes, Simon clinked his champagne glass with the tip of his spoon. "Okay, everyone, it's time for the happy couple to cut the cake."

Simon took pictures as they cut the cake and gently fed it to each other. Then Simon toasted them, wishing them success and long life.

"I'd like to say a few words, if I may?" Ashley turned to C.J., surprised he wanted to speak openly.

"I've known Austin personally for only a short time, but I feel like I've known him my entire life. When I realized he was someone my mom knew as a teenager, I started tracking his career through the financial pages. Nothing was ever written about him that disappointed or contradicted the person my mom had spoken about, or that I had conjured up in my mind. Even still, I was completely unprepared for the day he walked back into my mother's life. Admittedly, I gave Austin a hard time and was skeptical about his intentions. I know it probably sounds immature or weak, but my mom is my rock."

C.J. looked at her and smiled, making her heart melt.

"I didn't realize how much I relied on my mom until now. The thought of someone else in her life didn't thrill me, in fact, it made me jealous. But after a few scuffles," he looked at Austin, who in turn raised his glass to C.J., "and a couple heart-to-hearts," he turned to her with an I-love-you smile, "I can say wholeheartedly I couldn't be happier for my mom and Austin. If ever there were two soul mates in the world, it's them. It just took them twenty-five years to find their way back to each other. So," with an upraised glass, C.J. looked at her and Austin, "here's to your future together. I love you, Mom, and Austin . . . you're growing on me."

The men laughed while the women cried. Ashley stepped forward and gave C.J. a hug. "Thank you. I couldn't ask for a more amazing son."

After a little more visiting, Ashley and Austin slipped away so they could be alone. They slow danced on the far side of the patio, the music playing softly in the background.

"Are you ready to go?" he asked.

"Yes, I think so."

"Do you want to bring your things into my room?" he whispered in her ear.

Ashley stumbled over her words. "Well . . . no, I mean, I would but . . . you know. . . what will people think?"

"That we're married." Austin gave her a devilish grin, then let her off the hook. "Go get changed. I'll meet you in the living room." He kissed her, slowly—thoroughly—before letting her go.

Ashley made her way to the other side of the house and carefully slipped out of her beautiful wedding dress. Pulling from her garment bag the red sleeveless summer suit she bought yesterday, she smiled. The raw silk material was elegant, but the double-breasted vest gave it a sportier feel. Even though Austin said to go casual, she still wanted to look nice wherever they ended up.

Austin watched Ashley set her suitcase by the front door, then walked into the living room, looking drop-dead gorgeous. *Wow!* He shook his head, still having a hard time believing she was actually his wife. He was enjoying the view of *his wife* walking toward the cake table when all of a sudden, she faltered.

Ashley!

He darted across the room. "Ashley, what's wrong?" he asked, trying not to draw anyone's attention.

"I just feel a little light-headed. It's nothing."

"What have you eaten today?"

Before she could answer, C.J. was by her side "Mom, what's wrong?"

"Nothing, really. I just haven't eaten yet today, and I'm feeling a little light-headed. I'm sure once I have something in my stomach, I'll be fine."

"Are you sure?" C.J. asked again, concern etched on his face.

"Yes. Really. I'll be fine."

Austin insisted Ashley eat a few crackers before they left, and asked Jenna to make up a basket of food they could take with them in the car. Even though Ashley insisted she was fine, Austin wasn't taking any chances.

It was nearing nine o'clock before they said their goodbyes,

Austin listened as Ashley rattled off a list of instructions, then reminded C.J. she had her cell phone with her—in case there was an emergency at the ranch.

"The ranch would have to be burning down for me to call you. Believe me, I have no intention of interrupting the few days you have together."

Austin shook his hand. "Thank you, C.J., I appreciate that."

With a final wave, they were off.

Once they reached the highway, Austin asked, "Now that we're on the road, do you want me to tell you where we're going?"

"Nope. As long as we're together, nothing else matters."

Austin reached across the gear shift and clutched her hand. "Then why don't you lie back and enjoy the ride, Mrs. Taylor. It's going to take us a few hours."

"Oh, I think it's going to take longer than that."

He laughed. "But you don't even know where we're going."

"Like I said, it doesn't matter. What *I do* know is this is the ride of a lifetime, and I couldn't imagine spending it with anyone else but you."

THIRTY-ONE

The ride home with C.J. was quiet. Willow knew he had to be dealing with a lot of emotions, so she didn't try to keep a conversation going. Unfortunately, that gave her more time to worry about what she would be going home to.

She watched as C.J. pulled his cell phone from his pocket and turned it back on. Immediately, it chimed.

"What the—"

"What's wrong?" Willow asked.

"I forgot to turn my cell phone back on after the ceremony, and now I have a slew of calls from the same number."

"Is it Ashley?"

"No. I don't recognize the number." He put the phone to his ear. "Sheriff's Office?" he repeated out loud. Willow sat, watching C.J.'s reaction. "This is Christopher Summers. Someone has been trying to call me from this—Yes, I'll hold."

"Why would the sheriff's office be calling you?" Willow asked.

He just shrugged.

"Yes, I'm here," He turned his attention back to his phone. "What? Are you sure? You did? Was anything taken? No, I understand. I'm on my way." C.J. disconnected the call and laid his phone on the center console.

"Someone tried to break into the office at the ranch."

"What? Are they sure?"

"The alarm was triggered. When the police got there, it looked like one of the windows had been tampered with."

"Did they catch anyone?"

"The officer said they'd explain more when I got there. I know it's getting late, but would you mind if I go to the sheriff's office before I take you home? They seemed anxious to speak with me."

"Sure, no problem."

Willow thought about calling Steven—to let him know she was going to be late—but decided against it. If he was going to have a fit over the car, she would rather wait and hear about it all at once. Though she hoped hearing about it would be her only problem.

Willow glanced at her watch as they pulled into the Sheriff station parking lot. *Steven is going to have a fit.*

"You okay?" C.J. asked as he helped her out of the truck.

"Fine." She quickly affixed a smile on her face as they walked into the building. When C.J. asked for Lt. Fulton, they were waved over to a small cubicle on the left.

"Lt. Fulton, I'm Christopher Summers." C.J. extended his hand as the lieutenant stood and returned the gesture.

"Sorry to bother you, Mr. Summers, but I wanted to talk to you about a few things. Do you have a Willow Jenner working for you?"

Willow gasped. "I'm Willow Jenner."

"Well, there was a Steven Boyer on the property when we got there. He swears he didn't do anything—that he was only there to fix his girlfriend's car—but it sounded a little too coincidental to us. He was pretty belligerent. Argumentative, even."

"He's telling the truth, officer," Willow explained. "I work at the Circle-R, and my car wouldn't start today. Steven went over to see if he could fix it."

The officer looked skeptical.

"It's true, officer," C.J. said, backing her up. "We were on our way to my mom's wedding and couldn't be late. Willow left her car at the ranch and called Steven to fix it."

"Where is Steven, now?" Willow asked, feeling like she was going to throw up.

"One of his buddies came by and picked him up. We brought him in for questioning but couldn't hold him on anything."

Lt. Fulton discussed the details with C.J. while she took a seat in the front lobby. She could only imagine what she would be going home to now. It was bad enough her car broke down, and Steven had gone to fix it, but to be taken to the police station and questioned . . . he would make her quit for sure.

Or do something even worse.

"Willow, are you all right?"

She jumped, not realizing C.J. was standing in front of her.

"Sure. I'm fine. Are you ready to go?"

"Yeah."

Willow stood, taking a deep breath, then walked with C.J. to his truck.

"What did the police say?" she asked, trying to sound

nonchalant.

"Lt. Fulton told me what he and his partner found when they arrived at the ranch, and which window was tampered with, so I could have it checked, and . . . that was about it."

"He didn't say anything more about Steven?"

"Well, he just explained again why they questioned him. They didn't like the timing of him being there and the alarm going off."

"But you straightened it out, right? I mean, they have no reason to question Steven further?"

"I repeated what we already told him. Steven was there to fix your car, and I have no reason to believe he would try to break in."

"Thanks, C.J., I appreciate you saying that."

The ride home was a slow, agonizing torture. Not knowing what she was walking into almost made her ill. She silently rehearsed what she was going to say if Steven was home, and what she would do it he wasn't. When C.J. turned his blinker on at Coldwater Canyon, Willow realized where he was going and stopped him.

"Don't turn, C.J., keep going straight."

"But I thought you lived on—"

"I moved. I live off Roscoe, now."

C.J. kept driving, staring straight ahead. "Are you living with Steven?"

"Yes." Immediately, she left embarrassed and began making excuses. "I didn't tell your mom because I know how she feels about things like that. But economically, it was the only way we could make ends meet. With me saving for school, it seemed like the only pract—"

"Why didn't you go to Mom? I'm sure if she knew money was tight, she would've given you a raise or maybe offered to loan—"

"Your mom is more than generous, C.J.," Willow butted in. "It's just with Steven between jobs and me saving for tuition, it was a way to minimize our expenses." Willow tried to sound convincing, even though her living arrangement was far from perfect. It hadn't been her choice to move in with Steven, but at the time, there was nothing she could do to stop it.

~®~

C.J. could tell—by the tone of Willow's voice—something wasn't right. He listened as she gave him directions to a pleasant neighborhood with tree-lined streets and newly built complexes.

"Right there; the one with the palm trees and arched balconies."

Willow pointed out a very nice apartment building on the right side of the street. Seeing that she wasn't living in a hole-in-the-wall made C.J. feel a little better. That is, until he turned to Willow and saw the anxious expression on her face. She was clearly upset and hesitated before getting out of the truck.

Feeling uneasy, he jumped out of the vehicle and walked around to open her door. She stepped to the curb, thanked C.J. for all his help, and turned to leave.

C.J. followed her up the walk.

She turned around. "C.J., I'm fine. You don't need to walk me to my door."

"I thought maybe I could introduce myself to Steven. I always like to be able to put a name to a face. Besides, I want to apologize for the misunderstanding, and let him know I set the story straight."

"That's not necessary, C.J. You didn't call the cops on him. He was just in the wrong place at the wrong time. It's no big deal, really."

C.J. could see the apprehension in Willow's demeanor, and it gnawed at him. Something wasn't right. He smiled. "Just the same, I'd like to apologize anyway."

Willow was freaking out.

What would Steven do when he found out she had been with another man, no matter how innocent it was? Because of his jealous tendencies, Willow hadn't told Steven it was C.J. she would be going to the wedding with. She knew he would take it wrong—and it was easier if he just didn't know—but with C.J. adamant about meeting Steven, she could only hope for the best.

At one time in her life, she would've prayed about the situation, but she refused to be a hypocrite. She would not pray to God when she knew how disappointed He was with the lifestyle she was living. She could hardly ask Him for help when she wasn't obeying His rules.

Climbing the stairs to her second-floor apartment was an exercise of sheer determination. Her knees felt like they were going to buckle with every step, and with C.J. on her heels, she didn't feel like she could stop and regroup. Pulling her key from her purse, she paused before opening the door. *Please be gone.*

As soon as she saw Steven wasn't in the living room, she announced her arrival. "Steven, I'm home and there's someone here who would like to meet you."

C.J. felt self-conscious standing in his getup from the wedding. He would've felt a lot more comfortable in his jeans and boots, than in linen and khaki. Oh well, he was here to check this Steven guy out, not the other way around.

"Just give me a minute," Willow said before disappearing into the other room.

A moment later, she stepped back into the living room, a man behind her. He was older than C.J. expected, and if he went off first impressions, Steven had trouble written all over him. He stood in the doorway of the hall with slicked back shoulder-length hair, a wifebeater T-shirt, his hands shoved deep into the pockets of his black dress pants, and a scowl on his face. His brooding eyes and dark complexion gave him what others might consider a mysterious quality. To C.J., it came across as attitude.

C.J. fought his intuition and smiled.

"Hi, I'm C.J. Summers. I'm one of the owners of the Circle-R Ranch. I want to apologize for the misunderstanding tonight." He extended his hand and held it there for a moment before Steven decided to shake it. He didn't say a word so C.J. continued. "I just wanted to let you know Willow and I corroborated your story. I told the police you were fixing her car, so there shouldn't be any more problems."

Again, Steven didn't comment; he just stared at C.J. and gave him a nod of acknowledgment. After a long, uncomfortable silence, C.J. realized Steven had no intentions of speaking to him. "Again, I'm sorry for any trouble it caused you." He flicked a look at Willow. "I'll see you tomorrow." When he turned to leave, Steven finally spoke.

"Maybe Willow shouldn't work at your ranch if there's going to be this kind of trouble?"

C.J. turned back around and saw the snide expression on Steven's face. He clenched his fists, trying to keep his anger in check. "I can assure you, the ranch is perfectly safe."

"Well, I don't know. What if Willow never got that ride to the wedding and was stranded there? It's a pretty secluded place. No one would have even heard her scream for help if there had been any real trouble."

He watched as Steven walked to the bar and took a swig from a glass sitting on the counter. C.J. was sure the clear liquid wasn't ginger ale, and that it wasn't Steven's first. The thought of leaving Willow with an inebriated Steven didn't sit well with him. The lieutenant had warned C.J. that Steven had a pretty big chip on his shoulder, and the nervous fidgeting Willow had done in the car told C.J. this was exactly the behavior she was expecting. He wanted to refute Steven's accusation regarding the safety of the ranch but did not want to incite him further. Instead, he gave him a gentle reminder.

"Again, let me assure you, the ranch is perfectly safe. In fact, it's nice to know our security system works so well. Sorry again for the misunderstanding. It's nice that I can finally put a face to the person Willow is always talking about."

Steven smiled coolly. "Well, Willow and I don't want to keep you any longer than we already have."

C.J. let himself out and stood on the other side of the door for a moment. He was worried about Willow. Steven looked like a man who could have a very short fuse.

Hopefully, he didn't just ignite it.

THIRTY-TWO

The drawn-out silence was deafening.

Steven hadn't said a word since C.J. left, but Willow could sense him watching her every move.

Feeling like her head was going to explode from pent-up anxieties, she went to the kitchen to get some aspirin.

Steven followed, then stood directly behind her. With his lips close to her ear and a firm hand on her shoulder, he asked, "Was he your ride to the wedding?"

"Yes, but only because—"

Steven squeezed down on her shoulder, causing her to whimper.

"I thought you said some broad owned the ranch?"

"I did. Ashley Summers and her son. I told you that, Steven."

"You also gave me the impression he was a snot-nosed kid." Steven spun her around to face him, applying pressure to both shoulders, shaking her abruptly. "How is it that you never explained to me that the *kid* you work with day in and day out, isn't a kid at all? Did it just slip your mind? Or maybe you never brought it up because your hiding something?"

"I'm not hiding anything, Steven. I promise."

He pulled her across the living room and shoved her into a chair. "Tell me the truth, Willow. What's going on between you two?"

"Nothing; absolutely nothing. I love you, Steven. What do I need to do to prove that to you? I gave up my apartment. I'm helping you while you're out of a job. I've never given you a single reason to doubt me."

He paced the room, then sat on the coffee table in front of her and leaned in close. The smell of alcohol on his breath made her gag. Turning away, she asked, "I thought you promised you weren't going to drink anymore?"

"I guess I lied."

"What else about tonight are you lying about?"

Willow knew the minute the words were out of her mouth, she

had pushed him too far. The back of Steven's hand came across her face quicker than she could react. Fire coursed through her cheek as Steven yanked her up by the placket of her cardigan and dragged her across the living room.

"Steven, please . . ." She scrambled to keep her feet under her.

"Shut up!" he yelled.

Shoving her across the bedroom, she stumbled backwards and fell to the floor. "Steven, I—"

Before she could say anything more, he kicked her one, two, three times.

"How dare you call me a liar?" he shouted. "I'm not the liar, Willow, you are. Tell me the truth. You were on a date with that guy, weren't you?"

"No." Willow tightened her body, knowing every time she disagreed, he would kick her.

Sure enough, she received another blow to the hip. She cried out. "Please, Steven, stop. You're hurting me. I can't live like this anymore."

"Is that a threat, Willow?" Steven pulled her up from the floor and flung her on the bed, pinning her hands over her head. "You're getting it somewhere else, aren't you? That's why you're threatening to leave?"

"No, Steven. I haven't been with anyone else. I just can't handle the lies, and the drinking, and the jealousy anymore. You're ruining yourself, and I won't allow you to take me down with you."

"Ruining you? Are you kidding me? I'm the best thing that has ever happened to you. And how do you repay me? By going out with another guy and flaunting him in my face. He's just a boy, Willow. I'm a man. Let me remind you what you'll be missing, if you walk away."

THIRTY-THREE

"Ashley, we're here." Austin leaned over and brushed his hand against her cheek. She opened her eyes with a flutter.

"Hi," she said with a sleepy voice. "I guess I fell asleep. I'm sorry."

He kissed her forehead. "Don't be. You needed the rest. Hold on." Austin walked around the car, opened Ashley's door, and helped her out and into his arms.

"Where are we?"

"A little place I know in Pismo."

With a hand on Ashley's waist, Austin led her up the flight of stairs to where the house was perched above the sand. When they got to the doorway, he buzzed in a code, and the door magically opened. Without warning, Austin swung Ashley up into his arms and carried her across the threshold. He kicked shut the door behind them and carried her straight to the bedroom.

Placing her on the bed, he followed her descent, covering her body with his. Looking into her eyes, he kissed her passionately. She responded in turn, though timidly. He felt the slightest apprehension and rolled onto his side. Propping himself up on one elbow, he caressed Ashley's arm.

"I didn't mean to attack you like that," he smiled. "I just couldn't wait any longer. I promise to be more gentlemanly in the future."

"Don't change your approach on my account." She pulled him close and kissed him hard. When she let go, Austin teased. "Wow, maybe I'm the one who should be worried."

Ashley giggled, "Why do you say that?"

"Because with a kiss like that, you could ask me for anything, and it would be yours."

"Leverage. I like that."

Austin placed a peck on Ashley's shoulder. "Stay put. I need to get the bags from the car. I'll be right back." Austin rolled off the bed and headed for the front door.

~Ⓡ~

Ashley sat up and looked around. Flameless candles illuminated the room in a soft glow. Plantation shutters covered a sliding glass door, and a white brick fireplace filled the opposite corner. Peeking into the bathroom, she was mildly disappointed there wasn't a jacuzzi or soaking tub. Instead, there was a large marble shower with a bench seat, multiple body sprays, and a rainfall showerhead. It was nice, and she knew it could be romantic, but the thought of standing naked in front of Austin seemed so revealing—something she would have to work up to.

When Ashley's thoughts drifted to intimacy, her heart raced, and her palms grew moist. She had never been with a man. What happened to her in New York was an act of violence, not love. Would she embarrass herself? Would she be clumsy and awkward? A tremor raced through her body.

Don't freak yourself out. Austin loves you . . . no matter how awkward and clumsy you are.

Taking a couple deep breaths, she continued her self-guided tour of the cottage. Anything to distract herself.

She was standing in the living room when Austin stumbled through the front door loaded down with all their luggage. He dropped everything in the entryway, nearly collapsing on top of the heap. Ashley laughed as he regained his balance.

"What . . ." Austin said, panting. "I didn't want to make two trips." He stood with his hands on his hips.

Man, how is it that he can make jeans and a simple polo shirt look so sexy? Ashley felt her skin heat.

"Did you look around yet?" he asked.

"Just a little."

"Did you go out on the deck?"

"No, I didn't get that far."

"Well, allow me." Austin placed his hand on the small of her back and escorted her out onto the deck. It ran the full length of the house, from living room to master suite.

With light from the moon, Ashley stepped to the rail and watched the crashing waves. "What a wonderful view."

"And that's not all. Look." Austin walked toward the sliding glass doors off the master suite and lifted the lid off a full-size jacuzzi. "What do you think of that?"

"Oh," Ashley moved to Austin's side, "It's perfect."

"And see those shades?" He pointed to opposite sides of the deck. "They pull down, giving us an unobstructed view of the ocean," Austin leaned close and whispered in her ear, "but complete privacy."

Once again, the temperature of Ashley's body spiked. She knew Austin was thinking the same thing she was. He was just bold enough to voice it.

"You're blushing, Mrs. Taylor. Can I take that as a sign of consent?"

"You can take it any way you like, Mr. Taylor." Ashley playfully nudged his shoulder, but the sudden movement caused her to stagger.

"Okay, that's it. No more racy conversations or innuendo until after you've had something to eat." Austin led Ashley back into the living area and plopped her down in front of another full-size fireplace. "You just relax. I'll make you a sandwich."

"But it's almost midnight."

"Hey, there is no such thing as time while we're here. We are going to do whatever we want, when we want."

Ashley just smiled as she curled up on the overstuffed chaise and closed her eyes. She was nowhere near falling asleep, but the comfort she felt was beyond compare.

When Austin returned with a tray full of food, she laughed. "I hope you don't expect me to eat all of that?"

"No." He sat down next to her. "Some of it's for me."

"I thought you ate at the house?"

"I did, but I have to keep my energy up." He turned to her, grinning from ear to ear. "I don't want to take the chance of faltering in any of our extracurricular activities."

She didn't respond, because she didn't know what to say. She was nervous. Beyond nervous. But she kept her feelings to herself.

Austin munched on his sandwich for a few seconds, then said, "I'm nervous, too, you know?"

"You are? You don't act like it. You talk about it like it's no big deal."

"Oh, believe me, it's a big deal. It's just how I deal with things. Keep them out in the open. State the obvious. Sometimes that helps eliminate the pressure for everyone involved. Is it working?"

"Yes . . . and no. I guess I don't know how I feel."

Austin moved the tray that lay between them and scooted closer to her. He gently kissed her shoulder, her neck, her cheek, and then whispered to her, "Why don't we stop talking about it and start moving in that direction?" Austin continued to kiss Ashley, his fingers lightly caressing her body. Finally, he stood, took her by the hand, and led her to the bedroom. There they experienced what they had waited a lifetime for.

THIRTY-FOUR

C.J. tossed and turned all night. He kept picturing the nervous look on Willow's face, while rehashing his conversation with Lt. Fulton at the police station.

Be careful, Mr. Summers. Steven Boyer has a reputation as a swindler—a real con artist. I wouldn't enter into any business dealings with him, if I was you. Watch your back. He shouldn't be trusted.

Just the fact that the police knew Steven was enough to make C.J. worry. The hesitant look on Willow's face when he took her home made it all the more difficult to leave her there. He knew by the set of Steven's jaw, he wasn't pleased to see Willow with another man—no matter the situation. Even so, he knew if he had stayed, he would've only made it harder on Willow.

C.J. got up and dressed, then started his early morning chores. He convinced himself not to over analyze the situation or jump to conclusions. He would wait until Willow came to work—test the waters—then decide if he should tell her what the police had to say about Steven's reputation.

Until then, he had at least two hours of feeding and watering to do.

When Willow woke the next morning, Steven was already gone. She tried to sit up, but every bone in her body hurt and her muscles cramped with even the slightest movement. Only one other time had Steven been so rough on her; the time she told him they were through.

Willow thought back over the last several months. The kinks in Steven's armor increasingly grew larger, while the suave man who had swept her off her feet slowly disappeared.

She should have known from his first outburst that something was wrong.

They had been at her place, watching a movie, when he received an important business call he had been waiting for all day. As the conversation progressed, Willow could tell things had not gone as Steven expected. His tone was sharp. Accusations flying. What started as a disagreement escalated to a yelling match. Then, in a fit of fury, Steven threw his phone against the wall. It shattered only inches from where Willow sat on the couch. She was terrified. He had always been the picture of composure. Nothing rattled him. But that night he completely lost control. Steven spent the next hour apologizing to her, promising over and over that it would never happen again.

That was the night everything changed.

His jaw tightened when she disagreed with him, and his fists clenched when things did not go his way. He hadn't hit her yet, but even then, Willow worried what would happen if his anger was ever directed at her. The longer she was with him, the more unstable he became. She was living in fear, wondering how she could end their relationship. She actually prayed Steven would come home from a night of partying with his friends and tell her he had found someone new. Unfortunately, that didn't happen before he decided they should live together.

What a shock that was.

She would never forget the day she came home from work to find her apartment empty, except for a note on the counter that simply read *SURPRISE!* She called Steven a dozen times on her way to his place, but they went straight to voice mail. When she walked into his apartment and saw her things stacked around the room and him sitting on the couch smiling, she was speechless. When she recovered from the shock, she completely lost it.

Willow yelled at Steven, telling him they were through, that she no longer loved him, and she refused to be controlled and manipulated by him.

He launched himself at her, pinning her against the wall with his forearm across her neck. He made it very clear he had no intention of letting her go and warned her what would happen if she tried to leave him. Then he gave her a taste of what she could expect if she ever threatened him again. He slapped her around, bloodied her lip, and gave her bruises she hid under long-sleeve shirts.

But it paled in comparison to the beating he gave her last night.

Willow lay in bed, not knowing what she was going to do. She had no car to get to work, and even if she did, hiding her condition from C.J. would be difficult at best. Even so, Ashley was counting on her to keep the office running, and if she didn't show up to work, C.J. might get suspicious and drop by unannounced.

Knowing she could not let that happen, Willow swiveled her legs over the side of the bed and eased herself to a standing position. Inching her way toward the hall, Willow tried to convince herself a hot shower would help soothe the aches in her body. As she neared the bathroom, she was startled to see Steven sitting in the living room. When he got up and walked toward her, she turned away and cowered in the corner.

"You're in no shape to go to work today. Call in and tell them you won't be there." It was a command, not a request.

"But I have too much work to do. Besides, I can't afford to take a day off. Especially now that my car needs repairs."

"Okay, then I'll call." Steven pulled out his cell phone and scrolled through his numbers.

"Steven, don't . . . I'll do it." Willow grabbed the phone from him.

He grinned, enjoying his manipulation.

"Hi, C.J." Willow watched Steven's smile turn to a sneer, and his hands curl into fists. She closed her eyes, so she could concentrate on what she would say, hoping she sounded convincing. "I know this is really bad timing, but I'm not going to be able to make it in today."

"Willow, what's wrong?"

She could tell C.J. wasn't buying it. His tone was too harsh and direct.

"I can tell something is wrong. I'm coming over there right now."

"No!" Willow shouted.

Steven lunged at her, trying to take the phone away, but she turned and continued to talk.

"C.J., just leave everything alone. I'll take care of the foul-ups when I get there." *Please let him understand.* "If you try to fix anything right now, you'll only make matters worse . . . do you understand?" *Please hear what I'm NOT saying.*

"I understand what you're saying, Willow. It's Steven, isn't it? You're in trouble and he's right there, isn't he?"

"Yes. But I can fix the problem. I just need you to leave it alone."

"You can't stay there, Willow. What if he gets violent?"

If you only knew.

"Enough talking." Steven lunged for the phone again, but Willow took a step back and muted it.

"I've got this, Steven. He's asking me a computer question. Just let me answer him, then I'll hang up."

"Put it on speaker," he demanded.

Willow switched the phone to speaker. *Please don't say anything, C.J. Just shut up and listen.*

"C.J., are you still there?"

"I'm here."

"Okay, *just listen,*" she paused, hoping he understood what she was saying. "What's done is done. Like I already said, you can't fix it; you'll only make it worse. I'll work on it first thing tomorrow. But right now, Steven and I have to figure out my car situation."

"Whatever you say, Willow. I just feel like I made matters worse."

"That's why you need to leave it alone. Don't try to fix anything. I'll be able to handle it tomorrow." She hung up.

"What was that all about?" Steven asked with glaring eyes.

"C.J. tried to retrieve some files from the office computer. He thinks he fouled something up and was waiting for me to come in and fix it. I told him—as long as he left it alone—it couldn't get any worse, and I would work on it tomorrow."

"What was that garbage about your car?" Steven took the phone from her and tossed it on the couch.

"I had to tell him something. I was fine yesterday. To say I was too sick to go to work would've only made him suspicious. Besides, we do need to figure out something regarding my car. I need to be able to get back and forth to work."

Steven ignored her, leaving her to wonder if he was even going to help her with her car.

"Look, Steven, I need to take a shower."

He turned, a titillating smile on his face. "Sounds good to me."

He followed Willow into the bathroom and pulled at her clothes. Inwardly, she cringed at his touch, wondering how he could abuse her, beat her, then expect her to be intimate with him.

His mind was twisted, and she didn't see a way out.

Forcing her mind and emotions to shut down, she willed herself to a place where Steven couldn't hurt her. She detached from her body, refusing to feel what was to come.

THIRTY-FIVE

Ashley stirred momentarily before opening her eyes.

"Hey, sleepyhead." Austin lay on his side next to her, his head on his pillow.

"Hi," she smiled.

"Did you sleep well?"

Ashley blushed.

"Well, other than that," Austin clarified.

"It was the most perfect night of rest I've ever gotten."

"Well, maybe we'll have to get into a routine and do the same things every night to ensure you a good night's sleep."

Austin was incorrigible, and funny, and the best thing that had ever happened to her. "I'm not so sure about that. How does that old saying go . . . 'variety is the spice of life.' " Ashley smiled.

Austin actually blushed. "Well, aren't you the little tease."

"Who said I'm teasing?" Ashley laughed. "Besides, as long as you're by my side, I'm sure to have a perfect night's sleep."

Austin pulled her close and wrapped his arms around her. There was an unspeakable peace in the silence.

"Do we have anything to make for breakfast?" Ashley whispered.

"Actually, they provide breakfast."

"They?"

"The hotel. There's a hotel just across the street. This beach house belongs to them. They'll be bringing us breakfast around ten-thirty."

"What time is it now?"

"A little after ten."

"Ten? Oh my gosh!" Ashley sat up, gathering the sheet against her chest. "I can't believe I slept that late."

"Well, technically, we didn't spend *all* our time sleeping." Austin reached out and lightly stroked Ashley's back.

"Now don't start that, Austin. You just said someone would be coming to the door in less than half an hour. We can't still be in bed when they get here." Ashley got out of bed, dragging the sheet with her as a covering. "Besides I need to take a shower."

"Okay!" Austin smiled mischievously.

"Uuh . . ." Ashley stammered, clenching the sheet tighter, not knowing what to say.

"What?" he asked.

Austin sensed her unease. She could hear it is his tone. But she didn't know how to tell him without hurting his feelings? "Austin, I uh . . . I don't think I'm ready for that. I would feel too self-conscious."

"Self-conscious? About what?"

"You know . . ." Ashley whispered as if she was saying something lewd. ". . . total nudity."

Austin grinned as he scooted to the edge of the bed, drawing Ashley near. "What do you call last night?" he whispered.

"It was dark; your vision was impaired."

"Oh, I'm not too sure about that. I have excellent night vision," Austin said playfully.

Ashley sighed, not knowing how to explain her feelings.

"I'm only teasing, Ashley. We have the rest of our lives to learn these things. You go take your shower; I'll wait for breakfast."

"Is that okay with you?"

"Absolutely. Now go take your shower, so I can take mine."

Ashley quickly showered, then changed into a comfortable pair of cargo shorts and a bright yellow tank top. She liked the way the sunny color accentuated what little summer tan she had left. When she walked into the living room, Austin sneaked up behind her and wrapped her in his arms. She squealed with surprise, then scrunched her shoulders when Austin playfully gnawed on her neck.

A tap on the door was followed by a pleasant voice. "Good morning. Breakfast."

"I'll get it," Ashley said. "You go take your shower, so we can eat."

While Ashley arranged their breakfast on the patio table, a light breeze played with her still wet hair causing strands to go this way and that.

When Austin joined her on the deck, he was wearing a pair of sweat pants but no shirt. Ashley took a double-take. His body was in such incredible shape; she couldn't help but stare.

"Okay, that's no fair. You're staring at me, but I can't stare at you?"

Ashley threw one of the linen napkins at him as he grabbed her around the waist and pulled her close. Resting his forehead against hers, he whispered. "I love you so much."

"I love you, too."

THIRTY-SIX

It was obvious Steven wasn't going to do anything about her car, so Willow arranged for a tow truck to go to the ranch, pick it up, and take it to the local auto shop she had used once before. Later that day, she eased down in one of the dining room chairs and called the mechanic, needing to know what the prognosis was and what it was going to cost to fix it.

"It's the starter, Miss Jenner. You're going to need a new one."

"Great. What's that going to cost me?"

"With parts and labor, between one hundred and fifty to two hundred dollars. If you want to go ahead and authorize the work, I could have it done by tomorrow at closing."

"Could you hold on for a moment?" Willow put the phone to her chest while she debated her options. She would have to dip into the money she had set aside for tuition. She hated to do that, but still had a little time to replace it before the first of the year. She would just have to cut back on her spending. Since her car was a necessity, she really didn't see that she had much of a choice. Bringing the phone back up to her ear, she gave the mechanic the go ahead and asked, "What time do you close tomorrow?"

"Six o'clock."

"And what was your name?"

"I'm Andre."

"Thanks, Andre. I guess I'll see you tomorrow around six. I might be cutting it close, but I'll call if I'm not going to be able to make it on time." When Willow hung up the phone, she stood, nearly bumping into Steven. She gasped. "I didn't see you standing there?"

"Obviously. Who's Andre, Willow? Another man you're keeping from me?"

Steven recoiled his hand, causing her to flinch and hurry to explain. "He's the mechanic working on my car. I told you, Steven, I'm not seeing anyone." Her hands were still up in protection mode

209

when he dangled car keys in front of her face.

"What's this?" Willow reached for the key chain with the Saturn logo.

Steven snatched it from her reach and grinned. "Your new car."

Willow was confused. "I don't understand. When did you buy it? And where did you get the money?"

"I have my ways."

Typical Steven. This was his way of apologizing for his actions. He would terrorize her, beat her, threaten her, and then try to make up for his behavior with a gift. Willow carefully hugged Steven, even though it hurt to raise her arms over his shoulders, but she did it anyway.

"Well, don't you want to see it?"

"Sure." Willow smiled but was more concerned with how they were going to pay for it. If she was accepted into vet school, she would no longer be working. Where would they get the money for car payments? "Oh, I'd better call the mechanic and tell him not to work on my car. I guess I won't need it now." Willow dialed the mechanic and asked for Andre.

"Andre, this is Miss Jenner. I don't need that starter after all. Yeah, I got a new car. Can you hold onto it for a few days? Okay, I'll call back before Wednesday to let you know what I'll be doing with it. Thanks."

Steven and Willow walked to the apartment's underground parking area. It took a second for her eyes to adjust, then she saw it.

"So, what do you think?" Steven said with a smug smile.

"It's really nice." Willow ran her hand over the hood and stopped at the driver's door. Steven pressed the key fob in his hand. It chirped, unlocking the door. Willow slid into the car and admired the interior while Steven got in on the passenger side.

"Nice, huh?"

"Very nice, but how can you afford it?"

"Well, actually, I can't afford it . . . but you can."

"What do you mean, I can? I don't have any extra money. It took me this long to save for my tuit—" Then it dawned on her where Steven got the money. Her money. "No, Steven." Tears flooded her eyes. "Please tell me you didn't use my tuition money."

He shrugged his shoulders. "I never really liked the idea of you going back to school. It's not practical when you already have a job. But this is. Admit it, you need a car, and I think you deserve to ride around in style."

Tears poured down her face. "How could you, Steven? You know how important school is to me." Willow got out of the car, slammed the door and ran back to the apartment. Sure enough, when she checked the old makeup case where she had hidden her money, it was gone. All of it. She slid to the floor by the dresser and cried. Steven stood in the doorway, hands crossed against his chest.

"Come on Willow, that vet school you want to go to is a joke. Who wants to give shots to dogs or put their hand up an animal's butt for a living? Besides, when I hit it big, you won't need to work."

"You . . . hit it big? Doing what? You don't even have a job."

Steven started across the room, but Willow surprised him. She jumped to her feet and ripped open her blouse. "Here let me make it easy on you, Steven." She pushed her skirt to the floor, stepped out of it, then got on the bed. "Here I am Steven. Your puppet. You've taken everything from me today. My dignity, my pride, my money, my dreams. You might as well make it a clean sweep. While you're at it, invite your friends over. They've always wanted to get a crack at me."

Willow could see the anger building in Steven's eyes, but she didn't care. What more could he do to her that he hadn't already done.

"Come on, Steven, what are you waiting for? Or is this too easy for you? Maybe you would prefer me to cower in the corner or beg you to stop. Maybe you're not man enough to enjoy it unless you're taking it by force. Maybe you're not man enough at all."

Steven's anger quickly turned to rage. He came at her with fury in his eyes.

Willow forced her eyes open, wondering what time it was. Piecing together what had happened, she remembered the first blow, and the one to her head. But everything after that was a painful blur.

She looked for the clock on the nightstand, but it had toppled over. Inching toward the phone, she looked at the time on the LED screen. She'd been out for three hours.

Pressing speed dial, she clutched the phone to her ear.

~®~

"Hello?"

"C.J.?"

All he could make out was crying and sniffling, but he

211

immediately knew who it was. "I'm on my way Willow; I'll be right there."

C.J. threw down the shovel he was holding and yelled. "I've got to go, Billy. Take care of things while I'm gone."

He didn't wait for an answer; he just ran to his truck and broke every speed limit on the way to Willow's apartment. It took him a minute to remember what unit it was, then knocked. There was no answer. He tried again. Nothing. Finally, he turned the handle and realized the door was unlocked.

"Willow? Willow, it's C.J.?"

Still nothing.

He walked to the back of the apartment and pushed open what he assumed was the bedroom door. When he saw Willow huddled on the floor, her head on her knees, the phone still in her hand, he thought he was going to puke.

He slowly crossed the room and knelt beside her, unsure of what he should do. He was afraid to touch her, terrified he might hurt her more.

"Willow," he whispered. "I'm taking you home. He's not going to hurt you anymore."

She sat trance-like. He wasn't even sure she heard him.

"Willow, let's get you off the floor." When he tried to scoop her up, she cried out in pain.

"Sorry. I'm sorry," he gasped, then gently placed her on the edge of the bed. That's when he realized she had nothing on besides the blanket clutched to her chest.

"Willow, you need to get dressed. Do you think you can do that?"

When she finally raised her head, he could see her face was a kaleidoscope of purples, blues and blacks, with dried blood smeared across her lips. He coughed and swallowed hard to keep the bile from his mouth.

"I need to get dressed," she whispered, clearly disorientated.

He stepped back. "I'll wait in the living roo—"

"Don't leave!" she cried out in a panic.

He hurried back to her side. "I'm not leaving, Willow. I just wanted to give you some privacy while you get dressed."

"Okay," she said timidly, "but please don't leave."

"I'm not going anywhere."

He watched as she limped toward the closet, whimpering as she clutched her side.

It was all he could do to watch her move around, each step looking more painful than the last.

"I'll be right outside the door, Willow. Where's Steven?"

"I don't know."

"Are you expecting him back tonight?"

"Later."

"Then take your time. I'll be right on the other side of this door."

C.J. closed the door and took a couple of deep breaths. He hadn't known what to expect, but he certainly did not expect this.

He looked around the living room from his vantage point in the hall. Sitting next to an ice pack on the coffee table was a towel with blood on it. He pushed the bathroom door open only to see more traces of blood on hand towels and in the sink. C.J. was beginning to shake. He could feel the rage building inside him, but knew he needed to get it under control if he was going to help Willow.

When the bedroom door opened slowly, Willow stood there in a pair of black sweat pants and a faded red T-shirt. She moved awkwardly to the living room in a catatonic state. She took her phone, her purse, her keys, and looked back over her shoulder. C.J. watched as she looked around the room, emptiness in her stare.

"Willow, before we leave, you need to decide something." C.J. tried to keep his words soft and his emotions calm.

She looked up at him with lucid green eyes. C.J. realized at that moment—even through redness and tears—how beautiful her eyes were. How beautiful she was. He choked back his emotions and asked, "Are you going to want to press charges? If so, you should probably stay here and let the police see the apartment."

Clutching her purse to her chest, Willow shook her head no.

"Are you sure, Willow? He shouldn't be allowed to get away with this."

Willow started crying as she continued to shake her head no. C.J. could barely hear her when she finally spoke.

"I want to go. Please, I just want to go."

C.J. didn't argue. He couldn't. He needed to get her out of here before Steven came back.

Once they were outside, Willow clutched the railing of the walkway, but she only took a couple steps before she nearly collapsed. C.J. caught her, and gently picked her up. She didn't refuse his help. She just buried her head against his chest.

There was no conversation in the car, the only sound was Willow's involuntary shudders. But when she moaned and doubled over, C.J. panicked. Flipping on his blinker, he changed lanes and said, "I'm taking you to the hospital."

"No!" She sat up and winced. "I don't want to go to the hospital."

"But you're in so much pain. You could have broken bones or internal bleeding."

She started to cry. "Please, C.J., just take me to the ranch. I'll be all right. I promise."

Clenching the steering wheel in frustration, he changed lanes again, and against his better judgement, headed for home.

When he pulled into the driveway, he parked as close to the front porch as he could get, then carried Willow into the house and upstairs. Placing her on the center of the bed in the guest room, he sat alongside her. She immediately rolled away from him and curled into a fetal position. C.J. wanted to puke.

"Willow, I need to find Billy and set up some plans for tomorrow. I'll be right back. Are you going to be okay for a few minutes?"

She nodded as she lay with her arms wrapped around herself.

C.J. walked slowly to the door, in case she had second thoughts, but she never looked up. He hurried down the stairs, out the backdoor, and to the guest house to find Billy. He pounded hard on the door.

"What's up?" Billy asked.

"I don't have a lot of time for details. But you need to get a hold of Jaime and see if he can give you a hand for the next few days. Tell him I'll pay him double if he'll do morning chores with you." Billy was about to interrupt, but C.J. held up his hand and quickly went on to his next instruction. "Get a hold of Sarah and see if she would be willing to answer phones for the next few days. Nothing difficult, just phones."

C.J. saw the puzzled look on Billy's face but didn't stop to explain. "There's a chance we might have some trouble tonight or tomorrow. Keep your eyes open for anything suspicious. Lock the main gates after closing. You can open them again tomorrow morning. I'm going to call the police and the security company. I'll be in the house if you need me, but I'm not sure how available I'll be. And, if Mom happens to call and you get to the phone before I do, don't breathe a word of this to her. Nothing. Understand?"

Billy nodded, then asked. "Does this have to do with the break in?"

"No, not really. Well, maybe."

"Has something happened to Willow?"

C.J. paused before answering. "Yeah."

He could tell Billy was looking for more of an answer.

"Look, Billy, I can't go into details. Not right now."

Billy's questioning look turned to one of assurance. "I understand. Don't you worry about anything. I'll take care of that laundry list of yours. You just do what you've got to do."

"Thanks Billy. I knew I could count on you. If you have any problems getting a hold of Jaime or Sarah, let me know."

C.J. hurried back to the house and called the sheriff's station. "Lt. Fulton, please."

C.J. was put on hold and listened to elevator music until the line clicked.

"Lt. Fulton." The man sounded irritated.

"Lieutenant, this is C.J. Summers. I think we might have a problem.

THIRTY-SEVEN

Austin and Ashley's first day together was picture perfect. The weather cooperated as if it sensed they only had a few precious days before . . .

They walked along the beach for hours, hand in hand, catching up on life. There was still a lot they didn't know about each other, so every so often—interrupting the comfortable silence of just being together—they would ask a random question, to help fill in the twenty-five-year void between them.

When they reached the pier, they decided to forgo lunch, and chose instead to snack on chips and salsa, cotton candy and caramel apples. They ate their calorie-infused choices without a shred of guilt, opting to live the next few days without rules or restrictions.

After lunch, they walked back to the beach house for an afternoon nap. Though Austin had a hard time keeping his hands to himself, he knew Ashley needed plenty of rest to maintain her strength. He was committed to making sure she went into surgery in the best possible condition.

While she rested, he made a few business calls and worked on his computer, then crawled into bed alongside of her. Ashley stirred but didn't wake up completely, just enough to snuggle closer to him. When the late afternoon sun began its descent, Austin placed a kiss to Ashley's forehead and whispered, "We have dinner reservations at seven o'clock. Should I cancel them?"

Ashley answered without even opening her eyes. "What time is it now?"

"Six."

"No, don't cancel. I have an hour to wake up and get ready."

Several minutes later, Ashley turned on her side. "It's beautiful outside."

Austin looked out the window and watched as the sun dipped to the horizon—burning the sky with streaks of gold and orange. "It is, but not as beautiful as it is in here." He rolled her to her back, kissed the tip of her nose, and smiled. "But if we don't start getting ready, we'll never make it in time."

Ashley glanced at the bedside table. "Austin, we have thirty minutes. It's just across the street, right?"

"Yes. But I've shown a lot of self-control these last few hours. If you stay in bed much longer, I can't be held responsible for my actions."

Austin pressed a kiss to her forehead, then rolled out of bed. Grabbing a pair of black slacks from the closet, he tossed them on the end of the bed and began to undress. While listing the restaurant's menu options, he picked up the slacks and stood ready to lace his foot through the pant leg.

Ashley smiled.

"What?" he asked.

"You're standing there in nothing but your briefs, and you ask me why I'm smiling?"

"Well," he dropped the pants on the floor, then crawled up alongside of her, "Maybe I should cancel our reservation after all."

With her hand to his chest, she laughed as she pushed him away.

"No, sir. You promised me dinner."

He hung his head in mock disappointment, then got to his feet. "Replaced by a cut of meat. Where's the love?"

Ashley threw a pillow at him, knocking him off balance as he tried once again to thread his foot through his slacks. He picked it up and wound up to throw it hard—watching as Ashley clenched in preparation—then gently tossed it on his side of the bed.

"Ashley, will you do me a favor?" he asked as he succeeded in pulling on his pants.

"Sure."

"Did you bring the dress you wore to the reunion?"

"Yes."

"Would you wear it for me tonight?"

"Did you really like it?"

"Are you kidding? I've always liked you in black."

"I know. That's why I wore it."

Ashley slipped from the bed, took her dress from the closet, then disappeared into the bathroom. Quickly, she splashed her face with water and changed into the dress. She pulled her hair up on top of her head, then decided to wear it down, knowing Austin preferred it that way. She emerged from the bathroom less than fifteen minutes later.

"See, I don't take that long. We still have twenty-five minutes to spare."

"Well then, maybe some dancing is in order."

Austin took her by the hand and led her into the living room. He set the Bose system to a jazz station then pulled her close. Silently, they swayed to the music. Austin loved the feel of Ashley's cheek nestled against his gray angora pullover, knowing she could hear every beat of his heart. The intoxicating scent that was uniquely hers swirled around him, making his head spin with gratefulness, love, and desire. Playing with the wisps of hair that danced around her shoulders, Austin pressed his lips to her ear. "Will you lose your hair?"

"No," she whispered back.

"I'm glad."

As much as Ashley wanted to ignore her future, Austin's question seemed to break the spell she was under. Back in the bedroom, she picked up her shoes, slipped them on, then joined Austin by the front door. As they crossed the beach, one thought kept cycling through her mind.

Only three days left.

"What are you thinking?" Austin asked as they rode the elevator to the rooftop restaurant. "You disappeared on me."

Ashley looked at him and smiled, not wanting to ruin the end of a perfectly wonderful day. "Just that I'm the luckiest woman in the world—with the most amazing husband."

He pulled her close and kissed her soundly. So consuming was Austin's kiss, she didn't even hear the elevator door open. However, a disapproving cough broke the spell.

An older couple—with their noses in the air—waited for them to exit the elevator.

Ashley was embarrassed, but Austin just laughed. "You'll have to excuse us; we're on our honeymoon," he explained while they stepped from the elevator, and the older couple marched in. "I'm sure you remember what that felt like?"

The older woman grumbled, "That's what hotel rooms are for, not elevators."

"Oh, but you see, we have a list of places where we want to have sex before the week is—"

The woman gasped as the elevator door closed.

Ashley slapped Austin on the arm, making him laugh even harder.

"I can't believe you just said that! What if they complain to the hotel staff?"

Wrapping his arm around her waist, he guided her toward the restaurant entrance. "Let them. I'm sure the staff will take one look at the permanent scowls on their faces, and politely ignore them."

"You, Mr. Taylor, are trouble."

He bounced a brow and smiled. "And don't you forget it."

After dinner, both Ashley and Austin laughed when they stepped from the elevator and into the main lobby.

"Even though the clientele might be a bit stuffy, dinner was wonderful. Good thing I'm having surgery. What they remove will help even out the weight I gain over the next few days."

Austin didn't crack a smile; he just pulled her closer and stared off into the distance as they walked back to the beach house,

Stroking his back, Ashley tried to reassure him. "It was only a joke, Austin. I have to start mentally preparing myself for this."

He squeezed her tighter. "I know, I know. I just want to pretend it away for a few more days."

Ashley stiffened and stopped, then looked up at him. "That's just it, Austin, we can't pretend. This is not make believe. It's real." She waited for him to make eye contact. "Are you sure you're going to be able to handle this?"

"Yes, Ashley." He cupped her face in his hands. "I can and will handle this, but I want the next few days to be just about us. Come Thursday, we can go back to reality." He leaned down and pressed his lips to hers, soft and gentle. Then looped his arm around her as they climbed the beach house stairs together.

"You know what sounds good?" Austin said as he pulled off his sweater and dropped it on the bed. "A nice relaxing evening in the jacuzzi." He sat on the edge of the bed and pulled off his loafers. "What do you say, Ash?"

"Sounds good." She was feeling tired from all the walking they had done and knew the warm water would be soothing and relaxing. Stepping across the bedroom to the dresser, she pulled out a two-piece swim suit. She had never owned a bikini before, always opting for the comfort of a one-piece. But she wasn't going for comfort. She bought it solely with Austin in mind.

In the bathroom, she quickly changed into the bikini. After tying the strings at her hips and behind her neck, she looked at herself in the mirror. *Not bad.* She smiled at her reflection. For forty plus years she'd worked hard, ate right, and it had paid off. Except for her funny tan lines, she looked pretty good. She only hoped she would be able to keep her shape after her surgery. Tying the sheer black wrap around her hips, she headed toward the deck.

Austin was already relaxing in the bubbling water—his head resting against the rim—when Ashley stepped through the sliding glass door. He opened his eyes, then quickly sat up straight. After a complete body scan, he whistled. "Wow! Is all that for me?"

"Yes. And you'd better enjoy it now because I'll never go out in public looking like this." Ashley removed her wrapped and stepped over the edge of the jacuzzi.

"Why not? You have a great body; not that I want you showing it off, but I don't understand why you're so . . ."

"Prudish?" She finished for him as she slowly slipped into the hot water and scooted over to sit alongside him.

"I didn't say that. I'm just letting you know you could put some twenty-year-old girls to shame. You've kept your body in great shape, but I don't mind that being our little secret."

Ashley smiled and rested her head back against his outstretched arm and closed her eyes. She laid there for a while, but when the water got too hot, she propped herself up on the rim.

"You okay?"

"Yeah, I just need to cool off for a second." A moment later, Ashley lowered herself back into the water, but she didn't rest against the side of the tub. Instead, she sat on Austin's lap. He opened his eyes and studied her for a moment, then reached out and played with a lock of hair that had fallen over her shoulder. "Did I tell you how beautiful you look tonight?"

"Yes."

"Did I tell you how great you look in that suit?"

"I think you might have said something to that effect."

Austin pulled her forward and kissed her, then whispered, "What if I told you, you would look even better *without* the suit?"

Ashley looked into Austin's eyes. Then reached behind her neck and allowed the ties of her suit to fall loose over her shoulders.

THIRTY-EIGHT

Willow hadn't moved from where C.J. had laid her on the bed. Her eyes were closed, and it appeared as if she was asleep. Quietly, he crept across the room to sit in the chair by the window. He sat, his eyes trained on her, until they closed in exhaustion.

He couldn't have been there very long when something startled him. He sat up straight, thinking he heard Willow say something.

He stepped around to the other side of the bed to see her face. She was still, her eyes closed, tears running down her cheeks. A small cry escaped her lips as she clutched the pillow she was holding. C.J. knew she was having some sort of nightmare and should wake her from it, but he was afraid he would startle her even more. Even so, when she flinched again, C.J. had seen enough.

Kneeling next to the bed, he carefully placed his hand on her shoulder and whispered, "Willow, you need to wake—"

She swung at him, then gasped in pain.

"Willow, you're okay. You're safe. It's just a nightmare. I'm not going to hurt you."

Her eyes snapped open and stared directly at him. Slowly, she pushed herself to a sitting position and began to cry in earnest. C.J. sat alongside her and gently placed his arm around her shoulder.

"It's okay, Willow. You're safe now."

Who am I kidding? It's not okay. She's been beat to a pulp.

C.J. held Willow for a while before he asked, "Are you hungry? Can I get you something?"

"Water," she whispered.

C.J. hurried to the bathroom and filled a glass with water. Giving it to Willow, he watched her hand shake as she lifted it to her mouth, wincing when it touched her swollen lip. She swished the water around, then spit it back into the glass. A pinkish tinge colored the water.

"Willow, would you like to take a shower?"

"I don't think I can stand that long; maybe a bath."

"Okay, I'll run some water for you." C.J. went to the bathroom and turned on the spigot. He dumped in some bubble bath, then sat on the edge of the tub, making sure the water temperature wasn't too hot. When he looked into the mirror, he saw Willow standing in the doorway, one hand braced against the doorframe, while the other was pressed to her stomach. She looked so pale, he was afraid she was going to pass out or throw up.

"Willow, are you going to be sick?"

"I don't think so, but I left some things at home that I need."

"That's okay. What do you need? I'll get it for you."

She closed her eyes. "They're personal things."

C.J. cringed at his stupidity, then reached for her hand. When she looked at him, he spoke softly, "Why don't you go look in my mom's room. I know she wouldn't mind."

Willow knew she was in no condition to argue with C.J. She just hoped she had the strength to walk that far. Slowly, she crossed the hall, then turned on the light to Ashley's room. Looking around, she realized it was only yesterday when she had been in this same room helping Ashley get ready for her wedding day. She had daydreamed about her own future.

And now my life is over.

Willow carefully walked to Ashley's bathroom—looked through the cupboards—relieved when she found what she needed. She had been bleeding since Sunday night, and today it was worse. She then looked in Ashley's dresser and took a few pairs of underwear and a bra. She'd left her apartment so quickly, she hadn't even brought a change of clothes. Of course, Steven had ruined most of her things anyway.

Willow looked at everything in her hands and felt complete and utter humiliation. After all, Ashley was her boss, and Willow had just rummaged through her drawers. What was she going to say? "Ashley, I borrowed a few of your personal things. Hope you don't mind. Why? Because I have a psychotic boyfriend who enjoys beating the crap out of me, and I've been too spineless to leave him until now. And that's only because your son pulled me out of there before Steven killed me."

What does it matter? You lost your pride the minute you allowed Steven to manipulate you. You didn't have the guts to leave him when you should have. Now you're paying the price.

She slowly walked back to the guest room using the walls and furniture to keep her balance. Leaning on the doorframe of the bathroom, she looked at C.J.'s reflection in the mirror. He was still sitting on the edge of the tub. When he glanced up and saw the things in her hands, he quickly looked away. Willow reached out for the countertop to steady herself, allowing the items in her hands to fall onto the counter.

"Willow, I'm afraid to leave you by yourself. You're so weak. What if you pass out?"

Willow knew she couldn't promise him she wouldn't, because she felt like she might. "I'll leave the door unlocked. I'll call if I need you."

C.J. nodded in agreement—even though he looked skeptical—then left the bathroom and pulled the door closed behind him.

Willow sat on the closed toilet seat and slowly undressed—every inch of her body tensing in pain. She was shivering by the time she stepped into the tub and was thankful for the warmth of the water against her skin. Leaning all the way back, she sank as low as she could go until the water was up around her shoulders. Though there was no shower curtain to keep the steam in the tub, the bathroom itself was soon filled with a warm fog. She gently washed her body, feeling every bruise and welt. And every time her stomach cramped, she ignored what she knew was happening. She tried to relax, tried to soak, but then her abdomen cramped with such force, she doubled over in pain. She feared the worst but could do nothing about it.

Maybe if she had told Steven she was pregnant, he wouldn't have beaten her. If she told him about the baby, perhaps he could have loved her enough to change. Instead, he proved to be the animal she had come to know.

With the water turning red around her, Willow pulled the plug and sat in the empty tub waiting for the hemorrhaging to stop.

C.J. heard the tub draining and Willow crying. He was worried and anxious but knew he needed to give her some space. Some privacy. So, he waited for her to come out. When she didn't, he knocked on the door. "Willow, are you all right?"

C.J. heard a strangled 'yes' but tried not to be alarmed. A few more minutes passed before he asked again. "Willow, are you sure you're okay?"

She answered with an anguished sob. "I don't know what to do,

C.J., but I can't let you see me like this."

"Willow, let me help you. Cover yourself up, I'm coming in."

C.J. slowing opened the bathroom door and saw Willow doubled over in the tub, a large towel around her shoulders—surrounding her body. When he stepped forward, his concern was replaced with horror.

There was no water in the tub.

Only blood.

Oh God, please, no. Don't let her die.

Willing himself not to cry—or lose it altogether—he tried to speak in a calm, controlled, tone.

"Willow, we have to get you to the hospital. I'm calling 9-1-1."

When C.J. turned to leave, Willow cried out, "No! Don't! I don't want to go to the hospital. There's nothing they can do for me."

"But you're bleeding internally."

"No." She grimaced, clenching her stomach in pain. "I'm miscarrying."

"You're what?"

"I'm pregnant. Was pregnant. I'm miscarrying." Willow began to sob uncontrollably.

Stunned, C.J. was momentarily paralyzed by fear. But when the shock wore off, he realized he needed to take charge of the situation.

"I'm going to let the water run. That way you don't have to keep looking at the—"

C.J. took another towel and laid it across Willow's pulled up knees, that way her body was completely concealed from him, which gave him the freedom to move around and try to make her comfortable.

Willow was shaking, so he turned on the towel warmer. After a few minutes, he placed a warm towel across her shoulders. It seemed to help her relax, so C.J. kept rotating cold towels for warm ones. He plugged the tub, so the water would run past her, then pulled it when it became discolored.

He watched for any sign of improvement, but every few moments, Willow's shoulders would stiffen, and a new contraction would rack her body. When it passed, she relaxed slightly, but used what strength she had to hold her knees against her chest.

C.J. could tell Willow was not going to be able to handle much more. He was about to say something, when her head rolled back, and he saw her lips turn white and her complexion blanch a sickening shade of gray. When she looked at him with panic in her

224

eyes, he knew exactly what was happening.

He quickly grabbed the cleaning bucket from under the sink, dumped its contents onto the floor, then held it to her chin. When her hair fell across her shoulders, he pulled it back away from the bucket as she lost what little was in her stomach.

"You need to go to the hospital, Willow. I don't know what else to do."

She cried harder. "There's nothing . . . you . . . can do. Please . . . just stay with me."

C.J. wanted to scream, feeling scared out of his freakin' mind. *What if she loses consciousness? She's lost so much blood. What if something ruptured from Steven's beating, and she really is bleeding internally?*

"Please, C.J." She reached out for his hand and looked at him as if he was her betrayer.

"Okay," he conceded, "but if you black out, I'm calling 9-1-1."

She sighed with relief while he dumped the contents of the bucket into the toilet.

Rotated towels.

Emptied bath water.

Filled it up again.

After what felt like an eternity, C.J.'s panic began to fade. Willow's cramping slowed, and the tub water didn't have to be drained as often. No longer throwing up, Willow rested her head atop her raised knees, every few seconds nodding off from exhaustion. Thankfully, she was no longer crying out in pain.

C.J. crouched alongside her. "Willow, you need to lay down, so you can rest. Let's try to get you to the bed."

"No, I don't want to ruin anything."

"They're only sheets Willow. They can be cleaned or replaced. Besides—" C.J. stopped, when he thought of something that could work. "Willow, will you be okay for a few minutes while I go get something?"

She nodded weakly.

C.J. bolted down the stairs two at a time, then hurried toward the barn. In the shed, where they kept medical supplies, he grabbed what he was looking for, then rushed back to the house. When he walked into the bathroom, he was surprised to see Willow had gotten out of the tub and was sitting on the toilet lid wrapped in a towel. Without saying anything, he left again and came back with his mother's robe.

"Here, put this on." He held the robe up but kept his eyes on the floor. He felt Willow slip her arms throw the sleeves, then saw a bloodstained towel drop at her feet. With the robe wrapped around her, Willow sat back down and began to cry.

"Are you still in a lot of pain?"

Willow didn't answer.

"I'll take that as a yes," he said, then lowered himself beside her. "Here, put your arm around my neck." Willow didn't even argue. C.J. could feel her shaking as he lifted her into his arms and carried her to the bed.

"Is this what I think it is?"

"Yes, it will work fine." He had grabbed one of the medical towels they used when birthing a horse. Using it would be easier than having to change the sheets.

Once he laid Willow down, C.J. knelt alongside the bed and watched as she curled into a ball. "I'm going to go get you something for the pain, okay?"

She just nodded, looking weak and frail.

C.J. grabbed a bottle from his medicine cabinet, read the label, and put it back. Reaching for something else, he quickly read, then hurried back to the guest room. When he got there, Willow was lying on her side with her hands on her stomach, but not clutching it, her eyes closed, her breathing less labored.

He leaned against the wall and sunk to the floor. He ran his fingers through his hair and just stared at her, finally allowing his tears to surface.

How could someone do this?

Looking at Willow, he saw her swollen lip and bruised cheek. It was beyond C.J.'s comprehension. A man, no . . . not a man, an animal did this. He sat staring at her as his tears began to fall.

Willow slept for almost an hour, before getting up. C.J. watched her cross the room to the bathroom, using the furniture for stability. It was obvious she was still in a lot of pain by the way she walked hunched over. When she sank to the edge of the bed, C.J. went and sat beside her.

"Here, take these." C.J. handed her three small tablets and a glass of water. She had a hard time swallowing with her jaw and lip so swollen and almost coughed up the pills. Finally, she was able to swallow them and wiped at the water running down her chin.

"How did I get here, C.J.?" Her voice was barely above a

REUNION

whisper and void of feeling.

"I came and got you." He knew that wasn't what she was talking about but didn't know what else to say.

"No, I mean, how did my life get so messed up?"

C.J. waited a moment before asking her what had been on his mind from the beginning. "When did all this start happening?"

Willow hesitated. "About three months ago."

"Are you kidding me?!" C.J. jumped to his feet. "You've been putting up with this crap for three months? You're lucky you're not dead."

Willow didn't respond. She only hung her head and brushed a tear aside.

Immediately, C.J. felt like a jerk. After what Willow had been through, a lecture was the last thing she needed. He knelt down in front of her and apologized. "I'm sorry, Willow. I shouldn't have said that."

"No. You're right. I knew he had a violent temper, and I stayed with him, anyway. I guess I got what I deserved."

"No! No, Willow, I didn't mean that." C.J. tucked the loose strands of her hair behind her ear. "Nobody deserves to be treated the way Steven treated you. I just don't understand why you didn't leave him sooner."

"I tried . . . once . . ." Willow's voice trailed off.

C.J. thought for a moment, then asked, "A couple months ago, you said you fell off a ladder. You had bruises on your arm. Is that when—"

Willow nodded before he could finish his sentence. "I don't know what to do. I can't go back, but where do I go from here?"

"You stay here. Problem solved."

"No, that would only cause more problems. If Steven finds out I'm here, he'll make trouble for you, Ashley, and the ranch. I don't want to be responsible for that."

"I've already notified the security company of a potential problem. They're going to start a night watch of the ranch, and I've talked to Lt. Fulton."

"You told the police?" She looked horrified. "C.J., I know this is my fault, and I'm the one who screwed up, but I don't need everyone else to know that."

"First of all, you didn't screw up, and this isn't your fault. Second, I didn't tell the lieutenant about you, I just confirmed that I thought his suspicions about Steven were right. He thought Steven

227

was responsible for the break-in, and now I agree. I told him I was expecting more trouble. He said he'd arrange for a patrol to cruise by the ranch throughout the night. He also said he would keep an eye on Steven and his buddies."

"How does he know who Steven's friends are?"

C.J. sat beside her on the bed. "Willow . . . what has Steven told you about his line of work?"

"Well, right now he's out of work, but when I first met him he said he was a financial consultant. I had no reason not to believe him. He went to work every morning, suit . . . tie . . ."

"Well, he does deal in finances, but I don't think he consults people first. Lt. Fulton said he's in with a pretty seedy group of guys. They're con artists. Gambling. Swindling. Ponzi schemes. That's why the police knew him."

Willow looked dumbfounded. "I had no idea."

"Where did you meet him?"

Willow laid her head down on the pillow and pulled her knees up to her chest. C.J. knew she was tired and in pain, but he also knew she was avoiding the question.

"Why don't you try to get some sleep. I'll be right here if you need anything."

Willow didn't respond. She just closed her eyes and curled into a tighter ball. C.J. got up from the bed and pulled the quilt up over her shoulders. He went to his room, splashed some water on his face, and changed into sweat pants and a T-shirt. Grabbing the blanket off his bed, he walked back to Willow's room and sat on the floor. Leaning against the wall, he closed his eyes.

C.J. heard Willow get up every hour or so.

Quietly, she slipped into the bathroom, then slowly crawled back into bed. After one of her trips to the bathroom, she sat on the edge of the bed and whispered, "C.J."

"Yeah. Right here." He got to his feet.

"Could you maybe get me some more medicine?"

"Sure." C.J. went to his room and grabbed the bottle that sat on his bathroom counter. He measured out three tablets, refilled Willow's water glass, and handed her the medicine. In the light cast from the moon, C.J. watched her wince when swallowing and noticed perspiration glistening on her forehead. He raised his hand to check for a fever; his sudden motion causing her to flinch.

"Willow, I just want to see if you have a fever." He waited a second to make sure she was okay, then gently placed his hand to her forehead. She didn't feel hot, just clammy. "You're sweating in that heavy robe. Let me get you something cooler to wear."

C.J. went through his mother's dresser drawers without even thinking about it. He found a spaghetti-strap nightie of soft cotton and held it up. It looked like it would be more comfortable; at least it would be cooler. He walked back into the guest room and handed it to her.

"This should be more comfortable."

Willow untied the heavy robe she was wearing and then looked at C.J. He turned toward the window and stared out at the moon, to give her some privacy. When he turned back around, Willow was just lowering the nightie over her head. Her exposed back was a combination of discolored bruises and swollen welts. He turned back to the window and felt like cursing God. If He was so loving and good, how could He allow another tragedy to hit so close to home?

He was taking Willow's assault personally.

Willow slipped under the covers and appeared to fall right to sleep. It would be dawn soon, and C.J. wondered what the day would bring.

THIRTY-NINE

When Austin woke up, he rolled over and slid a hand across the sheets. When he felt only emptiness, he opened his eyes. Pulling on a pair of shorts, he went in search of Ashley. He saw her sitting on the deck, wrapped in her robe, feet up, and writing. Sliding the glass door open, Austin walked up behind her and pressed his lips to the crook of her neck. "Good morning, Mrs. Taylor. What are you doing up so early?"

"Early!" she chuckled. "It's already eight o'clock. Where I come from, this is the late side of morning."

"What are you writing?" Austin leaned back against the deck railing.

"A letter."

"To who? We'll be home by tomorrow."

"It's to C.J. I just wanted to put my thoughts down . . . in case things don't go as planned on Friday."

Austin crossed the deck, nudged her feet down from where they rested on the tabletop, and squatted in front of her. With his hands resting on her thighs, he glanced at an envelope laying on the table, then looked up at her. "Is there a letter there for me, too?"

She nodded, a tear landing on his hand. "Austin, I just want to be realistic. I don't want to miss the chance to say the things that are important to me. I'm confident God is going to perform a miracle in my body. He already has by allowing the doctors to catch it in time. Even so, if His plan is different than what we expect, I don't want to leave without telling you both how special you are to me, and that I expect you both to live full lives even if I'm gone."

He took the tablet from her lap and laid it aside. Cradling her face in his hands, he stroked her cheek with his thumb, wiping away more tears. "Then let me tell you how special you are to me." He took a moment to gather his thoughts, then looked into her eyes. "Ashley, if God had come to me and said, 'I can let you have Ashley for three days and then she's mine, or I can spare you the

230

pain and not let your paths cross at all,' I would have taken these three days. I've lived knowing you were the missing piece in my life, and now you're here. I can't imagine the rest of my life without you. Even so, if—" his words faltered.

"It's okay, Austin, I know—"

"No. Let me finish." With tears streaming down his face, he cleared his throat and started again. "Even so, if this is borrowed time, I'm thankful God allowed me to experience your love—if only for a few days."

Ashley reached out and pressed his head to her chest. They held each other as they cried, knowing each day they had together was a precious gift from God.

A gift to be treasured and lived to the fullest.

FORTY

Staring at the window, Willow watched as dawn pierced through the blinds. It was morning. A new day. But what did that mean for her? She looked at C.J. slouched in a small chair, a blanket crumpled on his lap—knowing there was no possible way he could've slept comfortably in that contorted position. But he'd done it anyway. Because of her.

Quietly, she walked to the bathroom and eased the door shut, then braced herself before looking in the mirror. She didn't even recognize the woman in the reflection. Eyes swollen from crying and discolored from bruising. Her left cheek distended. Her lips puffed up and blue. She stepped back further from the mirror until she could see most of her body. Slipping the spaghetti straps from her shoulders, she let the nightie fall to the floor. Covering her chest with her arms, she turned and saw the welts and bruises that crisscrossed her back. Then she pressed her hand to the purple flesh at her pelvic bone, knowing it was the blow that had caused her to lose her baby.

"Willow, are you all right?" C.J.'s voice was calm, but she could hear the concern in his tone.

"Yes, but I'm not descent. Please don't come in."

"But you're sure you're okay?"

"Yes. I think I'm going to try to shower."

"Are you strong enough for that?"

"I think so. I just want to be able to wash my hair."

"Use the bench and sit down as much as possible. I'll be right here if you need me."

Willow moved carefully, figuring if she took it slow enough she would be fine. Reaching into the freestanding shower in the corner of the bathroom, she turned on the water and adjusted the temperature before stepping inside. Leaning against the side wall for support, she stepped under the rainfall showerhead and let the water run over her body. She felt every cut and every bruise, the water both soothed and stung. When she felt her legs begin to shake, she reached for the shampoo and body wash from the corner shelf then took a step back and sat down on the bench seat. Lathering her hair—the best she could—she worked on the areas matted with blood. By the time she was done rinsing her hair, her strength was gone. She sat for a few minutes, not wanting to move, but knowing the warm water wouldn't last forever.

Getting to her feet, she turned off the water and carefully stepped onto the cold tile floor. She wrapped a towel around her body and sat down on the toilet seat, her hair dripping in her face. She tried to put her hair up in a towel, but to no avail. The motion of dropping her head forward was making her queasy, so she just sat there with her eyes closed.

"Willow, are you decent?"

"I guess, if you could call it that."

C.J. slowly opened the door and stepped inside. "I brought you a change of clothes. Just a simple dress, no buttons, no zippers. I thought that would be easiest."

When Willow met C.J.'s eyes, she quickly looked away. The stark reality of what had happened the previous night seemed magnified in the harshness of daylight. She felt embarrassed. Humiliated. The condition he'd seen her in was appalling. C.J. was her boss and had seen her almost completely naked. He'd been every bit a gentleman, but that didn't erase how Willow felt about herself or the situation.

"C.J., I think the worst is over. If you don't mind, I would like some privacy now."

"Sure, Willow. No problem. If you need something there's an intercom by the door. Would you like me to help you back to bed or get you some more medicine for the pain?"

"No, just leave me alone."

C.J. was surprised. Not by Willow's words, but her tone. Of course she would want some privacy; she had just been through a horrific ordeal. But her tone seemed almost . . . accusatory.

He went back to his room, showered, changed, and lingered upstairs for over an hour—just in case Willow called out for him. When all was quiet, he hurried to the kitchen to make breakfast. Keeping in mind she probably couldn't handle much, he scrambled two eggs and spooned some applesauce into a bowl. He poured some juice and set it on the tray. Going outside, he plucked a daisy from the front porch planter and put it in a vase. *There.* He smiled—pleased with himself—then headed back upstairs.

Balancing the tray on one arm, he knocked lightly on the door.

"I'm resting."

"But you also need your strength. I fixed a light breakfast. Nothing too—"

"I said I'm resting . . . and I'm not hungry."

"But Willow, you need to eat. You've lost a lot of blood, and you're very weak."

Silence.

"Can I at least bring the tray in?" C.J. tried again.

No answer.

"I'm going to leave it outside the door, okay? If you get hungry, it will be here." C.J. walked downstairs, frustrated.

He wanted to be mad but knew that wasn't fair. Willow was dealing with both the physical pain of Steven's assault and the emotional toll of losing a child. She would need time and space to process all she'd been through.

While cleaning up the kitchen, C.J. saw Billy walking across the yard. He went to the backdoor and called to him. Billy quickly changed directions and met him on the porch.

"How is she?"

"Not good. How about Jaime and Sarah, did they show?"

"Yep, no problems there, but when I unlocked the gate this morning, the security patrol stopped and gave me this." Billy handed him a piece of paper, giving the description of a car and a license plate number. When C.J. looked back at Billy, he explained further.

"The night watch said that car went back and forth at least half a dozen times last night between the hours of ten and four."

"Thanks, Billy. You doing okay? I mean, can you keep things going for me?"

"Sure thing, C.J., but I better get to it if I'm going to stay on top of things." Billy gave him a pat on the shoulder then left. C.J. went back inside agitated, knowing Steven was going to cause more trouble. He called Lt. Fulton, gave him the license number and told him what the security patrol had said.

"So, what set this Boyer character off?" Lt. Fulton asked. "Have you had problems with him in the past?"

"No. Sunday was the first time I met him, after I talked with you.

But you're right. He's trouble. And I think he's going to come looking for me."

"So, this involves the girl?"

"Excuse me?" C.J. was trying to stall. He didn't want to lie to the police, but he didn't want to compromise Willow's trust.

"The girlfriend . . . Willow Jenner. She was with you when you came to the station, but she said that Boyer was her boyfriend. Is this some kind of love triangle?"

"Absolutely not! Willow is an employee of the Circle-R Ranch and a friend. We were returning from a business function when I got your message to come to the station."

"Uh huh. Whatever you say. But the real issue here is Boyer, and we can't do anything if he hasn't broken the law. Just because you think he *might* be a danger isn't enough to bring him in."

If the lieutenant only knew. If he could see Willow's battered body, then he would have evidence of the threat Steven posed.

"Mr. Summers?"

"Yes, I'm still here."

"Look, we're going to treat this as an attempted break-in but other than that, there's nothing I can do."

"Can you at least run the plates and see who the car is registered to?"

"Sure, I'll see if it's Boyer."

"Thanks, lieutenant." C.J. disconnected the call and looked out over the ranch. *Now what?* He wasn't sure what to do next. He didn't want to leave Willow alone, but it was obvious she didn't want his company either. Deciding to stay close to the intercom, in case Willow tried to use it, C.J. opted to do some computer work in his room.

Needing to get some more supplies from Ashley's bathroom, Willow slipped into the hall. That's when she saw the tray sitting by her door. She cringed, feeling guilty for the way she had treated C.J. She knew he was only trying to help, but that didn't minimize her humiliation. Slowly, she bent and picked up the white daisy he had placed in a small vase. It made her smile. *Why couldn't more guys be like him?*

After getting the needed supplies, Willow put them in the bathroom, then returned to the tray. She took the bowl of applesauce, what looked like a glass of pineapple juice, and the small glass vase. She sat up in bed while eating, then lay back down to rest. She looked at the single daisy on the night stand until she could no longer see it through the blur of tears. She closed her eyes and was finally able to fall back to sleep.

FORTY-ONE

Though Ashley and Austin's day got off to a melancholy start, they redeemed it with a lot of holding, touching, and embracing. They had an insatiable appetite for each other and spent the rest of the morning satisfying it.

"Do you want to go into town and do some shopping?" Austin asked as he softly stroked her arm.

She sighed, tucked comfortably against his chest, enjoying the warmth of his skin next to hers. "No. I just want to stay like this the rest of my life, you holding me, no responsibilities, no phones, no doctors, no nothing."

"Okay, what do you say I call the front desk and tell them this room is occupied indefinitely?"

"Wouldn't that be great?"

"Yes, but not needed." He hugged her close. "We'll have days like this after your surgery, Ash. I know you can't see that far yet, but I can, and the future looks amazing."

They rested for a while more before Austin swung his feet to the floor and pulled his shorts on. "I'm going to make you some lunch."

"With what?" she asked."

"The room comes with a fully stocked pantry. Who knows what I'll find. Any requests?"

"Whatever you make will be just fine." Ashley smiled, snuggling deeper under the covers. She only intended to close her eyes for a few minutes, but the next time she glanced at the clock, a half hour had passed. Deciding to take a quick shower, she hurried to the bathroom.

She stood transfixed as the waterfall shower head sheathed her with warm water and the body jets lightly massaged her muscles. It was heaven. She knew she was taking longer than she intended, but it felt oh so good.

When she thought she heard a knock, she stopped what she was doing and listened. *Nothing.* Lathering her hair, she heard the knock

237

again. This time she was not mistaken.

"Yes?"

She listened to Austin's muffled voice but couldn't make out what he was saying. Something about 'being hunched over the bed.' Trying to rinse shampoo from her hair and listen at the same time, she hollered, "What? I can't hear you."

"I said—"

Ashley gasped, startled that Austin was standing just the other side of the beveled glass door. She looked at the blurry form that was his, knowing he was looking at the blurry form that was hers. He slid the door open just a few inches, so he could speak. Instinctively, Ashley crossed her arms over her chest, and Austin—ever the gentleman—did his best to keep his eyes focused on her face.

"I said I would bring you lunch in bed."

"Oh, okay. I'm almost done here."

"That's a shame." He smiled, a twinkle in his eyes.

"I could extend it . . . if you'd like?"

Austin's brow arched with surprise. "Is that an invitation?"

Ashley didn't answer; she just slid the door further, so Austin could step inside.

FORTY-TWO

C.J. checked on Willow every hour or so. He would tap on her door and ask if she was okay. She would answer in a whisper, usually telling him she was resting. When he checked on her before lunch, she didn't answer, so he quietly pushed open the bedroom door and saw her curled up in the chair, asleep. He glanced around the room, discouraged when he saw the bowl of applesauce was only half empty, but when he saw the vase that held the daisy perched on her nightstand, it made him smile. He was glad he'd placed it on her tray.

His goal for lunch was to get her to eat a little more than a half bowl of applesauce. Keeping her sore jaw and swollen lips in mind, he made tomato soup and stacked a choice of crackers on the side of the bowl. Carrying the tray upstairs—careful not to slosh the soup too much—C.J. only made it halfway up when Willow screamed. He bolted the rest of the way, dropped the tray on the hall table, and threw open the door. She was thrashing about and crying, deep in the grip of a nightmare.

He was at her side in two broad steps. Sitting on the edge of the bed, he pulled her to his chest. She was combative and screaming, but he didn't let go. "You're all right, Willow. No one is going to hurt you." She kept struggling against his hold, trying to break free. He waited for her to take the step from nightmare to reality. When she did, her body went limp, and she began to shake.

"He was right there," she cried. "I was sure of it. I could hear him. I thought he was right there."

C.J. rocked her back and forth gently stroking the back of her head. "It's okay, Willow. It was only a nightmare. You're safe here. I promise you; you're safe."

Her skin was moist with perspiration, and strands of her long hair clung to the side of her face and arms. When C.J. finally loosened his hold on her, she scooted up to rest against the headboard. She covered her face with the palms of her hands, then rolled on her side, away from C.J.

"I brought you some lunch."

He got up and went back into the hall to get the tray. The soup had splashed all over everything, but there was still a little in the bowl. "I can get you some more crackers. These are kind of soggy."

She continued to face the window as she spoke. "Just put it over there. I'll eat it later."

"But it'll get cold."

She said nothing.

Willow was back to silent mode.

"Use the intercom if you need me. Okay?" Without an answer, C.J. left the room frustrated and discouraged.

As soon as Willow heard the door click, she took the tray and rested it across her lap. She sipped at what was left of the soup and even ate the soggy crackers.

After lunch, she tried to rest, but her abdomen was still cramping, making it difficult for her to get comfortable. She slid deeper under the covers, clutching her stomach, willing her tears to dry up.

She thought about the life she had carried. *Her baby.* Though she never would've chosen to bring a child into her and Steven's relationship, the thought that she had lost a baby overwhelmed her. Greater still was the realization that she was responsible. She had allowed herself to suffer Steven's abuses, but knowing her child was an unexpected casualty tore at her heart. She mourned the child she would never know, as she fell back into a fitful sleep.

It was dusk when Willow carefully made her way downstairs. She held onto the banister and took each step one at a time. About halfway down she decided she'd bitten off more than she could chew. She sat on the steps for a moment to gather her strength. Her stomach continued to knot and release as she curled up with her head to her knees.

"Hey, what are you doing out of bed?" C.J. stood at the bottom landing.

"I was coming down to see you, but I kind of ran out of energy."

"I made pasta for dinner. It should be pretty easy to eat."

With the sun sinking fast, C.J.'s face was a mix of shadows. She couldn't see his expression, or read his eyes, but hated the hesitation she heard in his words.

"I'm sorry, C.J.; I haven't been very nice to you today." Overwhelmed with emotion, she had to take a breath before continuing. "I just can't even put into words how humiliated I feel."

He knelt on the step in front of her. "I know I can't change the way you feel or what you've gone through, but you have nothing to be embarrassed about."

She looked at him, rolling her eyes. "Nothing? You don't think the fact that you saw me half naked, found out I have a deadbeat boyfriend who uses me as a punching bag, and was stupid enough to get pregnant, doesn't warrant complete humiliation on my part?"

"I thought you were going to die, Willow." C.J. said, his eyes demanding her attention. "Nothing else matters. I mean, it does, and I hate that you've gone through so much, but all I could think about was you dying, and me not being able to do anything to help you."

"I don't think I could've died. I know it looked bad, but women have miscarriages all the time."

"I think you would've died if I hadn't gotten you out of that apartment."

The reality of his point chilled her.

"Look, dinner is ready." C.J. changed the subject. "Why don't I help you upstairs, and then you can eat something."

He helped her to her feet and with one hand to her waist and the other cupping her elbow, he slowly helped her back to the guest room.

"C.J., maybe you could bring a tray for yourself, so I don't have to eat alone."

He smiled and nodded. "Okay, I'll do that."

It took a couple of trips to the kitchen, but C.J. had dinner set up on two TV trays to her room. They sat facing each other, Willow on the right side of the bed while C.J. sat in the overstuffed chair in front of the window. He moved and fidgeted, clearly uncomfortable. She wanted to laugh because he looked so ridiculous. He could barely see over his tray from his low position in the chair, and he kept hitting the legs of the tray with his knees. Then, when he tried to scoot to the edge of the cushion, he nearly tipped the whole thing over. Though Willow found it amusing, she could tell C.J. was getting frustrated.

"You know, you could just sit on the bed. I promise not to bite."

~®~

C.J. wasn't sure what prompted Willow's change in attitude, but he wasn't going to question it. He dug himself out of the chair and picked up his tray. Though there was room to sit beside Willow, he thought better of it. Carrying his tray, he took a seat at the foot of the bed, giving her some space. Sitting almost shoulder to shoulder, at a right angle, he couldn't see her face, but as long as she wasn't pushing him away, he would take what he could get.

Stealing a few glances over his shoulder, he kept checking to see if Willow was eating. Though she hadn't touched the garlic bread, and the salad looked as if it had only been pushed around, he could tell she'd had some of the pasta. It was a start.

Silently they ate, but C.J. wanted to say something to break the very loud quiet between them. But what? If he talked about the ranch, it would only remind Willow of the work she was supposed to be doing, and he didn't want to talk about the wedding, because ultimately, him taking Willow home is what led to all this. *I guess I could—*

"C.J., I'm sorry I've put you on edge." Willow interrupted his thoughts. "I didn't mean to be so harsh with you. I guess I just feel so . . . so . . ."

He waited while she searched for the right word.

"Exposed."

"I understand." He took a few more bites, swallowed, then added, "But I still think you need to see a doctor."

"I don't need a doctor, C.J.; I'll be fine. What I need is to figure out where I go from here."

"What do you mean? You're staying on the ranch."

"C.J., Ashley and Austin are coming home on Thursday. I don't think I should be here when they arrive. Ashley will have a lot on her mind, and I don't want her to be the least bit distracted or upset. And you know as well as I do, if she finds out, she's not going to settle for the abridged version."

C.J. didn't agree verbally, but knew Willow was right. His mom's surgery was in three days. She didn't need to be worrying about the ranch, or Willow, or anything else for that matter. She needed to concentrate on herself for a change. He thought a moment, knowing there had to be a solution.

"Okay, I have an idea," he said.

"What?"

"Would you consider staying at Austin's?"

"What?" She turned to him. "Are you kidding? I can't go there. I don't want Austin to know about this anymore than your mom. Don't you realize how humiliating this is? What would you say to him, anyway? Excuse me, Austin, but Willow got knocked up by her boyfriend, and then he beat the crap out of her, causing her to miscarry. She wasn't smart enough to leave him, and now she looks like a truck hit her. Can she lay low at your place while she sorts out her screwed up life?"

Willow's tears did nothing to calm C.J.'s anger. Upset at her crude appraisal of her situation, he tossed down his fork and got up from where he was sitting. "I need to get some fresh air." He walked toward the door, but Willow wasn't through.

"Easy for you, isn't it?" she shouted. "You can get up and walk out. I, on the other hand, can't walk away. Not from the bruises, or the pain . . ." C.J. turned around and watched as Willow swiped at an errant tear. ". . . not from the nightmares or the fact that I just miscarried my—"

The floodgates opened, and with her head in her hands, Willow began to sob.

Feeling beyond horrible, C.J. sat on the bed beside her and cautiously draped his arm around her shoulders, hoping the physical contact didn't freak her out. Willow collapsed against him—her head pressed to his chest—and allowed her tears to fall. Stroking her arm and hushing her cries, C.J. came up with another plan.

"What if you stayed at Billy's?" he whispered. "It would only be for a day. Mom comes home Thursday but will leave first thing Friday morning. Then, she'll be in the hospital until Monday or Tuesday. You can stay at Billy's Thursday and come back Friday, after Mom leaves. That will give you a few days to recoup and figure out your next step."

"I don't want to stay here, C.J., or involve Billy. It would only lead to more questions. I'll call one of my friends or go to a motel."

"No way! I'm not convinced you're out of the woods. I'm not dropping you off at some motel only to find out later, you fainted or collapsed. And I don't want you at a friend's house where Steven could hunt you down. I want you where I can keep my eye on you."

"Regardless of what I say?"

C.J. knew it was time he took control. Willow's health was in the balance, and he was not going to take any chances. "Look, Willow," his voice was firm yet gentle, "I feel responsible for you, and I think Austin's is the safest place for now. It's secluded and out of the way."

"You're worried about Steven, aren't you? You think he's going to cause trouble."

"Don't you? How do you think he's handling the fact that you walked out? Or that you could be at the police station right now pressing charges? He could land in jail, and he knows it. I don't want to give him a chance to get anywhere near you."

Willow didn't say anything, she just sat next to him, sniffling, regaining her composure. Finally, she asked, "So, what do you think we should do?"

C.J. got up, pacing with nervous energy. "I'll call Austin and try to get him to call me back without Mom knowing. I'll give him a quick rundown and ask to use his house. I know he'll say yes."

He waited for an argument of some sort, but it never came. Willow was quiet, and C.J. knew her mind was fast at work. Moving the tray that held her half eaten dinner, he bent down in front of her and looked into her downcast eyes.

"What are you thinking?" He knew she was, because her foot was tapping, and she kept turning her hands over in her lap.

"I'm afraid." Willow's eyes met his. "I'm afraid to be alone."

C.J. put his hand on top of hers. "I know, Willow, and I would be there with you if I could, but I need to be here when my mom comes home. If I'm not, she'll know something is up."

"I know, C.J., and I would never ask you to be with me instead of your mom. Ashley needs you right now more than ever. It's just that Austin's is so far away."

C.J. looked at Willow. She looked so fragile, like she was ready to break. Brushing a strand of hair from her eyelash, he said, "You're right. I don't want you to be afraid any longer. I'll figure out something else." He pushed himself up to his full height and walked to the window.

C.J. contemplated several ideas. He couldn't take her to any of his so-called friends. They would try to put the make on her, even if she was incapacitated, and he was sure Willow's friends all had links to Steven, so that was no good. Even so, he knew she couldn't stay here. The stress on his mom would be too great a risk. It seemed like Austin's was the only solution, if it wasn't for the fact that she'd be there by herself. C.J. continued to think, and then it hit him. *Jenna. Maybe Jenna could stay with Willow?* He knew Willow would argue about just one more person knowing her situation, but it was worth a shot.

He mulled over his plan as he gathered up their dishes. Willow's plate was almost full. She'd barely eaten anything. Another reason he wanted to make sure someone was checking in on her. There was no other way. She needed to go to Austin's. He braced himself for an argument, then said, "I really think Austin's is our best solution, but I could call—"

"I agree," Willow interrupted. "It's only one night. Even if I stay up the whole time watching movies, I can do it."

C.J. was stunned, but thankful. "That's great, Willow. I'll leave Austin a voice mail. Hopefully, he can find a time to call me back when he's away from Mom." C.J. collapsed the trays and leaned them against the wall. "Willow, I did have another suggestion, so you wouldn't have to be by yourself." He waited to see if she was willing to hear it, before he continued. She looked at him, listening. "You hit it off with Jenna at the wedding, right? What if I ask Austin to give her a call? She seems pretty nice. I bet she'd be willing to stay with you. In fact, from what I hear, she crashes at Austin's all the time."

Willow cringed at the idea of involving just one more person in the mess that was her life. Though she and Jenna clicked at the wedding, it would be so humiliating to explain how she'd gotten to this place. On the other hand, Willow didn't know how she would handle being by herself. She told C.J. she would do it, but the thought of being by herself was terrifying. Her heart raced with panic, and she felt like she would throw up just thinking about it. She'd held it together so far, but that was because C.J. was just a room away. Being across town, in a strange house, with strange noises, and no one to talk to, it was enough to put her over the edge.

"I wouldn't mind Jenna's company, if it's not too much trouble."

C.J. smiled. "Great. I'll make the call."

Austin saw C.J. name on the screen of his phone.

This can't be good. He insisted he wouldn't call unless there was an emergency.

"What's up, C.J.?"

"Austin, I didn't expect you to pick up."

"I wouldn't have, but my phone almost vibrated off the counter. I answered out of reflex."

"Is Mom right there?"

"No." Austin glanced out the sliding glass door to where Ashley was lounging in the hot tub.

"Can you talk for a few minutes?"

Austin heard something in C.J.'s voice. Worry. Anxiousness. He wasn't sure, but he could tell it was important. Not wanting Ashley to overhear, he put down the sodas he'd gone to get from the kitchen, then stepped further away from the sliding glass door.

"C.J. what's wrong?"

"It's a long story, and I doubt I'll be able to give you all the details. Just let me get out the specifics, then if Mom interrupts, you can hang up."

"Okay," Austin's worry went up another notch.

"Willow needs a place to stay when Mom gets home. I was hoping she could use your house."

"Sure, but can you at least give me some details? This is kind of coming out of left field."

"In a nut shell, Willow's boyfriend beat her up when she got home from the wedding. She's been staying here, but I think it will be too stressful for Mom to see her in this condition. Willow's terrified to be alone, so I was thinking, maybe Jenna would be willing to stay with her at your place? I know this is asking a lot, but Willow's in no condition to be by herself. If you could call Jenna, or give me her number, I'll—"

"You're right, this would be too much for your mom to handle." Austin's head was spinning with a thousand questions. "Quite frankly, it's almost too much for me to handle."

"Tell me about it."

Austin could hear the weariness in C.J.'s voice.

"Okay, jot this down." Austin rattled off Jenna's cell number. "I'll try to call her myself—to give her a head's up—but I might not get the chance without your mom becoming suspicious. If you haven't heard from me by tomorrow, go ahead and give Jenna a call. I'm sure she'll want to help." Austin saw Ashley through the sliding glass door. She was craning her neck, trying to see what he was up to. "Look, C.J., I've got to go, but tell me this, are you in any danger? This boyfriend, does he know where to find Willow?"

"I'm pretty sure he knows she's here, but I've already called the cops and our security company."

"This sounds pretty serious, C.J.; I think your mom and I should come home."

"No!" C.J. shouted, then lowered his voice. "Don't do that,

Austin. Mom deserves this time, and I would feel horrible if you cut it short for nothing."

"If you've already involved the cops, it doesn't sound like 'nothing.'"

"Austin, you'll be home Thursday. I just have to get through tomorrow."

Out of the corner of his eye, Austin saw Ashley stand up in the hot tub, craning her neck looking for him. "C.J., your mom's getting suspicious. I gotta go."

"Then, go. We'll be fine."

"Okay, but if there's trouble—if you even sense there's going to be trouble—call 9-1-1, then call me."

"I will. I promise. See you Thursday."

Austin laid his phone on the counter, feeling guilty. Ashley deserved to know what was going on, but C.J. was right. She didn't need one more thing to think about before her surgery. When he saw Ashley stepping out of the hot tub, he grabbed the sodas from the counter and hurried outside. "Hey, where are you going?"

She stopped, one foot in, one foot out. "Looking for you. I thought you deserted me."

"Are you kidding? That would be a self-inflicted punishment." Austin handed her a soda and waited for her to step back inside. When he got in, he pulled her down beside him.

"What took you so long?"

"My phone rang, and I had to catch it before it vibrated off the counter. Then I was thinking what we should have for dinner. You know, go out, stay in, delivery?"

"And what did you decide?"

"That I wasn't hungry enough to decide." He slipped further into the water, his head resting on the edge, Ashley's head on his shoulder. "Come on, let's enjoy this a little while longer, then we can figure out dinner."

FORTY-THREE

Steven sat with his friends, anger building in his fists. It had been two days, and Willow still had not come home.

"Face it, dude," Derek said with a raised beer bottle, "you got dumped. Your woman found herself another man, and now you're out of the picture. His friends laughed, but Steven had had enough. He threw his beer bottle against the wall, nearly hitting Carlos in the head.

"Hey man," Carlos snapped, "we're just yanking your chain. She was all wrong for you anyway. She was always such a downer. 'Steven, don't drink,' 'Steven, do this,' 'Steven, don't do that.' Come on, man. No one wants a nag around all the time. You're better off without her. Besides, now you can find yourself a really fine woman who's open to having a little fun, you know . . . someone who's willing to spread the love."

"Yeah, man," Derek added, "Willow didn't know how to share; she didn't get it that we're brothers. What's yours is mine, and mine is yours. You got plenty of ours, but none of us got any of yours." The guys continued to laugh and make foul jokes.

Steven grew angrier the more he thought about Willow. He knew that cowboy friend of hers had something to do with her disappearing act. He sat clenching and unclenching his fists. He wasn't going to let either one of them get away with making him look like a loser or a fool. He might be better off without Willow, but *she* most certainly *would not* be better off without him, not after he got through with her.

After C.J. talked with Austin and finished doing dishes, he checked on Willow. She was up and sitting by the window. She had combed her hair and pulled it back in a knot, and had her feet pulled up under the hem of her dress.

"How are you feeling?"

She shrugged her shoulders. "I just wish the aching would stop. Every muscle in my body hurts. If they would at least take turns, I could handle it better." Willow smiled slightly.

He sat on the edge of the bed. "So, I talked to Austin."

Immediately, her smile was gone. "What did he say?"

"He wanted to come home, but I convinced him not to. I told him the basics, and he said using his house was no problem. He's going to try to call Jenna, but he also gave me her number. If I don't hear from her by tomorrow afternoon, I'll give her a call."

"Was he freaked out?"

"A little, but I assured him everything was under control."

C. J. could see Willow shrinking into herself and did not want to lose what ground he'd gained. "Hey, how about a movie? You've been cooped up in this room for the last two days. A change of scenery would be good."

Willow looked like she was actually considering the idea. After a minute, she slowly got up from the chair. C.J. grimaced as much as she did with each measured step that she took.

"Maybe this isn't a good idea. If you're not feeling up to—"

"I'm fine, C.J., and a movie would be a welcomed distraction."

"But I could bring my computer in here, and you could watch it while you're resting. I don't want you to exert what little energy you have."

"I made it halfway down the stairs last time. The only reason I stopped was because I was afraid I was going to fall. I won't be afraid if you're there with me."

C.J. held her stare as her words echoed in his mind. *I won't be afraid if you're there with me.* It was then he realized he wanted *to be there* for Willow for the rest of her life. The flood of emotion that washed over him was both startling and scary.

"C.J., is something wrong?"

"No . . . no, I was just thinking about our movie choices." He quickly shook off the feelings that had hijacked his heart and offered Willow his arm for support.

They took the steps one at a time. Willow braced herself with one hand on the banister, and the other tucked in the crook of C.J.'s arm. She made it to the great room and sat on the sofa with a sigh. Little beads of perspiration glistened on her brow, and her cheeks were flush. C.J. brought her a drink of water and sat on the ottoman in front of her.

"That took a lot out of you, didn't it?"

"I can't believe how incredibly weak I feel. I was strong as an ox three days ago. Now I have legs made of Jell-O."

"You've been through a lot. Your body might not bounce back as quickly as your determination." C.J. hunched down in front of the entertainment center and started flipping through DVDs. "So, what should we watch?"

"How about something with a happy ending?" Willow tucked her feet up under her and sank deep into the sofa, using the rolled arm of the couch as a pillow.

"Are you cold?"

"Maybe a little."

C.J. grabbed the afghan from the basket on the fireplace and laid it over her, then took a seat on the couch next to her feet. He picked up the controller and press play. Mel Gibson's, *Forever Young* filled the screen. "Have you seen this one before?"

"A long time ago, but I remember liking it."

They watched the movie in silence for about twenty minutes. C.J. used the time to process his newly discovered feelings for Willow. Then he realized his blunder. "What was I thinking?" He jumped up and walked toward the kitchen. "A movie without popcorn? Where are my manners?" Rummaging through the pantry shelves, he held up three different packets. "What do you prefer? We have light, buttered, or kettle corn?"

"Kettle corn sounds good."

Willow watched the movie while C.J. popped popcorn and poured sodas. He hadn't been paying attention to the movie, but when he returned to the great room, Willow was in tears and clenched up tight in the corner of the couch. A fight scene C.J. completely forgot about played out on the screen. He quickly grabbed the remote and turned off the movie, then sat next to her and hung his head.

"I'm so sorry. I totally forgot about that scene." C.J. pushed his fingers through his hair, his hands coming to rest at the back of his neck. Willow's sniffles softened but seeing her in tears again was like a stake through his heart. "I'm really sorry." He didn't know what else to say.

"It's all right. I overreacted. I guess it just took me by surprise, and I don't know . . . it just kind of . . ." Her words drifted off as she wiped her face with the back of her hand. He handed her a napkin, and she quickly dried her tears. "It was stupid of me to react that way."

Without the glow from the television, the room was almost completely dark—except for the yard lights filtering through the windows.

"I guess we could use some light in here." C.J. got up to turn on a lamp when Willow grabbed his hand.

"Can we leave it off?"

"Sure." C.J. sat down and pushed himself back against the couch cushions. It was too quiet, but he was at a loss of what to say. He started thinking about his Mom's surgery, and the fact that Austin was going to be a fixture in his life. He hadn't had much time to dwell on the changes that were coming his way. Willow's situation pretty much monopolized his thoughts. Even so, as they sat in total darkness, he thought about his mom, Austin, the ranch, and his undeniable feelings for Willow.

". . . met him at a bar."

"What?" C.J. barely heard her whispered words.

"You asked me where I met Steven. My friends took me to Chesterfield's for my birthday, and he was there at the bar."

Chesterfield's had a reputation for being a singles hot spot. It was a restaurant/bar, but everyone went there for the dancing. C.J. had been a few times but thought the clientele was sketchy.

"My friends and I were at the bar waiting for our table when Steven struck up a conversation with me. I remember thinking he looked so suave and sophisticated in his expensive looking suit, silk tie, and briefcase at his side. He had successful businessman written all over him."

Successful schemer and conniver is more like it. C.J. thought to himself.

"Kathy, one of my friends, noticed we were hitting it off, so when we got up to leave, she slipped Steven my phone number. He called the following night and asked me out on a date. He was older; I was flattered. That seems like an eternity ago."

C.J. waited for her to continue. When she didn't he asked, "Did he know about the baby?"

"No, I was afraid to tell him. He'd been on edge and moody lately, so there never seemed to be a good time to bring it up."

"This kind of thing happened a lot, didn't it?"

She nodded. "Sometimes worse than others. But Steven had never lost his temper to the point of hitting me where the bruises would show."

Willow's comment was so casual; it almost made C.J. sick. She

251

came to expect abuse as a normal part of life.

"Why did you move in with him, if you knew about his temper?"

"I didn't. He moved me. I came home from work one day to find my apartment empty. He had moved all my stuff while I was at work. He thought it was this amazing surprise. I was terrified. I knew then I had no place of escape."

"When you called me about missing work, I could tell something was wrong, but you were telling me to stay away. Why? Why didn't you let me come get you then?"

"I thought I could handle him. Steven was so upset about my car, and the police, and you bringing me home; I knew if you came over it would only make matters worse." Willow shook her head. "But then I made things worse all on my own."

"What happened?"

"Steven accused me of seeing other men. No matter what I did or said, he never trusted me. That started it. Then, when I found out he bought a car with the money I was saving for tuition, I completely snapped and said some pretty crude things. I guess I wanted to belittle him as much as he had belittled me over the last few months. I pushed him over the edge."

C.J. had to fight to control his anger. On some level, Willow was blaming herself for Steven's brutal behavior. He wanted to set her straight, but arguing with her was not the answer, so he kept his negative comments to himself. "Willow, why don't you go to the police? Steven already has a shady reputation. If you press charges, he'll go to prison where he belongs."

"Steven is too manipulative for that. He'll turn this around and make it all my fault, and since I never left him, I am to blame. Steven will walk away scot-free, then come after me."

"You're *not* to blame, Willow. The police will believe you; you have the bruises to prove it."

"You didn't see how Lt. Fulton looked at me at the police station, did you?"

"I'm not following."

It doesn't matter, okay." Willow's tone went up an octave. "It's bad enough I let this happen. I'm not going to let someone else point out my stupidity. I think Steven's driven that point home already."

"Willow, I didn't mean to upset you. I just feel so frustrated that I can't do more to help."

"Are you kidding me? I couldn't have made it without your help.

You got me out of there. You kept warm towels on me when I was cold. You held my hair back while I got sick. You've made me meals and held me while I cried, even though I was being mean and ugly toward you. I can't even begin to think how I can repay you for all you've done."

C.J. felt her hand slip over his. He turned his hand around and gave hers a squeeze.

"Press charges," C.J. said, stoically.

"What?"

"If you want to repay me, press charges. Don't let Steven get away with this."

She pulled back her hand. "I can't, C.J.; it's not that easy."

"Sure it is. You walk into the police station and tell them you were assaulted. You let them know Steven is dangerous, that you need police protection, and you want to press charges."

"Sure. Right. Easy." Willow snapped. "And then they'll sit me down and question me about every detail of my life. My friends, my family, my living arrangement, my sexual activity. They'll ask if I'd been drinking the day of the assault—if my judgment was impaired or my recollection of the events skewed. Then they'll ask me about you, and what sort of relationship we have. I'll paint Steven as an abuser, while they paint me as a woman pitting two men against each other. I'll be treated like a criminal, C.J., with no assurance they'll even believe me. I can't handle that mentally or emotionally; I just can't."

"Okay, let's forget I even said anything." The emotion in Willow's voice was his cue to change the subject before she lost it all together. "We won't talk about Steven anymore, but I did want to ask you about your car."

"Oh shoot!" Willow snapped. "I was supposed to call the mechanic and tell them what to do with it. I guess I'll need it fixed after all. I'm sure Steven will be more than happy to keep the Saturn."

"Saturn?" C.J. repeated.

"What?"

"He bought you a Saturn?"

"Yeah. Why?"

"The security patrol said a gold Saturn kept driving by the ranch Monday night."

"That had to be Steven." Her voice cracked with emotion. "He's going to cause trouble, C.J., I just know he is."

"Don't worry. He wouldn't be stupid enough to pull something in broad daylight, and the security patrol is out until dawn. Billy's locking the front gates at night, so he can't even get near the house."

A lengthy silence permeated the room.

"Come on, Willow, let's pick out another movie. Maybe Disney this time." He crossed the room to the entertainment system and opened the cupboard of DVDs. "How about—"

"You know what, I'm not feeling too hot. I think I'll just take a bath and go to bed."

C.J. noticed the way Willow clutched her stomach when she stood, and how slowly she moved. She had lost so much blood, and he knew a miscarriage could pose dangerous complications. She wasn't going to complain, that was obvious. So, he decided he would do a little research on the Internet once she went to bed. It would help to know what the medical world suggested to a person in her condition, and if it was 'being seen by a doctor', he would be more insistent.

Once Willow was asleep, C.J. went to his room and clicked his computer out of sleep mode. Typing *post miscarriage* in the address bar, he waited for a list to populate. Scrolling through the recommended sites, he clicked on one and started reading. It explained that cramping could last a few days, and it wasn't uncommon for bleeding to last seven to ten days. That gave C.J. a little peace of mind. Even so, it also recommended being examined by a doctor to be sure the miscarriage was complete. Then it went on to list complications such as hemorrhaging and infection, spiking his anxieties once again. C.J. realized, no matter what, he had to convince Willow to see a doctor.

For the time being, he decided to put the doctor discussion aside and started compiling a mental list of things that would have to be done before Thursday. First, he would find out where Willow's car was and arrange for it to be fixed. Then, he would figure out how to get Willow's things from her apartment.

When his phone rang, C.J. pulled it from his pocket and saw that it was Austin. "Hello."

"How's Willow?" Austin whispered.

"Stubborn."

"Look, C.J. I can't talk long. I left a vague message on Jenna's voicemail letting her know to expect a call from you, but you'll have to fill her in. I didn't want Ashley catching me on the phone, so I had to be quick."

"Okay, I'll call her right now. Did you tell her it was an emergency?"

"Yes, but that was about all."

"Thanks, Austin. Hey, how's Mom doing?"

"Highs and lows. We've had a great few days, but now it's getting a little harder to block out the inevitable."

"But she's doing okay?"

"She is. Ashley's strong, C.J.; we're going to get through this."

It took C.J. a minute to gather his composure before calling Jenna. He dug out of his pocket the scrap of paper he'd written her phone number on and dialed. She picked up on the first ring before he even had time to figure out what he was going to say.

"Jenna, this is C.J. Summers. Austin said he left you a message."

"Yes, he did, and he said it was an emergency. Has something happened to your mother?"

"No. Mom's fine and so is Austin." C.J. paused for a second before explaining the situation. "This is kind of a bazaar story, so if you don't mind, bear with me. I'll try to explain the best I can. Do you remember Willow, from the wedding?"

"Sure. We talked for quite a while and decided we would get together for lunch or something. Why?"

"How's Thursday?"

" 'How's Thursday', for what?"

C.J. took a deep breath. "Willow is going to be staying at Austin's place for a few days. I was wondering if you would be available to hang out with her Thursday and Friday; just so she's not alone?"

"C.J., if Uncle Austin said Willow could stay at his house, I'm sure he's fine with her being there alone. It's not like he needs someone to watch her."

"No, but Willow does."

"I'm not following," Jenna said, sounding confused.

"Look, Jenna, there's no easy way to say this; Willow's boyfriend beat her up Monday night." C.J. heard Jenna gasp, but continued. "She stayed here the last few days because she can't go back to her apartment. But if my mom sees her in this condition, she'll freak out. Austin and I don't want her stressed before her surgery, so Willow's going to stay at his place. If you could hang out with her on Thursday and Friday, it would be a big help."

"Ahh . . . sure . . . yeah . . . I can do that."

C.J. could hear her apprehension. "If it's a problem, Jenna, we'll figure something—"

"No. No . . . really, it's not a problem. I didn't mean to hesitate, I guess I'm just a little shocked."

"Believe me, I know how you feel."

"I absolutely want to help, C.J., really I do, but Friday morning I planned on being at the hospital with Uncle Austin, you know, just to provide a little moral support. So, if Willow can handle being by herself for a couple hours on Friday, I can be there the rest of the time."

"That would be great. We'll figure out something else for Friday morning. Do you think you could meet us at Austin's Thursday morning?"

"Sure. How about nine o'clock?"

"Perfect. That will give me plenty of time to get back to the ranch before my mom gets home. I want to be able to spend some time with her, you know, before her surgery."

"Okay, I guess I'll see you then."

"Jenna, I'm sorry to drag you into this, but I really didn't know what else to do."

"No, it's totally fine. I'm glad I can help. But C.J., how's Willow doing?"

"She's pretty banged up, and she . . . well, you two can talk about the rest of it when Willow gets there. But it's not just the physical, Jenna; she's struggling emotionally. She's embarrassed, humiliated, and blames herself. Willow's convinced it's her fault for letting things get so out of control."

"That's ridiculous! I don't care what she did or did not do, nothing justifies violence. Her boyfriend had no right to use her as a punching bag. No matter the circumstances."

"I know, but Willow's struggling. Maybe if she hears if from someone other than me, she'll believe it."

"Well, I'll do what I can to help.

"Thanks, Jenna, we'll see you Thursday."

FORTY-FOUR

When Ashley woke up, fear clutched at her lungs, making it hard to breathe. Slowly, she reached for her nightgown where it lay on the floor by the nightstand and slipped from bed. With her gown pressed against her chest, she stood at the foot of the bed and watched Austin sleep. His hair was disheveled, his rugged chin shadowed with scruff, and his bronzed chest raised and lowered with every breath. It was hypnotic, watching him breathe.

She felt peace.

Strength.

Hope.

A plea rushed from her lips. "Please, God, don't take this from me," she whispered, then hurried to the bathroom before her first tear could fall. She sat on the lid of the toilet, clutching a towel to her face, silencing the sobs racking her body. She was scared. Terrified. She had told herself for weeks that her strength was in the Lord—He would see her through—no matter the outcome. But the last few days had been like a dream; a fairytale. It gave her a glimpse at what she had to look forward to with Austin, and she didn't want to miss out on a single second.

She challenged God to show her His might and His mercy, even as she cried with fear. After a few minutes, she splashed some water on her face, and found her footing. It was the last day for Austin and her to be together before real life took over. She didn't want to be sad or pensive.

She wanted it to be perfect.

The day was a complete bust, and C.J. had no one to blame but himself.

After spending the previous night scanning the Internet for information, he was determined to convince Willow to see a doctor. When he brought her breakfast, he explained to her most every article he'd read, recommended seeing a doctor to ensure a miscarriage was complete. When Willow refused to listen, he'd told her about the article titled, *Fever. Infection. Infertility.*

Unfortunately, his scare tactics backfired.

Instead of conceding, Willow kicked him out of her room, but not before informing him 'it was her body, and he had no right lecturing her on what she should do with it.' She punctuated her argument by slamming the door in his face and refusing to talk to him further.

He was beyond irritated and ready to read her the riot act but refused to speak to her through a closed door. Figuring she just needed some time to cool off, he left her alone for the afternoon. He didn't push at lunchtime when she didn't answer him or unlock the door; he just left the tray of food on the floor outside her door and told her it was there when she got hungry. He did the same at dinner, even though his patience was running thin.

However, when she refused to talk to him at the end of the night, he had reached his limit. He wasn't only angry, he was hurt. Everything he'd done in the last seventy-two hours was out of concern for her safety and well-being, but she was treating him like he was part of the problem. All he'd wanted to do was protect her, help her, see her whole again. Sure . . . maybe he hadn't handled every conversation perfectly, but it wasn't like he was an expert in miscarriages, crazy boyfriends, or physically and emotionally battered women.

It was not fair.

He lay in bed, staring at the ceiling, letting his anger fester. Then he remembered the way Willow looked huddled on the floor of her bedroom, beaten and broken. Hearing her painful cries as her body contracted and bled. The sadness in her eyes at the realization she'd just lost her baby. The terror in her voice when she spoke about Steven, afraid of what he would do next.

His anger turned to anguish. His self-pity to a self-imposed reprimand. *You selfish, jerk! Thinking about yourself, your feelings. Fairness? You're worried about fairness? What part of what happened to Willow is fair?*

He may have witnessed a nightmare, but Willow had lived it. Every blow. Every contraction. Every terrifying moment.

I need to fix this before she does something stupid.

All he could think about was Willow nixing their plan for tomorrow and trying to do something on her own. The thought of her going back to her place, or Steven finding her at one of her friends, made him want to puke.

He didn't care what he had to do. He would apologize, tell her he was completely out of line, anything to ensure she didn't do something desperate.

Hopefully, she would put her safety before her pride.

~®~

Ashley could not have asked for a more perfect day.

They had walked the beach, visited the pier, strolled through shops, ate cracked crab, and watched as surfers caressed the waves.

Heading back to the beach house, the bright orange sky was just beginning to fragment into multicolor shades of sunset, and the slightest breeze played with her hair. Holding her sandals, so she could feel the moist sand press between her toes, she walked hand in hand with Austin.

"Today was perfect," she said, smiling up at him. "Except for the fifty times you stopped someone to take our picture."

Feigning surprise, he pressed his hand to his chest. "Whatever do you mean?"

"Oh my gosh, Austin, the lady in the souvenir shop, the man fishing on the pier, our waiter, and every jogger who ran by us."

"*Every* jogger? Don't you think you're exaggerating, just a little?"

She laughed. "Not one bit."

"Well, excuse me for wanting pictures of what we did on our honeymoon."

Ashley raised her eyebrow.

"Ashley Anne. . . you know what I mean."

"I hope so, because I think the other stuff is considered illegal."

Austin laughed. "You brazen woman, you." He reached down to the water swirling at his feet and splashed her. She squeezed her eyes shut and stiffened her shoulders. "Austin Carrington Taylor, you stop that this minute or—"

"Or what?" He splashed her again.

"I'll retaliate."

He laughed, inciting her even more.

"Oh, you don't think I will?" she taunted.

"Oh, you will. You're just no match for me." He splashed her again.

"Is that a veiled threat?" Ashley bent down, tossing a handful of water at him.

"Oh, there's nothing veiled about it, sweetheart. It's a downright challenge."

Austin sprinted toward her, but she quickly darted up the beach. When he caught up with her, he grabbed her around the waist, and softly tackled her to the sand. She laughed as he removed the straw hat she was wearing, laid in on the sand, then placed his phone inside it. Ashley rolled beneath him, saw both humor and determination in his eyes and realized what her lot would be. So she resorted to begging.

"Okay, Austin you're right."

He held her arms as she squirmed.

"I admit it, Austin, I'm no match for you."

He pulled her to her feet, chuckling. "Good, I'm glad we agree on that." Then he tossed her up into his arms and clutched her wiggling legs.

"Austin, don't! Please don't!" Ashley couldn't contain her laughter even though she knew she was completely at his mercy. "Austin, you win; you win!" He continued toward the water, undeterred. Ashley clasped her hands behind his neck and held on tight. "Okay, Austin, if I go in, you're going in with me!"

They both were laughing as he walked into the surf up to his knees, his rolled-up khaki pants turning a darker shade of tan.

"Okay, do you want me to count you off—so you can be prepared—or just drop you?"

"Austin Taylor, don't you dare!"

"Okay, counting it is." Austin started swaying. "One . . . two . . . three!" Austin let go of Ashley, but true to her word, she didn't let go of him.

He stumbled into the water, landing right on top of her. They laughed like they had never laughed before. Austin rolled to the side and sat up on his knees while Ashley got handfuls of water and tossed them at him. They wrestled and splashed as the sun continued to set, carrying on like children without a care in the world. Finally, when they stopped and caught their breath. Austin stood and extended his hand to Ashley. "Are you ready to call it quits?"

"Sure."

When Ashley gripped his hand, she tried to pull him back down, but Austin was ready for her. He pulled her up so hard, she smacked right into his chest, almost sending them tumbling backwards.

"You know me too well."

"And I'm so thankful I do." Smiling, he walked up the beach and retrieved her hat and his phone.

Ashley turned to the ocean and took a deep breath, inhaling the memory. She closed her eyes and tipped her head, letting the setting sun warm her face. She piled her hair on top of her head, and felt the wind pull at the hem of her dress. She wanted to remember this day for the rest of her life. She wanted to come back on their first anniversary and do it all over again.

She wanted time. Lots of time.

"You're stunning."

Ashley turned around to see Austin standing with his phone raised.

"That's not fair! You can't take a picture of me like this! I look like a drown rat!"

"Too late." He shrugged.

Teasingly, she started to march up the beach without him. "You, Mr. Taylor, can walk by yourself, and think about your behavior."

"Okay, but from where I'm walking, that dress of yours is pretty see-through. Are you sure you want to punish me so severely?"

Ashley brought her hands up to cover her chest and swung around to face him. "Austin, don't just laugh, give me your sweater."

"But I'll be cold. Besides, it's wet and you'll—"

"Austin!"

"Come on," he laughed. "It's not like you're naked. I'm sure no one will notice. Just walk faster."

"Austin, you have two options, either give me your sweater, or you'll be on the couch for the night."

"Nah, no deal. You wouldn't punish yourself like that. However, I will give you my sweater for a kiss." Austin pulled the navy-blue sweater over his head, the muscles in his stomach flexing, against the cold breeze, then he lowered it over her head, trapping her arms inside. He took his payment, wrapped his arm around her shoulders and walked back to the beach house.

By the time they reached the stairs, they were both cold. The sun was completely gone, and a light breeze had come up from the shore. Shivering, they hurried up the steps that led to the deck and peeled away their layers of wet clothing. Austin removed the lid from the hot tub and fired up the jets. They both sank into the warmth of the rolling water and rested their heads against the foam siding. They turned to each other simultaneously and broke out in uncontrolled laughter. A whimsical night in the water would be the last time they would be able to display such reckless abandon—for a little while anyway.

Tomorrow, they would be heading home.

Back to reality.

Back to the unknown.

FORTY-FIVE

Thursday had come.

Ashley stood on the deck of the beach house trying to soak up the scents and sounds that would always remind her of this time with Austin. The distinct smell of the sea and the sand. The light hush from the softly crashing waves. The cry of the gulls overhead. It had been the perfect honeymoon, but now, they had to pack up their memories and prepare themselves for what was to come.

Glancing at the gloomy gray sky, Ashley sighed. It was overcast and cold; the first clouds they'd seen all week. It seemed fitting that even the weather shared in their somber mood.

Ashley and Austin were silent as they packed, neither of them sharing what was obviously on their minds. They passed each other a few times as they crisscrossed the bedroom but didn't say a word. Finally, Austin reached out to Ashley and pulled her into an embrace. "God is bigger than this, Ash. You know that, right?"

Ashley kept her face pressed to his chest, holding on to him like her very life depended on it. "Will you remind me of that when I have my head over a bowl?"

"Absolutely. I'll even hold your bowl for you." Austin squeezed her tight and held her.

Ashley tried so hard to absorb his strength, knowing she would need it in the days to come.

After Austin put their luggage in the car, Ashley took one final glance at their ocean retreat, praying they would be back next year to celebrate their anniversary. She looked to the ocean. The waves had turned tumultuous, but the sky had split open, sharp rays of light slicing through the clouds.

Please, God, be that for me. Slice the darkness. Shine your light. Give me hope and strength to endure what lies ahead.

C.J. heard the rattle of pipes overhead, his cue Willow was up and moving around. He'd been awake for hours, unable to sleep with the merry-go-round of thoughts circling through his mind. His mom coming home. Her surgery tomorrow. Austin being a permanent fixture in their lives. Willow's state of mind. Her willingness to go to Austin's after their blow-up yesterday. Keeping her safe from Steven. Pretending everything was okay.

It was a lot of mental juggling.

Climbing the steps two at a time, he slipped into his mom's room to get some clothes and other things for Willow to take with her to Austin's. He had washed and returned what Willow had already worn and hopefully put them back in all the right places.

Being careful not to mess up his mother's drawers, C.J. intentionally pulled items from the bottom of the stacks, hoping his mom wouldn't notice anything was missing. Entering her bathroom, C.J. looked at the empty boxes in the cupboard and quickly wrote down brand names and box colors, so he could replace them before his mom got home. Stepping to the back of her walk-in closet, C.J. slid a few hangers aside before stopping on a floral sun dress. He didn't recognize it and figured since he'd found it sandwiched between a winter coat and an old bathrobe, it wouldn't be anything his mom would miss. He pulled it from the hanger and lapped it over his arm. With his arms full, he hurried to his room and pulled an old duffel bag from the floor of his closet, then returned to Willow's room.

With his ear pressed against the door, C.J. heard the shower still running. Trying the handle, he was relieved to find it unlocked. Slipping inside, he laid everything on Willow's bed, then went back downstairs to finish breakfast.

Slumping against the kitchen counter, he hated that everything he just did, and his plans for the rest of the day, revolved around deceiving his mom, even though he and Austin had agreed it was for her own good. They weren't deceiving her as much as they were protecting her. They would tell her about Willow's situation when the timing was right—but before her surgery was not that time.

"I'll just be glad when all of this is over," he mumbled to himself as he fired up the griddle.

But when would that be?

C.J. knew they hadn't seen the last of Steven. There was no way his narcissistic ego would allow Willow to walk out on him without retribution. He would want the final say.

That's what C.J. was afraid of.

Steven was clearly psychotic and extremely violent. He'd thought nothing of beating Willow to the point of unconsciousness over her belittling comments. What lengths would he go to, to punish her for walking out on him?

C.J. didn't like the answers filling his thoughts and had to shake off the fear building inside him. *Willow is safe here, and she'll be safe at Austin's with Jenna.* He had to believe this, or he would drive himself crazy with worry.

Willow stood under the cascading water, allowing the warm shower to soothe her pain. She had hoped to feel better today since she would have to travel; unfortunately, she still felt achy and sore.

When she emerged from the bathroom, she saw a duffel bag and a pretty floral dress lying across the bed. It made her cringe. She had been horrible to C.J. yesterday. Absolutely horrible. When all he was trying to do is help.

She'd always known he was one of the good guys.

C.J. was nice to everyone, his staff included. When he was with his students, he used gentle words and showed an extreme amount of patience, especially when working with the younger ones, and he was just as kind with his staff. He was a hard worker—who gave one hundred and ten percent—and expected the same from anyone who worked for him, but he was fair.

Why couldn't I have gotten involved with someone more like him?

After getting dressed, Willow tried to straighten the room as best she could then carefully walked downstairs, pleased she'd been able to make it all the way on her own. It gave her hope that her body was recovering.

"Hey, you made it down all by yourself. That's a good sign." C.J. smiled as she carefully took a seat on one of the barstools and rested her arms on the counter top.

"I'm sorry about yesterday, Willow," C.J. blurted out. "I had no business telling you—"

"No, C.J., I'm the one who's sorry. I was rude and belligerent. I don't know what I was thinking. As they say, beggars can't be choosers, so I need to take what I can get." When she saw his shoulders sag in disappointment, she groaned. "I'm sorry; I didn't mean it like that. You've been amazing. I don't deserve a friend like you. You're going through so much with your mom's health issues and Austin. It's not fair that you've had to put up with my crap, too. I'm sorry I've put you in the middle of all this."

"Don't be sorry, Willow, just don't push me away, okay?" His words were firm, but his eyes were soft.

"Deal. I will try to keep my tantrums to a minimum." She smiled, hoping he would do the same. When she saw the faintest smirk, she asked. "So, what is the plan for today?"

"Well, I talked to Jenna," C.J. said as he slid a plate of pancakes smothered in syrup in front of her, then poured more battered on the griddle. "She's going to meet us at Austin's at nine. I'll get you settled there, do some shopping to replace the things in Mom's room, then stay home and visit with her and Austin for the evening." C.J. plated his pancakes and doused them in syrup. "Tomorrow, I'll go to the hospital in the morning and stay until Mom is out of surgery. When I know she's doing okay, I'll come back and get you."

Willow pushed her pancakes around on the plate after taking only a few bites. "What did you tell Jenna?"

"I told her your boyfriend beat you up, and you were in pretty bad shape."

"Did you tell her about the miscarriage?"

"No, I didn't think it was my place. I told her you didn't want to be by yourself right now and could use the company. She was more than willing to help out."

Willow took a few more bites, while C.J. inhaled his pancakes standing up. Leaning against the kitchen counter, he looked at her and asked, "Are you going to be okay?"

She nodded.

"You sure?"

"I'll be fine." She forced herself to smile.

"Okay. I'm going to make sure the house is straightened before we leave. Why don't you rest down here? I'll only be a few minutes."

Willow sat on the little loveseat in the front room and stared out the window—anxious about what the day would bring—wondering what Steven was doing. He hadn't even tried to contact her. Willow didn't know if she should be relieved or worried. Deep down, she did not think Steven would let her go that easy, but maybe he was done with her. *Maybe he doesn't care enough about me to risk getting into trouble. Maybe he's afraid I'll involve the police. Maybe he . . .* Willow's eyelids fluttered. She forced them open and sat up straighter, not wanting to fall asleep. Unfortunately, her body proved uncooperative.

Willow heard her name, felt a hand on her shoulder. She recoiled, waiting for a blow to follow, but it didn't. Opening her eyes, she saw C.J. standing next to her. She exhaled the breath she was holding. *It was only a nightmare.*

"Sorry, I didn't mean to startle you," C.J. said, a painful look on his face.

"It's okay. I must have fallen asleep." She took a few deep breaths, urging her heart back into a normal rhythm.

"I just wanted to know what shop your car was at, so I could contact them and authorize the work."

"I don't have the money to fix it, at least not right now." She saw the I'll-take-care-of-it look in C.J.'s eyes. "And before you say anything else, the answer is, no. You're not going to pay for it."

"But it's no big deal."

"It is to me."

"Then consider it a loan. You can pay me back later."

"I'm not going to borrow—"

"Be practical, Willow," he cut her off. "It needs to be fixed. You might as well get it done while you're at Austin's."

She knew he was right. No matter what her plans were for the future, she needed her car. "Okay, but I'm going to pay you back out of my next check. In full."

"We can discuss it la—"

"There's nothing to discuss. I'm going to pay you back as soon as I get paid."

"Fine. Just give me the name of the shop."

She knew he only agreed to shut her up, but that was fine. She would pay him back as soon as she got paid. Every dime. "Gibson's Auto on DeSoto."

C.J. disappeared into the kitchen and came back a short time later.

"What did they say?"

"It should be fixed by Monday." He offered her a smile. "Are you ready to go?"

She nodded, then slowly got to her feet. C.J. picked up her duffel bag from where it sat on the floor. Walking out to his truck, Willow noticed C.J. glancing from side to side and out toward the street.

He was expecting trouble.

Tossing the duffel onto the backseat, C.J. held her door until she was inside. He scanned their surroundings again as he walked around to the driver's side of the truck. Then, with an encouraging smile, he drove through the gates.

FORTY-SIX

Steven slammed his hand against the steering wheel the second he saw Willow sitting in the passenger seat. "You lying little slut!" he shouted as the truck drove by. He waited for a few cars to pass before pulling from the wooded area that had served as the perfect camouflage. "You're going to pay for this, Willow. So help me, you and your moron boyfriend are going to pay." He followed at a distance, even though he wanted to get right behind the truck and slam it into oncoming traffic.

"You're crazy if you think you're going to get away with two-timing me," he mumbled, swearing and cussing as he followed them onto the freeway. "No one two-times Steven Boyer. Not even a cheap piece of trash like you." The angrier he got, the harder his foot pressed on the accelerator until he was almost parallel with the back bumper of the truck. Immediately, he backed off and dropped behind a large SUV, chastising himself for not staying in control.

With his focus on the pickup a few car lengths in front of him, Steven thought of the many ways he could exact his revenge. *Willow will be easy.* He thought to himself as he stayed hidden in the flow of traffic. *The things I could do to her.* His pulse raced at the thought of it. "And you, cowboy . . . I'm going to introduce you to a whole new level of pain. Believe me, you'll think twice before stepping out with someone else's woman again." He laughed, looking forward to their impending meeting.

Forty minutes later, Steven pulled to the curb; a lifted Escalade offering the perfect concealment. From there, he watched as the cowboy stopped at the entrance to an exclusive housing development known as *The Estates*. An older man in a gray uniform leaned out of the guard shack and talked with him. At the same time, a blond woman pulled up on the opposite side of the shack, waved, then got out of her car and walked to where the guard was talking to the cowboy. After a few minutes of conversation, the uniformed man wrote something on a clipboard, then allowed the arm of the gate to swing up.

As the truck disappeared through the gates, Steven quickly devised a plan to get some much-needed information. He pulled across the street but stopped short of the guard shack. Immediately, the uniformed man seemed suspicious, but Steven just smiled, knowing he could finesse his way past the middle-aged rent-a-cop. As he approached the small security booth, Steven zeroed in on the glassed-in bulletin board. *A Night of Jazz. Join us for an evening of music and dancing. The Equestrian Center, Saturday—*

"Can I help you?" the guard asked in a no-nonsense tone.

Steven looked up. "Yes. I'm so sorry to be a bother, but I guess I got a bit turned around. Would you happen to have a map I can borrow?"

The guard took in Steven's tailored suit and Italian loafers, then smiled. *Dress for success I always say.* It was the exact reaction Steven had hoped for. He'd seen it time and time again. When you appear to be a person of affluence, people tended to be more trusting.

The guard unfolded a map across the small surface area in the little outpost, and Steven stepped up to get a closer look. He acted as if he was viewing the map, but his eyes darted around, looking for anything that could be of help. He spied the clipboard hanging on a nail labeled 'visitors'. Then saw the license number of the truck Willow was riding in written on it.

"Where were you headed, young man?" The security guard asked. "Maybe I can be of help."

"Ah, there it is," Steven haphazardly pointed to the map. "I see where I went wrong. Hey, thanks, buddy, you've been a great help." Before further conversation ensued, Steven jogged back to his car and U-turned around. *All I have to do is get my license plate number on that list. Then I'll be in.*

Before pulling into traffic, a white van with a pool cleaning emblem on the side panel turned in front of him and drove up to the gate. Steven watched in his rearview mirror as the driver spoke with the security guard. After the guard referred to his clipboard, the automatic arm lifted, and the driver proceeded through the gate.

Steven smiled.

Pulling his phone from his pocket, he dialed. "Carlos, yeah it's me, Steven. Hey, I need a favor and I thought you might be the one to help me. Does your cousin still do landscaping in *The Estates*? That's what I thought. Okay, this is what I need."

Jenna watched in her rearview mirror as C.J. followed her into Austin's circular driveway. He hurried around to the passenger side of the truck and helped Willow out. Jenna couldn't help but notice how slow Willow walked and how she braced herself against C.J.'s arm.

Hurrying to unlock the front door, Jenna stood in the entryway waiting for them. Willow's head was down, so Jenna couldn't see the extent of her injuries, but the stress on C.J.'s face was clear.

Then Willow looked up.

Jenna muffled a gasp, trying hard not to show shock or alarm, but inside, she felt like she was going to be ill. Willow's discolored complexion and the swelling under her eye made her face look lopsided and a bit distorted. Jenna didn't consider herself naive. She knew physical violence and abuse against women was a problem in today's society, but seeing it in vivid black, blue, and purple made it all too real.

"Do you want to lay down? Or would you feel better sitting in the living room or even on the patio?" Jenna tried to sound normal, like she was welcoming a friend for a weekend stay, not someone who should probably be in the hospital.

C.J. looked at Willow and waited for her answer.

"The living room would be fine," she said quietly.

The three of them walked slowly to the sofas, then took a seat. "I'm sorry to involve you in this, Jenna," Willow said. "I hardly know you, and here I am making a great second impression."

"Willow, what happened is not a reflection of who you are. I'm just glad I could help, and that you thought enough of me to call." Jenna glanced from Willow to C.J.

"C.J., you probably need to get back. Willow will be fine with me; I promise." Jenna gave him what she hoped was a reassuring smile.

C.J. turned to Willow and grasped her hand to get her attention. "Remember . . . no heroics. You and Jenna have my cell number. If you need anything—anything at all—just call me, okay?"

"I'll be fine, C.J., really I will."

"Okay. I'll check in with you after Mom gets settled." Without even thinking, C.J. placed a kiss to the top of Willow's head as he got to his feet. He did it instinctively. A reflex.

Willow looked up at him a little startled.

"I'm sorry, Willow, I don't know where that came from."

"It's okay. I know you're just trying to make me feel safe."

Jenna walked him to the door.

"I think she is past the worst of it," he whispered as he opened the front door, then turned back to Jenna. "But please pay attention to how she looks and how she acts. Willow won't say anything if she starts feeling worse. She's embarrassed enough that we had to involve you. But if your instincts tell you something is wrong, or something has changed, call me right away."

"Don't worry, C.J., everything is going to be fine."

He felt uneasy as he pulled from Austin's driveway. In a sense, he felt like he was abandoning Willow. He'd come to feel personally responsible for her safety. Even though she was somewhere Steven would never find her, the anxiousness he felt soured his stomach.

Willow watched as Jenna and C.J. exchanged a few words by the front door, then Jenna walked back into the room with a less than believable smile on her face. "Would you like something to eat?" she asked.

"No, we had breakfast before we left."

"Good. I'm glad. I mean . . .that you have an appetite, that is. Not that I wouldn't want to fix you something to eat. Because if you're hungry . . . just name it. I can fix any—"

"No. I'm fine. Really."

"Okay." She smiled sheepishly.

Willow sat with her hands in her lap and her eyes closed, hoping Jenna would just go about her day and pretend she wasn't even there. However, when she opened her eyes, Jenna was sitting in the overstuffed chairs across from her, a perplexed look on her face. Willow knew Jenna probably had a hundred questions but was too polite to ask.

After more silence, Willow decided to take the initiative and break the silence between them.

"Jenna, I know you must have a hundred questions. Since I involved you in this mess, it's only fair that I answer them. Ask what you want. I won't be offended; I promise." Willow pulled her feet up under her and laid a hand on her stomach. Jenna glanced at

Willow's stomach and then back to her face but said nothing.

"Okay, I'll just tell you what happened." She took a long breath then began to explain. "I should have left Steven the first time he hit me, but I didn't. I believed him when he said he was sorry and swore to me, it would never happen again. Everything was fine for about a week or so. He brought me flowers, took me to a beautiful restaurant, even sat through a musical—something he absolutely hated. It was like we were dating again. Then, about a month ago, he came home drunk after one of his business deals fell through." Willow felt her heart rate accelerate at the memory and needed to take a deep cleansing breath to calm herself.

"You don't have to tell me any of this," Jenna said, looking close to tears. "It's really none of my business."

She continued anyway.

"That night, I told him drinking never solved anything. He slapped me and told me to mind my own business. After that, the hitting and shoving happened more often. As the abuse escalated so did his threats. He reminded me over and over again, if I ever left him or told anyone about our *relationship*, I would be sorry. I believed him. I was afraid to stay, but terrified to leave. Then . . . when C.J. brought me home from the wedding, Steven accused me of cheating on him and beat me up pretty bad. Up until that point, he'd been careful not to bruise me where it was noticeable. But this time, there was no way I could hide the bruises or swelling. When I called in sick, C.J. knew something was wrong. I told him to let it go, and I would explain it to him later. Then, Steven took my savings—every penny I put aside for tuition—and blew it on a new car. It was the last straw for me. I said things to Steven that pushed him over the edge. I thought he was going to kill me. Instead, he beat me unconscious."

"No!" Jenna gasped, a tear streaking down her cheek.

She shook her head and continued. "When I came to, I didn't know what to do; so I called C.J. and he took me to the ranch. I know I should have gone to the police, but I was afraid Steven would retaliate—not only against me, but against C.J., the ranch, maybe even Ashley. Steven also has the uncanny knack of always landing on his feet. I was afraid he would turn everything around and somehow get the police on his side."

"But, Willow, you have the bruises and injuries to prove what he did. Even if he accused you of cheating, he still assaulted you. The police would have no choice but to lock him up."

"But it's my word against his. He could tell the police anything. It doesn't matter that I have bruises; it doesn't prove he's the one who gave them to me. I'm afraid he'll sweet-talk his way out of the charges, then come after me or C.J. or both of us. I can't take that chance. This is my mess. I can't let C.J. or Ashley pay for my mistakes."

"But, Willow, you can't let him—"

"I know I need to do something!" Willow snapped, then softened her tone. "But I have to figure out what that is. With Ashley's surgery and her new husband, there's no way I can stay at the ranch and put this on her. Obviously, Austin agrees, or he wouldn't have allowed me to stay here."

Jenna sat back against the sofa cushions—her shoulders slumped—clearly trying to digest all she'd been told. Then she asked, "Is it painful for you to walk or are you just weak?"

"Both. My muscles are sore, and I've lost a lot of—" She paused, then realized she needed to be straight. From what she could tell, Jenna seemed pretty mature for her age and deserved the truth. After all, she was helping her out even though they were almost complete strangers.

"Jenna, I was pregnant."

Shock registered on her face.

"I miscarried and lost a lot of blood. So, I'm pretty weak and the cramping hasn't gone away completely."

"Have you seen a doctor?"

"No, I'll be fine; I just need to rest and recover."

"A miscarriage is nothing to fool around with, Willow. If your body doesn't completely . . ." She cleared her throat. ". . . completely, expel everything, you're putting yourself at risk. I could make an appointment for you where I work?"

"Where do you work?"

"I help out at a doctor's office as a receptionist and file clerk. Since I want to pursue a career in medicine when I graduate, Nancy is letting me intern a few hours a week. She's an Ob/Gyn, so I know what I'm talking about. She sees girls all the time after miscarriages or botched . . . aah . . . other medical conditions. She's really great. Nancy has a heart for young girls and volunteers a lot of her time with troubled youth."

Willow laughed, sarcastically. "Is that how you see me? As a pathetic, screwed up girl, who needs an intervention or hand holding? I'm a woman, Jenna. And even though it's my fault for not leaving Steven sooner, I don't need just one more person passing judgment on me."

Jenna visibly wilted. "That's not what I meant at all," she whispered, as her eyes welled with tears. "In fact, I meant the exact opposite. The last thing I would ever call Nancy is judgmental. Her number one priority is the well-being of her patients. She offers advice if they ask for it but doesn't push her beliefs on anyone. And if you don't want to talk, she won't pressure you. She has a 'no questions asked' policy. She just wants to be able to provide a safe environment where girls . . . and women can be treated without fear of being exposed, accused, or reprimanded."

Willow hated herself for being so rude to Jenna when all she was trying to do is help. "I'm sorry I snapped at you, and I appreciate you wanting to help. I'll think about it, but right now, I just want to rest."

"Okay, but you shouldn't wait too long. You could get really sick."

Willow closed her eyes, pulled the afghan from the back of the couch, and draped it over her shoulders and legs, hoping Jenna would get the hint.

"You're right. You need your rest," Jenna said, "I'm going to do some laps in the pool. Call me if you need anything."

After hearing Jenna walk away, Willow allowed herself to relax. Even though she'd snapped at Jenna, she found talking to her easier than talking to C.J. Of course, Jenna had two things going for her that C.J. lacked.

First—she was a girl.

Second—she wasn't her boss.

FORTY-SEVEN

Ashley was quiet on the way home, spending most of the time staring out the passenger window, looking like she was a hundred miles away. Occasionally, Austin would reach over and squeeze her hand. It expressed what he wanted without the need for words.

"Ash, I'd like to know more about your surgery, but if you don't want to talk about it, I can ask the doctor tomorrow."

She sat up a little straighter and cleared her throat. "I can tell you the basics, or at least what I remember. When Dr. Allen first told me the kind of surgery he wanted to do, I went home and Googled it to death. I probably read a hundred articles, each one explaining things slightly different than the last. If you want a more definitive answer you need to ask Dr.—"

He squeezed her hand again and tried to give her an encouraging smile. "Just tell me what you know."

"Okay. It's called a laparoscopic assisted vaginal hysterectomy."

"Wow. That's a mouthful. How about in layman's terms?"

"It's better than an abdominal hysterectomy. Well, not necessarily better, but easier. Actually, it's not easier either; it takes longer. The surgery, that is. But my recovery time will be easier. Not easier, faster. Only a few weeks instead of—"

"Ashley," he chuckled at her ninety mile an hour explanation. "I'm having a hard time keeping up."

"That's all right; I'm confusing myself. I mean, I know what I want to say, I'm just having a hard time saying it."

"What is the doctor going to do? Tell me that."

"He'll remove everything, the uterus, cervix, ovaries, tubes. If he's concerned with the possibility of remaining cancer cells, he'll remove tissue and have it biopsied. If he feels I need radiation, I'll go back in a couple of weeks. He'll decide how many treatments depending on what the labs tell him. That's why doing it laparoscopically is better. My recovery time will be faster, so I can get the radiation done sooner."

"Will you have to stay in the hospital for the radiation treatments?"

"No, it's considered an outpatient procedure."

"Isn't it going to be hard on your body to go back and forth? I thought your recovery time from the surgery would take weeks."

"Like I said, doing it laparoscopically will make my recovery time faster. And since doctors encourage a low level of activity to help you regain stamina after surgery, going back and forth to the cancer center shouldn't be that big a deal. I mean, I know I'm going to be fatigued, but if my prognosis is good, I might not have to do radiation at all."

Austin asked a few more questions but could tell Ashley was getting into her head and needed a change in topic.

"Do you want to stop and get something to eat? You said you wouldn't be able to eat after lunch, so it's now or never. Name it. It doesn't have to be healthy. Mexican food. Ice cream. Pancakes. Popcorn. You can even order a whole plate of french fries, and I won't steal a single one." Austin tried lightening the mood, but Ashley continued to gaze out the passenger window.

"I really don't have much of an appetite. Besides, if we keep going, we should be home around noon. If I'm hungry then, I'll have some broth."

Austin was quiet, but inside, a riot of thoughts raced through his head. He started to pray, hoping to calm himself.

"It seems fitting, does it?"

He turned to Ashley. "What does?"

"The ocean."

They were skirting the Pacific, the sky still overcast. Austin looked to see gray, turbulent water. Churning and swirling.

"It's amazing how the sea reflects the stages of life. Sometimes it's calm and tranquil. Offering enjoyment. Other times it's dark and unsettling, hinting at the turmoil that rests just below the surface."

"You're going to be fine, Ashley." Austin once again reached for her hand and gave it a squeeze. "No amount of waves are going to keep you down. Besides, I am going to be right there, helping you keep your head above water."

FORTY-EIGHT

After C.J. got the house back to normal, he went to check in with Billy.

Billy explained that he planned on making himself scarce during Ashley's brief stay. He was no good at hiding his feelings and was afraid he would say something he shouldn't. Sarah was still answering the phones in the office, so C.J. went to thank her for coming in on such short notice. Sarah was a great temp who worked for them whenever his mom went on an extended movie shoot. Sarah was in her thirties, newly married, and didn't want to be strapped to a full-time job. She and her husband wanted to start a family right away, so she only worked part-time.

"Hi, Sarah. I just came by to thank you for filling in on such short notice."

"No problem, C.J., I would do anything for your mom, but I must say, I was shocked to find out she was on her honeymoon. I didn't even know she was seeing someone, and hearing she had cancer, that was another shocker."

"I see the rumor mill is alive and well."

"Bad news travels just as fast as good. How is she doing? This must have really thrown her for a loop."

"Her surgery is tomorrow. I guess we'll find out more then."

"And where's Willow? Did she already leave for that veterinary school? I thought that wasn't until the first of the year?"

"No. She's just a little under the weather."

"Wow, bad timing for you? I guess it was a good thing I was available."

"You have no idea." He smiled. "Well, I have some things to get caught up on before mom gets home."

Excusing himself, he went into his mom's office and turned on her computer. The payroll information was already keyed in, but he needed the check forms in order to print it out. He chuckled. His mom would be shocked to see how much he knew about the business side of the ranch. She just assumed he never listened when it came to the details. He listened. He just didn't want the responsibility.

After a few minor glitches, he had payroll printed, signed, and ready to go. He handed the checks to Sarah and asked her to pass them out, but not before thanking her again for filling in. As he walked back to the house, he saw Austin pull into the driveway. He waited until Austin was parked, then went over to the passenger door and helped his mom out. He gave her a hug and asked, "How are you doing?"

"I'm doing fine. It's inevitable now, so I just want to get it over with."

C.J. looked at Austin, who signaled him to help his mom into the house. "You two go ahead. I'll get the luggage."

He led his mom into the great room. She immediately walked over to her favorite spot on the couch and sank into the cushions, drawing her legs up under her. She gazed out the picture-window that looked over the ranch and smiled.

After her swim, Jenna stood in the kitchen trying to decide what to make for lunch. The discoloration on Willow's cheek was obvious, as was the swelling and small cut on her lip. *I need to make something soft, and not too difficult to eat.*

Scrolling her phone for options, she found a recipe for a crust-less quiche. After making sure she had all the needed ingredients, Jenna went to work dicing peppers and grating cheese. Once the mixture was poured into the ramekins and placed in the oven, Jenna checked on Willow. Seeing that she was asleep, Jenna took a seat at the dining room table and clicked through her phone to the book she had downloaded earlier that morning.

Even though the novel was the latest release from her favorite author, Jenna could not concentrate well enough to read—not with a bruised and battered Willow sleeping in the other room. After glancing at the time every few minutes and re-reading the same page for the third time, Jenna laid her phone on the table and checked on Willow again, but the only thing on the couch was the rumpled afghan.

While looking at the pool and patio area, motion in her peripheral caught Jenna's attention. Willow was exiting the hall bathroom and walking toward her.

"Lunch should be ready in about ten minutes. Are you doing okay?" Jenna asked.

"Fine. Thank you." Willow sat back down on the couch.

Jenna returned to the kitchen and waited for the oven timer to go off. Pulling from the oven the cookie sheet that held the ramekins, she sat them on the stove top to cool. "Do you want to eat at the dining room table or in the living room?" Jenna yelled as she closed the oven.

~Ⓡ~

"The dining room is fine."

Jenna swung around and gasped. "You startled me. I didn't know you were right behind me."

"Sorry. I didn't mean to sneak up on you. I just wanted to see if there was anything I could do to help?"

"Sure, why don't you ice some glasses. I'll have tea; you can pick out whatever you want."

Willow watched as Jenna carefully set the black ramekins on deep red plates then disappeared into the dining room. When she returned and picked up the tray of sliced fruit sitting on the counter top, Willow followed Jenna to the dining room and placed their tall pilsner glasses on the table. She took a seat across from Jenna, who smiled and asked, "Do you mind if I say grace?"

"No, not at all."

"Dear Lord Jesus, we come before you now with thankful hearts."

The thought chilled Willow because she was anything but thankful.

"We're thankful because you kept Willow safe through her ordeal and allowed C.J. to be such a blessing to her in this most difficult time. We ask that You restore her heart. Help her to see that though life is difficult and sometimes beyond what we can comprehend, You are there for us to turn to. We also pray for a miracle to take place in Ashley's body. Guide the doctors tomorrow and give them wisdom. I thank You for the amazing gift of love You have given her and Uncle Austin. May they have many years to cultivate it together. Bless this food, may it be tasteful and easy on Willow's stomach. Thank you, Lord. Amen."

Willow felt guilty and self-centered. Jenna's prayer reminded her she wasn't the only one experiencing difficulties. Ashley was going through a monumental trial of her own, and poor C.J. was getting it from all sides. Not only was he worried about his mother's health and her instant relationship with Austin, he had walked smack dab into the mess that was her life and now had to worry about repercussions from Steven.

She realized how selfish she had been, dwelling on her own pain and loss, not even considering that things could have been worse.

Maybe God—in His omniscient, all-powerful way—did protect me. Maybe I should thank Him that I don't have to subject a child to my violent life with Steven as a father. Maybe one day I will, but right now, I'm angry. He could've spared me the physical pain and emotional suffering, but He didn't.

Willow knew she had fallen out of favor with God when she moved in with Steven, but couldn't He see she had no choice? It wasn't what she—

"I guess you're not much of a quiche fan."

Willow realized she'd been ignoring Jenna and was only poking at her food.

"No, no, it's fine. Actually, it's quite good. I just zoned out for a minute." She quickly put a forkful of the custardy mixture into her mouth.

"I'm not going to say I know how you feel," Jenna said as she rolled a grape around on her plate, "because I can't even imagine going through what you did. But I do remember how I felt when a guy I dated got out of hand. He was a few years older than I was, so I was flattered. He seemed like a solid guy. Decent. Polite. We went to a beach party/barbecue and were having a great time. After the party, he drove me to my mom's house, so I could change my clothes. When he realized no one was home, he assaulted me."

Willow flinched, dropping her fork, clanging it against the plate. "Sorry, I didn't mean to do that." She picked it up and placed it on the table. "What did he do?"

"He just assumed I would have sex with him. When I refused, he called me a tease and tried to make me feel guilty. He said if I was willing to wear a skimpy bathing suit in public, he thought he deserved a little more in private. He tried to force himself on me, but I fought back. When he hit me, I think he realized he'd gone too far. He got up and left without saying a word. I never talked to him again."

"Maybe if I had fought harder, sooner . . ." Willow stared at her lap, thinking of all the things she should have done.

"Willow, you can't blame yourself. It was different for me. I was on a date, not in a relationship. You were trapped with nowhere to go. I'm just glad it's over, and you're safe."

Then why didn't she feel safe?

Even though she was at Austin's—a place Steven wouldn't know where to look for her—Willow still had an uneasy feeling she couldn't shake. She knew Steven too well. He wasn't going to give up. *That's not how he operates. He doesn't let go . . . he gets even.*

"Willow, I've got the perfect solution for those aching muscles of yours. Why don't you use the Jacuzzi? It will help eliminate some of the soreness." Willow tried to refuse, but Jenna cut her off. "You can use one of my suits. In fact, I'll even join you." Jenna cleared the table, then led Willow down the hall to her room. Willow looked around and couldn't help but smile.

"Let me guess, pink is your favorite color?"

Jenna laughed. "Well, it used to be. It's been a few years since Uncle Austin fixed this room up especially for me. I don't have the heart to tell him I've kind of out grown it."

Jenna walked to her dresser and pulled out a very expensive designer swimsuit. "Here you go, this one should fit you. In fact, it will probably fit you better than me. I don't have what it takes to fill out the top. You, on the other hand, have a great figure."

Willow cringed, not at all proud of her body or the way she looked.

"Don't you dare feel embarrassed about your body," Jenna scolded. "You're beautiful, and nothing Steven said or did can take that away from you." Jenna handed Willow the suit. "Your stuff is in there," Jenna said, pointing to the room across the hall, "and there's a guest robe in the closet. Help yourself."

Willow disrobed in the adjoining bathroom, and with her back to the mirror, she stepped into the swimsuit and pulled it on. However, as she turned, her reflection caught her attention. She thought about what Jenna said, and looked at herself, trying not to focus on the bruises. She never considered herself beautiful or breathtaking, but at one time, she at least thought of herself as attractive. That was before Steven made her feel so ugly.

She ran her fingers through her long bronze hair, remembering how much she hated it when she was a kid. Back then, her hair was vibrant red, and she had freckles everywhere. But as she got older, her hair turned a deeper red, and she tanned better than most redheads—which helped camouflage the freckles around her nose and cheeks. Her petite figure finally blossomed into something with a few more curves, and even though she never got taller than five-foot three, she really didn't have much to complain about. *Then why wasn't it enough for Steven?*

"Willow, are you okay?" Jenna knocked on the door.

Once again, Willow had disappeared into her own little world, her way of ignoring reality. "Yes. I'll be right out."

She followed Jenna to the spa, but sat on the rim, only dangling her feet in the water.

"I'm so sorry." Jenna cringed, pinching the bridge of her nose. "I didn't even think about the fact that you couldn't go in the water. I was only thinking of your aching muscles."

"It's okay; this feels great. In fact, the steam on my face feels wonderful." The two of them sat for a while without say much. Willow closed her eyes, enjoying the warm, moist air on her skin.

"So, are you attracted to C.J.?"

Jenna's question caught Willow by complete surprise. She answered with a quick, firm, "No!"

"Why? Is he seeing someone?"

"No. Not anymore."

"So, why aren't you interested? I mean, if I saw him day after day, I think I'd be interested."

Willow was thankful her steamed complexion hid the heat of embarrassment. "I guess I've never thought of C.J. in that way. I know that probably sounds strange, but when I first started working at the Circle-R, he was in a pretty serious relationship. Even though I thought he was attractive, I valued Ashley's respect too much and needed the job too badly. I didn't want to do anything to cause waves. When C.J. broke off his relationship with Heather, I was already involved with Steven."

"So, what about now?"

"He's still my boss, Jenna. It wouldn't be right. Besides, he has a pretty high moral standing. I'm sure I've crossed the line on many areas he would find unacceptable." Willow thought for a moment what it would be like to be with someone as decent as C.J. "No . . . he deserves someone special, and I'm sure one day he'll find her." Willow decided to change the subject because it was making her extremely uncomfortable. "So, tell me about your Uncle Austin. He seems like a pretty stand-up guy."

Jenna went on and on, singing the praises of Austin Taylor. She loved him to death; that was obvious in the many adjectives she used to describe him. She explained about her mother and father's divorce, that she didn't get along with her stepdad, and that was why she spent so much time with her uncle. He taught her how to ski, rock climb, and how to drive. He hosted her sleepovers and pool parties, and even took her out on dates. It was obvious, in Jenna's eyes, Austin could do no wrong.

"I couldn't believe it when Uncle Austin told me about Ashley on the way home from the reunion. It's amazing; that's what it is. Absolutely amazing! They have lived within an hour of each other for all these years. I mean, I feel bad for the time they've lost, but it's so romantic that neither of them ever married; that they never fell in love with anyone but each other."

Willow was listening as Jenna continued. When a cramp pulled at her stomach, she tried to conceal her discomfort and casually applied some reverse pressure to her abdomen. Unfortunately, her subtle movement didn't go unnoticed.

"Come on, Willow, let me make an appointment for you tomorrow. I'm sure Nancy would fit you in. I can come home from the hospital after Ashley's surgery, pick you up, take you to the doctor, and then get you settled back at the ranch. As easy as that."

"You're going to the hospital tomorrow? C.J. didn't tell me that." Willow felt a slight pang of fear.

"I'm sorry. I know C.J. was going to try to work something out. I just feel my place tomorrow morning is with Uncle Austin. He'll need some moral support while Ashley's in surgery."

"No, you're absolutely right. That's where you belong. C.J.'s going to come get me after he sees his mom. I'll be fine until then. Especially here." Willow tried to sound confident even though she was freaking out inside.

"Let me drive you home, after we stop by Nancy's office. Please, Willow. You really need to be seen by a doctor."

She thought for a moment. "No questions asked, no hassles, no lectures?"

Jenna held up her hand as if she was giving an oath. "Absolutely not. I swear. Like I said before, Nancy's an amazing doctor. Because she's a Christian, she talks about abstinence, and the dangers of unprotected sex, but she would never risk a patient's health by using her position to lecture or preach. Please, let me set up an appointment for you. It's really important you get medical attention."

Knowing she should do the responsible thing, Willow conceded. "Okay, I'll go."

FORTY-NINE

C.J. had just taken a large drink of his soda when his mom asked, "Where's Willow?"

He choked, then took a few minutes to compose himself. "Willow was feeling sick. She said how sorry she was not to be able to see you before surgery but didn't want to jeopardize your health. The payroll still got done, she just thought it would be best if she stayed away until after you got home from your surgery."

C.J. chose his words carefully. Everything he said was accurate, even if he was bending the truth slightly. He could see the disappointment on his mom's face but tried to ignore it.

He watched as Austin sat down next to his mom and nestled beside her. She rested her head against his chest and immediately fell asleep. C.J. wanted to be angry, wanted to be the one caring for his mom, but looking at them, he realized Austin was exactly who his mother needed right now. They looked perfect together, except for the anxiousness he saw in Austin's eyes.

When C.J. made eye contact with him, Austin mouthed, *How's Willow?*

"Okay for now," he whispered. "I'll fill you in while Mom is in surgery."

Austin nodded, then closed his eyes, and rested his head against the back of the couch.

C.J. slipped outside in search of Billy.

What was supposed to be a quick conversation with Billy, turned into one question, dilemma, or situation after another. Handling the little things didn't bother him. Feed questions—no problem. Barn maintenance—easy enough. Shifting of exercise routines—simple. However, when the vet arrived to administer annual inoculations, and asked to talk to C.J.—regarding Dominus—his pulse/rate shot through the roof. He could not handle just one more thing.

After taking a few deep breaths, C.J. found Dr. Larsen standing

285

outside Dominus' stall.

"Billy said you wanted to talk to me?"

Dr. Larsen turned around, confused. "Actually, I asked to speak with Ashley."

"I would prefer you talked with me. My mom is having surgery tomorrow, and I don't want to upset her."

"Nothing serious, I hope?"

"Actually, it is. She has cancer." His words sounded blunt, even to his own ears.

Shock twisted the contours of Dr. Larsen's face. "C.J., I'm so sorry. I had no idea."

"Then you can understand why I don't want her worried about Dominus?"

"Not only that, but I think I have my answer."

"I don't understand?"

"I'm talking about this." Dr. Larsen took a step back from the door to Dominus' stall.

C.J. saw the classic signs of cribbing. *Why didn't I notice this sooner?*

"Not only this, but while I've been here, I've heard him pawing. I went ahead and examined him, but couldn't find anything physically wrong with him, though I did notice he didn't finish his feed. Now I know why. It's not physical, but emotional. Dominus is depressed or anxious, or both."

C.J. peered into Dominus' stall and clicked his tongue. Dominus glanced over his shoulder but ignored C.J., choosing instead to give him a clear view of his rump. "Dominus," he tried to get the stubborn horse's attention. "Come on, boy." He rattled the halter that hung to the side of the door.

"Showing his backside is another sign of depression," Dr. Larsen said. "It all makes perfect sense. The relationship between horse and rider is very connected, very intuitive. Dominus senses something isn't right. If Ashley has spent less time riding, even grooming him, Dominus feels that difference and surmises something is wrong."

"But Mom won't be able to tend to him for a couple of weeks, maybe longer. What do I do in the meantime?"

"Well, if the stress is affecting his adrenal glands, magnesium will help. I'll leave some supplements with you. Other than that, make sure he's getting lots of attention in Ashley's absence. He'll still miss her, and be moody, but his temperament type calls for plenty of praise and adoration. Even while bathing and grooming, he needs to hear words and tones of affirmation. So, whoever is tending to him, make sure they're really hamming it up."

"Okay." C.J. sighed. "I'll do my best."

"Make sure he's eating and stroke his ego. I'll stop by in a few days to check on him." Dr. Larsen smiled.

"I'd appreciate that."

When C.J. finally made it back to the house, the great room was empty; his mom and Austin gone. Figuring they turned in early, C.J. slipped upstairs and called Jenna.

"Willow's resting. I hate to wake her."

"No. Don't wake her, but you're sure she's doing all right?"

"I promise. She's doing as well as can be expected. I even convinced her to see a doctor."

"How did you do that?"

"Long story. But it's someone I work with. Someone she can trust."

"Thanks, Jenna. I don't know what else to say."

"I'm glad I could help. So . . . tell me . . . how's Ashley and Uncle Austin doing?"

"Same as Willow. As well as can be expected."

"Well, I guess I'll see for myself at the hospital tomorrow."

"Crap! I never got a chance to tell Willow you were going to be gone in the morning."

"That's okay, I explained it to her. I can tell she's still nervous, but I convinced her, there's no way for Steven to know where she is."

"Thanks, Jenna, I guess I'll see you tomorrow."

Plopping on his bed, C.J. laced his fingers behind his head. Staring at the ceiling, he hoped Willow was doing okay, and wished he was there to make sure she was. *I don't understand why I never noticed her before.* That wasn't true. He had noticed her, but never with the attraction he felt for her now. *I'm reading too much into this. I'm having a knee-jerk reaction because she was hurt.* He was in protection mode, that's all there was to it. He'd always thought of Willow as a girl—a sweet, young girl. But everything had changed. He now saw her as a vulnerable young woman. A woman he wanted to get to know better. *I can't tell her how I feel. Not now anyway.*

She needed time. Time to heal. Time to figure out what her next move should be. He didn't need to put undue pressure on her, and he certainly didn't want her to feel a twisted sense of obligation if her feelings for him never progressed past friendship.

As he wrestled with his thoughts, he heard a familiar knock on his bedroom door.

"Come in, Mom." C.J. scooted back against the headboard, while his mom pulled one leg up on his bed and sat down.

"Sorry I zonked out on you earlier."

"It's okay. You seem pretty wiped out. How was the beach?"

She smiled. "Amazing. Incredible. Perfect in every way. Austin made me—"

He held up his hand. "I think I'm going to stop you right there. I definitely *don't* want to hear the details."

She slapped his leg, laughing "I wasn't going to give you *details.* I was just going to *say,* Austin made me forget everything, even if it was only for a few days."

"How are you feeling now?" he asked tentatively.

"I'm okay. Anxious, I guess."

"Yeah, me too."

"I'll probably be in the hospital until Monday, possibly Tuesday." She cleared her throat. "C.J., in case I don't get the chance to tell you—"

"Stop it, Mom. You're going to have plenty of chances to tell me all kinds of things."

She gently placed her hand on his leg. "Christopher, please. I want you to know what a wonderful life you have given me. You and I had a tough start, but we made it. No one could ask for a better, more loving son than I have in you. I know you're struggling with your relationship with God right now, and I know you find it hard to believe He loves us if He's willing to put us through so much. But you have to realize something else. You have to understand how much God loved you from the start."

His shoulders stiffened, and he turned toward the window.

"Christopher, listen to me. Before you were even born, God protected you. Even though the world told me an abortion was okay because of my circumstances, God spoke to me and convinced me you were a child, not a mistake or a situation. God spared you, so we could have these twenty-four years together. If it's His choosing to call me home now, I would like to know you thought it was worth it. That you wouldn't trade a single moment for anything, because that's how I feel. I am choosing to thank God for our time together, not curse Him for cutting it short. If something happens, C.J., and I can't share the rest of your life with you, I pray you will be able to thank God for the time we did share. Please know I'll be looking forward to the time we're reunited in heaven. You won't stand me up, will you?"

Tears fell down C.J.'s face unchecked. He pulled his mother close and sobbed uncontrollably. She stroked his head like she had done so many times before when he was a little boy.

"I love you, Mom, and I want you to know, I won't do anything to hinder our reunion when the time comes. But I'm convinced God brought you and Austin together to give you something special. Not just for a week, but for years to come."

They held each other for quite some time, then his mom pressed a tender kiss to his forehead and got up to leave.

"I'll see you in the morning, Mom. I love you."

"I love you, too."

Once she closed the door, C.J. melted against his pillow. He muffled his cry while he pleaded for more days with his mom, then repaired his shaky relationship with God.

Austin crawled into Ashley's bed while she showered. Though he would have rather joined her, she had just come from talking with C.J., and he could tell from her red, glassy eyes, they'd had an emotional conversation. Thinking she needed some space, he lay in bed and prayed for tomorrow.

When Ashley emerged from the bathroom, she looked so amazingly beautiful, he was speechless. Her blond hair piled on top of her head, and a white lace nightie with thin straps and a plunging neckline clung to her body.

When she turned off the bathroom light, the remaining light from the bedside lamp washed the room in a warm glow. As she walked toward the bed, she pulled the clip from her hair, allowing her tendrils to cascade over her shoulders. She pulled back the covers and slid between the sheets, then scooted close to Austin and laid her head on his exposed chest.

The feeling was transcendent. Incomparable. The warmth of her body pressed next to his was euphoric and the clean floral scent that was hers and hers alone filled his senses.

Please, God . . . don't take this woman from me.

He held her close, caressing her arm as he reigned in the emotion tugging at his heart.

"You're awfully quiet, Mr. Taylor," she said as she stroked his chest.

He swallowed hard. "That's because you take my breath away. That nightie you're wearing, Mrs. Taylor, is quite lovely."

"I bought it for our honeymoon, but never had an opportunity to wear it."

"So why are you wearing it now?" Austin whispered as he slipped the thin strap from her shoulder.

"Because I bought it as your wedding gift and wanted to give it to you."

"I appreciate that, but I'm perfectly fine with what you have been wearing."

She smiled. He could feel it against his chest. "Then can I assume it was at least appreciated as gift wrap?"

"Absolutely."

Ashley looked up into his eyes. Austin reached down and covered her lips with his.

No more words were said.

No more words were needed.

FIFTY

Unable to quiet her inner turmoil, Willow lay in bed, staring at the ceiling. The shadow cast from the small lamp on the side table had been her focal point for hours. Even though she repeated her mantra—*I'm safe. Steven can't find me here*—the noises of a strange house had kept her awake. She closed her eyes and tried for the umpteenth time to come up with a plan of action—what she would do, where she would go? But the same question gnawed at her. How? How was she supposed to move on when she had nothing? No money. No car. No clothes. No tuition. No place to go. Even if she was accepted into the program she applied for, she no longer had the money to pay for it. One thing she did know, even though the very thought of it made her want to retch; she had to go back to Steven's apartment. There was no way around it. She'd left behind something important—something she needed. She didn't know when or how, but she would have to figure it out before Steven dumped her stuff, if he hadn't already.

Maybe I should go home. I could always start over there.

It wouldn't be the perfect situation—far from it. Even so, she would at least have a place to stay and a roof over her head while she figured out her next move. But going back to Colorado? Being with her mom? It was far from ideal.

Then there was C.J.

Though she tried to ignore her growing feelings for him, they were right there at the forefront of her mind. Intellectually, she knew she was experiencing some sort of knight in shining armor syndrome. C.J. was her hero. Her protector. He swooped in and saved her from the evil villain, rescued her from a life of torment. She was romanticizing what happened. She was confusing gratitude for attraction. C.J. was a decent guy. He couldn't help but do the right thing. That's just who he was and how he was raised. What he did, he would have done for anyone. His actions weren't motivated by attraction, but by his own moral compass.

291

Willow groaned, hating that she was acting so pathetic. She needed to keep her emotions in check. C.J. was her boss. A respectable guy. A prized catch for any woman.

Any woman but me.

After taking a long, hot shower, and getting dressed, Willow tiptoed passed Jenna's bedroom door, only to see her standing in the entry way.

"Good morning," she said quietly. "There are muffins on the stove and fresh coffee in the pot. I'll call you when we know something. Let the machine answer the phone. When you know it's me, pick up. Otherwise, let it go to voicemail."

Willow wrapped her arms around her midsection, her anxiety getting the better of her.

"If you get nervous and stressed, give me a call. I'll talk you through it. I left my number next to the phone. And remember, you have an appointment with Nancy at two o'clock." She looked at her watch, then smiled. "I've got to go, but I'll see you a little later, okay? And Willow . . . you're going to do fine."

When Jenna closed the door, the click of the lock, punctuated Willow's isolation.

She was alone.

By herself.

With no one to help her.

She knew her fear was without merit. Steven hadn't even tried to contact her and had no idea where she was.

As long as he doesn't cause trouble for the ranch, I'll be okay.

Ashley lay on the gurney, her complexion as gray as the blanket covering her.

Austin stood on one side of the gurney, doing his best to look positive as he stroked the back of her hand with his thumb. C.J. stood on the other side, wearing his emotions on his sleeve.

Dr. Allen appeared, greeted C.J. with a firm handshake and a pat on the back, then introduced himself to Austin with an extended hand. "I hear congratulations are in order."

"Yes, sir."

"Well, I'm going to take very good care of Ashley," he said with a smile, then proceeded to give a brief explanation of the surgery and recovery time. "Ready, Ashley?" he asked, sounding upbeat.

She nodded, then squeezed Austin's hand.

"We'll see you in a couple of hours, okay?" Austin leaned down and pressed a kiss to her forehead.

Ashley just nodded, her pre-surgery meds already taking effect.

Dr. Allen assisted the technicians in rolling Ashley through the double doors, while C.J. and Austin stood unmoving, unable to speak.

Austin looked at C.J., knowing he was scared, his life with his mom probably flashing through his mind. Austin swallowed deep, thinking about the future, and all he wanted to do with Ashley, nowhere near prepared to say goodbye so soon.

God's got this. He's in control. It's going to be fine.

When they finally found their way back to the waiting room, Jenna stood. "I'm going to get you guys something to eat." Austin tried to refuse, but Jenna didn't listen.

Once she walked away, Austin turned to C.J. "So, fill me in on Willow."

"Well, it started the day of the wedding. Willow's car broke down, so I gave her a ride. When she called to tell her boyfriend, he jumped all over her case, like she'd done it on purpose. I could hear him yelling at her over the phone. He sounded like a real jerk. Anyway, to make a long story short, the alarm went off at the ranch, coincidently at the same time Steven was there to fix Willow's car. He denies having anything to do with it, but the police think he's responsible because of his shady reputation."

"Wait a minute," Austin interrupted. "Willow's dating someone with a shady reputation?"

"Yeah. The police already have a file on him. How's that for bad taste? They took him down to the station and questioned him, but didn't have any evidence, so they had to let him go. The fact that he was at the ranch at the same time was circumstantial, since he had what appeared to be a valid reason for being there."

"But if he didn't do it, wouldn't he have seen who did?"

"Exactly! Anyway, fast-forward to later that night, when I dropped her off after the wedding."

"Her apartment?"

"*Their* apartment."

Austin raised a brow.

"I'll explain that later. Anyway, Steven knocked her around in a jealous rage, and accused her of cheating. He tried to apologize by buying her a car, but when Willow found out he used her tuition money to buy the car, she unloaded on him. More angry than afraid, she let him have it verbally, and in turn, Steven let her have it physically. He beat her so bad, she could barely walk."

"Is she okay now?" Austin asked, concerned.

"Yes and no. You should have seen her, Austin. I couldn't believe it. Her face was swollen, and her lip was split. She had bruises all over her body and blood in her hair. It was awful. The worst part was . . . she was pregnant, and the beating he gave her was so severe it caused her to miscarry. But I didn't know that. I thought she was bleeding internally."

Shoving his fingers through his hair, Austin realized this was worse than he expected. "Why didn't you take her to the hospital or call 9-1-1?"

"I wanted to, but she refused. That's when she told me she was miscarrying. Eventually, her bleeding slowed, so I watched and waited. I told her, if she blacked out, I was going to call 9-1-1. Luckily, it didn't come to that."

Austin shook his head, finding it all so unbelievable. "How is she doing now?"

"Better, I guess. But she still looks pretty messed up."

"How are *you* doing? That's a lot to handle."

"I'm doing okay, but I'm worried about Steven. Willow doesn't think he'll give up without a fight. That's why I asked Jenna to stay with her. Of course, he'll never find her at your place, so Jenna's not in any danger. But we are taking extra precautions at the ranch. Locking the gates at night. Heightened security. Keeping the police informed. I guess there's not much more we can do, unless he actually tries something."

Jenna was back with two trays of food and a caddy of coffees. She divvied everything out, then took a seat next to Austin.

"Well, Willow is welcome to stay at my place, as long as she needs," Austin said. "Besides, Ashley and I will be at the ranch until she's recovered." He took a swallow of coffee, then turned his attention to Jenna. "How are you and Willow doing?"

"Good. She's jittery, but that's to be expected. I did convince her to see Nancy. She has an appointment at two o'clock."

"So, how'd you get her to agree?" C.J. asked. "I've been trying to get her to a doctor since day one."

"I work at a doctor's office. Dr. Cummings is not just a great doctor; she's an exceptional person. Nancy does volunteer work at shelters and abuse centers, so she's used to seeing women in crisis. She's kind, gentle, and not judgmental. Dr. Cummings realizes when a woman has been through something like what Willow went through, a reprimand only adds insult to injury. A person questioning a woman about her choices, insisting she should have left sooner, or should have known better, is the last thing a battered woman needs to hear. Nancy's desire is to show the love of Christ, not disapproval. She warns patients about STDs, and recommends taking certain precautions, but other than facts, she helps take care of their physical needs without a lot of probing questions."

"That's great." C.J. paused, sipping his coffee. "Then I guess you two are getting along okay?"

"We're doing great. I'm sorry about the circumstances, but I enjoyed talking with her last night."

C.J. turned his attention back to Austin. "So, do you think Mom's going to be upset we didn't tell her about this? I realize I dragged you into it, but I just didn't want her to worry about anything before she went into surgery."

Austin didn't answer him. With the mention of surgery, he glanced at his watch.

Two hours to go.

FIFTY-ONE

Even though Steven had devised a plan to get into the estates, he still didn't know where Willow was staying.

What was the guy's name?

He remembered her talking about the wedding. Her boss was marrying some rich guy, and they were getting married at his home. When Steven put two and two together, the pieces fit.

Rich guy.

Gated community.

The cowboy driving Willow to the exclusive neighborhood.

That has to be where Willow's staying, but what was the guy's name?

He hadn't been listening, not really. When Willow came home gushing about a wedding, high school sweethearts, cancer . . . he couldn't care less. He was in the middle of saving a major deal from slipping through his fingers; he didn't have time for her stupid wedding crap.

What was his name? He thought some more.

Taylor, Tyler, it was something like that. He paced, trying to remember what she'd said. *It was Andrew something . . . Andrew Taylor . . . Andrew Tyler.* He thought for a moment, what angles he could work, then he called the information center for The Estates.

"Could I have the main gate please?" He waited while he was being connected. "Yes, I noticed a suspicious car on my street, driving slow. Could I give you the license number, and you tell me if it is an authorized vehicle?" Having memorized the cowboy's license plate while following them, he rattled it off to the person on the phone.

"Sir, that license number matches a guest of Mr. Austin Taylor."

"Taylor, you say. I thought he lived over on Saddleback Road."

"No, sir, he's at ten Rocking Horse Road. I'll call him and let him know this is an inconvenience to you."

"No need for that. His guest is probably out for a drive or got turned around. It just seemed suspicious to me. Thank you for your help. Please don't say anything to Mr. Taylor. I would hate to come off as an over-reacting neighbor."

Steven grinned to himself as he disconnected the call. He had the address. Now to get onto the property. He dialed Carlos.

"Yeah, Carlos, is everything set up with your cousin? Thanks, man, I owe you one. Where's your cousin now? I'd like to swing by and thank him."

Steven cruised down the street and passed the landscaping vehicle. He looked around but did not see any of the workers. Pulling a U-turn, he approached the truck slowly. When he was sure no one was watching, he rolled down his window, pulled the magnetic sign from the side of the vehicle, and drove away.

Now he had everything he needed.

He just had to wait for the right time.

C.J. was pacing, unable to sit still any longer. Two and a half hours had passed without a word. Then he heard the automatic doors and looked up to see the doctor walking his way. He rushed toward him. "How is she?" he blurted out before Dr. Allen could speak. Putting a hand on C.J.'s shoulder, he said, "Let me tell everyone at once."

They walked the remaining few steps to the waiting area where Austin stood—Jenna clutching his arm.

"She's fine. The surgery went just as we hoped."

They sighed in unison. "Thank God," Austin whispered.

"Ashley's been moved to recovery; you'll be able to see her in a little while."

"What's next, Dr. Allen?" Austin asked. "Will Ashley need radiation?"

The doctor rubbed the back on his neck, looking torn. "Though I feel confident we were able to get all the affected areas, radiation would be a safe measure to use. It's not that uncomfortable, though it can cause a level of fatigue. Even so, the amount of reassurance it can provide is invaluable. I'd like to go that route but let me think on it a little more." He glanced at the clock on the wall. "I need to go, but I'll make sure someone comes and gets you when Ashley's ready for visitors. I'll be back this evening to see how she's progressing."

Austin extended his hand to Dr. Allen; C.J. did as well, but when the doctor walked away, C.J. turned, not wanting anyone to see the tears in his eyes.

"I feel the same way, C.J.," Austin said.

When C.J. turned around and looked at Austin, he saw a pillar of strength. Stalwart. While C.J. felt ready to crumble. When Austin pulled him into a firm embrace and patted his back, words were not necessary.

C.J. took a moment to gather his emotions, then cleared his throat. "I'm going to call Willow and let her know Mom's okay." He started for the elevator, but when he turned back to say something, he saw Austin hug Jenna, and release the emotion he'd tried so hard to contain.

When the phone rang, Willow hurried to the machine, so she could listen. Hearing C.J.'s voice, she grabbed for the receiver. "Hello."

"Willow, Mom's out of surgery and everything went fine. The doctor sounds like he's leaning toward radiation, but it's just precautionary."

"That's great, C.J. Have you had a chance to see her yet?"

"No, she's still in recovery. How are you doing?"

"I'm fine, but . . . uhh . . . when do you think Jenna will come home?"

"I'm not sure. I mean, she was here more for Austin's sake than Mom's. We're just waiting for someone to come get us, so we can see Mom. There really isn't any reason for Jenna to hang around; I'll see if I can get her to leave."

"No. Don't do that. I don't want to be pushy or ruin her plans. I'm just being paranoid."

"No, you're not. You have every right to feel the way you do. But don't worry, either Jenna or I will be there soon."

"Thanks, C.J., for everything." Willow quietly hung up the phone and looked around the house, knowing she was acting ridiculous. She closed her eyes and took a deep, cleansing breath.

I'm safe.

Steven can't hurt me here.

Steven drove the rental truck up to the guard shack at the front gate, glad to see it was a different man on duty than the one he had spoken with previously.

"Yeah, I'm bringing some equipment for Peterson Landscaping. They were supposed to arrange it with you."

The guard glanced at the magnetic sign on the side of the truck. "No one's contacted me." His tone was firm.

"Well, I sure as heck didn't drive up here for my health. I've got a piece of equipment they need to finish up the lawns at the Equestrian Center—for that big shindig tomorrow. I don't know about you, but I sure wouldn't want the homeowner's association having a conniption because you didn't let me in. Call them. I'll wait." Steven stared ahead. Calm and cool.

"I don't have the phone number of the lawn service."

"Here," Steven offered his phone. "It's on speed dial. Number two. Just ask for Carlos."

The guard seemed perplexed, but finally snatched the phone from Steven's hand. He pressed two and held the phone to his ear. "I need to talk with Carlos. Carlos? Hey, I'm with Estate security, and I've got some guy here saying you need some equipment. Yeah . . . dark hair . . . medium build . . . okay, but if you guys have this kind of problem again, you need to let us know. We can't let just anyone in without proper authorization."

Steven grinned to himself as the guard reached for the visitors clipboard. The guard wrote down his license plate number and allowed Steven to drive on through.

Smooth as silk.

Steven drove through the sprawling estates, not really knowing where he was going. He doubled back a few times before finding Rocking Horse Road. Driving slow, he spotted a rambling ranch style house with a simple "10" on a brick post out front. Steven glanced at the open garage door, with a car inside. If someone was with Willow, that would complicate things.

He decided to lay low.

He didn't want any surprises.

Just Willow.

FIFTY-TWO

Austin followed C.J. into the dimly lit room. Looking at Ashley—pale, eyes closed, her petite hands hooked to an IV and some monitors—Austin had to remind himself what the doctor said earlier. *She's going to be fine.*

They each took their place on either side of the bed. When Austin softly brushed his hand against her cheek, her eyes opened momentarily. Smiling, she reached for both their hands before drifting back to sleep.

It was another hour before Ashley's grogginess wore off. She opened her eyes and again smiled at them both, then tried to push herself to a sitting position. When she winced in discomfort, C.J. stood. "I'll get a nurse."

A nurse followed C.J. into the room and introduced herself.

"Mrs. Taylor, I'm Barbara," the woman's voice was elevated and matter-of-fact—obviously trying to be heard through the fog Ashley was in. She placed a small push-button devise into Ashley's hand then explained, "If you feel any discomfort, you can push this button, okay?"

Ashley nodded in understanding.

"But if you need anything else, push this button right here." The nurse guided Ashley's hand to the button on the side of the bed. "Okay?"

"Button in hand for pain. Button on bed for help."

"You got it, sweetheart. Now, let me explain one more thing. You have two very handsome men here who are going to vie for your attention. But you need your rest in order to regain your strength. Kick them out when you're feeling tired, or press the button, and I'll do it for you."

The nurse smiled at Ashley but winked at Austin. As she stepped away from Ashley's bed, Austin followed her out into the hallway. "She's allowed to medicate herself?" he whispered.

"It's perfectly safe, Mr. Taylor. It will send a controlled dose of pain medication to her IV. She can't over medicate, but it does make it easier for her to get the relief she needs without waiting for someone to answer a buzzer. But we will also be checking in on her periodically to see how she's doing. Don't worry, Mr. Taylor, she's going to be fine." The nurse gave a polite smile, then walked away.

When Austin stepped back into the room, he saw Ashley press for medication. It was only a matter of seconds before the strained look on her face softened.

"Well," C.J. said, plopping down in the chair he'd pulled up next to Ashley's bed. "I guess we might as will get comfortable."

Austin dragged the other chair over and sat facing Ashley. It was a while before her eyes opened in earnest.

"How'd I do?"

"You did great, honey." Austin got up and kissed her forehead again, then her nose, and finally her lips.

"How'd you guys do?"

"We did great."

Jenna waited for a landscaping truck to complete his U-turn, then pulled into the driveway. When she walked into the house, Willow was standing in the living room waiting for her. Jenna could tell by the fake smile on Willow's face, she was a nervous wreck.

"How's Ashley?"

"The doctor said the surgery went as planned, and Ashley is doing fine."

"That's great!"

"How about you? How did you do while I was gone?"

"Fine. I'm still jumpy, but that's because I know this isn't over yet. Steven's not the type to concede, even if he doesn't want the prize."

Jenna watched as Willow nervously twisted and pulled at her hands.

"I think I should go talk to him," Willow said, sounding stronger than she looked. "I need to tell him we're done, get my things, and see for myself if he's going to let me go or not."

"You can't meet him by yourself, Willow. He's too dangerous. But if you were to file charges against him, the police could escort you to get your things."

Willow's shoulders stiffened. "You talked to C.J. about this at the hospital, didn't you?" she snapped. "Did he ask you to convince me to go to the police?"

"No, I just think what happened to you is unfair. But letting Steven get away with it, is just as unfair. What if he turns around and does this to the next woman unlucky enough to fall into a relationship with him? How would you feel then?"

Jenna looked at Willow's fallen expression and realized too late that her words had been harsh. Condemning. "I'm sorry, Willow. I didn't mean to put that on you."

"It's all right. I've thought about that myself. I just don't know if I can handle the questions I would have to answer if I went to the police. It was hard enough involving you and Austin, but at least you guys are giving me the benefit of the doubt. The police won't. They'll have to be impartial. They'll be very direct, probative. And when they find out this isn't the first time, they'll blame me. And they'll be right. This is my fault. If I had left Steven when—"

"Don't do that, Willow. This is absolutely *not* your fault. The only person to blame is Steven."

Willow and Jenna were working in the kitchen when Austin and C.J. pulled into the driveway. Willow felt her pulse race and was surprised how excited she was to see C.J. When the men walked into the kitchen, C.J. brushed up alongside of her and looked at her with the serious eyes she'd become so familiar with over the last few days.

"How are you doing?"

"Pretty good." She smiled, trying to be convincing.

"Jenna told me you have a doctor's appointment later today. How do you feel about that?"

"Nervous. Jenna assured me the doctor she works for won't be critical or judgmental. I just want to get through it, take whatever recommendations she gives me, and leave." Willow thought to herself for a moment and then asked C.J. "Will I go back to the ranch or stay here?"

"What do you want to do?"

"Well . . . I like being here with Jenna, and I feel safe and all, but I'd rather be at the ranch, if that's okay? It's just more familiar."

"Sure. Jenna can drive you to the hospital after your appointment, then I can take you home from there."

"But if that's too much of a hassle, I can—"

"It's not a hassle, Willow. Besides, it will be nice to have you there when I get home." C.J. smiled, offering her the reassurance she needed.

Jenna handed C.J. two plates of pasta just as Austin's cell phone chimed. Austin pulled it from his pocket and spoke quickly, then disconnected the call.

"Was that the hospital?" C.J. asked.

Austin shook his head. "It was Simon. He just wanted to let me know he has the pictures from the wedding, in case I want to pick them up and take them to Ashley."

Willow saw the relief on C.J.'s face, reminding her once again, of all he was trying to juggle. She hated that she was making a hard situation even more difficult on him. *I've got to handle this on my own. Once I get back to the ranch, I'll figure out how to handle Steven by myself.*

The four of them ate and made small talk, trying to act like everything was normal. Then, all too soon, Willow watched as Austin and C.J. pulled from the driveway and headed back to the hospital.

FIFTY-THREE

Steven smiled when he saw the sports car drive away.

He thought for sure his plan was blown when less than an hour ago, the car pulled into the driveway—the cowboy and another man going into the house. But it didn't matter. He wasn't going to let it detour him. He just had to be patient and wait for another opportunity to present itself.

Knowing he couldn't stay parked in one place too long without drawing suspicion, he drove around for a few minutes, until he saw a house under construction. There were plenty of vehicles on the site, so he decided it would be the perfect place to ditch his truck for the time being.

Wearing a jumpsuit and carrying a clipboard, he made his way back to Rocking Horse Road, looking official, stopping to read meters, like he belonged.

Now was his shot. He still didn't know who was in the house, but he knew who wasn't.

You lose, cowboy.

Running toward the garage, he used the foliage separating properties as coverage. Pressing up against the brick exterior, he waited. No shouts. No screams.

So far, so good.

Ditching the clipboard, he scanned the area for surveillance equipment. Seeing none, he worked his way toward the front door, navigating around thorny rose bushes while still trying to use the shrubbery for coverage. As he moved closer to a garden window, he heard voices. He stopped and listened. Though it was too muffled to make out what was being said, he learned two things.

Willow wasn't alone.

And, the person with her was a woman.

He grinned. *Easy enough.*

With the front door as his goal, he had one more obstacle to overcome—getting past the large bay window that overlooked the circular driveway. Still able to hear the voices—in what he assumed was the kitchen—he decided to go for it. With adrenaline pulsing through his veins, he sprinted to the front porch. *Yes!* He was excited. Euphoric. With each obstacle he overcame, he felt energized. Invincible.

Locked. The door was locked. He twisted and pulled, but it wouldn't budge. Swearing, he pulled the knife from his pocket and tried to jimmy it. Quickly, he chipped away at the wood nearest the latch, but it was no use.

His excitement quickly turned to anger.

Standing on the front porch, he felt exposed. He had a decision to make, and he needed to make it quick. He still didn't see any security cameras, so he could just knock, keep his head down, then pounce as soon as they opened the door. *But there's two of them.* If they both didn't come to the door, one of them could get away.

No. He needed to be sure.

He had to be in control.

He couldn't take the chance of Willow getting away.

She belonged to him.

Slinking to the far end of the house, he hurried around the corner to the backyard. There, he saw a small patio with french doors. *Perfect.*

He hugged the wall until he stood alongside the multipaned doors. Again, he waited and listened. *Nothing.* Taking a chance, he peered through the glass. *A bedroom.* He rattled the handle; it too was locked. *No problem. I'll just break one of these panes—*

Fisting his hand, he pulled the sleeve of the jumpsuit over his knuckles and was ready to shove it through the pane of glass nearest the handle, when he saw a shadow in the hallway outside the bedroom. A millisecond before he moved, he saw Willow walk into the room.

Flinging his body against the wall, he held his breath. When he didn't hear her scream, he smiled. *Luck is on your side today, Mr. Boyer. Luck is on . . . your . . . side.*

Steven stood out of sight but watched Willow through a reflection in one of the panes of glass. The longer he watched, the more his rage simmered.

How dare she leave me! Her place is with me. Not here. Not with that filthy cowboy.

He would teach her a lesson she wouldn't soon forget.

Taking a step toward the door, his foot snagged on a potted

plant, causing it to scrape against the patio tile.

~®~

Willow gasped and spun around toward the patio. She stood still, waiting to see if she heard the noise again, but convinced herself she was only imagining it. Sighing with relief, she looked in the mirror over the dresser, frustrated to see bruises still discolored her face. *I look like a freak.* She had hoped to resemble a normal person before going out in public but realized she would have to do some doctoring of her own to hide the blues and purples coloring her complexion.

She unzipped the makeup bag Jenna had volunteered and pulled out a compact. When she raised it to smooth on some powder, her heart stopped dead. She dropped the compact and swung around to see her fears come to life.

Steven.

Standing on the patio.

Hatred in his eyes.

Willow screamed and ran from the room, plowing into Jenna.

"Steven's here! He's on the patio!" she cried hysterically.

Jenna grabbed Willow's arms firmly, holding her still. "But that's impossible. He doesn't even know where you are?"

~®~

As Jenna tried to calm Willow, she heard the crashing of glass. *It can't be?*

"He's here! He's going to kill me!" Willow sobbed, nearly crumbling in Jenna's arms. Then, with a burst of strength, Willow pushed away from Jenna, stumbling backwards. "Get out of here!" she whispered frantically. "He'll kill you, too! You need to get out of here!"

"Not without you," Jenna whispered, doing everything she could to control the terror rising inside her.

Jenna hurried Willow toward the pool, to her childhood hiding place. She didn't look back, she only hushed Willow's sobs as she pleaded with God. *Please, please, please, let both of us fit inside. Don't let him find us.*

FIFTY-FOUR

Austin and C.J. were quiet as they exited the main gate, each of them lost in thought. Austin was thinking how happy Ashley would be to see their wedding pictures, when he slammed on the brakes. "Shoot!" he snapped, as he whipped the car back around.

C.J.'s arm shot out, stopping him from hitting the dash. "What are you doing?"

"We have to go back. I forgot my phone."

"Are you sure?"

"Pretty sure." Austin waited until he pulled up to the gate entrance, then threw the car into park. Lifting his hips off the seat, he checked each of his pockets. "I put it down after talking to Simon. It's sitting on the dining room table."

"You can't go a day without it?" C.J. groaned.

"Not today. With Ashley in the hospital, and Jenna taking care of Willow, I don't want to be without communication."

"Good point."

"Back so soon, Mr. Taylor." The security guard chuckled.

"I left my phone at the house. You'll see me again in another ten minutes."

Jenna covered Willow's mouth, trying to muffle her terrifying cries. Leading her to the lower deck of the pool, she opened the camouflaged door that housed the pool's pump and chemicals. It was Jenna's favorite hiding place when she was a child. Of course, she was much littler then.

Please, God, let us both fit.

She pushed Willow inside and pressed in beside her. When Jenna closed the door behind them, they were immediately plunged into darkness. Willow shook with fear beside her, sobbing softly.

"He won't find us," Jenna whispered, "as long as he doesn't hear us."

Jenna felt Willow struggle to lift her arm and knew the minute Willow put her hand over her mouth. In complete silence, Jenna continued to pray. *Please, God. Make him go away.*

Jenna heard nothing, praying God had answered her pleas. Unfortunately, the quiet only lasted a few minutes.

"I'm gonna find you, Willow! And when I do, you'll be sorry you ever left me! Do you hear me!" He cussed and swore as they listened to crashing sounds and heavy footsteps. "I don't want to hurt your friend, but I will if you don't come out and go home with me! Right! Now!"

Jenna wrapped her arms around Willow and whispered assuredly in her ear, "We're going to be okay. We just need to stay quiet."

Please, God. Protect us.

Not wanting to put pressure on the magnetic door, Jenna tried to scoot further into the cubby. When she moved she felt a tug on the hem of her blouse.

No, no, no!

Her shirt was stuck on the hinge of the door. Carefully, she tried to pull it loose, but it wouldn't budge. Cringing inside, she continued to call on the Lord.

Steven wandered through the house, looking for something that would tip him off. An opened door. A noise. A piece of furniture out of place. But he found nothing.

"I know you're here!" he shouted as he toppled over a lamp. "You're only making this worse for you and your friend! Did you hear that, girlfriend? Willow's not worth it! She's a liar and a cheat! Tell me where she is, and I won't hurt you." He waited, but nothing happened. With all self-control gone, he yelled at the top of his lungs. "I. Will. Find. You!"

He stood, overlooking the indoor pool, panting as he scanned the planter beds that surrounded it. He was burning up with rage, sweat running down his face. His chest palpated with anger.

He couldn't give up.

He had to find them.

He would silence Willow for good.

When he turned to walk away, something caught his eye. Squinting, he saw a swatch of material lying against the rock face, alongside the pool. When he looked closer, he realized it wasn't lying against the rock, it was embedded in the facade. That's when he saw it. The outline of a door.

He grinned. *Ollie, ollie, oxen free.*

"You know, Willow, none of this would've happened if you hadn't been mixing it up with your boss." His tone was calmer now. He was back in control. "We were supposed to be together. Why couldn't you see that? Why did you have to go and ruin everything?"

~Ⓡ~

Steven's voice was getting closer and closer.

When Jenna felt a tug on her blouse, she knew they'd been found. Tears rolled down her face. There was nothing she could do. They were trapped.

"I'm sorry, Willow," she whispered so quietly. "I'm so sorry."

Pulling her arms from around Willow, Jenna decided she wasn't going out without a fight. With all the strength she could muster, she rammed her shoulder into the fiberglass door and sent it swinging.

Jenna watched as Steven fell to the concrete deck, and almost into the pool. She moved as quickly as she could, but Steven regained his footing and grabbed her before she could get away. Struggling to break free, Steven shoved her with such force, she stumbled backwards onto the pool deck and hit her head on the jagged rock border.

Her vision quickly blurred to black.

~Ⓡ~

Willow huddled in the dark space, tears streaming down her face.

Steven bent low and looked at her with a satisfied smile. "Looks like you've backed yourself into a corner, Willow."

"Please, Steven, don't do this."

"It's time to go home, Willow. Back where you belong."

Willow shook her head, trying to gather all the strength she could. "I won't go, Steven. It's over between us. Just let me go."

Steven clenched his jaw, and screamed vile, profane things at her. Then, he pulled a knife from his jacket, and walked over to where Jenna lay motionless alongside the pool.

"Move right now, Willow, or so help me, I'll cut your friend into little pieces."

Willow gasped. "No, Steven, don't." She quickly scooted

forward from where she was wedged in the small space, but not quick enough for him. Steven grabbed her arm and dragged her out the rest of the way. He yanked her up by her hair and pushed her against the rock wall, pinning her with his body. He smothered her with vicious, loveless kisses, causing her stomach to turn. She tried fighting him off, but he only applied more pressure. Pressing his bleeding hand to her neck, he held her tight; the knife still clutched in his hand.

"You realize, Willow, this isn't going to work out. You've ruined everything. I could never trust you again. And I certainly can't let you or your friend live. You'll turn me into the police. No, unfortunately, this is where it ends."

Steven dragged the knife down her side and pulled back.

Clenching her eyes shut, Willow waited for the knife to plunge into her side. Instead, something fell on her, knocking her into the pool.

Willow struggled to orientate herself. She couldn't focus, and she couldn't breathe. *I'm drowning.* Her mind was blank, her lungs burning for air. She had no idea why she was in water, but she knew she couldn't last much longer. Feeling solidity under her feet, she pushed off, trying to break the surface, but her head slammed into something in her path. Moaning, she sank once again to the bottom and looked up.

A pool. I'm in a pool. But why? And who are the people splashing above me? And why aren't they helping me?

As her lungs reminded her that she didn't have much time left, it all came back to her.

Steven.

A struggle.

Jenna.

None of it made sense, but it didn't matter. Unless she got some air in her lungs, she would die wondering.

Swimming toward the side of the pool, Willow tried once again to break the surface. She reached up and grabbed the edge of the pool, gasping and choking for the air she'd been denied. Clinging to the side of the pool, she turned toward the commotion in the water.

C.J.!

C.J. was in the water. . . with Steven!

The sun shone through the floor to ceiling windows and glinted off something shiny in the pool.

A knife.

Steven had a knife in his hand and was pointing it at C.J.

C.J. had a grip on Steven's wrist, doing what he could to keep the sharp blade away from him, but Steven fought violently.

That's when she saw blood in the water.

No . . . God . . . not C.J.

Willow tried to get close enough to the two men, so she could help C.J., but it was no use. They tumbled and splashed and wrestled each other, pushing her underwater, knocking her out of the way. Willow fought to get to the side of the pool, clutching it with what was left of her strength.

In horror, she watched as Steven lunged at C.J., forcing him underwater, then raised the knife over his head. She screamed. But the blast of a gunshot drowned out her cries.

Willow looked up to see Austin standing on the upper landing, a gun in his hand. When she turned back, Steven was on top of C.J., blood tinting the water.

"C.J.!"

She watched as he pushed himself away from Steven's lifeless body and quickly swam to her side. C.J. grabbed her and held her close. "You're okay . . . you're okay . . . he can't hurt you anymore." He kept repeating over and over in her ear.

Willow held him in a death grip, terrified to let go. She watched as Austin jumped from the upper deck to the lower deck and crouched next to where Jenna lay in a heap.

"Austin, is she okay? She was trying to protect me. It all happened so fast. I . . ."

Gently, he roused Jenna. Semi-coherent, she reached for the gash on her head, winced, then looked around frantically. "Where's Willow?"

"It's okay, Jenna. She's right here. Everything is going to be all right."

C.J. pulled Willow's shivering body from the pool and held her close, wrapping her in his arms, assuring her it was over.

"Wait a minute," Willow pulled back and saw blood oozing from his sleeve. "C.J., you're bleeding."

He removed his shirt, exposing the slice on his arm.

"He stabbed you," Willow gasped.

"It's nothing." He quickly wrapped his shirt around the wound and held it tight.

"Come on," Austin said as he held Jenna close. "We need to call the police and see to these wounds."

Willow watched as Austin guided Jenna up the steps—the side of her face covered in blood, her hair matted with streaks of red.

"Come on, let's go," C.J. whispered, his good arm firmly around her.

She nodded, then turned to the pool where Steven's lifeless body lay on the bottom.

"Don't look, Willow," C.J. turned her into his chest. "You don't need to see that."

They all sat in the main living room, stunned into silence. It all felt so bizarre, like a horror movie come to life. Steven was dead. Austin shot him. There was blood everywhere. On C.J. On Jenna. On her. The nightmare was over, or had it just begun? She watched as Austin stood, walked toward the dining room, and picked up his phone.

FIFTY-FIVE

"Yes, I need the police and an ambulance at 10, Rocking Horse Road. I just shot an intruder." Austin disconnected the call, without waiting for further instructions or offering any more information. The police would be there soon enough. He would talk to them when they arrived.

Grabbing a hand towel from the kitchen, he returned to the living room where Jenna was sitting and scrutinized the back of her head.

"Ouch!" she hissed.

"Sorry, I just wanted to see if you're going to need stitches."

"Do I?"

"I don't think so. Here, hold this." He gently pressed the towel to the back of her head. "How are you doing, otherwise?"

"I'm okay. Shocked, but okay."

"What happened?"

"It was crazy," she whispered. "Willow started screaming that Steven was outside on the patio, then I heard glass breaking. I knew we wouldn't be able to out run him, so we hid in my cave."

Austin smiled. "The pump house."

She nodded, then started to cry. "But my shirt got caught in the door. When I felt Steven tugging on it, I knew he was going to kill us." She collapsed against his shoulder, sobbing. "I pushed the door open as hard as I could, knocking him down. I tried to run, but he caught me and shoved me to the ground. The next thing I remember is you hovering over me." She pushed back and looked him in the eyes. "How did you know? How did you know something was wrong?"

He shrugged. "I didn't. I forgot my phone and came back for it."

She threw her arms around his neck, crying. "I will never tease you again about being old and forgetful."

Austin held her for a few minutes, then stood. "I need to check on Willow and C.J. before the police get here."

She nodded in understanding, then asked, "Can I change my

clothes?"

"Not yet, honey, we need to wait for the police to get here before we do anything."

He turned and looked to see C.J. and Willow huddled together, shivering in their saturated clothing. He pulled some blankets from the antique trunk next to the fireplace and draped them around their shoulders.

"Thanks, Austin," C.J. said as he pulled the blanket around Willow.

"How's the arm?"

"It hurts, but I'm okay."

"Good. I called the police and asked them to send an ambulance. They should be here soon. Just sit tight."

Austin hovered over the three of them, while distant sirens grew louder. As he processed all that had happened, he offered God a silent prayer of thanks for His hand of protection over Jenna, C.J., and Willow. Though what they experienced was extremely traumatic, they had survived. Undoubtedly, each of them would carry emotional baggage from the day's events, but the fact still remained—they were alive.

For that he was truly grateful.

Austin watched as police cars, black sedans, and an ambulance populated his driveway. He opened the front door, then held his hands up in a nonthreatening manner. "I'm Austin Taylor, the owner of the house, and the one who placed the call," he said to the man approaching him—his badge clipped to the waistband of his slacks, right next to where his hand hovered over his weapon.

"You shot an intruder. Is that correct?"

"Yes. He's in the pool."

"Dead?"

Austin nodded. The word hitting him like a punch in the gut.

"Where is the gun now?"

"In the living room, on the coffee table. It's still loaded. There are three more people in the house, each of them injured."

After the cop determined Austin wasn't a threat, he introduced himself as Detective Michaelson and led him into the living room. "I'm going to ask you to have a seat, Mr. Taylor, while we secure the premises." Several officers—uniformed and plainclothes—converged on the house and scattered. 'Clear' echoed throughout the house. A cop in a black suit carefully removed the weapon from the table and slipped it into a plastic bag.

When the paramedics walked into the living room—medical bags in hand—Austin pointed to Jenna, then C.J. and Willow. "She has a gash on her head. He has a knife wound, and she was knocked out and swallowed a lot of water."

As the medics split up to see to everyone's injuries, Detective Michaelson reappeared. "Follow me, Mr. Taylor."

The detective walked to the far side of the house and into Austin's private office. "We'll talk here, if you don't mind." He motioned for Austin to sit in one of the chairs customarily reserved for visitors, not in his usual place behind his desk. Detective Michaelson swung the matching chair around to face Austin.

"Okay, Mr. Taylor, why don't you tell me what happened? Then I'll ask a few questions of my own."

"I don't know for sure what happened before I got here, but when I arrived, I could see the front door had been tampered with. C.J. and I entered the hou—"

"C.J.?"

"The young man sitting on the couch."

The detective wrote something down. "Go on."

"We entered the house quietly until we heard shouts from the vicinity of the pool. That's when I ran to my room and got my gun."

"Is the gun registered?"

"Yes, sir."

The officer noted that, then looked at Austin to continue.

"When I heard a splash, I ran to the upper landing and saw Steven and C.J. struggling in the water. Steven had a knife in his hand. Willow was in the water too, clinging to the edge of the pool. Jenna was laying on the ground next to the stairs. Unconscious."

"Steven is the intruder?"

"Yes."

More writing. "Okay, go on."

"Everything went so fast. Steven gained the upper hand and was holding C.J. underwater. He raised the knife above his head, his intentions clear. I fired one shot, hitting him in the chest. C.J. helped Willow out of the pool, and I went to check on Jenna."

"Did anyone check on the assailant, to confirm he was dead?"

"No. I was too worried about Jenna. She's my niece. I could see she was bleeding, and even with all the commotion, she hadn't moved. C.J. was busy helping Willow out of the pool—checking her for injuries. By the time Jenna came to, and Willow assured C.J. she was fine, Steven had been underwater for several minutes. I just assumed he was dead."

"Okay, Mr. Taylor, what is your relation to C.J. and Willow?"

"C.J. is my wife's son. Willow is—"

"What is his full name?"

"Christopher John Summers."

"But he's not your stepson?"

"No. My wife and I just got married on Sunday."

"Congratulations."

Austin couldn't tell if he was serious or being sarcastic.

"And Willow?"

"I don't know her last name. She's an employee of my wife's and Steven's ex-girlfriend."

The detective looked at Austin. "So, is this a lover's triangle gone bad?" he asked belligerently.

"No! It's not like that. Steven was abusive and violent. C.J. was only trying to protect Willow."

"How so?"

"Willow called C.J. earlier in the week after Steven beat her. C.J. took her to the ranch so she could—"

"What ranch?"

"The Circle-R Ranch. It's where Willow works, and it's owned by C.J. and Ashley—my wife. Willow recuperated there for a few days but was afraid Steven would cause problems if she stayed at the ranch. So, C.J. brought her here; someplace Steven wouldn't be able to find her. Or so we thought. I have no idea how he tracked her here, but I'm absolutely sure his intentions were to harm her, most likely kill her. Why else would he have a knife on him and break into my house?"

"And you're sure he broke in? Willow didn't invite him in?"

"No. He was *not* invited. Like I said, the door was jimmied. When he couldn't get in that way, he must've gone around the back, because he broke in through the guest room's french doors."

"This assault that took place on Monday, was a police report filed?"

"No. Willow didn't want to involve the police. She was too afraid. Look, detective, I know you probably have a thousand more questions, and I promise my full and total cooperation, but my wife is in the hospital recovering from surgery. If I don't show up there soon, she'll worry and expect an explanation. She doesn't need to deal with this right now, not if she doesn't have to. And I certainly don't want to have to explain to her why her son was stabbed. So, if you don't mind, I would like to change my clothes and get to the hospital. You and your men can stay here and investigate as long as you like, and I can stop by your precinct tomorrow and answer any follow-up questions you have."

The detective continued to ask Austin questions, ignoring his plea to leave. Austin tried to be as cooperative as possible, but with every second that passed, he knew his plan to shelter Ashley from this disaster was going up in smoke.

"Okay, Mr. Taylor, I know you're anxious to see your wife, so that's all for now. I'll be in contact with you later today or tomorrow. We will be staying until our investigation is concluded, but you're free to go."

After changing his clothes, Austin walked back to the living room to check on everyone. C.J., Jenna, and Willow had been separated. Jenna sat at the dining room table with a female officer, while one of the paramedics worked on her head.

"How is she?" he asked the technician.

"She'll be fine. She has a good size knot behind the laceration, but her vision is clear, and her pupils are responsive."

"She always did have a hard head," he teased.

"Uncle Austin! A little sympathy for the patient."

"Oh boy . . . I know that tone. You're going to milk this for all it's worth, aren't you?" He coughed, trying to camouflage the emotion he was feeling. When he thought about what could've happened . . . it was almost more than he could handle. "Does she need to see a doctor?"

"She can, if it would make you rest easier, but other than a nasty headache, she's going to be okay. No stitches. She opted for Dermabond."

"Jenna," the officer interrupted. "I have a few more questions."

Austin reached for her hand and gave it a squeeze. "I'm going to check on C.J. and Willow really quick, then I need to get to the hospital before Ashley figures out something is wrong. I'm going to call Simon to fill him in and ask him to arrange for security and see about getting this place put back together after the police are done. I'll tell him to call you when he has things lined up." He brushed her hair back from her face. "You really need to call your mom. I would, but she's not going to be very happy with me."

"You're telling me," she teased. "And she thinks my parties get out of hand."

"Are you going to be okay?"

Her smile quickly vanished. "Are the police staying?"

"Yes. They'll be here until they're done with the investigation."

"Okay. What about C.J., is he all right?"

Austin glanced to where C.J. was being helped onto a gurney. "I think they're taking him to the hospital. Let me go check on him." Austin crossed the room to the entry way. "How is he?" he asked the paramedic who was getting C.J. ready for transport.

"He's lost a lot of blood and is going to need some stitches. Even so, I think he'll be out of the hospital before the day's over."

C.J. looked at Austin, clearly frustrated. "I don't need an ambulance. I'm fine. I could probably even drive myself to the hospital."

"Oh no you don't! You might feel okay, but your gray complexion says otherwise." Austin turned to the paramedic. "Can you take him to Memorial?"

"Sure."

Austin smiled at C.J. "That way I can check on you and your mom."

"What if someone tells her? She'll freak."

"No one is going to tell her. Now, behave yourself and don't give the doctors a hard time. I'll catch up with you in a little bit."

"What about Willow? Is she going to the hospital?" He craned his neck around Austin, to where Willow was sitting on the couch.

"My partner's working on her now," the paramedic cut in. "But if I'm reading her body language correctly, I'm going to say it's a 'no.'"

C.J. looked Austin square in the eye. "I don't want her left alone. I know Steven is . . . gone, but Willow isn't as strong as she wants everyone to think. She's been to hell and back and shouldn't be left alone."

"Don't worry, C.J., Jenna and I will take care of her. I promise."

~®~

Willow shook her head, then stopped, feeling like she was going to throw up.

"Miss, please . . ."

She couldn't stop shaking, even with a blanket wrapped around her. She felt numb. Disoriented. Everything happened so fast. Every time she closed her eyes, she saw Steven's body at the bottom of the pool.

"Miss . . ."

She looked at the technician kneeling in front of her. "I said I was fine." *Liar.*

"There's bruising and swelling on your face, and a considerable amount of blood on your clothes. I know you're cold, but if you could remove the blanket, I could—"

"It's not my blood." She pulled the blanket tighter around her shoulders.

"Miss, you've suffered a very traumatic event. You might think you're okay, but you could have injuries you're unaware of."

"And I told you, I'm fine," Willow snapped.

Jenna came out of nowhere and sat down on the couch next to her. "Look, I think she's just shaken up. Besides, she'll be seeing a doctor later today for a preexisting appointment." Jenna draped her arm around Willow and smiled.

"Thank you, Jenna," Willow whispered.

"So, you're refusing medical treatment?" the technician asked.

"Yes." Willow chanced a look at the man crouched in front of her and could tell he was annoyed.

"Then I'm going to have to ask you to sign a form, stating that you're refusing medical aid."

He got up from where he was kneeling and walked away. Willow watched him cross the room to where C.J. was propped up on a gurney. The medic said something to his partner, then continued out the front door.

Willow stood on shaky legs and walked to C.J.'s side.

"I'm so sorry, C.J." she whispered.

"Hey," he reached for her hand and gave it a squeeze. "You have nothing to be sorry about. None of this is your fault."

"Of course it is." A tear slid down her cheek. "You're hurt, and it's my fault."

"No," he said firmly. "It's not. And my arm is going to be fine. I just need a few stitches." He gave her hand another squeeze. "What about you? The medic said you were refusing treatment. You should have a doctor check you out. You could be—"

"I'm fine. And I still plan on seeing Jenna's doctor friend, okay?"

The medic walked over and handed her a clipboard, explaining what it said as she signed it. When she was done, she watched the paramedics finish packing up their gear.

"Hey," C.J. gave her hand a tug. "You're going to be okay, right? You'll stay with Jenna, and ask her for help if you need it?"

She pulled the blanket closer. "I will."

Standing at the bay window, Willow watched as they loaded C.J. into the back of the ambulance. Once the doors were closed, Austin got in his car, snaked his way through the sea of vehicles, and followed the ambulance out of the driveway.

"He's going to be fine," Jenna said, as she hugged Willow close. "Come on, you should be sitting down."

They turned around just as the police heaved the black bag that held Steven's body, onto a second gurney.

Her knees went weak.

Jenna braced her, so she wouldn't fall down, then led her to the sofa. Willow watched as they wheel him away.

Her nightmare was finally over.

Steven couldn't hurt her anymore.

She struggled with her emotions and started to cry.

Jenna held her close and hushed her cries.

It took a few minutes, but when she regained her composure, one of the detectives sat across from them and asked some more questions. Actually, it was the same questions. Over and over again. Willow wanted to shout at him to leave them alone. But she didn't. She understood they had a job to do. She just wanted the whole thing to be over.

"When will we be able to start cleaning up?" Jenna asked, as the man stood to walk away.

"Not until the investigation team is done. We'll let you know."

"Can we use the other rooms to shower and change?"

"We'd appreciate it, if you didn't. Not until we've had a chance to clear each room."

"But everything happened on the west side of the house."

"Miss," Willow heard irritation in the detective's voice. "This is a homicide investigation, not just a break in. We need to be thorough."

"Homicide?" Willow didn't even consider the ramifications for Austin. "Mr. Taylor saved our lives," she snapped. "Steven had every intention of killing us. He told me so! You can't charge Mr. Taylor with murder!"

"We understand that, Ms. Jenner," he said in a more compassionate tone. "That's why we want to be exhaustive in our investigation. We want to make sure the evidence supports your statements. I promise, as soon as we're done, someone will let you know."

Jenna watched as the last of the police made their way down the driveway and to their cars. She cringed when she saw the crowd that had formed along the edge of the street. *Poor Uncle Austin. He going to get filleted at the homeowners meeting that's sure to be called.* With an arm around Willow's shoulders, she led her to Austin's bedroom. "Sit here. I'll be right back with something for you to change into."

Standing in the doorway of the guest room, Jenna shuddered. Broken glass. Splintered doorframe. Overturned chair. She closed her eyes. *Thank you, God.* The realization of what they just survived was almost incomprehensible.

Shaking off the morbid thoughts, she pulled a few items from Willow's bag, then hurried back, not wanting to leave her by herself for too long. When she returned, Willow had not moved. She sat with a catatonic-like stare on her face, her hands clenched in her lap. Jenna lowered herself beside her, on the edge of the bed. After a few minutes of silence, she asked, "What are you thinking?"

"I don't know. Nothing. Everything."

Jenna waited for her to say more, but she didn't. "Willow, don't get lost inside your head. Tell me what you're thinking, how you're feeling."

"I don't know what to feel, Jenna," she whispered. "Relieved? Numb? Guilty?"

"You have nothing to feel guilty about. What happened is not your fault," Jenna said firmly.

"Isn't it?' Willowed turned to her. "If I had left Steven sooner, this wouldn't have happened. I could've prevented all this if I had been stronger. Steven would still be alive."

"And you would be dead," Jenna raised her voice. "Do you really think if you'd left him sooner, he would have reacted differently? He hunted you down. Broke into someone else's house. Held you at knifepoint. Thank God it happened now, when you had somewhere to go. What do you think would've happened if he'd gotten you alone? He was psychotic. He chose his fate by the life he led. Yes, it's horrible it came to this. But thank God, you're alive."

Willow's shoulder's sunk, weighed down with remorse.

"Look at me, Willow." Jenna reached for her hand, wanting to encourage her with strength, but Willow's face was so drawn and ashen, Jenna welled up. "I am not glad that Steven is dead, but I am glad that you're safe and never need to worry or hide from him again. There's nothing wrong with feeling safe, Willow."

Tears slid from the corners of Willow's eyes. They were quiet tears, but Jenna could see they were also tears of hope. Hope for a new beginning. Jenna hugged her close and waited until Willow took a cleansing breath.

"Look, we need to get out of these clothes. The chlorine smell is killing me." Jenna put the items she'd taken from Willow's bag and laid them on her lap. "Take a shower and get dressed. You'll feel a little better. Nancy should be here in about an hour."

"Your doctor makes house calls?"

"No, my friend makes house calls. It just so happens that the doctor in her comes along."

Jenna smiled as she left the room.

FIFTY-SIX

As Ashley broke through the fog caused by the pain medication, she focused on her surroundings. Reaching toward the side of the bed, she felt someone take hold of her hand.

"Hi honey, how are you feeling?"

It took all the energy she had just to turn her head, but when she saw the outline of Austin's features, a small smile pulled at her lips.

Surely the surgery hadn't erased her ability to think or speak, but it seemed so difficult to get both her mind and lips to respond at the same time. She closed her eyes, swallowed, and tried again.

"I feel like an elephant is sitting on me. But the nurse said I could keep pressing this button whenever I feel pain." Ashley's words were slow and deliberate. She tried to smile, but when she looked at Austin, she noticed something in his eyes—apprehension, fatigue.

Something is wrong.

"What is it, Austin? What aren't you telling me? Did something go wrong?"

"No, nothing went wrong, Ashley. Everything went as planned."

The smile on his face was for her benefit, but Austin had never been good at masking his feelings.

"Where is C.J.?" A feeling of dread came over her. *Why isn't C.J. here?* Wild horses couldn't keep him away at a time like this, unless something was wrong.

"He's just down the hall. I think he's trying to do the gallant thing and allow us some time alone. After all, we are still newlyweds." Austin leaned over Ashley and placed a few kisses on her forehead and cheek.

Austin used distraction as an ally. He knew he couldn't upset Ashley with the truth, but he did not like deceiving her—even if it was for the right reasons.

He watched as Ashley began to drift. When he heard the evenness of her breathing, he carefully laid her hand aside and quietly left the room. He needed to check in on C.J., make sure he was doing okay. Hopefully, Ashley wouldn't wake and find him gone.

Hurrying to the ER, Austin asked about C.J. Stating he was family, a nurse led him down a corridor of beds separated only by movable curtains. When he got to the last partition on the left, he peered around it and saw C.J. sitting on the edge of the bed. Shirt off. Arm bandaged. A doctor giving him instructions. They both looked at Austin as he stepped forward.

"How are you doing, C.J.?"

Perturbed by the interruption, the doctor asked, "Who are you?"

"He's my son." The words came out as if Austin had said them a thousand times before. There was a familiarity in them. A rightness. He looked at C.J. for an adverse reaction, but there was none. Instead, C.J. shook his head slightly and glanced at him with a halfhearted grin.

"Your son was very lucky, Mr. Summers. It was a penetrating wound but missed the brachial artery. He'll feel stiff for a few days, and have a small scar, but other than that, he'll be just fine."

"So, he's free to go?"

"Yes," he answered, then reached inside the pocket of his medical coat. "But I'm going to write a prescription for the pain. You don't have to take it if you don't want to," he directed his instructions at C.J., "but I would suggest taking it at bedtime. No sense losing sleep while you're trying to recover."

The doctor handed the scribbled prescription to Austin, along with C.J.'s discharge papers. "I hear your son was quite the hero today, Mr. Summers. Something you can be proud of in this day and age. Most of the young men I treat are getting into trouble, instead of doing something to stop it."

"I'm very proud of C.J., and he is his mother's pride and joy." Austin looked at C.J. with admiration. *So, this is what it feels like to be a father.* He shook the doctor's outstretched hand before the man moved on to the next patient.

C.J. lowered his feet to the floor and started to put on his shirt. When Austin saw the bloodstains, he stopped him. "Here, take mine." He quickly unbuttoned his long sleeve, blue micro plaid shirt, leaving him only in his dark blue T-shirt. "I know you'd prefer the T-shirt, but it won't hide your bandage. Your mom has already asked about you once, and if you're not there the next time she wakes up, there'll be no stopping the onslaught of questions."

C.J. slowly slid his bandaged arm into the cotton shirt, then craned his other arm around until he caught the dangling sleeve. After pulling it up over his shoulders, he tried buttoning the shirt, but his bandaged arm wouldn't cooperate.

"Here, let me do it." Austin stepped forward and started on the second button down.

"Gee, you take this fatherly thing pretty serious, *Mr. Summers*," C.J. teased.

Austin looked up from what he was doing. Seeing the humor in C.J.'s eyes, he smiled. "Look, if I had taken the time to correct the doctor or try to explain our relationship, he'd still be standing here."

"I think you explained our relationship pretty well."

The change in C.J.'s expression from humor to seriousness caught Austin off guard. Swallowing past the knot in his throat, he rolled up the sleeves to just below C.J.'s elbows. "I know it's not flannel, but it will have to do."

They walked toward the elevator in silence, a silence no longer laced with strain, but with comfort.

Their relationship had turned another corner.

FIFTY-SEVEN

Squeezing her eyes shut, Willow tensed each time the doctor pressed or probed. Though she was gentle, and used words of comfort, it did little to mask the pain.

"Sorry," Nancy whispered as she took off her gloves. "I know that was uncomfortable, but I needed to be thorough. The bruising on your right side worried me. I felt some swelling, but no breaks, so that's good. Ibuprofen and ice should help with the pain and swelling. Are you having a hard time breathing?"

"No. It's uncomfortable, but not stabbing."

"Good. I want you to take at least one deep breath every hour. If it's too painful to do that, I want you to give me a call, okay?"

Willow nodded anxious to know the rest. "What about . . . everything else?"

"You won't need a D&C, if that's what you're asking?" she said with a reassuring smile.

Willow sighed with relief.

"The bleeding patterns you described are within the normal range and should continue to taper off. Your discomfort should also decrease a little each day, but since you have other injuries, it might be hard to distinguish. If you're still bleeding in a week or the amount of bleeding increases, I'll want to see you again. The same with heavy cramping. Aching is normal, but if you're cramping is so severe it takes your breath away, it could mean something more serious. Try not to worry, though. You need to channel what energy you have into the healing process."

"Okay."

"Willow, I'm sorry for your loss," Nancy reached out and took her hand. "A miscarriage is a very emotional event for a woman, regardless how she conceived, and you've already been through so much physically and psychologically. The days ahead are going to be difficult. Lean on your friends or call me. Don't try to process all this on your own."

Willow did not know how to respond. She didn't deserve people's sympathy. She'd been so upset when she found out she was pregnant—angry even. She blamed God, thinking Him callous and spiteful. She was convinced He'd allowed her to get pregnant as a form of punishment. Now that *punishment* was gone, and Willow was devastated. She didn't deserve people's pity; she deserved to suffer. But her child didn't.

She started to cry.

Nancy squeezed her hand even tighter, but Willow pulled her hand away. "It's my fault." She stood and walked to the sliding door overlooking the pool, but a flash—the memory of C.J. and Steven wrestling in the pool—made her turn away. "It's my fault. I never wanted this child. I didn't want Steven's child. I was angry and bitter. I'm a hypocrite; I don't deserve anyone's sympathy."

"This isn't your fault." Nancy walked over to where she stood. "Lots of women are overwhelmed when they find out they're pregnant. It's not the right time, they're not ready, or like you, they're in a difficult relationship. But that doesn't mean the woman wishes her child was dead. Willow, you didn't want your child to die. You are not responsible for what happened."

"I am. I am responsible," she sobbed. "I should have left Steven the minute I found out I was pregnant. I knew his temper. I knew what he was capable of. But I was afraid. I put my fears ahead of the safety of my child. I'm to blame. It's my fault."

Willow sunk to the edge of the bed, and completely lost it.

Nancy sat with her, letting her cry.

Letting her mourn.

After getting up and splashing water on her face, Willow apologized for her meltdown. Nancy just nodded, then gave her some gentle advice, a brochure of dos and don'ts after a miscarriage, two business cards for women's counseling centers, and her own.

"Now, remember, you can call me anytime. You have my card. When I have your test results, I'll give you a call. Hang in there, Willow. Just take one day at a time."

After Nancy left, there was a muffled tap on the door. "Can I come in?" Jenna asked as she opened the door slightly.

Willow rested against the headboard. "Yes."

"How are you feeling? Nancy said you were doing pretty well— all things considered. Did you feel comfortable enough with her?"

"Yeah, she was very nice. You were right. She does have the

best interest of her patients at heart."

"Well, I just wanted to check on you, and let you know, if you hear a male voice, don't panic. Simon is here, and he's going to take care of the repairs and security. Why don't you rest a little bit, while I talk with him, and then I'll take you to the hospital to meet up with C.J."

Willow scooted to the edge of the bed. "I'd rather wait in the living room if you don't mind." She stood. "I just don't want to be alone."

~®~

Ashley couldn't make sense of what she was seeing.

C.J. was standing by the side of the bed, holding her hand. *But why is he wearing Austin's shirt?* She knew the pain medication could mess with her mind, but this was so bizarre. *Did I dream that Austin was wearing that exact same shirt?* She pushed the thought from her mind, so she could concentrate on what C.J. was saying.

". . . I said, your color looks good." C.J. squeezed her hand as he spoke.

"I know. You always look good in blue."

~®~

C.J. grinned at Austin.

His mom wasn't making much sense, but the doctor said she could be a little out of it for the remainder of the day. The two of them sat with her until evening—taking turns walking the halls, stretching, and making hourly visits to the vending machines.

Austin has just come in from one such visit, when he glanced at his watch.

"Look, C.J., I'm going to sleep here tonight. Why don't you go back to my place, get some rest, and bring me a change of clothes in the morning?"

"Are you sure?"

"As long as your well enough to drive?"

He nodded. "My truck is an automatic, it won't be a problem. But I think I'm going to take Willow back to the ranch. She'll feel more at home there now that Steven's . . . well, now that she's safe. Is there anything else you need from your house, other than clothes?"

"No. But let me ask you something. How much do you know about this Steven guy?"

"Not much, why?"

"It makes me nervous thinking Jenna will be at the house by herself. I mean, we don't know if this guy had friends helping him or buddies who are going to be seeking revenge. I'd feel a lot better knowing she's not at the house alone. She could go home, but then I would have to explain to my sister how Jenna got tangled up with a deranged gunman. I'd rather save that conversation for after Ashley's home. Do you think she could stay at the ranch with you and Willow? I mean, you still have the security presence, right?"

"Of course. No problem. But what if she won't come? She seems pretty independent."

Austin laughed. "So, you noticed that."

"Yeah, she definitely—Uh-oh." C.J. looked at the T.V. monitor on the wall while reaching for the controls on Ashley's bed rail. He turned the volume up a few notches as Austin's house came into view.

". . . we still don't know the details of the case, but we do know there was at least one fatality, and others injured in what seems to be a home invasion in this very exclusive neighborhood. We will be bringing you more details as they become available. This is Evan Jones at *The Estates*. Back to you in the studio."

C.J. and Austin turned to each other and knew they were going to have their work cut out for them. Not only keeping this from his mom but trying to keep things under wraps for privacy sake.

"I better get over there. I don't want Willow strong-armed by the media. She can't handle just one more thing right now."

C.J. headed to Austin's, not knowing what he would find. When he got there, he was met by a string of media vehicles at the front entrance and three guards on duty.

Isn't that always the case. Beef up security after there's been a problem.

He pulled up to the guard shack and told the man on duty he was on the visitor's list.

"Too bad, buddy, only residences are being allowed in."

"But I have to pick up someone." The guard looked at C.J. more intently.

"Hey, you're one of the fellas who got hurt in this whole mess," the security guard said, just loud enough for one of the media vultures to hear.

"Over here, Jerry. This guy was part of the incident."

The cameraman swung over to the side of C.J.'s truck and

flipped on a light, nearly blinding him. The man with the microphone hurried to the driver's side window, shoved the mic in C.J.'s face, then asked a string of questions, not even acknowledging that C.J. answered with a firm "no comment." Feeling trapped, C.J. looked over his shoulder to back up, but the swarm had him surrounded.

Finally, a policeman came over and addressed the press, warning them if they didn't stay in the cordoned off area, he would throw them off the property. He then leaned into the vehicle and spoke to C.J.

"Can I see some I.D., please?"

C.J. pulled out his wallet and flipped it open. "I'm here to pick up Willow Jenner. She's expecting me."

The officer spoke with the guard, made a few calls, then escorted C.J. to the house. The patrol car pulled to the curb in front of the house, allowing C.J. enough room to turn into the driveway. As C.J. got out of his truck, he watched the cop approach the unauthorized camera crew that was responsible for the report he'd seen on TV.

C.J. entered the house to find Willow tucked in a ball, asleep in one of the chairs. Jenna was in the office area off the kitchen making phone calls. When Jenna saw C.J., she acknowledged him, but held up her hand so she could finish her phone conversation.

"What happened, C.J.?" she asked after clicking off the phone. "How did reporters get past the gate and the police? The phone is ringing off the hook with people calling to make sure Uncle Austin is okay."

"It looks like a camera crew got past security and filmed out front. Anyone who knows where Austin lives would have recognized the house. The story is leading the news. Something like this doesn't usually happen in such an exclusive, gated community. We saw the report while we were at the hospital, so Austin doesn't want you staying here tonight."

"No problem there," Jenna huffed. "My mom called, nearly hyperventilating. She's coming to pick me up."

C.J. saw movement out of the corner of his eye and turned to see a man walking down the hall, his phone pressed against his cheek.

"C.J., you remember Simon, Uncle Austin's business partner?" Jenna whispered. "He's here to arrange for security and take care of the mess."

C.J. nodded and shook his hand, while Simon continued with his phone conversation.

"He's trying to line up as many repairmen as possible, so Uncle Austin doesn't have to worry about it."

C.J. waited for him to pace back down the hall, then turned to Jenna. "How's Willow doing? Did your doctor friend come by?"

"She's doing as well as can be expected. Nancy said physically she's as good as she looks. Battered and emotional. Her ribs are badly bruised, but other than that, she doesn't expect any other health issues. She gave her a prescription for antibiotics, and Willow has pretty much slept since Nancy left. She's struggling with Steven's death. She feels guilty—thinks she's to blame. I tried talking to her, and she knows in her heart this isn't her fault, but her head is still playing mind games with her."

A knock at the front door interrupted their conversation and caused Willow to stir. C.J. answered the door and let in the policeman who had escorted him to the house.

"So, how'd the camera crew get in?" C.J. asked, with attitude.

"Evan Jones lives here. He snuck in his crew and got an exclusive. They're gone now."

"But the damage is done," Jenna snapped. "The house has been on the news, and now the phone is ringing off the hook. The owner of the house has arranged for private security to come in for the night, and the rest of us will be leaving." Jenna handed the cop Simon's business card. "He'll take over from here."

"That's not necessary, folks. We'll make sure no one comes near the house."

Jenna rolled her eyes. "All the same, I think private security is best. These people have a relationship with the owner and will handle the job with confidence."

The officer shrugged. "It's your call. I'll be outside when you're ready to leave." He closed the door as he left.

"What's happening?" Willow asked from where she was curled up on the chair.

C.J. crossed the living room and sat on the coffee table opposite her. "The news is carrying the story of the shooting."

Panic filled Willow's face.

"Don't worry," C.J. reassured her with a gently placed hand on her knee. "No names have been given. The only real information they have is that someone was shot, and they've shown a picture of the house. Jenna's mom is coming to get her, and I'm taking you back to the ranch, okay?"

"How's Ashley?"

C.J. recognized Willow's attempt to change the subject, but let it go. "She's doing well. We should know more tomorrow when the doctor has some results. Austin is staying with her tonight. She's still pretty incoherent."

"You should be with your mom, not worrying about me."

"There's nothing I can do there. If anything comes up I should know about, Austin will call."

Willow gently caressed the bulge of bandage under the sleeve of C.J.'s shirt. "How are you doing?"

"I'm fine. After the doc got it all cleaned up, it was barely a scratch."

"And how many stitches did this *scratch* require?" Willow raised her eyebrow.

"One or two. . ." He tried to play it off, but the seriousness in Willow's expression made the truth pop right out. ". . . or twelve."

"Twelve is *not* 'barely a scratch.' Does it hurt much?"

"No, it's stiff, but I'll tell you what did hurt was that blasted tetanus shot. I swear they used a needle the size of a twig of straw." C.J. chuckled, then turned the conversation back to Willow. "So, are you ready to get back to the ranch?"

"More than ready."

FIFTY-EIGHT

When Austin awoke the next morning, it took him a minute to recognize his surroundings. The chair that converted to a bed was more comfortable than it looked, allowing him a pretty decent night's sleep, considering the circumstances. Sitting up, he stretched, then turned to see Ashley staring back at him. He smiled and walked over to her bed. Leaning over the rail, he kissed her on the lips—lips that once again held color.

"Good morning, beautiful. How are you feeling?"

Ashley had a strange expression on her face that Austin couldn't quite decipher.

"Better, considering the wool I have over my eyes."

Austin didn't know what to make of her statement. Ashley seemed alert and not in as much pain, but why wasn't she making sense?

"I guess the medicine still has you a little loopy, because that didn't make any sense." He was trying to be lighthearted because he didn't want to hurt her feelings, but he could see she wasn't going to let it drop.

"No. I might be speaking slow, but believe me, I know exactly what I'm saying. You see, I woke up last night and couldn't get back to sleep. You seemed comfortable, so I didn't want to wake you. Imagine my surprise to see a picture of your house on the late-night news." Ashley slowly pushed herself up to a sitting position, wincing as she laid her arms across her chest and stated very firmly, "Spill it, Taylor! You have some explaining to do."

He sighed.

"Is it that bad?" Ashley's playfulness quickly vanished when he didn't have a ready answer. "Did something happen to Jenna?"

"Jenna's fine," Austin said, knowing he should have had this moment all planned out. He knew he was going to have to tell Ashley, but now that that time was here, he was drawing a blank on how he should start.

"I saw the tail end of the report so the only two pieces of information I have is that there was some sort of home invasion and it happened at your house. Now . . . I've been patient all night, but if you don't start filling in the blanks, I'm going to march down to the corner newsstand and find out for myself."

"Hold on, Ashley. Just give me a minute to figure out where to start."

"Start by telling me everyone is okay."

Austin reached for Ashley's hand and held it firmly. "Everyone is going to be okay."

" 'Going to be?' Who's hurt?"

"Ashley do you want me to tell you what happened, or just tell you the outcome?"

"I want you to tell me who's hurt?"

He knew he had no choice, so he just said it. "Jenna has a slight bump, C.J. needed a few stitches, and Willow is recovering from a very traumatic experience."

"Willow? But they said it was a home invasion. What was Willow doing at your house?"

"Okay, Ashley, this is where you have to stop long enough for me to explain, or else we're going to go in circles, and you're going to get yourself all worked up."

Ashley dropped her head back into her pillows. Austin could tell she was already drained from her little outburst and was getting herself all worked up.

Just then a nurse stepped through the door and approached Ashley's bed. "Everything all right in here? Your heart rate is a bit elevated. Are you in pain, Mrs. Taylor?" When Ashley didn't respond, the nurse looked to Austin for an explanation.

"I was telling her some disturbing news. I warned her not to get worked up, but she's pretty bullheaded."

"Okay, Mrs. Taylor, your husband is right. You can't let yourself get worked up right now. You need your strength for your recovery. I want you to close your eyes for a few minutes and take a couple of deep breaths, okay?"

~®~

Ashley did what she was told, but her mind wouldn't stop racing. The *what, who, and whys,* multiplied, but nothing made sense. The only thing that gave her a measure of comfort was the fact that Austin had been in her room throughout the night.

If he was here all night, it can't be that bad.

Or so she tried to convince herself.

"Mrs. Taylor, I need you to relax."

She looked at the nurse, to Austin, then to the monitor that betrayed her. Knowing she would not get any answers until her heart rate improved, she closed her eyes, and took slow, even breaths.

After a few minutes, the nurse stepped away from the monitor. "Okay, Mrs. Taylor, I'm going to go for now, but I'll be back if I see another spike like that." She turned to Austin. "And I'll give him the boot," she said with a smile, "if he's the one responsible for jeopardizing your condition. And that would be a real shame." She left the room, still smiling.

Ashley turned to Austin, and calmly asked again, "So, what happened?"

Austin took a deep breath, pulled a chair to the side of her bed and began to explain.

Willow felt more rested than she expected.

After arriving at the ranch last night, C.J. walked her to what was now being considered *her room*. When she lay down on the bed, exhaustion completely consumed her. She figured she would be up all night with nightmares and flashbacks, but she didn't remember waking up, not even once.

Still wearing Jenna's dress and wrapped up in the bed quilt, it was the sunrise that had awakened her.

It was a new day.

A new start.

When she stood, she felt achy and sore, but not as weary. Walking to the bathroom, she refused to look at herself in the mirror. She didn't want her outward appearance to weaken the hopefulness she felt inside. Stepping into the shower, she felt a renewed strength—strength that had eluded her the last few days. The warm water kneaded her muscles and made her feel clean again. Wrapping her hair in a towel and another around her body, she crossed the bedroom to the foot of the bed. Movement to her left caused her to turn. C.J. was standing next to the window, the old fashion crank in his hand.

When C.J. saw Willow standing with only a towel wrapped around her, the attraction he felt for her ignited. There was no more hiding the truth. It wasn't just the need to protect her—because Willow no longer needed protection—it was desire that made his heart race and his body flame.

He didn't realize he was staring, but when Willow took a step back and held the towel tighter across her chest, he snapped to.

"Sorry, I . . . I didn't mean to intrude. I knocked but you didn't answer." He finished cranking the window open, then stood with his hands in his pockets. "I was just letting in some fresh air. It's a beautiful day outside, and it seemed a bit stuffy in here." Not sure what to say next, he hurried toward the door. "I'll be downstairs making breakfast. Come down when you're ready. No rush."

C.J. descended the stairs at lightning speed. His heart was going a mile a minute, and he felt like his body was on fire.

I'm in trouble. Deep, deep trouble.

Working at the stove, C.J. knew the minute Willow walked into the kitchen, but he didn't turn around, afraid he might say or do something stupid.

Willow took a seat at the breakfast bar across from where he was cracking eggs into a bowl.

"You know, C.J., with you having to go to the emergency room, and being at the hospital with your mom, I never got a chance to apologize for everything that happened or thank you for all you've done for me." Willow paused, but he didn't look up, sure what he was feeling was written all over his face. "I want you to know, I don't think I could've made it without you. I would've given up."

C.J. poured the scrambled eggs into a pan, pushed them around, then folded the mixture into itself. "You don't need to apologize. None of this was your fault."

"It *was* my fault. I involved you. And when I think of what could've happened, I freak out all over again."

C.J. looked up. "But it's over, so let it go."

"'Let it go?' Steven could've killed you!"

"But he didn't. And for the record, I involved myself."

Willow didn't comment, she just watched as he worked at the stove.

"What I don't understand," C.J. said as he salted and peppered the eggs, "is how you endured so much for so long. I can't imagine what it must have felt like, living in fear every time you went home." He turned to the oven and pulled out English muffins with slices of melted cheese on them. After pushing the eggs around for a few more minutes, he tipped the pan over the muffins and allowed the eggs to tumble out.

"So, what's next?" he asked as he set a plate in front of her. "Do you think we're going to have problems with Steven's friends?" He leaned against the cabinet behind him, holding his plate in one hand and a fork in the other. "Are they the type to retaliate?"

"I don't think so. The only friends Steven had were people he could use and manipulate. Once he got what he wanted from someone, he usually cut them lose. Derek and Carlos were pretty tight with him, but they've both done jail time. I don't see them sticking their necks out for Steven, especially now that he's . . . gone." Willow cleared her throat as she pushed the eggs around on her plate.

"That's good to know. Now, why don't I pray so you can do more than push your food around?" He chanced a smile before bowing his head.

"Lord, I don't know what to make of all this. I'm glad Willow is safe and that nothing worse happened to her or Jenna. I know this didn't take You by surprise, but Lord, help us understand how to deal with the issues that face us now. I pray nothing will happen to Austin because of the shooting, and I pray that when Mom finds out, she's able to deal with it without endangering her health. Be with Jenna while her parents try to comprehend all that happened. Thank you for your protection, as veiled as it was. Bless this food and give Willow the strength she needs. Amen."

"Thank you for praying, C.J. You know, I've been so wrapped up in me, I didn't even think about the fact that Austin could be in trouble for the shooting. The police will see it was self-defense, or defense for someone else, right?"

"I'm sure they will, once they get all the facts in order."

Willow and C.J. were quiet as they continued eating. C.J. poured two glasses of orange juice, setting one in front of Willow, and chugging the other in just a few swallows. When he was done, he placed his plate and glass in the sink.

"Willow, I thought we could go to your place today and get some of your things. Do you think you could handle being back there?"

"Will you stay with me?"

"Every step of the way."

~Ⓡ~

It took over an hour for Austin to explain to Ashley everything that had transpired—from C.J.'s phone call on their honeymoon to the break-in at the house. He didn't know all the details regarding Willow's injuries or what led to Steven's shocking behavior, but it didn't matter. Not anymore.

Ashley looked stunned and was obviously having a hard time absorbing all that had happened in the last few days. "I can't believe you kept this from me?"

"It was for your own good."

"My son was nearly killed, and you didn't think I should know that?"

"Come on, Ash, what went on at the house happened after you were in surgery. None of us could've predicted something so over the top. We still don't even know how Steven tracked Willow down."

"But I don't understand, how did you know to go back to the house?"

"I didn't. It just so happened that I left my cell phone on the counter. When C.J. and I went back for it, we noticed the door had been tampered with, then heard yelling. We crept inside and saw Steven by the pool holding Willow at knife point. The next thing I know, C.J. leaps on Steven, sending all three of them into the pool. I went for my gun in my bedroom and was going to fire a warning shot, but when Steven arched his arm back with the knife directed at C.J., I knew I didn't have time. I had a clear shot, so I took it."

Ashley flinched at Austin's admission.

"I had no choice, Ashley. Steven had the upper hand. He was going to kill C.J. if I didn't do something."

"Are you okay? That had to be awful for you."

"I've tried not thinking about it." He felt bile rise at the back of his throat and took a deep breath to maintain his composure. "When I saw C.J. struggling with Steven in the pool, I knew I had no choice."

Ashley clutched his hand.

"Hey," he smiled, not wanting her to worry further. "What's important is everyone's okay. Traumatized, but okay."

"What happened next?"

"I checked on Jenna, and C.J. pulled Willow from the water. Once we knew they were okay, I called the police. They came.

Paramedics came. It was chaos."

"And now?"

"The house is a crime scene. Jenna has a bump on her head. C.J. has a cut on his arm with twelve stitches. And I think only time will tell how this is all going to affect Willow. She has been through an awful lot in the last few months, so I think we'll just have to wait and see."

"What about you, Austin? Are the police going to charge you with Steven's death?"

"I don't know, Ash. I mean, it's obvious Steven was deranged." Austin could see worry creasing the edges of her eyes. "Don't worry, Ashley, I've given the police my full cooperation, and told them I would be available for further questions. I have nothing to hide. I acted out of fear and defense for the lives of other people."

Ashley continued to pepper Austin with questions, and he had to reassure her several more times that C.J. was okay. Finally, he asked for a break. "How about we take a breather, so I can at least get cleaned up?"

"Okay." She squeezed his hand, then pressed her palm to his cheek. "Thank God you're okay—that everyone's okay." She closed her eyes, but he knew sleeping was the furthest thing from her mind; she was just letting it all sink in.

Walking to the bathroom, Austin leaned over the sink, splashed some water on his face, then helped himself to the sterile items in the bathroom meant for Ashley. He unwrapped the toothbrush and comb, then used both to make his appearance a little more suitable. After readying himself for the next round of questions, he exited the bathroom and saw a nurse leaning over Ashley. His heart skipped a beat, thinking something was wrong. Panic must have been evident on his face because she quickly assured him everything was fine.

"Don't worry, Mr. Taylor. This is all routine."

He relaxed and waited until she finished, but then the dietitian came in with a breakfast tray. When she walked out of the room, it took only a second for Ashley to ask her first question.

"How is C.J. holding up? It sounds like he's had to deal with a lot. He has to be freaking out."

"You'd be very proud at the way he's handled everything, Ash. I don't think I was that mature at his age."

"When do you think he'll come to the hospital?" Ashley quickly brushed a tear aside. "I just want to see him for myself. Wait a minute. I wasn't dreaming last night. Was C.J. wearing your shirt yesterday when he came to see me?"

"Yeah, he was in emergency getting stitched up, but his shirt was bloody. How did you remember that?"

"I just remember seeing C.J. and wondering why he was wearing your shirt. I figured I was either hallucinating or dreaming, so I didn't say anything. At least now I know I'm not going crazy."

Ashley looked over the food tray that had been left for her. "Care to join me in a decadent bowl of oatmeal and sliced fruit?"

FIFTY-NINE

C.J. could tell Willow was hesitant as she slowly approached her and Steven's apartment. She got out her keys and tried to insert one into the lock, but her hands were shaking so bad, she dropped them.

"Here, let me do it," C.J. said as he bent to pick them up.

"It's the one with the red ring on it," she whispered.

He found the right key and opened the door. The apartment was much the way he remembered it, except for the addition of even more beer cans and liquor bottles littering the coffee table and kitchen counter.

Slowly, Willow crossed the room, as if she feared disturbing something or someone. C.J. followed closely, wanting her to feel safe.

The bedroom was in shambles. It looked like Steven had been searching for something and destroyed Willow's belongings in the process. Her dresses and blouses were ripped in two. A pile of empty perfume bottles, spilled makeup containers, and costume jewelry were piled in the center of the bed, caked together by the powders and liquids. Willow quietly walked through the room to the bed. Grabbing a pillow, she removed the case, and used it to gather the things that hadn't been ruined. The stench from the pile of jeans and T-shirts at the foot of the bed was almost unbearable. A mixture of spilled beer and bodily fluids, if C.J. had to guess.

Willow gathered up a few pairs of shoes that looked unscathed and picked through another mound of clothes on the far side of the room. She dumped most of the contents from an untouched dresser drawer into the pillow case and gazed around the room on the verge of tears. Then she moved the chair from the corner of the room, to the door of the closet, and stood on it.

"Wait. Hold on. What are you doing?"

"I hid some things in an old purse at the top of the closet." Willow strained to grab it, while clutching her side, but it was still out of reach.

"Here, I'll get it." He helped her down then stood on the chair. "What am I looking for?"

"The straw purse in the top right corner."

C.J. grabbed the purse, surprised at how heavy it was. He handed it to Willow, who was visibly relieved to see the contents were still there. She hooked the large purse over her shoulder and slowly looked around the room. After adding a few more things to her makeshift nap sack, she turned to leave.

"There's nothing else for me here."

Willow walked backed into the living room and looked around.

"Is there anything here you want to grab? Like the dishes or some of the furniture?"

"No. I'll tell the building manager to keep the cleaning deposit and do whatever he wants with the stuff."

"But you could use some of it when you get back on your—"

"No!" Willow snapped. "I don't want it. Any of it."

"Okay. That's fine." C.J. reached for her, stroking her arm. "But what about Steven's stuff?" he whispered. "Does he have any family?"

"No." Willow said before hurrying out the front door.

They walked to the manager's apartment on the first floor. When a woman opened the door, she quickly stepped forward and pulled Willow into a hug. "I just saw the news, honey. I'm so sorry."

"Thank you, Mrs. Benson," Willow said as she pulled away. "Look, I don't want anything that is left in the apartment. So, if it's all right with you, I'll just forfeit the cleaning deposit and let you and your husband take care of everything."

"Of course, dear. That will be just fine. Is there somewhere I can reach you, in case I have any questions or find something that looks valuable?"

C.J. pulled out his wallet and handed her a business card. "You can reach us at this number if you have any questions."

Mrs. Benson looked at the card, then at C.J. with a smile. She rested her frail hand on Willow's forearm and gave it a squeeze. "I'm glad to see you have someone to take care of you."

It was obvious the woman knew Willow's relationship with Steven wasn't a pleasant one. Angered, C.J. wondered how many of her other neighbors knew Willow was being abused but did nothing to stop it.

Carrying Willow's stuff to the truck, C.J. opened the passenger door and swung the bundle into the backseat before Willow got in.

Closing the door behind her, he crossed to the driver's side and climbed in. Turning the key in the ignition, he looked straight ahead and asked, "Your landlord knew, didn't she?"

Willow nodded. "She tried to help in the beginning. When Steven would leave in a tantrum, she'd check in on me—make sure I was okay. When he came home drunk, she'd offer me a place to stay until he sobered up. But when Steven found out, he started causing trouble. Intimidating stares. Obscene trash left in front of their door. He even wrecked an apartment after they got it ready for a tenant. The Bensons are old and retired. They couldn't handle that kind of turmoil, so they just looked the other way. I don't blame them. I don't blame anyone but myself."

"Willow, you have to stop thinking like that. It's obvious Steven was psychotic. You didn't have a choice. You were in survival mode."

She didn't say anything, she just turned toward the passenger window and leaned her forehead against the glass.

The ride back to the ranch was frustratingly quiet. C.J. didn't want to pressure Willow into carrying on a conversation, but he didn't want to be shut out either. He knew she needed space to come to terms with all that had happened, but he was afraid if she got too into her head, she would spiral.

When they got home, C.J. took Willow's bundle of stuff to the laundry room. When he went to dump it out on the utility table, Willow reached for it. "I can do this," she said.

He swiveled the bag out of her reach. "I'll do it. You need your rest."

When he shook out the pillow case, a few items tumbled to the floor. Willow quickly snatched them up and snapped, "I said, I can do it!"

C.J. looked at the bra and underpants clutched to her chest and cringed. Feeling like an idiot, he turned to the washing machine and explained its idiosyncrasy. He then pulled down the soap, fabric softener, and stain remover from the upper shelf, so Willow wouldn't have to reach for them.

"If you don't mind, I'd like to get to the hospital in the next hour. Why don't you get a load started, and then we can go together?"

"You go ahead. I'll just stay here and get this done."

"Are you sure? I know Mom's going to ask why she hasn't seen you, yet."

"Tell her I'm holding down the fort. That will make her feel better. Besides, I might go over to the office and spend some time getting caught up."

"You don't need to do that, Willow. The office can wait."

"I know, but I want to keep busy. Besides, if I do routine things, maybe I can convince myself everything is going to be all right."

"Everything *is* going to be all right. You just have to give it time." C.J. watched for a moment as she fiddled with the pile of clothes. "You're sure you're going to be okay?"

"I'm sure," her words were brisk. "You don't have to babysit me anymore. I'll be fine."

C.J. tried not to take offense to her tone. He knew he had to give her room to adjust and not take her mood swings personal. Even so, what he wanted to do was pull her close and tell her how he felt.

"Okay then . . . I guess I'll go. I'll pick up lunch for us while I'm out. Remember, Billy's around, so don't let him startle you."

Willow didn't acknowledge him; she just kept sorting.

C.J. drove to the hospital on autopilot, his thoughts still on Willow. Debating the pros and cons of telling her how he felt, he stepped off the elevator and saw Austin and the police detective from yesterday talking in the hall. He approached silently, but the conversation broke off as soon as he appeared.

"Thank you for your cooperation, Mr. Taylor; we'll be in touch." The policeman looked at C.J., nodded, then walked away.

"What was that all about? And why did he come here to talk to you? What if Mom overheard, or better yet, he walked into Mom's room and introduced himself?"

"She knows, C.J."

"What?"

"She saw it on the news last night. I told her everything this morning, well . . . as best as I could, anyway."

"What did she say? How did she take it? Is she okay?"

"Whoa, C.J.," he put up his hands. "She's fine. Upset we kept her in the dark, but she understands why we did it. Now she's just trying to wrap her head around all that happened."

"I bet she gave you an earful."

"You could say that." Austin chuckled, then asked, "How's Willow doing?"

"Okay, I guess. We went to her apartment to get some of her stuff. And you know what that son of a–"

"C.J.!" Austin snapped, then whispered, "You need to keep your voice down."

Looking around, C.J. saw he had the attention of some of the nursing staff. He smiled apologetically, then lowered his tone before continuing. "You know what that *jerk* did? He ruined her stuff. He shredded her clothes. Dumped out her makeup and perfume bottles. Trashed everything."

"Is she okay?"

"Yeah. It was a mess, but she handled it pretty well."

"Where is she now?"

"At the ranch doing laundry. She was able to salvage some of her clothes, but they were bathed in beer and . . . bodily fluids."

Austin winced. "Do you think she's doing well enough to be alone?"

"She said she was." C.J. paced a few steps from Austin, ran his hands through his hair, then walked back. "I don't know what to do. I didn't *want* to leave her alone, but she acted like she didn't want me around. So, I figured I didn't have a choice and needed to give her some space." He stared down the hall, wishing the answers were written on the wall. Shaking off the feeling of helplessness, he asked Austin about Jenna.

"She called me this morning, and said she was doing fine. Then my sister got on the phone and read me the riot act, accusing me of intentionally putting Jenna in harm's way. Once Carrie calmed down enough to listen, I explained what Jenna had already told her. Even so, she wants Jenna to stay put for a few days and take it easy. I can't say that I blame her."

"No sense talking in the hallway you two," Ashley yelled from her room. "You'll just have to repeat it all for me anyway." Both C.J. and Austin laughed at the determination that epitomized his mom. They walked into her room to see her sitting up, hands folded in her lap.

"Hi, Mom." C.J. leaned forward and gave her a kiss.

Ashley reached for his hand, tears in her eyes. "How are you doing?"

"I'm fine." He squeezed her hand knowing she needed to be reassured. "Really, I am."

"How's Willow? It must have been awful for her. Did you even know she was having these kinds of problems at home? She never said anything to me, and I guess I felt like I was prying when I asked about her personal life. She seemed so private. I had no idea this was the reason why."

C.J. waited until his mother was done with her ribbon of

questions and comments.

"No, Mom. I didn't know either."

"What happened, C.J.? I mean Austin had some details, but said he was still in the dark about what led up to all this."

"He beat the crap out of her, Mom; that's what happened!" Once again, C.J. was too loud, so Austin got up and closed the door. "Sorry! I'm still a little wound up by all of this."

"Of course you are. The last few days must've been a nightmare for you."

C.J. just nodded, afraid his emotions might seep out with his words.

"Willow must be devastated. Did she still have feelings for this Steven guy? I know that sounds ridiculous, but I've read stories where women still love the man they're with, even if he's abusive."

"No. She didn't love him; she was terrified of him. This wasn't a one-time thing. He's been abusing her for months." C.J. looked at his mom, a knot lodged in his throat. "But that's not all, Mom. Willow was pregnant."

Ashley gasped.

"He beat her so severely, she miscarried and lost the baby."

"Oh, C.J., no."

He took a long breath. "I just don't get it. How can a man tell a woman he loves her, then beat her to a pulp; not just once, but over and over again. It's sickening. And, I don't care how bad it sounds, I'm glad Steven's dead. Better him than Willow." C.J. saw the concern in his mother's eyes. He knew his words were cold and calloused, but he didn't care.

"How's your arm?" She asked, staring at his sleeve.

"It's nothing. The stupid tetanus shot hurt more than the cut." C.J. glanced at his arm, then turned his attention to Austin. "What did the detective have to say?"

"They figured out how Steven got past security at the gate. He told the guard he was there to deliver a piece of equipment to another landscaping crew. He had a landscape insignia magnet on the side of the truck, and his license plate number somehow made it on their visitors list. So, everything seemed to check out. They're still investigating what the connection might have been to the other landscaping crew. He did his homework to get through the gate, that's for sure."

"What about you? They're not going to charge you with anything, are they?"

Austin was about to answer him, when Dr. Allen entered the room.

"Good morning, Ashley. How are you feeling?" He walked to the side of her bed.

C.J. took a step back to get out of the way but watched as Austin took a step closer and reached for his mom's hand.

"Well, I no longer feel like a truck hit me, maybe just a minivan. But why don't *you* tell me how I'm doing, then I can go from there?"

"The surgery went very well. I'm confident we were able to get all the questionable cells."

"Radiation?" his mom quickly asked.

The doctor glanced at him and Austin, then smiled at his mom. "I still feel radiation would be beneficial."

C.J. watched disappointment shadow her face. "When?" he asked.

"In a couple of weeks," the doctor answered C.J., then turned back to Ashley. "Outpatient. Monday through Friday. Just like we discussed. I know you were hoping to avoid further treatment, but I feel the benefits far outweigh the negatives."

She nodded, looking more tired than ever.

"C.J.," the doctor turned his attention back to him. "I hear you were quite the hero yesterday."

He felt anything but that, with the condition Willow was in. "No, sir. I was just helping out a friend."

"Wrestling with an armed suspect is a little more than 'just helping out a friend.' I'm glad to see you weren't injured further."

"Me, too," Ashley said, even though her eyes were closed.

"Well, I'll leave you three to your visiting," the doctor said as he reached out and shook his and Austin's hand. "Ashley, make sure you get your rest."

She opened her eyes long enough to agree, then as soon as Dr. Allen left the room, she drifted back to sleep.

Austin signaled C.J. to follow him out into the hall. "Want to grab something for lunch?"

"Nah, I'm going to pick something up on the way home. I don't want to leave Willow by herself for too long. But we'll be back later this afternoon. I think it will help Mom to see for herself that Willow is doing okay. I'll talk to you later, Austin."

SIXTY

"Willow, it's just me. I picked up some lunch." C.J. announced his arrival as he walked through the kitchen, tossed his keys on the counter, and put down the fast food bags. He waited for a response, but there was none.

Heading upstairs, he saw her bedroom door ajar. After tapping lightly, he pushed the door open, but she wasn't there. C.J. broke out in a cold sweat. "Willow! Willow!" He hurried to the laundry room where he was met by the tumbling rhythm of the dryer, but Willow wasn't there either. Trying not to panic, he remembered she said something about work. *She's probably in the office.* He rushed around to the office door. "Willow!" he yelled, then pushed the door open.

She was sitting in her normal place—at her desk—headphones on. *Thank God.* He placed his hands on his waist and took a deep breath.

Willow looked up from her work and pulled her headphones off. "C.J., what's wrong?"

"I didn't know where you were. I guess I panicked."

"I told you I wanted to catch up on some work."

"I forgot. I guess I'm still in defense mode."

"Well, I'm fine now, so stop worrying." Willow's words were sharp and to the point. Then she turned back to her computer screen and started typing.

"But I brought lunch."

"I'm not hungry!" she snapped. "And I'm not going to get any work done if you keep interrupting me."

"Fine, but you still need to eat if you hope to regain your strength."

"I think I can judge my strength just fine, thank you. I'll be in when I'm done."

Before C.J. could answer her, Willow put her headphones back on and proceeded to ignore him.

C.J. walked out of the room, not only dumbfounded, but angry. He did not deserve to be treated like an interruption. He knew Willow's emotions would rise and fall, but it hurt that she wanted to distance herself from him. He stomped back to the house, wolfed down his food, then went in search of Billy.

He and Billy walked and talked for more than an hour. Billy caught him up on the ranch as C.J. caught him up on everything else. Billy listened, completely speechless.

"Who would have figured a sweet girl like Willow was dealing with such a lowlife," Billy huffed. "She sure hasn't had an easy go of it, has she?"

"No, she hasn't."

The two men stood quietly, each lost in thought.

"Well, I know someone else having a hard time of it," Billy said with a smile. "Knight has been having a conniption these last few days. I think he feels you've deserted him."

"Then I'd better set him straight." C.J. smiled and shook Billy's hand. "Thanks for everything. I don't know what we would do without you."

"Well, you better not be planning on finding out anytime soon because you're stuck with me. Got it?"

"Got it." C.J. chuckled as he walked over to the stables.

At least Knight will welcome my attention.

"Hey boy, how you doing?" C.J. said as he stepped inside Gallant Knight's stall and stroked his neck. Knight acted aloof, like he was actually giving C.J. the brush off. "I know, I know, I deserve that. I've been ignoring you lately. But I'm here now with a peace offering. A midafternoon rubdown."

C.J. set down the tack caddy on the shelf in the corner, picked up a curry comb, and started brushing. "Have you missed me? I bet you've been talking smack about me to the ladies." He continued brushing in small circles from Knight's shoulder across to his hindquarters. "Sorry I haven't been out to see you in the last few days, but it couldn't be helped. You wouldn't believe the trouble I've gotten myself into."

Willow sat at her desk, tears running down her cheeks. She didn't mean to be so rude to C.J., it was just that she felt . . . well . . . she really wasn't sure how she felt, and that made her even more upset. She knew her feelings for C.J. were growing, but also knew she could never let them show. He was a great guy, who deserved a great girl, not someone loaded down with baggage like her.

But there was one thing he did deserve from her.

An apology.

After drying her face, Willow walked to the stables, keeping her head down, not wanting anyone to see the bruising on her face. Luckily, everyone was busy doing their own thing, so other than a few waves, no one stopped her.

She walked the corridor but didn't see C.J. anywhere. Figuring she would look out back by the practice rink, she kept walking. As she neared the tack room, she thought she heard whispering. Not wanting to intrude on a private conversation, she stopped. But when she turned to leave, she realized it was C.J. who was whispering, and it was coming from Knight's stall. Quietly, she approached, then smiled. C.J. was talking to his horse.

She found it endearing. C.J. was a hunk of a man, but here he was, whispering and cooing to Knight, his four-legged friend.

Knowing she still needed to apologize, she stepped closer. C.J. had his back to the door, so he didn't see her right away. Which was good, since she still did not know what she was going to say. Gathering her nerve, Willow watched as he tossed a curry comb in a caddy of grooming equipment, then reached for another brush.

She took a deep breath. *Okay, here it goes.* "C—"

"Take my advice, Knight, stay away from women. They are the most confusing and troublesome animal of them all."

C.J.'s words stopped Willow short.

Knight whinnied, and C.J. laughed. "Okay, so you know what I'm talking about. It's like taking a punch to the gut, and for what? So, they can kick you to the curb when they don't need you anymore."

Willow quickly backed away and hurried out of the stables.

So, under all your kind words and thoughtfulness, you think I'm trouble. Well, Mr. Summers, you don't have to worry about me causing trouble anymore. I can take care of myself.

"Ya see, Knight, just when you think you have women figured out, they change on you. I want to be there for Willow, help her through this, but she acts like she wants nothing to do with me."

C.J. changed brushes again and stroked Knight's mane.

"Maybe I was confusing her need for protection with something more." He slowed his ministrations as he inwardly addressed his feelings. *Maybe, now that she doesn't feel threatened, she no longer wants me around.* C.J. felt a twisted combination—equal parts sadness, anger, and misery. *I'll give her space, if that's what she wants. I mean, I'm certainly not going to be the one to put undue pressure on her. But this sucks!*

C.J. knew his feelings for Willow had changed into something so much more than just friendship. And while he felt wounded because she was pushing him away, he also realized he was being selfish. He'd had two interactions with Steven. And even though they were volatile and tragic, he was ready to put them behind him. But Willow . . . she'd had months of physical and emotional abuse. At one time, she'd cared for Steven. To think she could process her feelings and emotions overnight and be ready to jump into another relationship with him, was being completely unrealistic.

He would have to wait.

Allow her time to recover.

Then, when the time was right, he would tell her how he felt.

I need to get out of here.

Even though he knew he had other things that needed his attention, C.J. saddled Knight, swung up onto his back, and headed for the hills. He didn't plan on being gone long, just enough to clear his mind.

When C.J. returned from his ride, he was glad to see Willow had eaten. The fast food wrappers were in the trash, only remnants of the burger remained. When he didn't find her in the house, he figured she'd gone to the office to catch up on work. He walked over there but stopped outside the door to coach himself. *No attitude. No pressure. Just ask the question.*

He opened the door slowly, not wanting to startle her. "Hey, I'm going back to the hospital. Want to come?"

She looked up at him. No, it was actually more of a glare. "I hate to be so *troublesome*, but I did have some questions for Ashley."

Why is she acting like that? "No trouble. I'm the one who asked." C.J. heard the sarcasm seep from his comment. *Come on, keep your attitude in check.*

Without saying another word, she stood, grabbed a pair of oversized sunglasses from the desktop, and walked right by him out to his truck.

He got in and started the engine. "Don't you need your purse?"

"What for?" she said with her arms crossed against her chest.

"I don't know. I just thought . . ." *Let it go. Change the subject.* He eased from the driveway and waited for a car to pass before pulling onto the highway. "Your car will be here on Monday,"

"What?"

"I made arrangements for the mechanic to deliver your car after it was fixed."

"Thanks. I'll pay you back as soon as I get paid."

"That's not necessary."

"Well, *I* think it is."

"Whatever. We can work out finances later."

"What's to work out? I just said I would pay for it when I got paid."

C.J. opened his mouth to say something but decided against it. He drove for a few miles before Willow broke the silence.

"I'm going to start looking for an apartment on Monday. Hopefully, I can find something by the weekend."

"You can stay at the ranch as long as you like. There's no rush."

"You've been very accommodating, C.J., and I don't want to overstay my welcome, or be any more trouble than I already have been. I'll find my own place."

"Willow, what's wrong? C.J. finally asked, tired of her snippy behavior. "You've been acting strange all day."

"Oh, really?" She looked straight at him, but her sunglasses hid her eyes. "How's a girl supposed to act when she's been beaten, miscarried a baby, watched other people get hurt because of her, and seen a man get killed? Sorry, but I didn't get the memo on the proper behavior to use when your whole life is falling apart."

C.J. didn't know what to say. Willow was right. He had no business putting expectations on her. Even so, he didn't want to be treated like he was part of the problem.

Once they arrived at the hospital, C.J. led Willow to the elevator. When they exited into the corridor, he placed his hand on the small of her back to guide her in the right direction. It was just a reflex. But when she stiffened at his touch, he dropped his hand to his side.

"Room two-eleven." He pointed.

Willow slowly poked her head into the large room. Ashley was sitting up and smiled when she saw her. "Willow, I'm so glad you're here."

Willow reached for Ashley's outstretched hand. Clasping it, she leaned in for a hug.

Austin stood and joined C.J. by the door. "While you two catch up, we'll go for a walk. I need to stretch my legs."

C.J. looked at Austin, puzzled. "But I thought—"

"We'll be back in a little while." Austin cut him off and pulled him from the room.

"What was that all about?" C.J. asked.

"They need to talk. It will be easier if we're not there."

He knew Austin was right. Willow needed to be able to talk freely. It was just that she was already putting such distance between them, he didn't want to give her the opportunity to shut him out completely.

SIXTY-ONE

"How are you, Ashley?" Willow sank into the chair where Austin had been sitting.

"I'm fine. But how are you?"

Willow's eyes filled with tears. She didn't expect her emotions to get the better of her. But somehow, she didn't feel the need to be strong in front of Ashley the way she did when she was with C.J. Tears she had tried to hide behind her sunglasses fell, and her shoulders began to shake. She laid her head down on the side of Ashley's bed and began to sob. She didn't want to fall apart; it just happened.

Ashley stroked Willow's head trying to bring her comfort but said nothing. She understood how important it was for Willow to let go of her bottled up emotions.

Ashley remembered back to how she felt when she fell into her grandmother's arms so many years ago. Assaulted, pregnant, running from her dad. The realization she no longer had to keep her feelings to herself had started the same flood Willow was experiencing now.

After a few minutes, Willow sat up, snatched a few tissues from Ashley's beside table, and blotted the tears under her sunglasses. "I'm sorry. I didn't mean for that to happen." She pushed the tissue into the corners of her eyes. "Here I came to see how you're doing, and I fall into a million pieces." Willow looked at Ashley, but quickly looked down into her lap.

Ashley saw the discoloration peeking out from under Willow's glasses and the swell of her lip. Her lunch rolled inside her stomach.

"Willow, would it help to know I have an idea how you're feeling?"

Willow stood and pulled the sunglasses from her eyes. "I don't mean to sound cold and uncaring, Ashley. I mean, I know you've

354

been through a lot with your surgery and all, but I really don't think you could possibly know how I'm feeling."

Ashley didn't miss the anger and disbelief in Willow's tone. "What if I told you C.J. was a product of rape, and that my pregnancy came at the end of an emotionally abusive relationship with my father?"

Willow's expression turned from anger to shock.

Ashley smiled softly at Willow, wanting to be transparent, so Willow would see her as an ally not a judge. "It's true. When I was seventeen, my father's business associate raped me. I was told to get an abortion because I was an embarrassment. I knew I couldn't do that, so I ran away and lived with my grandparents."

"But I lived with the guy, Ashley. I knew he was violent, and I wasn't even smart enough to leave. I put myself in that position. I got what I deserved."

"No! That's not true, Willow." Ashley's voice was firm, but compassionate. "Don't believe what the world would tell you. I blamed myself for years, telling myself I got what I deserved. I know now that's not true. No one asks to be abused or mistreated, and no man has the right to force himself on a woman, regardless of the situation. You should be proud of yourself, Willow. You're a survivor, not a victim. As long as you don't blame yourself, you'll get through this, but it's a choice only you can make."

Fresh tears trailed down Willow's face. "I had no idea you'd been through so much. I always just thought you were some kind of super woman."

Ashley laughed

"Well, you are. You're beautiful. Successful. Wealthy. You've raised a great son all on your own. I've always seen you as a woman who knew exactly what she wanted in life and worked hard until she got it."

"Well, now you know not everything is as it seems."

"Does C.J. know . . . about your past?"

"Yes. I told him when I thought he was old enough to understand. He struggled with it for a while, but I think he came to realize how special he is. It was because of C.J. that I came to know the Lord. It was because of him that we now own the Circle-R Ranch. You see, God seldom removes the consequences of our bad choices, but that doesn't mean he can't use them to bring about the good he desires for His children."

Willow sat back down, looking confused. "But you're saying

355

God allowed all that stuff to happen to you. And you're fine with that?" She shook her head. "I don't think I'm capable of that kind of acceptance."

"I wasn't fine with it, Willow. My relationship with the Lord wasn't repaired overnight. I'm just saying God can forgive our wrong choices, and He can heal our broken bodies. Even so, the forgiveness He gives us can only be felt after we forgive ourselves."

Willow twisted her hands together in her lap. "Maybe if other people weren't hurt, I'd be able to accept things better. But Jenna was assaulted, C.J. almost got himself killed, and Austin will have to live with the fact that he killed a man. Knowing all of this could've been avoided if I hadn't been so stupid, that's what I'm having a hard time with. God can punish me. I'm all right with that. I deserve it. But allowing everyone else to suffer, that's not fair."

"Well, just know that no one blames you for what happened. You're the victim, Willow, not the culprit. What's more, you're going to remain a victim if you keep beating yourself up."

Willow pressed the tissue back under her glasses, then smiled. "Okay, enough about me. I came here to see how you are doing."

Ashley explained to Willow what the next few weeks would probably look like, and made sure Willow still felt up to the workload. They were talking about upcoming orders when a light tap on the door interrupted them.

Austin and C.J. walked into the room. Austin bent over the bedrail and placed a kiss on Ashley's forehead, while C.J. leaned against the wall under the television. They visited for a few more minutes, but all the while she struggled to keep her eyes open.

"Okay, everyone," Austin said. "I think we need to call it quits. The guest of honor is falling asleep on us."

Ashley quickly opened her eyes. "I was just resting my eyes."

"That's okay, Mom. I need to get back to the ranch anyway. If I leave Billy in charge much longer, he's going to think he owns the place." C.J. stepped forward to give her a kiss goodbye.

"I'm glad he's been a help. Sometimes he can be such a fussbudget." Ashley spoke, but her eyes were slipping close.

"He's been great, Mom. I don't know what I would've done without him these last few days. There's no way I could've handled all this stuff without his help."

~⑧~

'Stuff?' That's all my life is to him. 'Stuff?'

356

Willow cringed as she walked toward the door.

"Remember what I said, Willow. It's your choice."

Willow turned toward Ashley and forced a smile. "Sure."

"Here, I'll walk you out."

Austin followed them into the corridor and stopped, when all Willow wanted to do was keep walking.

"Hey, why don't we meet at The Clubhouse for dinner? My treat. I thought it would be nice to do something normal for a change. You know, no doctors, no hospitals, no guns." Austin teased.

"Sounds great to me." C.J. looked at his watch. "Let's see if we can go . . . oh, I don't know . . . let's say, four hours without any trouble."

I can't believe it. He's actually making fun of everything that happened.

"Okay. I'll call ahead for reservations."

Willow started walking toward the elevator while C.J. and Austin were still making plans. The doors opened as soon as she got there, so she stepped inside and pressed the 'G', then did nothing when the doors started to close.

"Hey!" C.J. stuck his arm in at the last second, tripping the sensor. The doors stopped, then opened wide. "I'm glad to see you're feeling better, but I didn't think this was a foot race." Willow moved to one side when C.J. stepped in. She watched him press the 'G' and waited for the doors to close again. She could feel C.J. staring at her, but she kept her eyes above the door, watching as the numbers lit up in descending order. When the doors slid open, she stepped out ahead of C.J. and hurried across the parking lot.

"So, are you going to tell me what I did wrong this time?" C.J. asked when he caught up with her.

She didn't have the energy or the patience. "I have work to do. Ashley's counting on me, and I don't want to let her down."

"Fine. Just take it easy, okay? You shouldn't be overdoing it."

Willow did not answer back. She just waited for C.J. to unlock the passenger door with the remote, then hopped in, wincing as she clutched her side.

C.J. pulled into the driveway, not having exchanged a single word with Willow the entire way home. She got out of the truck, slammed the door shut, and walked straight to the office.

Shaking his head in frustration, he stormed into the house and paced. *What am I doing wrong? Why is she being so cold?* He stopped. *Maybe Mom said something to upset her.* He thought about it for a moment. *No. She was fine until she hit the elevator.* He paced some more. *This is ridiculous! I can't pretend to know what she's thinking. I just need to give her some space.*

Needing to work off his own pent-up frustration, he headed to the stables. The minute C.J. whistled, Knight bobbed his head out of his stall, ears perked. "Hey, boy, ready for round two?" he asked, as he stroked Knight's withers. "And this time, we're going to tear it up."

An hour later, C.J. was exhausted.

But it was a good exhaustion.

He was tired and sweaty, but it felt good. Running Knight had been exactly what he needed. It helped him focus on something other than what had happened in the last few days. Even so, if he and Willow were going to meet Austin for dinner, he needed to get showered and changed.

Taking off his boots and socks on the back porch, he pulled off his shirt as he crossed the kitchen to the stairs. Swabbing the back of his neck with his balled-up shirt, he took the stairs two at a time, plowing right into Willow. She plopped backwards with a moan, and C.J. quickly braced himself on the stair behind her so all his weight didn't fall on top of her. "Are you all right?" He pushed himself to the side and squatted next to her.

Willow was eye level with C.J.'s well-defined chest. "I'm . . . uh, I'm fine." She pushed herself up the few steps to the landing and stood.

"Willow . . ."

She turned around, but he grabbed her arm. "I said I was sorry."

"Fine, you're sorry. It's no big deal." Willow glared at his hold on her arm.

He quickly let go.

She tried to walk around him, but he would not let her by.

"What's gotten into you?" he asked. "You act like I have the plague or something."

"I have more laundry to do." She tried again to sidestep him only to find herself staring—once again—at his very bronzed, very muscular chest. "Look, C.J., I don't feel like going out to dinner and I'm in no mood for games, so if you don't mind . . ."

"Neither am I, so why don't you tell me what's wrong, so I can stop playing guessing games."

Willow crossed her arms and leaned back into the wall. "Nothing is wrong."

"Right. Nothing. That's why you're being cold, distant, and you cut me off whenever I try talking to you. I'm not the enemy, Willow."

C.J. stepped back with his hands on his waist, like he was waiting for an explanation. But she didn't say a word. Instead, she turned around, walked into her room, and shut the door.

A second later, C.J. barged in, startling her.

"I don't deserve this, Willow."

She swung around, anger racing through her veins. "I'm so sorry, Mr. Summers. You're right. You don't deserve this *stuff* or the *problems* I've caused you, or the *trouble* I've been. I promise I will be out of your hair as soon as I possibly can."

She pushed passed him and stormed downstairs.

C.J. stood with his chin to his chest, muttering to himself. "You handled that one like a pro, Mr. Summers. You sure do have a way with women."

He didn't know if he should just go take his shower or follow Willow and make sure she was okay. He knew she wouldn't want his help, or his apologies, but he needed to make sure she hadn't left the property completely.

He trudged down the stairs, feeling more tired with every step. He walked carefully across the yard in his bare feet trying to avoid the rocks and thorns. When he reached the office door, he heard crying. *Great. Now what do I do?*

How did you give someone their space, without letting them feel like they were all alone?

The phone started ringing in the house, sending C.J. running back to the porch, every step more painful than the last. Rocks and gravel stabbed his feet and dug into his heels. By the time he reached the house, he could barely walk. Dropping alongside the end table, he picked up the phone.

"Hello!" C.J. yelled.

"Whoa, what has you so riled up?"

"Nothing!"

"It sounds like a very loud nothing."

"I picked up a splinter or a rock in my foot."

"How'd you do that?"

"I . . . it doesn't matter. Look, Austin. Willow and I don't feel much like going out tonight. I'll come by the hospital later to visit mom, but I think we'll pass on dinner."

"That's what I was calling about. Ashley is really wiped out. I think today was a little too much for her. The nurses did a lot of poking and prodding, and even had her up walking around. She's pretty exhausted, so I thought maybe she might be able to get some extra sleep if she didn't have to stay up talking to us."

"But she's okay, right? I mean this isn't a setback or anything?"

"She's fine, C.J., just tired."

"But I don't want her to get the impression, I was too busy to come by. Are you sure she'll understand?"

"I'm positive. I'll tell her I asked for a quiet night."

"Okay."

"Are you sure everything is *okay*? You sounded pretty upset when you answered the phone."

"I guess I'm just not being sensitive enough with Willow. It seems whatever I say she takes the wrong way. She's already talking about finding another place to stay. I don't get it."

"She just needs time to adjust."

"Yeah, I know, but I don't like being the object of her wrath." *Or listen to her cry. Or watch her wince in pain.*

"Hang in there, C.J. It will get better."

"Right. Hey, say good night to Mom for me, okay?"

"Sure thing. We'll see you tomorrow."

C.J. sat on the floor, picking the gravel out of his feet, struggling to remove a few stubborn thorns that were too small for his big, fat fingers. Hobbling to the kitchen cabinet, he pulled out the first aid kit and found a pair of tweezers. He tried to contort his body, so he could see the thin slivers still in his foot. But after about ten minutes, he got so frustrated, he threw the tweezers across the room. He decided to take a hot shower instead. Maybe it would help work the splinter out, or at the least, improve his disposition.

SIXTY-TWO

Willow sat at the desk doing nothing. She was already caught up on all her work and too tired to cry another tear. She thought about what Ashley had said. It was her choice to be a victim or a survivor. She knew it was true. As long as she allowed self-destructive feelings and belligerent behavior to control her, she was letting Steven win.

She needed a fresh start.

Picking up the phone, she dialed Colorado.

"Hello?" With the receiver over one ear, Willow plugged the other, straining to hear her mother. The noise in the background sounded like she was at a sports bar during playoffs.

"Mom, it's Willow. Can you hear me?"

"Willow, my baby girl," she said in the sickening sweet tone Willow hated. It's what her mother always called her . . . when she was drunk or wasted.

"Turn that crap down, Jimmy, I'm trying to talk on the phone. I'm sorry, baby girl. What were you saying?"

"I just called to say hi, and to see how you're doing."

"I'm out of detox, if that's what you mean." Her mother's voice switched from sweet to bristly.

"No, Mom, I was just calling. I thought I could come visit, you know . . . maybe catch up."

"Oh, baby, now isn't a good time," her mother whispered. "You see, I got this new guy. He's really cute, but pretty young. If he knew I had a daughter near his age, I think he'd freak. He's been really good to me, baby. His name is Jimmy. So, you see, now wouldn't be a good time. You understand, right?"

"Sure, Mom. I understand."

"So, how's my baby girl?"

"Great, Mom. Just great."

"That's good. Okay, baby, so we'll talk again real soon. Kiss, kiss."

Pressing the palms of her hands against her eyes, Willow refused to shed another tear over her mother's abandonment. As far as she was concerned, her mother could go to–

Willow jump when the phone rang on the desk. She sniffled, then put on her most professional voice. "Circle-R Ranch, how can I help you?"

"Hi, Willow, it's Jenna."

She sighed. "Hi, Jenna. How are you doing?"

"I'm, fine. How about you?"

"I'm hanging in there, I guess."

"How's C.J.?"

"C.J.?"

"Yeah, you know, tall, blond, handsome. Willing to walk over broken glass for you."

"I'd think twice about that last one. Right now, I'm a bigger imposition to him than broken glass."

"Did you guys have a fight or something?"

"No, I just know he'd rather I get on with my life instead of causing him so much trouble."

"I don't think we're talking about the same guy. The C.J. I saw cared a lot about you. I could see it in the way he looked at you and the way he talked about you. I don't know what you're seeing, but I'm sure you must have your wires crossed."

"He felt sorry for me, Jenna. He felt like he had no choice but to protect me. Now he doesn't. End of story."

"But, Willow—"

"Jenna, look, I appreciate you calling and checking up on me, but I'd rather not talk about C.J."

"But—"

"How's your head?" Willow quickly changed the subject. "Are your parents being cool about the whole thing?"

"My mother's suffocating attitude is more painful than the bump on my head. She makes it sound like I was on death's door. I finally got her to understand there wasn't anything Uncle Austin could have done to prevent this. She was so mad at him; she acted like she was going to sue her own brother."

"I'm sorry you had to go through all that, Jenna, and I'm sorry you got hurt in the process. I have no idea how Steven pieced together my whereabouts. He must have followed C.J. and me."

"Are you doing okay about all that? You know . . . Steven's death?"

"I cleaned out my apartment today. He tried trashing everything that was mine. The only things I was able to salvage were some of my clothes. He must have passed out before he got to the dresser drawers because everything else was either stained, or he took a knife to it."

"Gee, I'm sorry, Willow, but hey, if you need a shopping partner someday, count me in."

Willow smiled. "Thanks, Jenna, I'll keep that in mind." Even though she knew it would be a long time before she could afford to do any real shopping.

"Look, I'd better go. Tell C.J. hi for me, and Willow, don't fool yourself. He really does care for you."

It was dark. There wasn't a single star in the sky as Willow walked back to the house. When she slipped into the kitchen, she looked around. C.J. wasn't there so she decided to help herself to some dinner. She looked in the cupboard and decided a hot bowl of tomato soup sounded good. She opened the can, poured it into a small pot, and added enough milk to make it creamy. While it simmered, she flipped on a light on in the great room. When she turned around, she saw C.J. walk by the kitchen door to turn a light on in the living room.

"C.J.?"

He walked through the kitchen and hobbled to the refrigerator.

"C.J., I thought you went to dinner with Austin."

"I wasn't hungry." His tone was quiet, monotone. He removed a soda from the frig and drank it from the can. He hobbled back across the kitchen and into the living room. Willow followed him as he plopped down on the couch. He was wearing a baggy pair of sweatpants and a ripped-up tank top, but to Willow, he looked like a million bucks.

"Why are you limping?"

"I have a thorn stuck in my foot." His voice was level. Void of feeling. He pulled open the paper and started reading.

"Why don't you remove it?"

"I already tried."

It was obvious he did not want to talk, so Willow went back to the stovetop where her soup was bubbling. She poured herself a bowl, found some crackers in the cupboard, and grabbed a soda. She blew on the soup, but it was still too hot to slurp. She sat at the bar, listening to the clock tick, feeling guilty. She knew she was responsible for C.J.'s bad mood, just like she was responsible for everything else that had gone wrong in the last few days. Sliding from the barstool, she walked to the living room to offer him some dinner.

"There's enough soup for two people, if you'd like some."

C.J. grunted, sounding disinterested.

Fine. I tried.

She returned to the kitchen, grabbed a few ice cubes, and dropped them into the soup. Without a word, C.J. limped through the doorway and took a seat at the bar. Willow didn't bother acknowledging him, she just poured the remaining soup in a bowl and set it in front of him. She took her seat at the bar, spun the bag of crackers toward him and said, "I know it's not the Clubhouse, but it tastes pretty good. Just be careful it's still really—"

Before Willow could finish, C.J. brought a large spoonful of soup to his mouth. He quickly spit it back into his bowl and took a huge swig of soda.

Willow laughed. She didn't mean to; it just came out.

"So, now I know how to put you in a good mood. It just requires pain on my part."

Willow got the strange feeling C.J wasn't teasing. In fact, his words sounded like an indictment.

He blew on the next spoonful of soup and chomped on some crackers.

"I didn't mean to laugh. Are you okay?"

"No. No, I'm not." C.J. turned his barstool to face her. "I want to know what I did to offend you. I feel like I'm walking on eggshells. I know you're dealing with a lot—and that's to be expected—but I want to be part of the solution, not the problem."

Willow slipped from the barstool and busied herself in the kitchen. She removed the pot from the stovetop and filled it with water. She was trying to figure out what to say. She knew what she overheard in the stables. C.J. thought she was a problem. Even so, Jenna insisted he really cared about her.

She was confused and didn't know what to say.

The longer she took to formulate an answer, the more agitated C.J. looked. Finally, he got up from where he was sitting and brought his dishes to the counter by the sink. Willow could not bring herself to face him, but she knew he at least deserved an answer.

"C.J., I don't want you to feel an obligation to look after me. I appreciate all you've done. In fact, I don't even know how I'll be able to repa—"

C.J. reached for her arm and pulled her closer. "Willow, I'm not looking for payback, and I don't want you to think you owe me anything. I just want to be there for you without feeling like I'm part of the problem."

"I'm sorry, C.J., but I can't help but think you got all tangled up in my problems by no choice of your own. Unfortunately, you were in the wrong place at the wrong time."

She worked up the courage to look at him, but the second she did, she knew it was a mistake. His clear blue eyes searched hers, looking for answers, causing her heart to leap.

This is wrong. I can't feel this way. C.J. is my boss; I'm his employee. I swore to myself I would never cross that line. I'm just having an emotional reaction to a difficult situation. I'm sure it's some kind of Prince Charming Syndrome. C.J. has slain the evil dragon, and I'm confusing appreciation for something more. Besides, he deserves someone better than me.

"Willow, did you hear me?"

She shook her head. "I'm sorry, what did you say?"

"I said, I'd like to think I was at the *right* place at the *right* time. I can't imagine what would have happened if you had never gotten away from Steven."

"And I'm grateful for your help, really I am. I just don't know how I'm going to repay you for all that you've done but—"

"I do."

"What?"

"I know how you can repay me."

"How?"

Before Willow could even comprehend what was happening, C.J. pulled her close and pressed his lips to hers. His kiss was deep, thorough, and though Willow was too stunned to return his show of emotion, she did nothing to stop him. When C.J. stepped back and looked into her eyes, she felt caught in his stare.

"Why did you do that?" Willow whispered.

"Because I wanted to. I've wanted to all week, but I was afraid of scaring you."

"So, why did you do it now?"

"Because I want you to know I have feelings for you. Not because I feel sorry for you, or because I feel obligated to help you, but because you're desirable. I want to get to know you for my own selfish reasons, not out of pity. I don't want to push myself on you, if you're not ready, but I don't want you to keep pushing me away either."

Her thoughts were a mosaic of contradictions. She wanted to feel his kiss again, but she wanted to be angry with his forwardness. She wanted to push him away, but she wanted to draw him close at the same time. She wanted to love again, but she wanted C.J. to have someone who was as wonderful as he was. He was settling if he decided to focus his attentions on her, and Willow knew he deserved far better. She knew she would have to take drastic steps to keep C.J. from throwing his life away on her.

"C.J. I'm flattered that you're willing to ignore the mess my life has become, but I don't think you should waste your time on me. I've decided to move back to Colorado."

She could read the shock on his face as he raked his hand through his hair and hobbled to the great room. "When did you decide this?" he asked.

"I called my mom today. She was really excited to hear from me." Willow faked a smile. "Our relationship has been kind of bumpy the last few years, so I think I'll take this opportunity to go home. Mend some fences."

C.J. turned to Willow, then returned to the kitchen. "But I thought you liked it here?"

"I do. I just think it would be best if I leave."

"When?"

"I'm still not sure. I don't want to leave you or your mom in a bind after all you've done for me. I guess I'll wait and see how well Ashley's recovery goes, then take it from there. I figure it probably won't be for another month. I just thought you should know."

His limp wasn't as noticeable as he crossed to the stairs.

"C.J., I can take that splinter out for you."

"No need, it's not that big a deal. Not now."

Willow finished in the kitchen, turned off all the lights, then checked to make sure the doors were locked before heading upstairs. Light filtered from under C.J.'s door.

I should talk to him, explain why I need to leave.

She reached for the doorknob but decided against it. There really wasn't much she could say. She just needed to leave him alone and let him sort things out for himself.

She went to her room and turned on the lamp next to the bed. Scooting up against the headboard, she pulled her knees to her chest. *Now what am I going to do?*

Colorado was no longer an option, but she couldn't stay on the ranch. It would be too difficult—too awkward. *Maybe I should head for San Diego or Monterey?*

She wanted to stay near the beach, but she also wanted a job working with animals. She groaned. *That's not asking for much, right? I'm sure there are plenty of businesses near the beach . . .that work with animals . . . willing to hire someone with limited experience. No problem.*

The reality was, she would have to take whatever she could find. *At least my car will be fixed.* But at what cost?

It didn't matter. She would pay back C.J. with the money she usually spent on rent, and offer Ashley something for room and board, but she would save every cent after that so when the time came to leave, she would have enough money to find a place to live. *And if that isn't enough . . .*

Willow walked over to the closet and picked up the worn straw purse she salvaged from her apartment. To anyone else, it looked like a ratty, old, handbag, but it held her most prized possessions.

Sitting on the bed, she pulled out the cigar box from inside her purse and opened it. One by one, she looked at the baseball cards her grandfather left her and remembered the conversation they had that day.

Sweetheart, these are for you, and only you. I know they don't look like much, but they're worth a pretty penny. Don't let your momma see them and don't tell her you have them. Consider them your rainy-day fund.

When he had told her their worth, she couldn't believe it, and swore she would never sell them. He hushed her promise and went on to explain why he was giving them to her.

Sometimes this world can be harsh, unfair. Look at your momma. She brought us such joy when she was little, but then she allowed alcohol and drugs, and people of bad persuasion to influence her life. Your grandmother and I never had much in the way of riches, but we have our faith, and tried the best we could to love her and offer help when she needed it. We tried to save her from herself, warned her the people she was running with were hurting her, but she would have none of it. When we told her we could no longer support her harmful lifestyle, she took off. We didn't see her for almost three years. Then, one day, she showed up on the door stoop, you in her arms. Right then and there, we set our differences aside and put no expectations on her. It was the only way we could be sure she wouldn't run off with you. Well, as you know, she hasn't changed much. But that doesn't mean you have to follow her path in life. You're bright and intelligent. You can do anything you set your mind to. But like I said before, sometimes life throws us curve balls, and you might find yourself down in the count. That's what these are for. Not to buy a shiny new car, or fancy things, but to use when you need it most. I know you'll do the right thing, and if you have to sell them, it will be because you had no choice. But remember, no matter what, you can't tell your momma you have them. She will sweet-talk you, guilt you, or pity you out of every single one of them. These are for you. Willow remembered the way he pressed them into her hands, with fingers that were frail and wrinkled. *And if life shines favor on you, it would do my heart good to have you pass them down to my great-grandson or great-granddaughter.*

Willow pushed away the tears, remembering her grandparents, and all they did for her while she was growing up. The thought of selling the cards made her sick to her stomach, but if things didn't turn around soon, she would have to sacrifice some of them, to get back on her feet.

She shuffled through the cards, remembering which ones were his favorites. He was really proud of his Sandy Koufax and Ted Williams rookie cards. Those would be the last to go. She remembered her grandfather told her the Hank Aaron card was worth about six hundred dollars all by itself. *And that was then.*

Taking a deep breath, Willow gathered up the cards, put them back in the box, and slid the box into the straw purse. She couldn't waste time living in the past when she needed to figure out what to do in her future. She would have to find time to research the cards on the computer to determine their value. If she was forced to sell, she wanted to know what she could get for the cards. Because, if she was going to rip out her heart and put a price on it, she would settle for nothing less than top dollar.

She stuck the purse back in the closet before running a bath, then sank into the warm water and tried to relax. She wasn't in as much pain as she had been, though her ribs were still pretty tender, and hurt when she moved the wrong way. Her bruises were multicolored and painful, but they also served to remind her how lucky she was.

Luck had nothing to do with it.

Willow's eyes opened wide and she sat up straight, nearly splashing water onto the tile floor. She could have sworn she'd heard someone. She took a few deep breaths to calm her racing heart, then sank back into the soapy water, realizing it must have been her subconscious talking to her. Thinking about her grandparents, had stirred up old memories. Conversations of luck versus faith. God's mercies versus trials.

It was true. It wasn't luck that had saved her. It was C.J.

She thought about him lying in the next room. It would be so much easier to tell him how she felt and let him take her in his arms.

But that would only be taking advantage of him after all he's done.

She knew he was probably suffering from the same shining knight syndrome, she was. He wanted to be the one to save her from herself, but he didn't realize what he would be giving up. She wasn't good enough for him. He deserved someone more like himself. He wasn't stupid like she was. When he found out about Heather's lifestyle, he broke it off. It proved he wanted a relationship that was pure and untainted by others. She couldn't offer him that. She was as used and worn as his old sweat pants and ripped up T-shirt.

Her bath water had suddenly turned cold, and Willow did not like where her thoughts were going. She would check the Internet tomorrow and see what she could come up with in the classifieds.

For now, she just needed some rest.

SIXTY-THREE

The next day when C.J. got up, he felt like he had a two-by-four stuck in his foot. The splinter had festered, and his foot was hot and swollen. He took a shower and pulled on his jeans, then went downstairs to see if he could find the stupid tweezers he'd thrown across the room.

He searched in the general direction he'd thrown them but didn't see them anywhere. He checked the floor, the end table, then pulled every cushion from the couch. Still nothing. After putting the cushions back in place, he knelt on the couch and looked behind it. There, in the corner . . .

He stretched and twisted, then turned his head sideways to gain a few more inches, but he couldn't grab them. Groaning, he made one more ditch effort. He touched them with his middle finger, but he couldn't pick them up.

"What are you doing?"

His head came up so quick, it cracked against the windowsill. He spun around and saw Willow standing with her arms crossed, and her face twisted in confusion. "Gees, you scared me." He rubbed his head, then turned back toward the wall. "Don't sneak up on me like that."

"I'm sorry. I didn't think coming downstairs for breakfast constituted sneaking up on you."

C.J. ignored her comment and stretched once again for the tweezers that were still out of reach.

"What are you trying to do?"

Muffling a curse, he stood up straight and punched one of the sofa cushions. "I lost a pair of tweezers behind the couch, and I'm trying to get them. My stupid arm's too fat and I can't reach them."

"Why do you need tweezers?"

He looked at her until she answered her own question.

"Oh, you still have that splinter in your foot?"

"Yep." He turned back to the couch.

"Would you like me to try?"

"What makes you think you could reach it?" he grumbled and groaned. "Your arms are too short."

"But they're not as muscular as yours." Willow knelt on the couch next to him. "Where are they?"

He pointed to the far corner by the end table.

"Switch places with me."

He got up, waited for her to scoot over, then knelt beside her. The cushions sank under his weight causing his arm to brush against hers.

Willow pressed her free arm to her midsection while she contorted her small frame. She wiggled and squirmed, grunted and moaned. When she sat back on the couch, her hand was empty.

"I told you your arms were too short. There's no way you can reach that far. Besides, you're just going to hurt yourself."

She looked at him, determination clearly written across her face. She tossed the oversized pillow from the back of the couch, onto the floor, then stretched her lean body once more over the side of the couch.

Try as he might, C.J. had a hard time turning his eyes away from Willow's petite, but curvaceous form. Having her so near scrambled his senses. He wanted to reach out and steal another kiss. Maybe if he could make her realize how he felt, she wouldn't leave. Willow pulled herself back from the edge of the sofa and held the small implement in front of C.J.'s eyes. "Ta-da!"

C.J. controlled his thoughts and reached for the tweezers. Willow snatched them away before he could grab them.

"Why don't you let me give it a try? I'll have a better vantage point than you."

C.J. didn't argue. He didn't care about the splinter; he just didn't want her to leave. "Fine." He turned and sat on the couch while she pulled over the rolling ottoman. She took a seat, then lifted his foot onto her lap. She examined it closely while C.J. drank in the warmth of her touch. "It's worked itself pretty deep, but at least I can see it. Do you want me to numb it first, so you don't feel me poking around?"

"It's only a splinter; I think I can handle it."

"Okay, cowboy, have it your way."

C.J. watched as Willow used her thumbnails to pinch together the skin surrounding the splinter. He yanked his foot back with a yelp. "Dang it! That hurt!"

Willow laughed as he rubbed the bottom of his foot. "I told you it would. You let it fester all night. Now it's going to take some massaging to get it near the surface."

"Massaging maybe, but if you press much harder with those claws of yours, you're going to draw blood." C.J. was still rubbing his foot when Willow pulled it back into her lap.

"I'm sorry. I'll try not to hurt you again."

Then don't leave. He looked at her, wanting to say it out loud. "Promise?"

"I'll try my best." She met his eyes, but quickly looked away.

Willow massaged his heel for several minutes, pressing hard at times, then releasing the pressure. She hunched down closer and grasped the tweezers. "Okay, I have a little corner of it sticking out. If you hold very still, I think I'll be . . . able . . . to get . . .it . . . . out." C.J. braced himself as Willow slowly pulled back on the tweezers. "Got it!" Willow held up the decent size sliver on the tip of the tweezers so C.J. could see it, then put his foot down on the ottoman. "Do you have a first aid kit somewhere?"

He pointed to the kitchen. "Last cupboard on the left."

Willow grabbed the kit, then sat back down on the ottoman. She opened the blue box and pulled out some items, before placing his foot in her lap. When he saw the iodine swabs, he pulled his foot back from her grasp.

"Oh, no you don't. That's going to burn like crazy. I think a Band-Aid will do just fine."

"Well, I don't, and you're not a doctor. It already looks infected. If you don't take care of it properly, it could get worse."

C.J. stroked his chin. "Hum, where have I heard that before? Funny, when I said it, it fell on deaf ears." He looked at Willow jokingly but saw she was not amused.

"Fine. Suit yourself." She dropped his foot to the cushion, smacked the bottle of medicine down on the end table and got up to leave.

"Willow . . . I was just kidding." His words did nothing to stop her. She was out the door before he could hobble to catch up with her.

He plopped on the couch, grabbed for a bandage, but instead took the iodine swabs from the table. He dabbed the painful antiseptic on his foot, then stuck the Band-Aid on it. After cleaning up the discarded paper wrappers, he walked slowly to the cupboard, and put away the kit. *What an idiot, I am!* He slammed the cupboard shut. *She was smiling and laughing, and I had to go and ruin it by reprimanding her.* He leaned against the kitchen counter and sighed. *When will I learn to keep my mouth shut?*

SIXTY-FOUR

Monday morning, Willow unlocked the office, turned on lights, fired up office machines, then dropped into her desk chair, still in a funk.

After she stormed out on C.J. yesterday, she pretty much avoided him the rest of the day. When he went outside to do chores, she made herself a quick lunch. When she heard him pull out of the driveway, she went to the office to use the computer. She searched the classifieds, and trolled Internet sites specializing in baseball cards and sports paraphernalia. When she heard him drive up an hour later, she hurried to her room and pretended to be resting. It felt childish and stupid, but she needed to put some space between them. She had to get her head on straight. If she was going to make a new start, she had to show some self-control where C.J. was concerned. It was for his own good. He might not see that now, but eventually he would.

Even so, though she told herself to focus on other things, her thoughts always circled back to him. It was frustrating. *How did I work here all this time without obsessing over him, like I am now?* The way he talked. The way he smiled. The way he looked in his wrangler jeans and worn-out boots. The way his T-shirts emphasized his broad shoulders and defined chest. The way it felt having his arms around her. The heat of his body. The feel of his strength.

Her heart fluttered, and her skin ignited. *Could C.J. tell? Did her eyes betray her or the color of her complexion give her feelings away?*

That's what she had been afraid of all along. Not that C.J. would find out, but Steven would; that he would somehow sense it, feel it, see it in her eyes. That's how she kept herself in check all this time. Survival mode.

A knock at the door forced her to put her thoughts on hold, at least for the moment.

"I'm here to drop off a red Honda." A well-built man in a mechanic's jumpsuit filled the doorway. "I'll need someone to sign for it."

"Sure thing." Willow came out from behind the desk and saw through the window her car sitting on top of a flatbed truck. She never thought seeing that old red Accord would make her feel so good. Walking toward the truck, she sensed the mechanic staring at her. Feeling self-conscious, she let her hair fall over her shoulder and across her cheek, hoping it would hide the discoloration still evident on her face. She glanced at him, only to see him smile at her with a little too much appreciation. She quickly looked away and tried not to let her nervousness show.

"What do I owe you?"

His stare turned into a smarmy sneer. "Oh, the repairs are paid for, but I wouldn't say no to a tip."

"Of course. Let me just get my purse." Willow turned toward the house, but he caught her by the elbow and pulled her back around.

"No need for that sweetheart, I'll settle for drinks at Dooley's."

C.J. was on the phone when the tow truck arrived. He finished his conversation, then walked out onto the front porch, just in time to see the driver grab Willow's arm.

He bolted.

Willow pulled free from the mechanic and was in the process of telling him off, when C.J. got to him, shoving the guy away from her.

"What the heck do you think you're doing?" He stood between Willow and the burly man.

"Hey, the little lady asked how she could repay me, so I told her."

"Well, the bill's already been paid for, buddy, so you can leave."

The mechanic crossed his massive forearms over his barrel chest, then widened his stance. "I don't believe the little lady gave me her answer yet, and since I don't see a ring on her finger—indicating this is any of *your* business—I think I'll listen to her." He stepped to the side, making eye contact with Willow. "Now, don't let this bully tell you what to do, sweet thing. I'll show you how a lady should be treated."

Not giving Willow a chance to respond, C.J. threw a punch.

The mechanic hit the dirt, then shook his head, clearly stunned that he'd been leveled.

"I said leave. The lady is not available, and you're on private property."

Rubbing his jaw, the mechanic got to his feet. C.J. was ready to hit the guy again, when Willow stepped in front of him. "If you're a gentleman, you'll do the polite thing and leave. Besides, I would hate for your boss to get wind of how you treated a customer."

C.J. took a step closer, but Willow stopped him.

The mechanic brushed himself off and walked to the driver's side of his truck, never taking his eyes off C.J. Then he turned to Willow. "You ever get tired of blondie, come see me. I'll show you what a real man can do for you."

C.J. lurched forward, but Willow held on tight.

He watched as the mechanic drove away in a cloud of dust, Willow still holding onto his arm. Then he realized, she was no longer holding on to restrain him, but holding on for support. Her arm began to shake, and without thought, C.J. pulled her against his chest and wrapped her in his arms. "I'm sorry I caused a scene." He heard her soft sobs even though she'd buried her face against his flannel shirt. "I saw that guy grab you, and I just kind of lost it."

He stroked her bronze hair as it shimmered in the sunlight, and then gently walked her back to the office. He sat her in the desk chair and swiveled it to face him. Squatting level with her knees, he tipped her chin up, so he could see her eyes.

"I'm sorry."

"It wasn't your fault, C.J. I must have given him the wrong impression. Maybe I deserve—"

C.J. stood and threw his arms up in the air. "Stop doing that! Stop blaming yourself for everything! The guy was a jerk and hit on you! That's not your fault!"

"How do you know that? Maybe I was flirting with him."

C.J. looked at Willow, annoyed. "And why would you do that?"

"To get what I wanted!" she snapped. "Look, I'm a person of many talents. I could tell the guy was interested, so I thought I would save a few bucks. You think you know me, C.J., but you don't. I've gotten plenty of things over the years by batting my eyes or tossing my hair."

C.J. was shocked but didn't believe a word of it. "That's not what you were doing. You were scared; I felt you trembling."

"That's because I was afraid you were going to get your head shoved down your neck. Look, C.J., I can handle myself just fine.

You, on the other hand, need to learn when to butt out." The phone rang, and Willow answered it like a seasoned professional; her voice calm and cool, even though he could see her hands were still shaking.

C.J. left in a fury—his fist clenched and his jaw set—as he headed toward the house. He knew she was lying. Her voice might be able to hide her fear, but her eyes could not.

He felt like punching something and came close to putting his fist through the wall. He didn't understand. He didn't understand why Willow would say what she did or want him to believe the worst. But . . . if those were the lengths she was willing to go to, in order to prove she was no longer interested in his help, then fine.

Message received.

Miss Jenner could fend for herself.

"No, I'm sorry. We are no longer accepting applications."

Willow watched as C.J. stormed out of the office.

"If you like, I can take down your name and number and contact you when an opening becomes available."

Quickly, she scribbled the pertinent information. When she hung up the phone, she crumbled.

She hated saying what she did to C.J., but it was necessary. He was too nice of a guy, too headstrong. Desperate times called for desperate measures. She needed him to let go, and the only way he would do that was to convince him he really didn't know her at all. If he thought she was more like Heather, he would drop her like a bad habit.

SIXTY-FIVE

C.J. tossed bales and shoveled straw for three hours straight.

With his white T-shirt clinging to the perspiration on his shoulders and back, he pulled off his hat, swiped at his brow with his forearm, then placed his hat back on his head. He took a deep breath and blew it out.

He'd done almost a full day's work in a matter of hours. His muscles were burning, and his sore arm was throbbing. He didn't care. Physical pain helped mask his emotional pain as he wrestled with his feelings.

He couldn't imagine Willow intentionally leading a man on, not after all she'd been through. But why? Why would she say that? Why would she act like that? He shook the thoughts from his mind and concentrated on the task at hand.

Working through lunch, C.J. buried himself in the chores of the ranch. He had just fixed a broken latch on a gate, when he stopped to watch Jessica Peterson go through her jumping routine. She was good. Very good for her age. Then again, her parents would expect nothing less.

He saw Mrs. Peterson pull April, Jessica's coach aside. He could tell from the woman's sharp mannerisms, she was unhappy about something. Whatever it was, they discussed it at length before April approached one of the jumps and lifted it a notch higher. She then walked over to Jessica, high in the saddle, and smiled. After a quick discussion, April patted the little girl's leg, then moved back to the rails. C.J. watched as Jessica rounded the far side of the rink and cantered toward the higher jump, a jump he never would have recommended for her age or size.

He straddled the rails, intent on stopping the little girl, but it was too late. Jessica took the jump, lost her balance, and lurched forward in the saddle. C.J. hurried across the rink and watched as she struggled to hold on. Clutching the reins in one hand, and the throat latch of the bridle in the other, she was finally able to pull herself upright. When he made eye contact with Jessica, her saucer-sized orbs were full of fear. Stepping into her path, C.J. brought Sugar to a halt.

"Hey, Jessica, that was some mighty fine jumping there, but I think you need to leave the bigger jumps to the bigger girls. I would hate for you to take a spill when it's not necessary." Jessica was all of nine years old. Blonde hair, blue eyes, immaculate riding habit, black felt cap and all. She looked at C.J. and spoke quietly.

"I don't like the jumps at all, Mr. Summers, but Mommy says if I want to be a champion one day, I need to be able to do a complete program."

She spoke in such a proper way and with the sweetest tone, it made C.J.'s heart melt. "Well, what do you want to do, Jessica?"

Her face lit up and her cheeks squeezed out a smile. "Barrel racing . . . like you." She blushed. "You go so fast and Knight is so swift. I know Sugar could do that if I let her. She's the best."

Mrs. Peterson and April walked over to where he stood beside Jessica and Sugar. "What seems to be the problem here?"

In response to her mother's sharp tone, Jessica sat up straight and her smile disappeared. C.J. watched the lighthearted dreams of a little girl vanish.

"Hello, Mrs. Peterson. I was just watching Jessica here with Sugar. You know, I've grown up around horses all my life, and I think Sugar would be a better barrel horse, than jumper." C.J. turned and winked at Jessica. Her grin was back, wider than ever.

"Yes, I would agree with you, Mr. Summers."

Jessica could barely contain her excitement. Then her mother continued, "That's why we're getting Jessica a new mount."

The corners of Jessica's mouth came crashing down. "No, Mother, please, I don't want a new horse. I love Sugar." Jessica laid her head down on Sugar's sturdy neck and stroked her beautiful mane. The Appaloosa nickered at Jessica's affection.

"Please, Jessica, it's just a horse. Daddy and I are going to buy you a new one. A Danish horse." Mrs. Peterson turned her attention to C.J., who was equally devastated at her disregard for Jessica's feelings. "Surely you've heard how prestigious the Danish stables are in the dressage community."

"Frankly, Mrs. Peterson, I think it's more important for the rider to feel a trust for his horse, a relationship Jessica and Sugar have right now."

"Well, yes, I know Sugar and Jessica have been together for a while. She's a good horse but if Jessica hopes to win in the future, she's going to need every advantage Mr. Peterson and I can give her."

C.J. rubbed at his chin with his gloved finger. Then, he lowered a steely gaze onto Mrs. Peterson. "I think it's you who worries about winning, Mrs. Peterson. I think Jessica only cares about riding." April, who had remained silent until now, looked at C.J. like he had just read her mind. They both looked at Mrs. Peterson who stood stiff and brittle.

"I am not paying for parental advice, Mr. Summers, only for the use of your stables and your instructor. I think I know what's best for my daughter."

"And I think I know what's best for the Circle-R. If you are not in need of our advice, then we are not in need of your patronage. We will not put our students in danger because of the selfish ambitions of their parents. Jessica and Sugar are welcome here, but we do not have a vacancy for a new horse."

The woman fumed. "I am not going to let some . . . stable boy tell me what I can and cannot do with my daughter. I am paying for space and boarding rights, and if I'm not mistaken, it's my name on the contract not Sugar's. I can replace her with whatever horse I choose." Mrs. Peterson wore her arrogance with confidence.

"That's where you're wrong," C.J. corrected her. "I know you think I am just some dumb cowboy who knows nothing better, but let me assure you, your impression is far from the truth. I'm the owner of the Circle-R and I make the rules. If you break your lease with Sugar, you'll lose your spot and you'll have to go elsewhere." C.J. grabbed the little fingers of Jessica's hands and gently squeezed them. "I'm sorry, Jessica. Just know that you and Sugar are welcome here at any time." April stood there stunned, Jessica was in tears, and apparently Mrs. Peterson was speechless as C.J. walked away.

He put his hat under the spigot at the far rink, filled it with water and lifted it onto his head. The cool liquid trickled down his face and neck and soaked into his already wet T-shirt. He replayed his conversation with Mrs. Peterson but wasn't sorry for what he had said. He was tired of seeing the affluent people of Malibu manipulate their children or try to buy their affections.

Fewer and fewer people came to the Ranch any more for pleasure riding. C.J. was beginning to think it was time to restructure the focus of the ranch. Maybe offering competitive training was attracting the wrong breed of people. He sat on the ground, back against a tree, and closed his eyes. He drifted off for a moment, until he heard approaching steps.

He assumed it was Billy ready to scold him for how he'd treated a customer. So, without opening his eyes, he started his excuses. "Before you say anything, Billy, I meant what I said, and I'm not the least bit sorry. If she wants to pull her membership, good riddance to her."

"Actually, I agreed with everything you had to say."

C.J. opened his eyes to see April approaching. She walked around the tree C.J. was sitting under and sat down in front of him.

"Thanks, April. It might not have been very professional of me, but I'm fed up with self-righteous, self-centered parents." He paused for a moment and then continued. "She had you raise the bar, didn't she?"

April stared at the ground. "I'm sorry, C.J., I shouldn't have let her bully me like that, especially when I think of what could've happened to Jessica. Mrs. Peterson is just so intimidating. I guess I caved in. I was afraid she would complain about me to you and Miss Summers."

"Mrs. Taylor."

April smiled. "Sorry, I forgot. Did she really run away and marry her high school sweetheart?"

C.J. had to smile at the giddiness in April's demeanor. She was just a teenager, and an easy pushover for a fairytale.

"Well, she didn't really run away and marry him. But yes, they did date in high school, and yes, she did marry him last week."

"Wow!" April shook her head in disbelief. "That has to be the most romantic thing I've ever heard. Is it true he's a millionaire, and they're on an around the world honeymoon?"

C.J. laughed out loud. "Where did you hear that?"

April looked sheepish. "One of the guys told me. He said that's why she's been gone."

His mom was coming home tomorrow, so he thought there was no reason to hide the truth any longer. Ashley had not wanted the staff to know about her absence, but he was beginning to think hiding the truth only brought more questions.

"Actually, my mom had surgery on Friday."

"What? Surgery? No one said anything about her being sick? I'm sorry, C.J. I didn't know. Is she okay now?"

"The surgery went well, but she needs to have radiation. You probably won't be seeing her out and about for a while yet."

"So, she and her husband will be living here?"

"While she recovers."

C.J. and April talked a few minutes longer. April glanced at her watch. "Well, the Timmons will be here at three-thirty. It was nice talking to you C.J."

"April . . ."

She stopped and turned to C.J. "Yes?"

"Don't ever let a parent or a student make you doubt your better judgment. Jessica could've gotten hurt today, and I know you would have felt terrible. You're a good instructor, take pride in that." C.J.'s voice was business-like. He wanted April to know he was serious. "And don't ever think we would side with a parent over you. You're a professional, and we respect that."

April had a look of pride on her face as she walked away. She was a seasoned professional, even at such a young age. She'd come to them when she was only five-years-old, as a rider. But as she grew up, the switch from rider to trainer happened naturally, and helped keep her out of the spotlight. Her parents had the wealth to open their own training facility, but her father's political ties and the sensitive nature of his business, made such a venture impossible, the security risk too great. But C.J. could tell April preferred it this way. When she was here, she was her own person, not her father's daughter. She appreciated the anonymity, and C.J. appreciated her exceptional talent.

Getting up from where he was sitting, he finished cleaning up around the back of stables. It was work he should have assigned to one of the hands, but he was thankful for the distraction.

It allowed him time to think about something other than Willow.

Willow closed the window blinds and returned to her desk.

Seeing April carrying on a conversation with C.J. bothered her. Probably because April was exactly the kind of girl C.J. deserved. She came from a prestigious family, was beautiful, bright, and shared C.J.'s love of horses. And the look on April's face when she walked away—clearly, she was smitten.

But she's too young for C.J. He's twenty-five, and she's only like seventeen or eighteen. C.J. wouldn't date someone that young . . . would he?

What's it to me? I'm the one who told him to butt out of my life.

Willow had no right to be jealous, but she definitely had to leave sooner than later. Even though she was willing to let C.J. go, she did not want to stick around and watch him move on.

SIXTY-SIX

Ashley awoke feeling a marked improvement. She wasn't as exhausted as she had felt the day before and the pain from her incision was starting to diminish. She turned to see Austin lying on the foldout bed, looking at her. "Have you been up long?" she asked.

"No, just admiring the scenery."

She laughed at the playful look on his face. "Oh, and I must be such a sight to see?"

Ashley watched as he pulled back the blanket covering him and stood to stretch. His clothes were rumpled and his hair disheveled. He yawned like he was tired. He definitely did not look like someone who had just woken up from a good night's rest.

"Luckily, tonight you get to sleep in a real bed and take a real shower. No more splashing your face or sleeping in chairs."

Austin sat on the edge of her bed and put his face down close to hers. Nuzzling her nose, he smiled. "Someone sure is bossy this morning."

Ashley used what energy she had to kiss him. It was deep and passionate, making her wish they were home and without the restrictions her surgery required.

"Sorry to interrupt." Dr. Allen cleared his throat as he entered, clipboard in hand. "Looks like the patient is recuperating nicely."

Ashley blushed. "You could say I feel like I've turned a corner."

Dr. Allen looked at Austin, then back at Ashley. He wrote something on the clipboard, then smiled as he closed the chart. "Everything looks good, Ashley. I'll work on getting your discharge papers in order. Someone will be by to give you post-op instructions, so be thinking about any questions you might want to ask."

"Thanks, Dr. Allen." Austin extended his hand.

"No thanks needed, Austin, just make sure she doesn't overdo it." He shook his hand, then Ashley's. "I'll see you in two weeks."

~Ⓡ~

Austin was heading for the cafeteria when C.J. walked through the sliding glass door of the lobby. "Hey, great timing. I'm just on my way to get a bite to eat."

"But I thought Mom was going home today?"

"She is, but there's a bunch of stuff they have to do first, and I was just in the way." Austin gave C.J. a sideways glance and noticed the set of his jaw. "How about you? You look upset about something."

"I'm fine!" he snapped.

"If you're so fine, why do you sound like you want to bite someone's head off?"

C.J. ignored him as Austin held the cafeteria door open.

Austin set a cinnamon roll and a coffee cup on his tray, then watched as C.J. loaded up his with a ton of food. "You going to eat all that?"

"No, I just thought I'd pay through the nose for hospital food, so I could throw it all away."

"Hey, whatever is eating at you, don't take it out on me. Or your mom."

C.J. was silent.

Austin paid for their food, then filled his coffee mug before taking a seat. C.J. had already downed half his sandwich.

"Come on, C.J., what's wrong? And don't say nothing. If it's none of my business, just tell me, but don't lie to me."

C.J. snapped his head up, so Austin braced himself for the 'it's none of your business' speech, then C.J. exhaled rather loudly. "It's Willow."

Austin sat up straighter, feeling a stab of concern. "Is she all right?"

"Yeah. I mean physically she's good . . . maybe too good," he mumbled, then took another bite of his sandwich.

Austin smiled. "You've fallen for her, haven't you?"

C.J. didn't answer right away, but when he did, his voice was brimming with emotion. "It wouldn't matter if I did. She's leaving." Again, C.J.'s tone and the voracity in which he was eating were clear giveaways.

He cared for Willow.

A lot.

"Where is she going, and why?"

"To live with her mom in Colorado. She *said* she wants to start over."

"And you don't believe her?"

"No. I think she's running."

"From her problems?"

"From me." The expression on C.J.'s face was a mixture of anger, pain, and confusion. "I kissed her."

Austin held back his smile, not wanting to anger C.J. more than he already was. "And?"

"And, nothing. She's not interested."

"Are you sure?"

"Yeah, she made it pretty clear. In fact, she's hardly talking to me." C.J. threw his napkin on top of his unfinished food.

Austin drained his coffee cup, hating to see C.J. in knots. Especially when he'd seen the way Willow looked at him when they were all at the house. Unless he had completely misread her, she was denying the fact that she was interested in C.J. But why?

The walk back to Ashley's room was quiet. C.J. was in his head, and Austin didn't want to say anything to set him off. When they got to Ashley's room, she was dressed, sitting in a chair, looking anxious to go, but when she saw C.J., she smiled.

"So, have you come to take your old mom home?"

"You bet. Are you ready to go?"

"More than ready. I'm just waiting for the final okay." Austin watched as she studied her son. "How's Willow?"

"She's in the office every spare minute she gets, making sure everything is up to speed."

"I'm glad."

Austin could tell Ashley was hoping for a more detailed answer, but she didn't push.

"You look tired, C.J. Are you sure you're all right?"

"I'm fine. Just getting back in the swing of things."

"Well, you've made me very proud with how you've handled yourself and everything that went on."

He chuckled. "You haven't seen the house yet."

C.J.'s mischievous smile told Ashley he was kidding, and that he was also trying to avoid talking about something else. Her bet was Willow. She knew her son. She could see how he felt about her whenever he spoke her name, but he was holding back.

"Mom, you should know . . . Willow's leaving."

"What?" Ashley was stunned. "Why? What happened?"

"She says she wants to start over, and she can't do it here. I guess she's talked to her mom and decided to move back to Colorado."

Ashley might not have known the problems Willow was having with Steven, but she certainly knew the problems she'd had with her mother. Willow had told her the reason she moved to California was because she could no longer watch her mother self-destruct. She took care of her through most of high school, tracking her down in bars, cleaning her up after binges, and holding off creditors. When Willow had enough, she left. Ashley knew it was tough love on Willow's part. She was a caretaker by nature, but she couldn't handle watching her mother kill herself with alcohol.

"Mom, what are you thinking?"

"What . . . oh, I was just thinking about why Willow came to California in the first place. Maybe things are better now with her mother."

"She made it sound like her mother was excited she was coming home."

"Are you all right, I mean with Willow leaving?"

"Hey, if that's what she wants to do, then let her." C.J. stood and stretched. "I need to make a phone call. I'll be right back."

Ashley scrunched her face and sighed.

"What?" Austin asked.

"Something is up. Do you know what it is?"

"Yeah, Willow says she's leaving, even though it's obvious she has feelings for your son. And C.J.'s willing to let her go, rather than admit how he feels."

"That's it, isn't it? I sensed it but wasn't sure if I was just being a hopeless romantic and reading into things."

"No, they're definitely denying their feelings for each other, but I don't know why."

"I do."

"How could you know? You've barely spoken to either one of them since all this happened."

"Because I know how I felt when I left you." She looked at Austin. "After what I'd gone through, I was humiliated and embarrassed by what I'd become. I thought you deserved more than what I could give you. I knew you would accept me and love me, but I didn't think that was fair. I didn't want you to do the right thing out of a feeling of guilt or obligation. I didn't want you to have to settle, so I made the decision for you."

Ashley paused as years of memories raced through her head. "I think that's what Willow is doing now. She's making the decision for C.J. She's trying to save him from who she is and the baggage she carries."

Ashley watched as Austin caressed the back of her hand, finally placing a kiss to her wedding ring. "Then you'll have to set her straight, let her know C.J. doesn't need to be saved."

~®~

When C.J. walked back into his mom's hospital room, she was already sitting in the wheelchair raring to go. He started gathering up the flowers from around the room, feeling bad that he never sent any. Then he realized they were all from Austin, except for a little teacup bouquet of yellow daisies from Jenna.

"Austin, I think I should be able to push Mom, while you figure out how to juggle the flowers, since you're the one who sent them all."

"No deal. You just want to race your mom to the elevator." Austin turned, tossed the overnight bag over his shoulder, and wheeled Ashley through the corridor leading to the elevator. C.J. followed with the five bouquets of flowers, knowing one false move and there would be petals everywhere.

C.J. waited in front of the hospital with his mom while Austin went and got his car. When he pulled curbside, C.J. waited until his mother was in the car before hurrying to his truck. After loading up the flower arrangements, he followed Austin home at a painfully slow pace.

When he pulled into the driveway, he immediately zeroed in on Willow as she walked to the passenger side of Austin's SUV. After Austin helped her out of the car, Willow stepped forward and gave his mom a gentle hug.

C.J. started loading up his arms with flowers, but when he saw all three of them walking toward the house, he shouted, "A little help here."

Willow turned back around and saw him juggling the flowers. She walked to where he was standing and took hold of the vase that was resting precariously against his chest.

"Wait. If you take that one, I'm going to lose my grip on the pink one."

"So which one do you want me to take?" Willow asked, sounding irritated.

"Forget it. I'll do it myself."

"Fine!" Willow walked ahead of him to the house.

Going slow, C.J. finally made it to the house and unloaded the vases on the kitchen counter. Hearing Willow and his mom talking in the other room, he scowled, then caught Austin staring at him out of the corner of his eye.

"What?" C.J. grumped.

"I didn't say anything," Austin whispered, "but I can sure see why she's keeping her distance."

C.J. was ready to fire back, when Willow came into view.

"I'll be in the office if you need me, Ashley. It's good to see you home again."

"It's good to *be* home."

Willow glanced his way before walking out the backdoor.

Once she was gone, Austin looked at him. "What was that all about?"

"I told you, she's not talking to me."

"Well, I can't say that I blame her, if all you're doing is snapping at her."

C.J. was ticked. He knew Austin was right, but he didn't need him judging him like that. "Look, the silent treatment started after she hit on the tow truck driver. And if you don't mind, it's none of your business." C.J. grabbed his hat hanging on the peg by the backdoor and left.

"What was that all about?" Ashley carefully scooted back against the couch cushions and looked to Austin for answers.

"I don't know, but he's right. It's none of my business. If he lets her go, he'll regret it and have to live with it."

"I'll talk to Willow when I get the opportunity. I'll explain to her that C.J. doesn't need saving."

"Well, it's nothing you have to worry about at this very minute. I didn't bring you home, so you could solve the world's problems. I brought you home, so you could rest and recover, before starting treatments."

"Ugh. I hate to think about going back."

"So, don't. There's no reason to worry about it right now. You've got a two-week reprieve." Austin sat in the oversized chair, stretched out his legs, and reclined his head. "So, just relax. That's an order."

Ashley watched as Austin's eyes closed. *Poor guy hasn't had a decent night's sleep for days.* She stared at the man she loved more than life itself, then closed her eyes and drifted off to sleep.

SIXTY-SEVEN

Willow was shutting down everything in the office—feeling the ache from a day's worth of work and a whole lot of tension—when April walked in.

"I saw Ashley is home. Do you know how she's doing?"

"I don't think I'm at liberty to say," Willow was matter-of-fact.

"Well, C.J. already told me about her surgery. So, I was just—"

"I'm sure Mr. Summers told you all you need to know. Miss Sum—, I mean Mrs. Taylor is a very private person and our boss. I don't think we should be talking about her in her absence."

"I wasn't talking *about* her; I was just going to offer my help, in case you could use an extra set of hands around the office. Sorry I asked."

After April left, Willow shut off the lights and walked to the house. Guilt gnawed at her because of the way she'd spoken to April. *You can't snap at everyone just because you're miserable. Grow up! The world doesn't rotate around you and your problems.* Willow slowed her steps as she approached the backdoor, not wanting another confrontation with C.J., especially in front of Ashley. Craning to see through the picture-window, she only saw Ashley standing by the breakfast bar, drinking some water. Relieved, she walked in and plastered on a smile. "Wow, you're looking good, but should you be standing up?"

"I'm a little weak, but being home is a lot better than lying in a hospital bed. How about you? How are you doing?"

"Me? I'm doing fine." Immediately she averted her eyes.

"C.J. tells me you're thinking about leaving."

"Well, yes, but only once you're doing better. I would never think of leaving you now when you need me most."

"And what about C.J.? How do you feel about leaving him?"

Willow looked around, still unable to make eye contact with Ashley. "I'm not sure I know what you mean?"

"Willow, let's sit down for a minute." Ashley reached out for her

391

hand and led her to the couch.

Willow didn't want to discuss C.J. with Ashley. He was her son. How awkward was that?

"Willow, I know what you're doing. I did it myself."

"I don't understand what you're talking about." She tried to sound casual.

"You're pushing C.J. away as a way of protecting him."

"That's ridiculous." Willow stood, twisting her fingers together as she paced.

"Then why are you leaving? Are things really that much better in Colorado?"

Willow felt as transparent as glass in front of Ashley. It was like she knew her every thought.

"Willow, I did the same thing to Austin. I felt he deserved so much better than I could give him. I knew if I told him what happened, he'd do the noble thing and stick by me, but I would've always wondered, did he love me, or just felt sorry for me?"

"Okay, then if you know how I feel, why are you questioning it?"

"Because what I did wasn't fair to Austin, and it won't be fair to C.J. either. I know my son. I can see he has very deep feelings for you."

"He feels responsible for me, like I'm a project he needs to fix. He deserves more than that, Ashley. Surely you want someone better for your son? Not another man's leftovers. Not someone who sees sex as a weapon." Willow was crying when Austin entered the room.

He stutter-stepped, looking completely uncomfortable. "Sorry, I didn't mean to interrupt."

"That's okay; I'm on my way out." Willow quickly wiped away her tears. "I'm going to grab a bite to eat, and then I'll be home. I'll make sure it's not too late." She left the great room, went upstairs, grabbed her purse, and left.

Austin sat by Ashley. "Well?"

"I was right. She's pushing C.J. away because she feels worthless."

"Are you going to talk to him?"

"I'll see. I don't want to interfere, but I'd like to know how he really feels about her."

"Well, you're going to get your opportunity."

Ashley followed Austin's glance to the backdoor. C.J. was taking off his boots on the porch. He walked through the door, looking exhausted.

"What have you been up to?" she asked.

"Stuff that's been stacking up for a while." He walked over to where she was sitting on the couch, sank to the cushion next to her, and patted her knee. "So, how was your first day home?"

"Good. Quiet." She paused slightly, questioning if now was a good time. *There isn't going to be a good time, you're just going to have to put it out there.* Clutching his hand, she smiled, "So, what happened between you and Willow?"

"Mom . . ." He got up from where he was sitting. "I need to take a shower."

"C.J., come on. Tell me you don't have feelings for her, and I'll drop it. End of subject."

He leaned against the bar, glanced at Austin then back to her. "Mom, you're supposed to relax and use your energy to recover. You don't need to worry about me. I've got things under control."

"Under control? You mean by ignoring it?"

"Mom, I really don't want to discuss this with you."

"Why?"

"Because Willow told me to butt out!" he snapped. "Just like I'm telling you to do!" He turned to leave.

"C.J., don't walk away. Austin's going to make us dinner, then we—"

"I'm going out."

When she heard C.J. stomp upstairs and slam his door, she started to cry. "I handled that like a pro." Wiping her tears as Austin sat down next to her, he draped his arm around her shoulders, gently pulling her close. She rested her head on his chest and asked, "Now what?"

"I think you have to let them sort it out for themselves."

"But Austin, I know Willow cares for him; I know she does. She just won't admit it to herself because she's afraid someone is going to get hurt."

"But think about what she's been through, Ashley. Do you honestly think C.J. will be able to handle that? I mean, I know he's a good kid, and I saw the way he took care of her when she really needed him, but maybe . . ."

"Maybe what?" Ashley winced as she sat up, feeling defensive.

"What are you saying, Austin? That maybe when C.J. thinks about it, lets his mind wander, he'll realize he really can't handle the garbage she's been through. Is that it?"

Austin sat up and looked deep into her eyes. "Ashley, don't make this about us. I love you, and I don't want you ever to doubt that, but it might not be the same for C.J. We already had a relationship before you left. I was in love with you before everything went sideways. C.J.'s feelings for Willow developed *because* they were thrown together in a tragic situation. It's different for them. You've got to let them do this their way."

Ashley eased back and once again, rested her head on Austin's chest. "I just don't want to see him get hurt. I don't want him to spend his life wondering what could have been, what should have been. I know what that's like."

"Me too, Ashley. Me too."

SIXTY-EIGHT

C.J. drove around for a while, then parked at the bluff at the end of the canyon. It's where he always went to clear his mind—helped him think. Leaning against the hood of his truck, he looked out over the ocean.

He loved her.

He knew he did.

But what was he going to do if she left for Colorado?

He thought for a while, trying to figure out why Willow was pushing him away after all they had been through. *Maybe there's more? Maybe it's not just the Steven thing? But what could be worse than that? Maybe there were other men? Maybe she's had other sexual relationships. Maybe she's on the run? She could be a criminal or a prostitute, or even—*

"What are you thinking?" he shouted, slamming his hand down on the hood of his truck, disgusted with himself. "She's none of those things, and you know it! She tried to protect her modesty when she was in the tub and told me how humiliated she felt. She wouldn't have cared about any of that if she'd slept around or been promiscuous." *It's because of the way Steven treated her. It has to be.* He raked his fingers through his hair. "Well, there's one way to find out."

C.J. got into his truck and drove home on autopilot. All the while he kept asking himself, what more was Willow hiding? He realized it was pointless. He kept picturing her in one absurd scenario after another, his imagination far worse than anything she could've possibly done, and yet he still didn't think it would matter. He loved her. That's all there was to it.

Now all I have to do is convince her of that.

When he got home, he found Austin in the kitchen straightening things up and turning off lights. "Hey, Austin, is Willow in her room?"

"No, she went out earlier and hasn't come back yet. Why?"

"I need to talk to her. Where's Mom?"

"She's taking her bath."

"Wait a minute . . ." for a quick second, C.J.'s thoughts were derailed. "I didn't think you were allowed to take baths after surgery?"

Austin laughed. "She begged, and the doctor said a quick bath would be okay."

C.J. shrugged, then headed for the front door.

"Where are you going?" Austin asked.

"I'm gonna wait for Willow on the porch. We have some talking to do."

C.J. closed the door and took a seat on the porch swing, reflecting over the last few weeks. It felt like everything had changed overnight. *Austin shows up out of nowhere, and already it seems natural having him around. Mom has surgery, and for once, she's the one needing peoples' help. And Willow and me, if in fact, there is a 'Willow and me.'* With his boot perched on the porch rail, he rocked the swing. *Okay, God, this is one of those times I could really use Your help. I need Willow to listen to me, to put her stubborn, bullheaded thinking aside, and let her walls down so she can actually listen. And . . . I . . . I even hate to think it, but if this isn't what You want, if this is a mistake, show me before I make a complete jackass out of myself.*

~®~

Austin knocked on the bathroom door, then leaned in. He found Ashley lying in the tub, head back, eyes closed, bubbles up to her shoulders.

"How does it feel?" he asked as he sat on the rim of the tub.

"Wonderful."

"I think your little talk with C.J. worked."

Ashley opened her eyes. "What do you mean?"

"C.J. came home asking for Willow. He's on the porch waiting for her."

"Oh good, now we just need to pray Willow listens and doesn't keep pushing him away." Extending her hand, she smiled. "How about offering me a little assistance?"

"It would be my pleasure." Slowly, he helped her up, and reached for the towel on the rack. Wrapping it around her, she used him for support, then stepped out of the tub and into his arms. Resting his chin on her damp shoulder, he whispered in her ear. "It feels so good to have you home."

"It feels so good to be home."

Austin turned down the bed quilt and covers, while Ashley dried herself off and slipped into a nightie. When she sat on her side of the bed, she let out a sigh of relief. "My own bed. My own pillow." Carefully, she laid down, wincing at the pain. After getting comfortable, Austin leaned forward and pressed a kiss to her forehead.

"I'm going to take a quick shower, and then I'll join you."

She raised a brow.

"I know, I know. We have limitations, but you lying next to me is gift enough. For now."

~®~

C.J. did not have to wait long. Willow pulled up in her red Honda and slowly climbed the front stairs. She didn't see him sitting in the shadows and jumped when she heard the creak of the porch swing.

"C.J.! What the heck are you doing out here? You scared me half to death."

He didn't speak. He just walked over to where she was standing and looked into her eyes.

"What? What are you staring at?"

"I want to know everything about you. I want to know what it is you're afraid to tell me, and why you keep pushing me away."

"Forget it, C.J.; it will never work." Willow reached for the door, but C.J. pulled her hand away.

"I'm serious, Willow. What is it? What are you afraid to tell me?"

"I'm not afraid to tell you anything. I just think you deserve better."

"But I *want* you." C.J. took another step closer and framed her face with his hands, then pulled her into a kiss. She didn't resist. But when he wrapped his arms around her and pressed his body close to hers, she pushed him away.

"C.J., why are you doing this?"

"Me? What about you? Why won't you believe that I want to be with you?"

She rolled her eyes and clenched her jaw. "Because anytime you've ever thought about the woman you would one day marry, was she covered in bruises or recovering from an abusive relationship? I don't think so. Look, C.J., I know you've saved yourself for the perfect woman. I'm not her."

"Is there more?"

"More?"

He reached out for her arms, holding her so she wouldn't walk away. "Willow, I already know all this. Is there something else you're not telling me?"

"Why do you keep saying that? Why do you think I'm keeping something from you?"

"Because, I already know about the abuse and your relationship with Steven. There must be something more for you to keep pushing me away."

"There isn't."

"Then why won't you believe me?"

"Because, I think over time, you'll realize this is just an infatuation. You risked your life for me, C.J., and I will be forever grateful. We will always have a unique connection because of what we went through. But I don't know if that is strong enough to build a relationship on."

"No," C.J. shook his head and planted his hands on his hips, "I disagree."

"What about April?"

"What?" C.J. strained to make the connection. "What does April have to do with this?"

"Are you telling me she doesn't interest you?"

"Why would you think I'm interested in her?"

"I saw the two of you talking earlier today. You seemed to be getting along pretty well, laughing and joking. She's the kind of person you deserve, C.J. She comes from an affluent family; she's beautiful, and she shares your love of horses. That's who you should be pursuing."

"Are you kidding me? She's only sixteen-years-old. She's just a kid."

"But she's a good person."

He started laughing at the idiocy of their conversation.

"Why are you laughing?" she growled.

"Because you are so freakin' stubborn! Instead of accepting the fact that I have feelings for you, you're trying to set me up with a little girl." He couldn't help but laugh, even though he could see it was making Willow even madder.

"Fine! Laugh all you want." She stormed off the porch.

"Willow. . ." C.J. caught up with her and reached for her arm to slow her down. She yanked it free, and even though she stopped, she refused to turn around.

"I'm sorry, Willow. I'm not trying to pressure you; I just want you to know how serious I am. Please don't move to Colorado, at least not yet. Give *us* some time to explore what we have. I know you have a lot of emotions and bad memories to sort through. I want to be the one who helps you forget. I want to be the one who shows you what real love is."

Willow was still and silent.

C.J. felt like he was speaking into the wind.

SIXTY-NINE

He said 'love.'

Willow's heart was pounding so loud in her ears she could hardly think. *Did C.J. mean it—as in 'I love you'—or was it just a figure of speech?*

Struggling, feeling confused and shaken, she listened to the battle her mind was waging with her heart. Her mind was telling her to leave, to put her feelings for C.J. aside, that it would never work out, and he would just end up getting hurt. But her heart . . . her heart was pleading with her to stay, to take C.J. at his word, and experience real love for the first time.

What do I do? Hold my ground or take a chance? Step back or move forward? Give in or let go?

Slowly, she turned around and stared into the hopefulness she saw in C.J.'s eyes. Releasing a cleansing breath, she took a tentative step forward. He smiled and took a step toward her. She took another, and he followed suit. When they were only inches apart, she reached for his hands. He quickly grabbed hers and pulled her closer. With his face just inches from hers, she stretched up, and pressed her lips to his.

It was a simple kiss, not asking or promising too much.

C.J. pulled back, brushing his lips against her ear. "Please tell me that wasn't a goodbye kiss?"

"Okay," she whispered.

"Okay, what?"

"I'm not saying goodbye."

When he brushed back a few stray strands of her hair and tucked them behind her ear, his touch sent tremors through her body.

"You mean you're not going to leave? You're not going to move to Colorado?"

Willow shook her head and smiled. "I'm—"

Before she could say another word, C.J. silenced her with an indulgent kiss. Wrapping her arms around his neck as tightly as he held her, she felt the warmth of his body pressing against her, and the beating of her heart bouncing off the muscles of his chest. She was falling. Too fast, and too hard.

When she opened her eyes, and saw C.J. staring at her, she felt embarrassed by her unbridled show of affection. Releasing her hands from behind his neck, she took a step back, trying to regroup, but he quickly wrapped his arms around her waist and pulled her back to himself.

"Hey, don't stop now," he teased.

But that was exactly what she needed to do. Though she wanted nothing more than to explore their newfound relationship, she was afraid things might get out of hand. She didn't quite understand it. Being with a man should be the last thing she wanted to do. But C.J. was different. Though there was passion in his kiss, there was something more. Tenderness. Protectiveness. She felt safe. Cared for.

Steven had always been so controlling and possessive. His frenzied desires constantly made her feel like she was only there to satisfy his needs. Their physical moments had never been about intimacy. To Steven, sex was an act not an expression.

What C.J. was offering was so much more. Being loved . . . she really did not know what that felt like. She never knew her father, and her mother always made her feel like an inconvenience, an interruption in her life. That's why she had fallen so hard for Steven. The thought of someone wanting her—being attracted to her—was intoxicating. So much so, she was oblivious to his flaws, to the little things other people would have seen as a warning sign. By the time she knew she was in trouble, it was too late.

"Hey, what's with the serious look?" C.J. asked, tipping her chin up, so he could look into her eyes.

Willow wanted to melt. C.J. was so handsome, so rugged. She imagined what it would be like to wake up in his arms, to hold him close. She wanted to please him, satisfy him, make him happy. *What am I thinking? C.J.'s not like that, he wouldn't expect that from me.*

She was weak . . . weak and pathetic. For so long, she had used sex to diffuse Steven's volatile behavior. If she took him to bed, got him to leave the liquor behind, she could soothe his temper, and if she was lucky, he would pass out. Other times, she had to give him what she promised.

She had to be honest with C.J. She had to let him know she would be too weak to put up defenses. But what would he think?

Would her confession make him think differently of her? Would he think her past situation was her own fault? Willow wasn't sure, but she no longer wanted to live in fear of unanswered questions or unaddressed issues. The moonlight filtered through the moving clouds, making C.J.'s expression harder to read. In the cover of darkness, she decided to let him know what she feared.

"C.J., I have to be honest with you. I'm . . . well, I mean . . .you should know . . . not that I wanted to . . . I mean I did, but not for the right reasons, even so, it was my fault that . . ." This was harder than she thought. Her embarrassment was outweighing her need to be open and honest.

"What is it, Willow? Just tell me."

"This is really hard for me, C.J." Willow stepped back and turned away from him. She drew her fingers through her hair trying to refocus. She scrunched the handful of curls in her grasp, as if she was trying to awaken her brain and make it more alert than her sense of touch. She jumped when she felt C.J. thread his arms around her and pull her back to his chest.

She relaxed against the strength of his form as he placed a kiss to the base of her neck. Maybe this would be better. She wouldn't have to look at his soulful eyes as she explained herself. "C.J.," her voice cracked, her mouth feeling drying as a bone. She cleared her throat and tried again. "C.J., I'm too weak. I mean . . ."

"Why didn't you say something? We can sit down."

"No, that's not what I mean." She pulled out of his arms and walked back to the porch, trying to figure out what to say. When he walked up the steps behind her, she tried again. "I'm afraid I'm not going to be very strong when it comes to a physical relationship." *There, I said it.* She waited for his reaction.

C.J. was quiet for what seemed like an eternity. Then, he walked toward her and turned her to face him. When she saw the look in his eyes, she knew she had to explain further.

"It's not you; it's me. I have a screwed-up perspective when it comes to sex. I used it as a bargaining chip for so long, as a reward system, or my way of waving the white flag. I'm afraid I'm going to default to it when I think something is wrong, or you're mad at me, or I've upset you. Or, if we're in a heated moment, I don't know if I'll be able to stop, or be the voice of reason. I won't want to disappoint you."

C.J. reached out and caressed her arms, sending a shiver from her head to her toes. "Then, I guess I'll have to be strong enough for the both of us." He pulled her into a hug and wouldn't let her go.

She held on tight, enjoying the steady rock of their bodies. "I've confused you, haven't I?" she said against his chest.

"No, I think I understand. I just hope I don't disappoint you."

She looked up at him. "You could never disappoint me." She shivered, and C.J. was quick to stroke her arms.

"Come on, let's go inside where it's warm." They walked into the house, but it was obvious C.J. didn't want the night to end. Leading her over to the couch, he sat and pulled her down beside him. Tucking her feet beneath her, she nestled under his outstretched arm. Words were not necessary, as they both processed all they had talked about. Soon, Willow felt her eyelids flutter. She was tired, exhausted really.

But she was exactly where she wanted to be.

C.J. played with Willow's long, silky hair as she sank further into the crook of his arm.

They had cleared the first hurdle.

Willow admitted she wanted to pursue a relationship with him but was afraid of her confused feelings. C.J. was already praying about their relationship, calling on God to give him wisdom and self-control. He wanted nothing more than to feel the warmth of Willow against him and enjoy the feel of her touch. But he would have to control his desires and be strong enough for the both of them.

Thinking Willow had fallen asleep, he was surprised when she whispered. "C.J., have you ever been with someone . . . intimately?"

He cleared his throat as a picture of Heather flashed before his eyes. He remembered some of the heated situations they'd gotten themselves into. They'd been out of line more times than he cared to remember, but thank God, they had never made the ultimate mistake.

"C.J., you don't have to answer if—"

"No, it's an honest question, and yes, I allowed myself to get into some pretty out of control situations, but I've never had sex if that's what you're asking me."

"So, do you consider yourself a virgin?"

"My body, yes. My eyes and my thoughts, no. I wish I could tell you differently. But I allowed myself to accept Heather's seductions as some sort of reward for controlling myself. My reasoning was wrong, and I now know why God's desire is for someone to share intimacy with only one person. I wish I could tell you I was coming to you without guilt, but I can't."

"Nobody's perfect, C.J."

"No, and I'm far from it."

"Don't be so hard on yourself. I don't know many guys your age that can say they applied the brakes before they went too far."

"Maybe. But what I did was still wrong."

"Okay, so neither one of us are perfect. Maybe this is our chance to start over."

He pulled her closer. "That's exactly what this is."

They sat a while longer, enjoying the warmth of each other. It was getting late, and they both needed to get to bed. C.J. nudged Willow to a sitting position and helped her to her feet. He held her close and pressed a kiss to her lips. It was firm, but her lips felt so soft.

Willow stepped back, ducking her head. "Okay, on that note, I think it's time we go to bed."

He playfully bobbed his eyebrows and was quickly rewarded with a slap on the arm. "Don't look at me like that. You know exactly what I mean. Besides, what did we just get done talking about?"

C.J. laughed, "I know, I know."

They walked side by side up the stairs, shared a simple kiss, then whispered good night. When C.J. closed his door, he shook his head in disbelief. The day had definitely ended better than it had started.

The click of shutting doors didn't wake Ashley, because she wasn't asleep. When she heard Willow and C.J. in the hallway whispering, she prayed it meant their relationship had turned a corner. Though it would be bumpy—navigating situations other couples didn't have to deal with—Ashley felt confident God had brought them together in His time and would help them through the rocky patches.

Reaching for Austin, she laid her hand on his bare chest, feeling the steady rise and fall as he slept. It lulled her into her own peaceful slumber.

SEVENTY

The next morning broke gloriously over the horizon.

Ashley stared out the window while Austin stirred beside her.

"Do you ever sleep in?" he asked, his eyes still closed.

"Nope. I don't want to sleep my life away."

"How are you feeling?" He reached forward and kissed her neck, then gently massaged the muscles in her back.

"Good. Even better than yesterday, and I thought yesterday was pretty good. I'm sure sleeping in my own bed and you within arm's reach has something to do with it."

"Well, you fell asleep shortly after I nodded off; I even heard you talking in your sleep."

"I wasn't talking in my sleep. I was praying." She rolled over to face him. "I think Willow and C.J. finally clicked last night. I could hear them in the hall."

"Ashley," he scolded, "you were eavesdropping?"

"I wasn't eavesdropping!" She gave him a playful nudge. "I just figured if they were talking civilly to each other, it had to be a good sign."

"Well, you know what I think is a good sign?" He stroked her jaw, running his thumb across her lips. "You have color in your cheeks, and your eyes are bright, and you look beautiful as ever."

After relaxing a little while longer, and enjoying the simple pleasure of holding each other close, Austin groaned, rolled out of bed, and pulled his jeans on over his thigh-hugging briefs. As he stretched, Ashley admired his sculpted physique.

"Hey, don't be parading around like that when you know I'm on restriction," she teased.

Austin pounced on the bed, startling her. She let out a screamed that sounded more like a gasp, then quickly covered her mouth. She giggled as Austin slithered his way across the sheets.

"Are you saying you find me irresistible?" His tone was low and menacing.

Ashley could feel the blush rush across her cheeks. "I would, but then your head wouldn't fit through the door, and you wouldn't be able to bring me breakfast."

Austin kissed the tip of her nose before crawling off the bed and grabbing a shirt from his duffel bag. "What would you like?" he asked as he walked to the door, pulling his shirt over his head.

"Umm, I don't know. Surprise me."

He turned and gave a quick bow. "For my bride, a banquet it shall be."

Ashley slowly got out of bed as she listened to Austin bounding down the stairs. Feeling a marked improvement in her mobility, she took a quick shower, then put on some comfortable clothes. When she walked toward the door, she noticed Austin's duffel on the floor in the corner, and realized she never cleared any drawers or closet space for his things. Even if they were going to make his house their home, he would need some room for when they stayed here.

Before she knew it, Ashley was going through her drawers, discarding clothes she never wore anymore. Thinking Willow was close to her size, she sorted and refolded the items she thought Willow might like, and put everything else in a discard pile, to be given away. *That's funny . . .*

She was rooting around in the drawers, searching for a few specific items she thought would look nice on Willow, when there was a knock on the door.

"Come in." Ashley answered from where she sat on the floor.

"Mom, what are you doing? You're supposed to be resting."

"I'm feeling pretty good today, so I decided to make room for some of Austin's things."

"Does that mean you've decided to live here?"

There was a hopefulness in his tone, she hated to disappoint.

"No, not really, but you know we'll stay here on occasion. When we do, Austin shouldn't have to live out of a duffel bag. Besides, I needed to go through my things anyway. A lot of this stuff I don't wear anymore, so there's no use packing it up and moving it to Austin's." She held up a peasant blouse with colorful stitching and embroidered flowers on it. "Like this. I can't even remember the last time I wore this." Ashley folded it and put it aside. "I thought Willow could go through this stuff and take whatever she likes before I give it to the Salvation Army."

"That would be great." C.J. sat on the corner of her bed. "I guess I should tell you, while you were gone, I let Willow borrow some of your things. She left her apartment so fast, she didn't bring any of her clothes with her. I didn't think you would mind."

"No, not at all, but that does explain why some things seem out of place." Ashley continued to sort and fold. "How is she doing?"

"I think we've cleared a few hurdles."

She looked at him, eyebrow raised.

"How would you feel about that?" he asked.

"You and Willow being in a relationship? I think it would be wonderful. I always thought you two would be perfect for each other, but both of you were involved with other people. I realize the situation isn't ideal, but I think the world of Willow, and she'd be getting a pretty great guy." Ashley smiled, but when she looked up, C.J. looked pensive.

"What's wrong?"

He leaned forward, pressing his elbows to his knees. "Willow is struggling with everything that's happened. She's embarrassed and thinks people will look at her differently. She's even tried pushing me away, insisting I deserve someone who doesn't have so much baggage. She blames herself for everything that happened, including the miscarriage. She feels God was punishing her because she got involved with Steven. I told her she couldn't be further from the truth, but I know she's worried about your reaction to us being in a relationship, in light of her situation."

Ashley had to admit she had her concerns. Since C.J. was a baby, she prayed for the perfect woman to come into his life. Someone he would fall head over heels in love with, marry, then experience love as it was intended, between husband and wife. She realized how unrealistic that was in today's society, but as a mother, she only wanted the best for her son.

"Mom, what are you thinking?"

Ashley looked up and could tell C.J. was concerned by her silence.

"Don't take this wrong, C.J. I love Willow like a daughter, but have you two talked much about other things?"

"What do you mean, 'other things?' "

"You know: likes, dislikes, past relationships, the fact that she's planning on going away for school. Things that matter other than the obvious attraction." C.J. was ready to object when Ashley raised her hand, so she could finish. "C.J., I'm not saying I don't approve. I'm just saying you need to make sure you know enough about each other before you decide to plunge into a relationship. Chemistry and physical attraction are wonderful, but honesty and compatibility are defining pieces in a relationship."

"But I don't think there's anything Willow could say that would change the way I feel about her."

"I'm glad to hear you're so sure of yourself. I just think it would be wise if you two could sit down and get everything out in the open. You've already had to face some pretty major issues. I don't think asking a few more questions will make things any more difficult."

"No . . . you're right, but I'm afraid if I ask too many questions, she'll feel like I'm doubting her and myself."

"Well, you need to do what you think is best. Again, I love Willow, and I think she's a wonderful person. But I also had no idea what was going on in her personal life. If I can miss something that major, I would hate for you to find out there is more you don't know about her."

"I understand what you're saying, Mom." C.J.'s smiled was reserved. The smile that meant he was listening, but not necessarily agreeing. "So, which stack is for Willow?"

His change in subject was Ashley's cue to leave well enough alone, and pray that some of what she said would sink in.

"Those there." She pointed to the stack on her left.

"Okay, I'll give them to her, so she can go through them."

"Actually, why don't you have her come talk to me? I feel like I haven't seen her forever, and I would like to see how she's doing."

"Mom, you're not going to grill her, are you? She doesn't need that kind of pressure right now. She shouldn't be expected to relive everything, just so she can update you."

"C.J., give me a little more credit than that. I just want her to know I'm here if she needs someone to talk to."

"Well, maybe after breakfast."

"Breakfast! I forgot Austin went downstairs to make breakfast. Here, give me a hand up." Ashley extended her arm from where she was sitting on the floor. C.J. carefully helped her to her feet.

"Want me to give you a hand going down the stairs?"

"I'll be fine, but you and Willow are welcome to join us. If Austin cooked anything like he did on our honeymoon, we'll have plenty."

"I'll see if Willow's up." C.J. left her amid the piles of clothes as she made her way to the door. Ashley held onto the banister and carefully took the steps one at a time. She was steady and barely winded. Her recovery was picking up, but she knew she would be back to square one way to soon.

"Smells wonderful." Ashley drew in a deep breath, almost able to taste the waffles Austin had stacked in the oven.

"Hey, I was going to bring this up to you." He glanced at the tray he already assembled with silverware, linens, and a bud vase with some wildflowers in it.

"That's okay. It feels good to be out of a room that consists of a bed and bathroom. I'd rather eat down here anyway." Ashley watched Austin as he continued to pour batter, turn bacon, check eggs, and stir orange juice. "Willow and C.J. might join us. Is that all right?"

"Of course. I was planning on making enough for everyone." Austin arranged a place setting at the bar where Ashley had taken a seat. "So, were you able to talk to C.J. about him and Willow?"

"A little bit. She's wary I won't give my approval."

"And?"

"Oh, I approve. Like I told C.J., I love Willow . . . as long as she's being honest with him. I mean, I thought I was a pretty good judge of character, but I had no idea she was living with her boyfriend. She brought it up once, said Steven wanted them to combine expenses. But after I gave my opinion, she never brought it up again. I didn't think it was my place to question her further."

"From what I understand, I don't think it was her decision to make."

"See, even you know more about the situation than I do. Like I said, as long as she's honest with C.J., and he doesn't have to worry about any more skeletons popping out of closets, I'm fine with them being together. I just hope they take it really slow."

"Smells good, Austin."

Ashley turned around as C.J. and Willow walked into the kitchen.

"I told you, C.J., I know my way around the kitchen. Being a bachelor for so long will do that for you."

Ashley felt self-conscious, wondering if C.J. and Willow had overheard her conversation with Austin. Unexplained, her words sounded harsh and judgmental, *exactly* what Willow didn't need. Hopefully, they would get a chance to talk . . . soon.

"Okay, everyone grab some silverware. Call out what you want, and I'll dish it up for you." Austin assembled the plates with the morning fare. Everyone took their helping and sat at the bar. "How about you say grace for us, C.J.?" Austin asked as he wiped his hands on a dish towel, after putting dishes in the sink to soak.

"Sure."

Ashley noticed how C.J. reached for Willow's hand and gave it a squeeze. Her heart skipped a beat to see the look C.J. bestowed Willow before closing his eyes.

"Dear Lord, what an awesome morning. Everything feels so right with Mom home and each of us ready for the rest of our lives. Thank you for Austin's love and care for Mom, and Willow's decision to stay. Thank you for this great breakfast, and for second chances. Amen."

Breakfast was shared along with lighthearted conversation. Ashley told Willow about the clothes she was getting rid of, and C.J. caught her up on what was going on around the ranch. He told her about the situation with Mrs. Peterson, and she assured him she would have handled it the same way.

"It must have put April in an awkward position, having a parent put such demands on her," Ashley said.

"It did, but I told her never to second guess her own instincts, especially where safety is concerned. I assured her we would always stand behind her decisions if they were made with the best interest of the rider in mind."

Ashley noticed Willow tensed when C.J. spoke about April. With all C.J. had told her, Ashley guessed Willow probably felt intimidated by April. But she had nothing to worry about. C.J. only had eyes for her.

With breakfast over, C.J. walked to the other side of the bar, so he could help Austin with kitchen detail.

"Willow, while they're doing dishes, why don't we go upstairs and go through the clothes I was talking about."

"Ah, sure," she looked at her watch. "I have a little time before I have to open the office." She smiled, but Ashley could hear apprehension in her tone. "Just let me go brush my teeth really quick, so I'm ready to go."

Once Willow was gone, C.J. leaned over the bar and whispered, "You're not going to interrogate her, are you? If Willow feels you disapprove, she'll—"

"Give me some credit, C.J.," she snapped, then softened her tone. "Remember, I know a little bit of what she's going through."

C.J. hung his head. "I'm sorry; I shouldn't have come at you like that. Just be careful, okay? Willow and I had a good talk last night, and I don't want her to second guess what we decided."

"Don't worry, we're just going to talk." Ashley slipped from the barstool and headed toward the stairs, but before she could put her foot on the first step, Austin came up behind her. "What are you doing?" she asked.

"Making sure you make it up the stairs incident free."

She rolled her eyes. "I think I can handle a few stairs."

"And I think I'm going to make sure you can."

Austin didn't help Ashley, but he walked every step with her just the same. When they made it to the bedroom, he gave her a kiss, and turned around. "I'll be downstairs if you need me."

Ashley walked to the edge of the bed and sat down.

"Knock, knock." Willow tapped on the doorframe.

"Come on in; I'm just catching my breath. I can't believe the stairs I'm used to running up and down a hundred times a day are actually exhausting me."

"But you look really good, Ashley. Twice as good as yesterday, and I'll bet you'll feel even better tomorrow."

"I hope so. I don't like this weak feeling. It makes me feel lazy."

"With the quick pace you're used to, a little R & R should be a nice change. With me in the office and C.J. taking care of everything else, you should just relax, take as much time off as you need. You could even recuperate at Austin's if you want to. We have this covered."

Ashley could tell Willow was making small talk out of nervousness, so she decided to cut to the chase. "Look, Willow, I'm going to be very honest with you. I didn't ask you up here just to go through my clothes."

"I kind of figured that." Willow's shoulders sagged. "Look, Ashley, I understand if you don't want me seeing C.J. If I was a mom, I wouldn't want my son seeing me either." Willow's whole countenance changed. Gone was her bright eyes and pretty smile, replaced by a downcast stare and an expression of failure.

"Come sit with me." Ashley motioned for her to join her on the bed. When she sat down, Ashley reached out and squeezed her hand. "Willow, I'm not against you and C.J. having a relationship. But I won't lie either; I do have some apprehensions."

Willow's shoulders slumped even further as if the weight of the world was pressing down on her.

Ashley pulled her close, hugging her to her side. "Willow, please don't look like that. I'm not trying to put more pressure on you. Just promise me, you and C.J. will be open and honest with each other. I know you've had a difficult childhood, and obviously a difficult few months. You need—"

Willow sat up straight and swiveled toward her. "I'll answer any questions you have, if that will make you feel better."

"You don't need to do that. Your personal life is none of my business. I just think you and C.J. need to be candid with each other if you expect to have a future together." Willow looked so dejected, Ashley felt close to tears. "Willow, you need to know, I think the world of you. In fact, I always hoped you and C.J. would someday get together."

"Really!" Willow finally looked at her and smiled.

"Of course! The minute I hired you, I thought you were smart, and beautiful, and there was just something about you I found so refreshing. And I assure you, my opinion of you hasn't changed because of your circumstances. You've made some difficult choices, and unfortunately, you've paid a very high price for them. I just want you to promise, no matter what obstacles you and C.J. come up against, you'll be completely honest with him. It's obvious he's crazy in love with you. I just don't want it to be a blind love. I think he'll be able to handle anything you tell him, as long as he knows he's being told the truth."

Tears slipped down Willow's face and fell onto her lap. Ashley reached forward and hugged her again. "I'm only saying these things out of love, Willow, love for both you and C.J."

"And I want you to know I would never do anything to hurt C.J. In fact, I tried to distance myself from him, but he told me I was making him miserable. He's seen me at my most vulnerable, and I've tried to be completely honest with him. I promise you, I won't ever do anything to compromise the trust C.J. has put in me, and I pray that my past will never be bigger than what we can handle."

After tears were dried and hugs were exchanged, Ashley and Willow went through the clothes stacked on the floor.

A few minutes later C.J. knocked on the door, then pushed it open. "So, how is shopping going at Ashley and Son?"

"Great."

"Do you have any jeans in there?"

"A couple pair, why?"

"I thought we could go on a ride."

"C.J., I need to open the office."

"I know, but later. We could go for a short ride before dinner."

"I don't know, C.J., I haven't been on a horse in a while. I'm pretty rusty."

"That's okay. I'll take it easy on you. Besides, it's just like riding a bike. It will all come back to you."

"More like falling off a bike. That part I remember really well."

"Oh, come on. You're not going to let an animal three times your size frighten you? What kind of vet would you be if you were intimated by your patients?"

"I'm not intimidated; I just have a healthy respect for things I'm unsure of." Willow grabbed the pile of clothes she'd chosen, got to her feet, and walked to the doorway C.J. still occupied. She turned to Ashley. "Thanks again . . . for everything."

"You're welcome, Willow. And if you ever need to talk, I'm here."

Willow smiled, then went to her room with her new wardrobe.

Willow stacked the clothes Ashley gave her on her bed. When she turned to leave, she ran right into C.J.

Gasping, she took a step back. "You scared me half to death. I didn't know you were right behind me. I thought you went to work."

"I have a few minutes. I just wanted to make sure you were all right—that Mom didn't give you the third degree?"

Willow shrugged her shoulders. "She's being a mom, worrying about you getting hurt."

"Sounds cryptic." He crossed his arms against his chest. "She wasn't too hard on you, right?"

"No. Nothing I didn't expect."

C.J. took a step toward her. "Good. Because I don't want you to have any doubts about us." He slipped his hands around her waist and nudged her closer.

Willow looked up into his sultry eyes, realizing this was going to be harder than she thought. When he lowered his mouth to hers, and gently pressed a kiss to her lips, she did nothing to discourage him. She felt C.J. smile against her lips before he kissed her again.

Then again.

Never had she felt so safe or so loved before. Free from fear, Willow wrapped her arms around C.J.'s neck, and allowed herself to let go. She loved everything about him. His scent. His taste. The texture of his lips. He was everything she could have ever hoped for in a man.

That's enough, her conscience prodded, when she held on tighter.

Don't let things get out of hand, her brain scolded, when his hands rested at the slope of her lower back.

Her still small voice was right, but she didn't want to listen.

Even so, when their kiss escalated from searching to indulgent, Willow pressed her hands to C.J.'s chest and broke their connection. "I need to get to the office. I'm already late," she whispered.

He smiled, still holding her close. "I'll talk to the boss and smooth things over for you."

It was just what Willow needed to hear to snap her back to reality. "No, you won't!" She stepped out of his arms. "I don't want preferential treatment. In fact, I don't even want people to know we're involved."

"What?" C.J. said, dumbfounded. "Why?"

"Because I don't want to be gossiped about, or for people to think you're playing favorites."

"But you *are* my favorite." He grinned. "Besides, it's not like you do the same work as everyone else. You run the office; everyone else works with the horses. I can't exactly push your workload off on them."

"I know, but I still don't want anyone to know about us. Besides, I think it will be a good thing. It will force us to remain professional throughout the day and help keep us from getting too relaxed with our feelings."

"Sounds like torture."

"It's called self-control, and I have every confidence you'll do just fine. Now, I have to go." Willow pecked his cheek, then hurried downstairs.

C.J. stood for a moment, hands at his hips, eyes on the carpet. He'd blown it.

It hadn't even been twenty-four hours since Willow told him she felt vulnerable with the physical side of a relationship. And what did he do? Put her in a situation where she had to put on the brakes—because he didn't.

He took a deep breath of acceptance and headed out for the day.

This is going to be harder than I expected.

SEVENTY-ONE

It was only a week after her surgery, and Ashley felt even better than she had hoped. The sharp pains had turned into small aches, allowing her to move more easily without as much hesitation. However, she sensed something was off with Austin. He was distracted—not entirely present. He was still the doting husband, maybe too much so, but other times, he was distant, or his brows would press together in silent concentration.

From where she sat on the couch, she watched him walk across the room, the morning paper tucked under his arm, his coffee cup pressed against his lips. When he took a seat in the side chair, he set his coffee aside, opened the newspaper, and immediately thumbed his way to the business section. As he scrutinized and scanned the page, it hit her.

Of course! He misses work.

"You know, Austin, I'm feeling really good today. Why don't you go to the office for a while, so you can see how things are going?"

He folded the paper closed and casually tossed it on the ottoman. "Why? I'm sure Simon has everything under control; he would've called if he didn't."

"But didn't you threaten him within an inch of his life if he called you for anything less than a financial apocalypse?"

He frowned. "I don't think I put it quite that way."

She laughed. "I believe your exact words were, 'If you call me for anything less than an economic landslide, you're fired.'"

He started to disagree, but when she raised a brow that dared him to do so, he just grinned.

"Okay, maybe I was a little overprotective of our time together."

Leaning over, she kissed him and smiled. "And I love you for it. But I'm doing fine."

"I just hate leaving you alone."

She chuckled. "I'm not exactly alone. C.J.'s here. Willow's here.

The crew is here."

"I guess what I meant was, I don't want you to be by yourself."

"Austin, I'm fine, and I'll feel even better if you go to the office and see for yourself that everything is running smoothly. You'll be more relaxed, and I won't feel as guilty."

"Hey," he stroked her cheek and frowned, "you have no reason to feel guilty. I'm exactly where I want to be."

"And I love having you here. But I'm not going to feel the least bit neglected if you take a couple of hours to be brought up to speed."

"Are you sure?" He walked behind the kitchen counter and set his coffee mug in the sink.

"Absolutely. Look, I'll see if Willow can make us a light lunch; it will give me another chance to talk to her and see how she's doing. Then you can dazzle me with another one of your fabulous dinners when you get home."

"Hey, wait a minute; I might go for a couple of hours, but I don't want to be gone *that* long."

"But your staff needs you. I'm sure they're getting pretty antsy for your return."

"Hah! You don't know Simon. I'm sure he's loving having ultimate control."

"You've never left him in charge before?"

"No. There's never been a time when I made myself unavailable. Even so, I trust him completely. He knows me well enough to make decisions on my behalf. But if I told him that, he'd want a bigger cut of the business, so you need to keep that between you and me." Austin chuckled.

"Well, when you see him, you can thank him for me, and let him know as soon as I get passed this next hurdle, we'll have him over for dinner. I bet he has a lot of stories he could tell me about you." Ashley smiled mischievously.

"Humm . . ." he stroked his chin. "Maybe I need to make sure Simon keeps his distance. I would hate for him to taint the illusion you have of me."

"Oh, I have no illusions. I know you're the most wonderful man in the world, and that I'm the luckiest woman on earth to have you."

"You're sure you don't mind?" Austin leaned over her, braced his arms on the back of the couch, and gave her a very affirming kiss. When he broke their connection, he smiled. "If I stayed home, we could spend the day doing more of this."

"Would you just go already, before I change my mind." She smiled and gave his shoulders a playful shove.

"Okay, but only if it makes you happy."

"It does. Now go."

"Fine. Let me get changed, then I'll come say goodbye before I leave."

When Austin came downstairs ten minutes later, he looked quite dapper in a pair of khakis, a navy dress shirt, and a blue silk tie.

"Wow! You had all that in your duffel bag?"

"I've learned over the years to pack a little of everything. You know, always be prepared." He leaned over and gave her another kiss. "I'm going to go out the backway and let C.J. know I'll be gone for a few hours, just so he knows to check on you from time to time."

When he closed the door, Ashley watched him walk across the yard and disappear inside the barn. She couldn't help but smile. *Wow, I love that man!*

Puttering around the house with no real agenda, Ashley watered a few plants, straightened a stack of magazines, and tossed out yesterday's newspaper. It took all of twenty minutes before she was back on the couch resting.

When Willow came in at noon, Ashley perked up and took a seat at the bar.

"Where is Austin?" Willow asked, as she pulled a few items from the refrigerator.

"I sent him to work. He needed to get out; he just didn't want to admit it."

"Oh, okay, then let me make you some lunch. What sounds good?"

Ashley looked at the spinach, avocado, and tomato Willow had set on the counter. "What you have there is just fine."

"Perfect."

Ashley visited with Willow while she assembled their salads. She asked easy questions to start with: How's the office going? Anything she should know about? Did she have any questions? Ashley was working up to the more serious questions when C.J. and Billy walked through the backdoor. Billy gave Ashley a gentle hug, then took a seat two barstools over from her. He asked how she was feeling, congratulated her on getting married, then launched into day-to-day ranch stuff without even missing a beat. Ashley tried to keep up with him but was more interested in the nonverbal communication going on between C.J. and Willow.

Ashley witnessed C.J. brush up against Willow and lean forward to give her a kiss. But Willow backed up and gave him an icy stare. She whispered something about Billy, but C.J. just chuckled and tried to kiss her again. When he got the same reaction, he frowned, shook his head, and spun around to the refrigerator. Yanking on the handle, he pulled out everything for deli sandwiches.

The four of them chatted through lunch, or at least three of them did. Willow did not say a word. C.J. kept having silent communication with her, but Willow answered with either a raised brow or a steely stare.

The men inhaled their food and went back to work in less than twenty minutes. As soon as the door clicked shut, Willow let out a frustrated huff.

"Tell me if this is none of my business," Ashley said, "but what just happened between you and C.J.?"

Willow tossed their utensils in the sink, then rinsed out their bowls. "I don't want anyone to know we're seeing each other, including Billy. I don't want to be gossiped about. C.J. thinks I'm making a big deal out of nothing. But for now, I want us to be professional during business hours."

"Oh, I see; you didn't like him leaning in for a kiss in front of Billy."

"No, I didn't. Billy is sweet and all, but he's a talker. He might let it slip." Willow wiped up the crumbs from the countertop, then shrugged. "Do you think I'm making too big of a deal out of it?"

Ashley shook her head. "No. If that's what you told C.J., he needs to respect your feelings. A relationship is about making decisions together and considering the other person's feelings above your own. It's definitely give and take."

"Then maybe I'm not considering his feelings? Maybe I am making a big deal out of nothing."

"I don't think you are. At least not right now. Maybe a couple of weeks down the road you'll change your mind. He just needs to give you some time."

"Thanks, Ashley. I didn't mean to put you in the middle, but I do appreciate your advice."

"Anytime."

At the end of the day, Ashley sat by the bay window and watched as the staff left. Wanting to avoid the well-intended—*how are you feeling*—comments and curious questions, she waited until everyone was gone before creeping outside and curling up in her favorite chair. Laying her head back and closing her eyes, she inhaled the scents of home. Earth. Hay. Even manure. It was the perfect medicine, and she allowed herself to bask in its familiarity, and the peace it brought.

"Looks like the patient is rehabilitating just fine without me."

Austin pressed a kiss to her lips as she pushed the fuzziness aside. Smiling, she opened her eyes. "I guess I fell asleep."

"That's good." Austin plopped down in the chair next to her.

"What time is it?"

Austin glanced at his watch. "Six o'clock. How long have you been out here?"

"About twenty minutes. I waited until the staff cleared out, but I just wanted to feel the sun on my face, even if it was only for a few minutes."

"It looks good on you."

"It feels good. *I* feel good. So good in fact . . . I'm rethinking the radiation."

"You're what?" Austin shifted to the edge of the chair.

"I'm rethinking the treatments. I feel so good. But if I start the treatments next week, I'll feel horrible again. Three weeks of horrible, and who knows how long after that."

"I don't agree, Ashley. And you don't know for sure how your body will react to the radiation. Dr. Allen said some patients have minimal side effects, if any."

"But the literature describes numerous side effects. Abdominal cramping. Nausea. Diarrhea. Skin blisters. Fatigue." She looked at him, eyes pleading for his approval.

"You can look at me with those puppy dog eyes all you want," he said in a soft, yet stern voice. "But you need to go through with the radiation. It's a safeguard you shouldn't ignore."

She growled, then whined, "But it feels so good to be in the sun and out of the house, spending time with Dominus. Just the thought of feeling miserable again is enough to make me want to scream."

He scooted closer and reached for her hand. "Well fine. Scream and get it out of your system, because you're going in next week and that's final."

Austin's no-nonsense attitude irritated Ashley, fueling her combative side. She was ready to unload on him, when he twisted around and picked up something from the side table. He sat a white square box on her lap.

"The pictures? They're done?"

"Yep, Simon's had them since Monday. He said if I hadn't come by soon, he would have sent them over. He says hi, by the way."

Ashley pulled the album from the box and opened the beautiful linen cover. "Wow!"

Simon had created a mock invitation with all the pertinent information and added his personal thoughts for their future. His words touched her, and she had to brush away her tears in order to see the pictures. Page after page, Ashley was blown away by the quality of Simon's work and the expressions he captured on their faces. The last picture in the album took Ashley's breath away. It was the most intimate picture Simon had taken while they were alone on the beach. He had developed it in black and white, which added to the romance. The sensuality reflected in the picture really captured the love Austin and she had for each other. Flipping back to the front of the album, she started all over again. What a priceless gift they'd been given. After looking through the pictures for a third time, she closed the book and sighed.

"I take it that's a sigh of approval?"

"Austin, these are wonderful. I can't believe Simon doesn't do this professionally."

"Don't tell him that. I need him at the office." Austin said with a teasing smile. "Actually, Simon has been approached before, but his photography is a hobby, and he's afraid if he turns it into a business, he won't enjoy it as much. He thinks he'll lose his creative eye. I don't argue because I don't want to lose him as a partner."

"Well, they're wonderful." Ashley stroked the cover. "Once I've got some more energy, we'll have to have him over for dinner, and maybe a ride. If he's interested."

"He'd love it. In fact, when I told him about the ranch, he got excited. He had a horse when he was a kid, and I guess he's thought about getting one again."

"Why hasn't he?"

Austin chuckled, "He'd have a hard time housing a horse since he lives at the marina."

"That's what we're here for. The Circle-R could board a horse for him."

"We're full, you know that, Mom," C.J. interrupted as he scaled the porch. "If we take on any more horses we're going to have to build that fourth stable you've been talking about." C.J. collapsed in one of the patio chairs and perched his hat on his knee. "Who are we talking about anyway?"

"Simon. Austin's partner."

Ashley extended the album for C.J. to see. Just then, Willow walked up the steps and sat in the chair next to him. C.J. had already opened the album so Willow scooted closer as he flipped through the pages.

"These shots are beautiful, Ashley. I had no idea he was a professional. I thought Simon was just a friend of yours." Willow glanced at Austin, where he casually leaned back in his chair and hooked his hands behind his head. "He is a friend, and he is a professional, but he prefers to keep it as a hobby."

"Will he do animals?" Willow asked, as she continued to flip through the book. "Because I would recommend him to some of your boarders, Ashley, for when they want portraits and Christmas cards, stuff like that. These are definitely better than what I've seen in the past. And if Simon doesn't mind being around horses—like most of the photographers who show up here—he's sure to get better shots."

"You're probably right." Ashley agreed. "Maybe you could talk to him, Austin. Invite him out here one day. Have him take some pictures and see what happens."

Austin raised an eyebrow and gave his head a nod in approval. Ashley moved to sit with Willow, where she was still looking at the pictures. Together, they commented on the best ones, which ones should be enlarged, and which should be developed in black and white.

C.J. stretched his long body and said, "So, who's in charge of dinner tonight?"

"That would be me," Austin said, his eyes closed. "I promised your mom a feast."

Ashley laughed, "You certainly don't look ready to cook a feast."

Willow popped up. "I'll make dinner."

Austin sat up straighter. "You don't have to do that."

"But I want to. It will make me feel like I'm contributing."

"Are you sure you feel up to it?" Ashley asked.

"Sure. What sounds good?"

C.J. quipped, "Food."

Austin agreed, "I'm not picky. Chef's choice."

"Ashley, how about you? What sounds good?"

She thought for a second. "Teriyaki chicken sounds good."

The guys agreed wholeheartedly.

"Okay, teriyaki chicken it is." Willow scooted the album, so it was only resting on Ashley's lap and stood.

"Wait a minute," C.J. said. "I get it now. You were supposed to go on a ride with me before dinner. This is your way of getting out of it."

"That's not true. I offered to make dinner, and my offer was accepted. Nothing more, nothing less." Willow could not disguise the smile creeping into her expression.

"Okay, if you say so, but you're not getting out of it. We'll just go after dinner."

Ashley listened to the exchange between C.J. and Willow, and found it amusing.

"Do you need any help?" C.J. asked from his relaxed position.

"You can help me cut the chicken if you'd like, but I have to defrost it first. I'll call you when I need you."

Willow closed the backdoor behind her, but C.J. continued to watch her through the picture-window, unaware that Ashley was watching him, his thoughts completely monopolized by Willow.

Ashley relaxed back against the rim of the chair and closed her eyes, but her smile never dimmed.

~®~

Gathering up the dishes in front of her, Willow walked toward the sink, turned the spigot on, and waited for the water to get hot.

"That was great, Willow." Austin said, as he pushed himself away from the table. Ashley and C.J. were quick to agree.

"Thank you. I'm glad you enjoyed it."

C.J. collected the serving dishes and set them on the drainboard, then leaned over Willow's shoulder and said, "Austin volunteered for kitchen detail, so we can still take our ride."

Willow looked at Austin. "I feel a conspiracy is at hand. Did you volunteer or were you strong-armed?"

"Oh, I volunteered. I firmly believe in sharing household duties. You cooked, so I'll clean."

Willow couldn't help but smile as Austin tried to play the part of innocent bystander.

"So, while you get changed," C.J. placed his hands on Willow's shoulders, turned her around, and gave her a light push toward the stairs, "I'll go saddle the horses."

Climbing the stairs, Willow felt a little apprehensive. How long had it been since she'd ridden? She grabbed a pair of jeans she had salvaged from home and pulled them on. She could tell by their loose fit, she had dropped a few pounds. Instinctively, she reached for her stomach, and felt her heart flutter. She found herself praying for her unborn baby as tears welled up in her eyes. She took a moment to splash her face and tried to cleanse the sadness from her soul. She didn't know how often she would have these small glimpses of what might have been, but she was determined not to allow them to prolong her recovery, physically or emotionally.

C.J. took a few minutes to talk to Dominus—stroking him, and his ego. Dr. Larsen was right. While his mom was recuperating, C.J. had asked everyone else to show him a little attention.

And it worked like a charm.

The extra affection was just what he had needed. He still wasn't eating as much as normal, but he had stopped cribbing, and when someone called to him, he no longer gave them his rump. But the best part was, his mom was feeling well enough to spend some time with him again. Not a lot, but enough for Dominus to know Ashley still loved and cared for him.

"Okay, boy," he stroked his withers a few more time. "I have some plans of my own for the evening. I'll see you in a little bit."

C.J. was busy saddling Knight and didn't hear Willow until her boot clanged against the bottom rung of the gate. Turning, he skimmed her with his eyes. Wearing a plaid button-down shirt, she'd gotten from his mom, he couldn't help but stare. The pink pattern was soft and feminine, but it was its slim fit accentuating the curves of Willow's petite frame that had his pulse racing in double-time. "Wow." The exclamation escaped his lips before he could stop himself. "I mean, that shirt looks nice."

"Thanks. I don't usually wear pink, but I like it."

C.J. did, too. Maybe a little too much. He turned toward Knight, took a deep breath to level his equilibrium, then led him out of the stall. "Are you ready?" he asked Willow as she fell in step beside him.

"As I'll ever be. But my riding skills are a little rusty, and I'm still not quite a hundred percent."

"You'll do fine." He reached out for her hand and smiled. She took it, then gently ran her other hand over the bandage on his arm.

"How are your stitches doing?"

"Good. Another week and they come out."

"Does it still hurt?"

"Nah. They itch more than anything. That's why I keep it wrapped. That, and I need to keep it clean."

When Willow looked away, he knew what she was thinking. "It wasn't your fault." He squeezed her hand, so she would look at him. "Come on, let's just enjoy the ride. No distractions."

"Okay." She smiled. "No distractions."

Once they were in the yard, C.J. led Knight to where Willow's mount was already saddled and ready to go. He looped Knight's reins around a post, then turned to give Willow a leg up. Once she was in the saddle, C.J. adjusted the stirrups. With his hand wrapped around her calf, he slipped her foot into the stirrup and gave her leg a squeeze. Looking up, he asked, "How does that feel?"

"Feel?" She squinted down at him, looking nervous.

"The stirrups? Is the length okay?"

"Oh, yeah." She stood in the saddle, then sat back down. "Feels good."

"Good," he smiled, then quickly mounted Knight.

With a nicker, C.J. led Knight toward the fence line on the back of the property, Willow on his right. The horses knew the routine and walked right up to the fence. Knight side shuffled so C.J. could lean down and slide the bolt on the gate. Once on the other side, gate bolted, they started up the hillside.

"So, remind me, who am I riding?"

"That's Gent."

"Gent? Why don't I recognize that name?"

"Because everyone else calls him Jester."

She groaned. "That name I know. Ashley had been working with him and said he could be a real pain at times. Why do you call him Gent?"

"Well, his registered name is Gentleman Jester. It's an apt description. One minute he can be a gentleman, the next he can be a real prankster."

"So, are you telling me or warning me?"

C.J. chuckled. "He's not that bad anymore. He's calmed down quite a bit, but if he decides to take you for a ride, shift your weight back in the saddle, and take up the slack in the reigns."

"Thanks, I'll keep that in mind."

C.J. watched Willow and could tell she was tense. But he knew it would only last a few minutes. Once she was able to relax, and take in the view, she would realize why riding was the perfect way to unwind after a busy day.

They didn't talk much, but C.J. was okay with that. He just enjoyed the two of them being together. Leading them up a narrow trail, Willow fell in behind him. When they finally crested the top of the mountain, the Pacific coastline came into view. C.J. stopped as Willow came up alongside of him.

"Wow! This is incredible." Her eyes scanned the horizon from one side to the other.

"That's why I wanted to bring you here." C.J. dismounted and lapped Knight's reins over a low-slung tree branch, then turned toward Willow. "Here, I'll help you." He walked closer. "Swing your leg around the horn." C.J. reached up and put his hands firmly around her waist. With her hands on his shoulders, Willow slid from the saddle to the ground, but C.J. was in no hurry to let her go.

They lingered. Unmoving.

Willow smiled up at him, closing one eye against the rays of the sun. "You can let me go now. I feel steady enough."

"But maybe I don't." He smiled, then let his hands drop to his sides.

Willow walked to the rim of the plateau while massaging the muscles on the backs of her legs. C.J. didn't laugh, but he had a hard time hiding his smile. When Willow turned around she caught him grinning.

"No laughing. I haven't been on a horse in years, and that was no small ride."

He put up his hands in surrender. "I'm not laughing; I was just admiring the scenery.

"Some scenery. I'm walking like a tired, old bulldog."

C.J. watched as she tipped her head back and drank in the sun. With her eyes closed, he quietly stepped behind her and slipped his arms around her waist. Pulling her back against his chest, Willow rested her head just below his chin and sighed.

Feeling his heartbeat jump to double time, he had to work to control his breathing. When he did, he asked, "Penny for your thoughts?"

"No way," she whispered. "What I'm feeling right now is priceless."

"You mean it couldn't get any better?"

Willow twisted around in his arms and slipped her hands around

425

his neck. "Well, maybe a little better." On tip-toes, she reached up, and he bent down, meeting her halfway.

What started out as a simple kiss turned into so much more.

Passion.

Urgency.

The still small voice of his conscience warned that danger was fast approaching.

Reaching behind his head, C.J. untangled Willow's fingers and took a small step back. Leaning his forehead against hers, his throaty whisper was barely audible. "I think we need to stop. If it gets any better, we're going to be in big trouble."

She looked at him, then quickly looked down. "I'm sorry," she said, before walking away. Sitting on a large boulder, she pulled her knees up to her chest and wrapped her arms around her legs.

It didn't take a genius to read her body language. He sat beside her on the rock and nudged her shoulder. "Don't shut me out, Willow."

"I'm not shutting you out," she snapped. "I'm just mad at myself."

"For what?"

"For *not* wanting to stop. For wanting to do everything I know we shouldn't." She glanced his way but only for a second. "I told you this would be a problem. I try too hard. I want you to be pleased with me. I'm afraid I won't be enough, so I offer more than I should. If I was stronger, if I had a little more self-worth, if just once, someone loved me for me and not for what they could take from me, my life wouldn't be such a mess."

"Hey," he wrapped his arm around her. "My love has only one stipulation, that you love me in return." He waited for her to say something, but she was silent. "Look at me, Willow."

Slowly, she turned toward him, tears glistening on her cheeks.

"You can't let your past dictate our future. There will be times when we disagree, or we argue. But that doesn't mean I will love you any less."

"How can you be so sure?"

He shrugged his shoulders. "Because I am. God brought us together for a reason, and I have faith He's going to see us through the good and the bad. The highs and the lows. You just need to believe in Him . . . and in us." He pulled her a little closer and kissed her temple. "Now, no more beating yourself up or questioning what we have. We're here to enjoy the sunset.

SEVENTY-TWO

With a week of radiation treatments behind her, Ashley was surprisingly optimistic. She wasn't feeling nearly as bad as she had expected. Yes, she was fatigued and experiencing some mild cramping, but nothing that could not be dulled by a couple of Ibuprofen. In fact, she realized she couldn't blame her fatigue and lethargy solely on her treatments. In the last week, Austin and she had turned into a couple of grade-A couch potatoes. Each day, after her treatment, they came home, ate lunch, lounged on the couch, and watched old movies. They laughed through *Groundhog Day,* cuddled during *Sleepless in Seattle,* and she couldn't help but sob when Shadow, an aging golden retriever, limped home in *Homeward Bound.*

Even so, whenever she took her bath or left the room for any amount of time, Austin was immediately on his phone, checking in with Simon or Victoria. Austin was coddling her, and acting like his time was his own, but she knew it drove him crazy being away from work. Well, tonight all that was going to change. She loved him for making her the center of his world, but she needed to get back to a normal schedule. Modified, but normal.

"Okay, here are our choices for tonight." Austin walked into the living room with three movies in his hands. *The Sandlot, The Fugitive,* or *The Three Musketeers.* He fanned the three DVD covers in front of her.

"Humm," she studied the covers. *"The Sandlot."*

"Good choice." He popped the DVD from the folder and walked over to the blue ray player. Once everything was cued-up, he sat down beside her, put his feet up on the ottoman they shared, and wrapped his arm around her shoulders, then asked, "So, have you figured it out yet?"

Ashley smiled to herself. She had recruited Willow to help her research Austin's movie choices. He'd given her ten at the beginning of the week and said they all had something in common.

It took Willow less than forty-eight hours to figure out the common denominator, but Ashley didn't let on that she knew.

"Come on, I told you, you had three guesses or until Saturday night to figure it out, whichever came first. Time's up."

She looked up at Austin, who was smiling proudly, thinking he'd stumped her. Of course, he would have without Willow's help. Ashley wasn't much of a movie person, except for the ones her horses were featured in, and Austin knew it. "Well, I don't remember any one actor being in all the movies."

"Nope."

"And I don't think they were all shot in the same location."

"Nope."

"Remind me again what I get if I guess right?"

He laughed. "Anything you want," he said smugly, so sure she didn't have a clue.

She tucked her chin and grinned, knowing she had him exactly where she wanted him. "Okay . . . my final guess is . . ." she drew out her answer.

"Come on; no more stalling."

"Okay, my final guess is . . ." She sat up straighter, a proud smile on her face. "They're all movies that were released the same year we graduated."

His jaw dropped open in stunned disbelief.

She threw her head back and laughed.

"You conned me. All week long you acted like you didn't know, that you didn't even have a clue. When did you figure it out?"

"On Wednesday."

"Wednesday!"

She laughed some more. "Yep. And now I get anything I want." She tapped her finger against her lip, pretending to be deep in thought. "Okay, I got it." She turned to him and smiled. "I want you to go back to work."

"What? No way."

"Are you reneging?"

"No. But that's off the table. My place is here with you, not at work."

"And if I was feeling even half as miserable as I thought I would, I wouldn't let you leave my side. But I'm doing fine." He was shaking his head as if he wasn't even listening. "You can still take me to my treatments, and we can still have lunch together. But after lunch, I want you to go to the office, at least for a few hours."

"But don't you get it?" he asked. "Why I chose the movies I did? I'm making up for all the dates we missed out on. These are all movies we would've seen together if you hadn't . . ." he locked eyes with her.

"Up and disappeared," she snapped, and immediately regretted it. "I'm sorry. I didn't mean to sound so snippy."

He stroked her arm. "And I didn't mean to make you feel bad. It was a stupid idea anyway."

"No, it wasn't." She rested her cheek against his chest and wrapped her arm around him. "Everything you do is so intentional. I love that about you."

He huffed. "Right. That's why you want to get rid of me every day."

She gave him a playful shove and sat up. "That's not true and you know it."

"Then why?"

"Austin . . . I have to get back into some kind of routine. I can't just keep laying around the house. If I do, I'll never be a hundred percent again. I need to start pressing myself a little. See what my limitations are, so I can build on them." She couldn't tell if he was thinking or stewing. She gave him a second or two, then said. "It's a compromise. You're with me half a day, and at work half a day. At least give it a try. If I crash and burn you can say, 'I told you so' and hold it over my head the rest of our lives. Deal?"

He still wasn't budging.

She cuddled closer and dotted his chin with kisses. "Deal?"

He smirked. "Don't start something you can't finish, lady."

"I have my follow-up appointment on Friday, after my treatment." She kissed him some more. "Now do you see why I have to build up my stamina?"

He pulled her down, across his lap, and kissed her soundly. "Deal."

SEVENTY-THREE

C.J. stared at the ceiling, waiting for dawn.

He'd been awake for hours unable to sleep, thinking about everything that had happened in the last month. His mom and Austin's marriage. Her surgery. Willow's attack. Steven killed. Radiation therapy. Phone calls and visits from the investigating detectives.

It was a lot to process.

And Willow was still struggling.

Each day was different. Most were good. Others were rough. Physically, she was fine. All outward appearances of her attack had faded, but emotionally, she still had her dark days. Steven had really done a number on her psyche, convincing Willow she was incompetent and stupid. Because of that, she struggled with feelings of inadequacy and was constantly striving to do more or try harder. She was a textbook people pleaser. She volunteered to make dinner every night and was always cleaning up around the house. And when groceries ran low, she did the shopping. On top of that, she ran the office like a well-oiled machine.

Unfortunately, every time C.J. saw a hint of improvement, a glimmer of confidence, the detectives investigating Steven's death would either call or come by the ranch with more follow-up questions. C.J. tried not to take offense; they were only doing their job. Checking every angle. Confirming every piece of information.

But for Willow, it was grueling.

The roller-coaster of emotions she was forced to relive every time her relationship with Steven was brought into question, dug deep into her soul, and stirred up her insecurities all over again. Even though the detectives were polite and sensitive when questioning her, the minute they left, a wall would go up, and she would close herself off from everyone. Sometimes it only lasted a few hours, other times, a few days.

C.J. constantly reassured Willow what happened between her

and Steven wasn't her fault, but he always saw a hint of unbelief in her eyes. When he came to the realization that working in the office was a type of therapy for her—because there she felt a sense of adequacy and control—he backed off and gave her, her space. Begrudgingly, he conceded to the professional relationship Willow insisted on during business hours but being kept at arm's length between eight and five, and practicing for state finals every night until dusk, gave them very little time together—just the two of them.

What he enjoyed best were evenings when they could just lay around the house and do nothing—maybe watch a sappy movie together or a silly sitcom, but it was rare for them to have the house all to themselves. His mom needed the downtime to recover from her treatments, and most times when he was done practicing, he'd walk into the house and find her and Austin curled up together in the great room. He had to bite his tongue and check his belligerent attitude on more than one occasion, reminding himself that they'd only been married a month. Even so, their star-crossed lover's behavior, at times, was hard to swallow. Especially since Willow and he were trying to mind such strict boundaries.

So, on nights when Willow didn't cook, they went out to dinner. Sometimes fancy, most of the time just fast food or the barbecue joint up the road. They walked the mall a few times and had driven to the beach on occasion. They even saw a couple of movies. New releases, not the ancient films his mom and Austin insisted on watching. Then they would end the day on the porch swing talking. Well . . . talking and kissing. He was careful to maintain a balance between Willow's insecurities and her vulnerabilities. He'd done his best to keep the physical side of their relationship from moving too fast, and for the most part, they did fine.

Until last night.

He cringed thinking about it, knowing he'd failed miserably.

The evening had turned chilly, so instead of spending time on the porch, they decided to go inside and play a card game. Knowing the game was all about speed, C.J. was afraid if they played downstairs they would be too loud and interrupt his mom and Austin's movie marathon. So, they sprawled out on his bedroom floor. They had a great time. They got crazy and obnoxious, and taunted each other until they were in hysterics. He found out Willow was very competitive and quite the card shark.

But after they calmed down and called a truce, they curled up on the old loveseat tucked in the corner of his room and started to watch a movie on Netflix. He stroked Willow's arm, loving the feel of her skin, and she snuggled closer, wrapping her arms around him. He felt his self-control beginning to wane, and should have gotten up right then and there, but he didn't.

Tactile senses trumped common sense, and before he knew it, they were crossing lines they shouldn't have. If it wasn't for hearing his mom and Austin laughing as they climbed the stairs, breaking the spell he was under, he's not sure he would have stopped.

Needless to say, he called it a night after that. But he could tell Willow was confused with his abrupt behavior. He didn't want to come right out and say they had blown it, because he knew she would blame herself. Instead, he made up a lame excuse about feeling a head cold coming on, and that he really should take some medicine and get some sleep. Especially since they were planning on going to church in the morning. He sounded like an idiot, but he didn't know what else to say. Not without hurting her feelings.

It certainly wasn't the best way to end the night, but it definitely was the safest.

Sighing, C.J. got out of bed, knowing he needed to help Billy with the morning feeding. For the hundredth time, he asked God for forgiveness and prayed for a better day.

~Ⓡ~

Willow was nervous.

She had tried on everything in her sparse wardrobe. Twice. And still wasn't happy with her choice. She wanted a dress that would hide the Willow she saw whenever she looked in the mirror. But, no matter what she wore, she felt her past was tattooed on her forehead for everyone to see.

She fidgeted with her purse while she looked out the passenger window, afraid she would do or say something stupid and embarrass C.J. This was his church. His friends. They would take one look at her and know C.J. deserved better.

Because He does.

"You're awfully quiet over there," C.J. said.

"I'm not feeling so good. Maybe I got whatever you had last night?" She turned to him. "But you seem better this morning."

"Yeah. Medicine and sleep usually does the trick."

"Then maybe I should go home and lie down."

"But we're already here."

The minute C.J. pulled into the church parking lot, her heart accelerated.

I'm going to be sick.

Taking deep breaths, she waited for C.J. to open her door and help her out of the truck.

Holding her hand as they walked toward the sanctuary, he leaned over and whispered, "Did I tell you how beautiful you look?"

She fidgeted. "Three times." She looked down at the floral sundress she was wearing. It was vibrant, with swirls of fuchsia and red. Its full skirt flared around her ankles, but the sleeveless bodice accentuated her petite figure. "But I still think I should have worn the pink dress with the white flowers. It's more feminine looking."

"If you looked any more feminine, I wouldn't be able to concentrate on the message."

Willow let go of C.J.'s hand and stopped.

He turned around. "What's wrong?"

"You said it yourself, this dress sends the wrong message."

"I did *not* say that!"

She couldn't do it. She couldn't go in there and have everyone judge her. She hadn't been to church since moving in with Steven; she felt too guilty. Steven just laughed at her and told her she was stupid for thinking *those people* were anything but weak and hypocritical, who used religion as a crutch and a smokescreen to hide behind. *You don't think they get drunk, have sex with their neighbor's wife, or cuss and swear at the jerk who cuts them off on the freeway? Grow up Willow. Don't be so naive.*

"I don't belong here."

"Come on, Willow," C.J. whispered as he reached for her hand, tugging her toward him. "Don't let Steven get inside your head."

He slipped his arm around her waist and gently led her through the massive doors, music already playing. They shuffled into the back pew on the far left of the sanctuary, and without even looking at the large screens on either side of the platform, Willow knew the words to the old familiar hymn. She sang them softly, C.J.'s strong voice harmonizing with hers.

She looked around, expecting to see people staring at her, dissecting her, sizing her up. But the few people who glanced her way only smiled.

They sang two more songs, then took their seats.

Announcements were made.

The preacher preached.

And before she knew it, they were singing the doxology.

She had survived.

Not only survived but felt comforted. The preacher's message was simple. *God cares for you. No matter what you do. No matter what others say. No matter how you feel about yourself. God. Cares. For. You. Period.*

It was as if the message had been prepared just for her.

C.J. held her hand as they made their exit through the crowd of people—the size of the crowd a little overwhelming. He nodded to a few people, waved to others, but thankfully, he didn't stop to talk or try to introduce her to anyone.

As they ascended the front steps, he asked, "So, what did you think?"

She smiled. "It was good. I really enj—"

Willow was interrupted by someone calling C.J.'s name.

When she turned around, she saw that the tinny voice was attached to a statuesque blond.

As the woman approached, she gave Willow a cursory glance, but her attention was definitely on C.J. "Where have you been keeping yourself? We've missed you and your mom."

He smiled politely. "I doubt that. In a church this size, you could go months without seeing someone."

"Maybe," the blond grinned, "*if* you weren't looking."

Willow looked away.

Is she serious?

I'm standing right here.

C.J. is holding my hand.

"The ranch has been pretty busy lately."

"Aren't you going to introduce me to your friend?" The bleached-blonde's second glance at Willow spoke volumes. She was sizing up the competition.

"Tara, this is Willow."

"Nice to meet you, Willow. Are you new in the area? I think I would've remembered if I'd seen you before."

Willow wasn't sure what Tara meant. Would she have remembered her because she was with C.J., or because there was something about her that would make her stand out?

"I'm from Colorado. Nice to meet you."

Tara barely waited for Willow to finish before turning her attention back to C.J., ignoring her completely.

"A bunch of us are having a barbecue on the beach tonight. Want to come? You can come, too." She shrugged in Willow's direction.

Please don't tell me these are the kind of people C.J. hangs out with away from the ranch?

Willow could not picture C.J. with anyone so shallow. Then again, Tara was gorgeous. Tall. Blond. Tanned. Her white halter dress hugging all the right curves. Willow's insecurities coiled around her like a noose. She was short, freckled from the sun, and could buy a month's worth of groceries for the price Tara paid for her dress and designer shoes.

Let's just go already. Willow wanted to yank on C.J.'s arm and get in the truck.

"Okay, maybe next time," Tara said.

Good. They were finally done.

"But, in case you change your mind, you remember the place, right? We went there together once?"

Willow felt like a deflated balloon.

C.J. had dated her.

She was his type.

They said their goodbyes, then walked to the passenger side of his truck. C.J. held the door for her as she got in, then walked around to the other side and jumped in. She could feel C.J. staring at her as he started the truck and back out of the parking space.

"Don't look like that, Willow. Tara is just a flirt, looking for some attention."

Willow didn't say anything.

"Come on, Willow, what are you thinking?"

"Nothing."

"Right. The windshield has just become so fascinating; you can't take your eyes off it."

Willow didn't appreciate his sarcasm. She closed her eyes and leaned her head back on the seat. "Actually, my head is hurting, and I'd like to go home."

"But we were going to go out to lunch." C.J. clearly sounded disappointed.

"I'm not hungry." Her words were soft, and her eyes stayed closed. She felt the truck swing a U-turn and was thankful C.J. was willing to let the conversation drop.

When they pulled into the driveway, she reached for the door handle, but before she could get out, C.J. caught her hand.

"I dated her twice, while I was getting over Heather. I was angry and looking for some easy attention. Tara was more than willing to oblige. But that was it. You have nothing to worry about."

"Thanks for telling me," she said, her tone cool, then waited for C.J. to let go of her hand, before getting out of the truck.

Once in the house, she hurried to her room. Stepping out of her dress, she flung it across the room, swearing she would never wear it again. After pulling on a pair of jeans and a simple blouse, she collapsed across the bed, debating about the way she was feeling, and if she had a right to those feelings.

Of course C.J. dated. He's a guy, not a monk. He was hurt and looking for someone to make him forget. C.J. has feelings for me, now. I know he does.

She told herself she had nothing to worry about, but the blackened areas of her heart dug at her festering insecurities.

She tried to sleep but found no rest.

Instead, she was plagued with images she tried to will away.

C.J. was fixing himself a sandwich when Austin strolled through the kitchen. "How was church?" he asked.

"Church was great. After church was lousy." C.J. tossed the mayonnaise laden knife into the sink and took a bite of his sandwich.

"What happened?"

"A girl I dated introduced herself to Willow, sending her into a tailspin. I told Willow I only dated her after Heather because I was looking for some easy attention, but I don't think I got through to her."

"What did she look like?"

C.J. just stared at Austin, not having to say a word.

"That good, huh?" Austin said, rubbing the back of his neck. "So, you think maybe Willow is feeling inferior?"

"I don't know why. Willow is gorgeous. She has nothing to feel inferior about."

"You know that, and I know that, but the mind can play horrible tricks on a person when they've been through an ordeal like Willow has. She might see herself as ugly because what she went through was ugly. She doesn't see herself in a positive light because of her negative relationship. You have to be patient with her, C.J. She needs time and space to process her feelings."

"But I think the more I leave her to her own thoughts, the worse she'll become. I want to reassure her that she's beautiful and attractive, and that I only have eyes for her."

The phone rang, but before Austin reached to answer it, he said, "Just make sure while you're busy convincing Willow of your feelings—and how beautiful she is—you don't cross lines you shouldn't."

C.J. inhaled his sandwich, while chewing on Austin's piece of advice. He understood what he was saying, all too well. But Willow needed to know he only had eyes for her.

"That's great news. Thanks. Yes. I'll be sure to tell her." Austin hung up the phone and let out a deep breath. "That was Detective Michaelson. They're done with their investigation. The shooting has been ruled 'an act of self-defense.' They won't be pressing charges."

"That's great, Austin!" C.J. set his plate in the sink, then backed toward the doorway. "I'm gonna go tell Willow. Maybe it will bring her out of her funk."

C.J. took the stairs two at a time, and was ready to knock on Willow's door, when he noticed it was ajar. Pushing it open a little further, he peered inside, and saw that she was sleeping. Deciding a nap would do her good, he headed for the stables.

I can tell her later.

Maybe that and a little rest will change her mood.

Austin went upstairs to tell Ashley the good news.

She'd woken up, not feeling well, and didn't have an appetite for breakfast. He suggested they stay home from church—so she could get a little extra rest—and was surprised when she didn't put up a fight. All morning long, he'd tried to stay busy, counseling himself not to panic. Fatigue was one of the main side effects of the radiation, not a sign that something was wrong. But still, seeing Ashley take a step backward was hard to watch. She'd made him promise not to say anything to C.J. or Willow. They were already struggling; they didn't need just one more thing to worry about.

Gently, Austin sat on the edge of the bed. "Hey, Ashley," he whispered.

Her eyes opened slowly.

"I just got off the phone with Detective Michaelson. I'm off the hook."

She smiled, still half asleep. "What do you mean?" She pushed herself up against the headboard.

He crawled over her and leaned his head against the headboard next to hers. "They're not pressing charges. As far as they're concerned, it was a 'tragic event with extenuating circumstances.' Case closed."

"That's incredible! Thank God." She reached up and kissed him.

He slipped his arm behind her shoulders and pulled her close. She snuggled next to him, and with her head pressed against his chest, and her arm wrapped around his torso, he listened as her breathing took on a slow, steady rhythm.

SEVENTY-FOUR

Willow stirred from a restless sleep.

For the hundredth time, she replayed the conversation between Tara and C.J. in her head and kept wondering the same thing. What else would influence their relationship? Is this how it would be every time they went somewhere? Girls today showed no pride or decency when they wanted to hook a man. Tara—a church girl no less—pretty much made a pass at C.J. with her standing right there. Some girls liked the challenge of knowing another woman was involved. As they say, 'All's fair in love and war.'

What a stupid saying.

Willow walked to the bathroom and stared at herself in the mirror. She saw glimpses of beauty in her reflection and tried to convince herself she deserved C.J. and all he had to offer. But then Steven's badgering and taunting words played through her mind. He constantly told her she was a mess, needy, and a drag on his patience—and the only reason he stayed with her was because they had great sexual chemistry. But it wasn't her performance he enjoyed. It was the hold he had on her, the intimidation tactics and manipulation he had mastered. She was a puppet; that's all she was to him.

But it's true.

I am a mess. I am needy.

Every time the detectives talked to her, she felt like she was going to puke. Then she would hide in her room and shut C.J. out. Her emotions flare at the littlest thing, like Tara talking to C.J. in the parking lot.

You're good in bed, Willow. It's your only asset.

She always hated when Steven said that to her, but maybe he was right.

What did she bring to a relationship, anyway? She did not come from money or have a lucrative career. She wasn't a stunner like Tara, and she wasn't even passionate about the latest cause trending on Facebook.

She'd once heard a professor say that people fell into one of three categories: passionate, focused, or reconciled. They were either passionate about a cause or their talents, focused on their career or their future, or reconciled to merely existing or mediocrity.

Growing up, she always saw herself as assertive and determined. But of late, she just cared about putting one more day behind her.

How pathetic.

She sat on the edge of the bed and flopped backwards.

So, what does C.J. see in me?

She thought about last night.

They had gotten lost in each other, and then just as quick, they started arguing. But for those few moments, Willow felt desirable.

Needed.

Wanted even.

C.J. didn't just tell her how he felt; he showed her.

And it felt so good, so different. With C.J., there wasn't any fear or pain.

I can't lose him. I will never find someone willing to accept me for who I am—or the baggage I carry.

She felt an urgency to find C.J. and convince him she was enough.

She could be his everything.

She just had to show him.

~®~

Austin slowly inched his arm from around Ashley's shoulders and slipped from bed.

Trying to work out the numbness, he flexed his fingers, and rotated his shoulder, then sat on the cushion of the window seat, and leaned back against the frame.

He stared at Ashley, watching her sleep.

God, I love her.

After a few minutes, he bent forward and pressed his elbows to his knees. Lacing his fingers together, he prayed for Ashley's next week of treatments.

. . . Amen.

Sitting up, he glanced out the window and saw Willow walking toward the stables. Knowing that's where C.J. went after their miscommunication, he took it as a sign that Willow was ready to talk. But then, he thought again. He knew Willow was feeling vulnerable and confused. *Making up, could lead to making out, which could lead to something more.*

Immediately, Austin shook off his thoughts.

He was jumping to conclusions.

He needed to give Willow and C.J. the benefit of the doubt. C.J. was a good kid. He certainly wouldn't take advantage of Willow when she was feeling so vulnerable.

But the discomfort in Austin's soul did not fade.

He paced in front of the window, waiting for Willow or C.J. to emerge.

~®~

Willow looked for C.J. in Knight's stall, then in the tack room. Walking the length of the stables, she accidentally kicked a feed bucket causing an echo to fill the corridor.

C.J. stepped out of the shadows.

"Are you looking for me?" He leaned against the doorpost, his arms crossed against his chest.

Just looking at him made Willow's blood rushed hot throughout her body.

"I wanted to apologize for the way I acted earlier today." Willow walked toward him, closing the gap between them.

She watched him watching her. She saw his eyes travel over her blouse, down her jeans, and up again. She could see the attraction he felt for her in his eyes. It made her feel beautiful. But when their eyes connected, they held for only a second before C.J. turned around and stepped back into the hay room.

Willow followed him, letting the door close behind her. When he kept pitching hay, completely ignoring her, tears filled her eyes. *He doesn't even want to look at me.*

Finally, C.J. stopped and leaned on the handle of the old wooden pitchfork. He removed his hat and wiped his brow in one quick motion, then replaced it as he spoke. "You have nothing to apologize for, Willow."

"Yes, I do. I was rude, and short with you. I had no right to treat you that way." She crossed the room and stood directly in front of him. Looking up into his eyes, she hooked her fingers in the belt loops of his jeans. "I want to make it up to you."

She raised up on her tiptoes and pressed a kiss to the base of his neck. Slowly, she allowed her hands to move up his chest and over his shoulders. With her hand on the back of his head, she pulled him down until his lips touched hers.

At first, Willow felt him resist. Her conscience taunted her. *See, he doesn't want you.*

Then I'll make him want me.

She was determined to prove to C.J. she was everything he needed. She held him closer, her breasts pressed against the buttons of his shirt. She felt his body relax. *See, he wants me. I just have to let him know it's okay.*

She kissed him some more, and soon he returned her kisses with passion of his own.

Willow took a step back, then another. C.J. followed her like they were fused together. When she felt a bale of hay press against the back of her knee, she bent down until she was sitting, then laid back, pulling C.J. with her.

Her heart was beating so fast, her head was beginning to spin. She wanted to be everything to C.J. and to prove it, she would show him the extent of her love.

~Ⓡ~

C.J. was lost.

Utterly lost.

His conscience was firing off warning flares left and right, but his hands were doing his thinking. With his body covering Willow's, his fingers traveled the length of her, outlining every curve. He dotted her lips with kisses, then brushed his lips against her chin and down the column of her neck. He was dangerously close to the scoop of her bodice and knew he should stop. This was not what God wanted for their relationship, but the small voice of reason was easily silenced by the desire he felt racing through his body.

When Willow reached for his hand, he thought she was putting on the brakes—having the strength he did not have to stop. Instead, she slid his hand under the gauzy material of her blouse, slowly guiding him toward the beating of her heart.

Suddenly, C.J. felt a rush of cold air swirl into the room. When he realized where it was coming from, he looked up and saw Austin standing in the doorway.

"I think you two had better stop."

~Ⓡ~

What have I done?

Willow was mortified by her behavior.

The passion she'd felt—wanted C.J. to feel—was doused as quickly as it had ignited. She no longer felt full of love. Instead, she felt empty of pride.

Both she and C.J. scrambled to their feet and stood with their heads down, unable to face Austin.

"C.J., why don't you go to the house? I'd like to talk to Willow for a moment."

Willow looked at Austin then quickly looked away—horrified and embarrassed. How would she ever face him again? He was sure to tell her, in no uncertain terms that her behavior was offensive and unacceptable. It was obvious he blamed her, or he would be talking to C.J. instead.

"It's not Willow's fault. I—"

"C.J.!" Austin shouted, then lowered his tone. "I want to talk to Willow. Alone."

Slumping onto a bale of hay, she wrapped her arms around her midsection and waited for the onslaught of ugly words Austin was sure to spew at her. But C.J. was still standing there, unmoving.

Looking up, she saw Austin and C.J. locked in a stare. C.J's fists were taunt. Austin's body tense. Like they were ready to come to blows.

"C.J.," Austin said calmly, "please go in the house. Don't make this harder than it already is."

Willow held her breath, afraid of what C.J. would do. When he glanced her way, she nodded. What choice did she have? Austin was not going to be denied his pound of flesh. She might as well get it over with. "It's fine, C.J."

"But, Willow, we need to talk."

"No, we don't. Not now," she argued.

He crossed his arms against his chest and turned to Austin. "This is none of your business. Willow and I are adults. We can handle this ourselves."

"I beg to differ."

"Come on, Willow," C.J. ignored Austin, and reached out his hand to her. "We don't have to list—"

"Just go, C.J.!" she snapped, wanting it to be over. "I'm asking you to leave. So, please, just go."

Looking shocked and betrayed, C.J. stormed away without another word.

Willow braced herself for what she could only imagine Austin was going to say. Fighting back the tears, it seemed like an eternity before he spoke, but when he did, he was calm, his words measured, not the ranting she had expected.

"Willow, I owe you and C.J. an apology."

She looked up, shocked. "You? This is my fault. I wanted to prove to C.J. how much I could be to him."

"But when I saw you heading for the stables, my gut told me to follow you. Instead, I waited . . . almost too long."

"So, I guess what you're saying is you expected this sort of behavior from me." Willow set her shoulders defensively. "Why else would you talk to me and let C.J. go on his merry way?"

"Willow, I wanted to talk to you because I'm concerned." He pinched his forehead, then rubbed his face. "Look, I'm going to lay all my cards out on the table like I would do with Jenna. If I offend you, I'm sorry. That's just the chance I'll have to take."

She watched him pace. It kind of freaked her out because Austin was always so calm. So cool. Even with everything that was going on with Ashley. Finally, he stopped, and looked right at her.

"Willow, you're a beautiful young woman. But because of your past, I think you feel the only thing working in your favor is your body. Steven made you feel ugly by the way he treated you. He was manipulative and demeaning. He brainwashed you."

She swallowed deep, not knowing what to say, but Austin continued.

"It was the only way he could hope to keep you for himself. He preyed on your insecurities. Made you feel like nothing. But, Willow, you are too beautiful, too smart, and have too many *other* assets to be treated like an inferior piece of flesh. Steven's gone now, and you need to let go of the person he created. You're intelligent and strong. Don't ever believe the lie that you are nothing more than an object for someone else's pleasure. Because if you do, you will allow Steven to ruin the rest of your life."

Willow was awestruck. Austin wasn't condemning her or punishing her. He was encouraging her. Loving her. She sat there speechless, her head down, tears wetting her jeans.

"Look at me, Willow."

When she looked up, his expression was stern, brows drawn together.

"Now for the father speech. If I ever find you two in such a compromising situation again, there will be repercussions. Do you understand?"

Willow nodded.

"I know you're both adults, but this kind of behavior is unacceptable in this house. Now, if you'll excuse me, I need to go talk to C.J. Are you going to be okay?"

Again, she nodded, not trusting herself to speak.

Austin left her in the hay room, but she quickly stepped out into the corridor.

"Austin," she called after him.

He stopped and turned.

"Thank you."

"You're welcome." He smiled and turned back toward the house.

Willow wanted to say so much more but didn't know how to express what she was feeling inside.

Austin stormed across the yard, wanting to rip C.J.'s head right off his shoulders. He knew better—was raised better.

Had more class than that.

He should have known they were reaching the danger point and put a stop to it.

But judging from the scene he'd walked in on, C.J. had completely lost the battle.

C.J. was sitting at the bar in the great room when Austin walked in. He was pale and looked like he was going to be sick. The minute their eyes met, Austin started in. "What in the world were you thinking?" he yelled, then lowered his voice, not wanting Ashley to hear. "You know Willow is vulnerable—know she is struggling. You should be *telling* her how much you care, not taking advantage of the situation. Do you know what you just did? You just reinforced every ugly thing Steven ever said to her."

C.J. jumped up. "You know what . . . I don't have to stay here and listen to this! I'm a grown man, not a child! Don't talk to me like I'm some punk kid you just found with your daughter!"

"But that's exactly how you were acting! You were taking advantage of a vulnerable girl! If that's what you think being a real man is, then I pegged you all wrong."

"That's not fair!"

"You're right! What you were doing was *not* fair."

C.J. looked ready to explode. He stared at Austin from across the room. Austin thought he might even charge him. Instead, C.J. shook his head, knifed his fingers through his hair, and sat down on the edge of the coffee table.

"I screwed up, okay! I screwed up big time! I didn't mean for things to get out of hand, but Willow was making it so easy, so inviting. I just lost it."

"Do you think that's what she wanted, C.J.? Sex? Do you think Willow would've felt better about herself if she'd been able to seduce you? She's struggling with who she is right now. She's convinced she's an object for someone else's enjoyment. And you were more than willing to prove her point. As much as she hated the way Steven treated her, she's going to have a hard time putting his conditioning out of her mind."

C.J. sighed, dragging his hand down his face. "I thought if I refused her, she would freak out and think I didn't want her anymore."

"That's a crock, C.J., and you know it! Admit it . . . you liked it and didn't want to stop." Austin realized his tone was getting loud again, so he took a minute to calm down. "You have to be stronger, C.J. You need to make Willow feel loved in ways other than physical. I'm not saying you can't touch her or kiss her. I'm just saying you need to be able to notice when she is trying way too hard to get your love and approval. Like today."

C.J. laced his fingers behind his head, his elbows on his knees. Austin could see his knuckles turning white, his hands shaking.

"Meeting someone you dated intimidated Willow," Austin said in a more controlled tone. "Feeling challenged, she needed to prove to herself she was worthy of your attention. It's times like that, you need to be a little more perceptive about what's really going on. You need to reassure her without letting your hormones do your talking."

C.J. had his head down, not saying a word.

"Do you see what I'm saying, C.J., or am I just talking to myself?"

"Yeah . . . I get it." He snapped to his feet, circled the room once, then slumped into the oversized chair in the corner. Shaking his head, he slammed his fist down on the arm of the chair. "I'm an idiot." He looked at Austin.

Austin stared back. "No, you're not an idiot; you were just acting like one."

"What did you say to Willow? I hope you weren't as brutal to her as you're being with me."

"No, I wasn't brutal, but I did tell her there would be repercussions if it happened again."

"Oh, right, that doesn't sound brutal at all, just humiliating. You gave her an ultimatum like you would a teenager. Did you tell her you were going to ground her, too?" C.J.'s words dripped with sarcasm.

"No. I told her I understood her insecurities and that I didn't fault her for her behavior. Look, we had a good talk, and I think I handled it fine. Cut me some slack. I'm new to this father thing, but I'm not a nonhuman. I remember what it was like to be young and have my hormones rage."

"Okay, okay." C.J. raised his hands to Austin. "I think I'll do better if I don't get a mental picture of you and my mom doing what we just did."

They sat in silence for a few minutes before Austin decided to check on Ashley. He was sure she overheard their heated conversation and didn't want her coming downstairs to investigate. When he got up to leave, C.J. stopped him.

"Austin?"

"Yeah?"

"I appreciate the advice, and I'm sorry I put you in such an awkward position. The truth is I'm humiliated and angry with myself for letting things get out of hand. I know better. I've preached to my buddies and defended my position against casual sex a hundred times. I can't believe I almost blew it—especially with Willow."

"Yeah, well, you can thank me by not letting it happen again."

Austin left C.J. with his thoughts and went upstairs to check on Ashley. She was curled up on the window seat. One look at her, told him all he needed to know.

"So, what was the big powwow about?"

Austin wanted to protect C.J.'s privacy but wasn't going to lie to Ashley.

"C.J. and Willow got into a situation that required a little intervention. But everything is fine now. C.J.'s feeling pretty cruddy, but he'd feel worse if he found out I told you about it."

"Did he listen to you?"

Austin sat next to Ashley, feeling a sense of pride. "Yeah . . . I think he did."

Ashley smiled. "So, how does it feel to dole out fatherly advice?"

"Terrifying. I wanted to string up both of them and yell my head off, but I knew that wouldn't help. If I wanted them to give me a chance, I knew I had to approach them like adults, and surprisingly enough, it worked."

"So, how far did they go?"

Austin sobered. "Not far in the grand scheme of things, but I'm not sure they would have stopped if I hadn't followed them." Ashley's worried look led Austin to explain a little further. "It's not like there were clothes strewn about, if that's what you're thinking. Let just say they got a little intimate with their sense of touch."

The look of disappointment on Ashley's face made Austin feel horrible.

"I expect better from C.J."

He looped his arm around her shoulders and gave her a squeeze. "I as much as told him that. He knows he crossed a line and is feeling pretty miserable."

"And what about Willow? How is she feeling?"

"I think she's confused. Steven really did a number on her, and it's going to take a lot of reconditioning for her to gain back her sense of worth."

Ashley rested her head against Austin. "I'm glad you were here for them. C.J. needs this kind of interaction, and so does Willow. Her father was out of the picture by the time she was in her teens."

"I'm glad I was here too. But, I'll be honest, I would rather look down a table of investors and explain a plunging bottom line, then do that again. Parenting is intense."

Ashley laughed softly.

Willow had slipped through the front door while C.J. and Austin argued in the great room. She was leaning against the headboard on her bed, her knees pulled up to her chest, when there was a knock at the door. She knew it was C.J. but wasn't sure how she was going to face him after what she had done.

C.J. didn't wait for her to acknowledge him; he just walked in and closed the door behind him. He stuffed his hands in his front pockets and stood at the foot of the bed. "Willow, I'm sorry for what happened. You deserve better."

Willow shook her head as she stood. "No, it was my fault, C.J. I let the thought of you with Tara freak me out." She sank onto the edge of the bed, her hands in her lap. "I didn't mean to be that aggressive. I'm so embarrassed."

C.J. moved to Willow's side and circled his arm across her shoulders. "And I'm sorry I caved. I had no intentions of taking advantage of you. I'm just afraid that . . ."

She looked at him. *This is it. This is when he tells me he's afraid it's not going to work out.* "You're just afraid . . . of what?" She had to swallow back the bile rising in her throat, not wanting to hear what he had to say.

"I'm afraid if I don't respond the right way, I'll send you into a tailspin."

"Respond the right way?" It wasn't what she'd expected. "I don't understand."

He sighed, "Willow, how would you have felt if I pushed you away earlier or last night during the movie?"

She thought about the frame of mind she'd been in, then looked away.

"That's what I thought." He reached for her hand, stroking her wrist with his thumb. "Willow, I'm not perfect. I struggle with self-control. Last night, and again today, I knew we should stop. But the feel of you next to me, the way you responded to my touch, I was afraid if I pulled away, you would misconstrue my actions and jump to the wrong conclusion."

"So, I'm being a tease? Is that what you're saying?" She tried to get up, but he wouldn't let go of her hand.

"No. That's not what I'm saying. But you're reacting the way I feared."

She pulled her hand away.

"Willow, you're still questioning my feelings for you."

"No, I'm not," she said stiffly.

"Then why did Tara upset you so much?"

She shot to her feet and spun around to face him, arms crossed against her chest. "Are you kidding me? The woman pretty much propositioned you with me standing right there. Everything about her screamed perfection: perfect body, perfect smile, perfect hair. And she probably has a pedigree to match. I can't compete with that."

He stood and crossed to where she was standing. Cupping her face in his hands, he looked her in the eyes, and whispered, "You don't need to compete for my affections, Willow. You already have them."

She brought her hands up, held onto his wrists, and dropped her head in defeat. "I'm sorry, C.J. I don't mean to be so needy, so compulsive."

"You're not needy. You just need to trust me. If I pull away from you, or you think I'm not into it, you can't freak out. I'm just trying to do the right thing and keep our impulses under control. I let you down today, and it kills me to think what would've happened if Austin hadn't stopped us. I don't want to be put in that situation again, but that means I need your help."

She looked into his incredible blue eyes, knowing he would never intentionally hurt her.

"If I pull away from you, you can't take it as a sign of rejection or disinterest. You just have to know I'm struggling and trying to protect us, okay? If I know you'll understand, I think I can be stronger. I just don't want to hurt your feelings."

"Okay. I'll try not to overreact."

He leaned over and gave her a kiss that was short, but full of warmth. "I love you, Willow."

"I love you, too, C.J."

"Good. Then let's move on to the next subject."

"Next subject?"

"Yeah. I'm starved. What do you say to Italian for dinner?"

The rest of the evening was spent in carefree enjoyment, a barrier lifted in their relationship. They ate at a nice little Italian restaurant in the Valley before coming home and relaxing on the porch swing, even though it was chilly. When they decided to call it a night, they quietly walked upstairs, hand in hand. C.J. stopped at Willow's door. "Thank you for such a nice evening." He kissed her temple.

"I'm sorry the day got off to such a rocky start."

"Hey, we're past that, okay?" He kissed her again, gently on the cheek, then wished her sweet dreams before heading to his own room.

Willow changed for bed and lay awake in the dark.

God, I know it's been a while since I talked to You, and I know You're disappointed with what I've done with my life. I didn't mean for it to go like this, but I'm trying to get things figured out. I wanted to get my life together before I came back to You, but I see now, that I can't do it on my own. I almost ruined everything with C.J., trying to do things my way, and I don't want to mess up anymore. God, please forgive me for the mistakes I've made. Help me break free from the past and start living for the future. I know I don't deserve C.J., but thank You for putting him in my life, and for the counsel that both Austin and Ashley have given me. I know I have a long way to go, but I'm glad I have a place to start.

Willow's eyes were open, and though she only saw darkness, she felt as if she had finally stepped back into the light.

SEVENTY-FIVE

C.J. had never wanted something so bad in his life. It wasn't about the winning; it was about so much more. As he sat atop Knight waiting to make his final run toward the championship, he thought about everything that had transpired in the last month.

His relationship with Willow flourished. It took Austin finding them in a compromising situation for them to grasp the importance of communication. No more unspoken expectations, wondering what the other was thinking, or trying to spare the other's feelings when something wasn't right. They talked about everything and promised whenever they were frustrated or feeling anxious not to give vague answers like: fine, it's nothing, or don't worry about it. C.J. discovered the difference between *feeling* love and being *in* love. And he knew Willow felt the same way, too.

His mom had given all of them a scare when she developed an infection between her first and second week of radiation treatments. She'd been outside doing more than she should, when she snagged her arm on some wire fencing, something she'd done a hundred times before. But with her weakened immune system, it flared into a nasty infection. Almost overnight, she developed a high fever, and the scratch turned an angry shade of red, causing her arm to swell. Immediately, the doctor put her on antibiotics, and got it under control. Even so, it wiped out what little energy she had. But she was in the stands today cheering him on, just like she'd promised.

Austin became a trusted ally. Not only because of the way he loved Ashley, but because of the time Austin invested in him. He talked to C.J. daily, showed genuine interest in his life, asked the hard questions, and made sure Willow and he didn't press the envelope or get in over their heads. In turn, C.J. confided in Austin things he couldn't discuss with his mom. She was amazing, and incredible, and had always been there for him, but issues involving temptation, desire, and sexual control were not conversations he wanted to have with his mom. Austin filled the gap nicely.

Sometimes he was too direct, which led to arguments, when C.J. felt Austin's concerns were unfounded. But in the end, C.J. knew Austin was only looking out for Willow and his relationship—just like a father should.

When the buzzer sounded, C.J. snapped from his thoughts, surged forward, and raced into the arena. Knight rounded each barrel at precisely the angle they had practiced. With a clean run, and posting the fastest time for the day, Knight and he cinched the championship. With a fist pump and a holler, he exited the arena an indelible smile on his face.

Ashley shouted from where she sat, while Austin and Willow jumped to their feet, cheering C.J.'s victory. Willow raced down the bleachers, as Austin stood there, looking every bit the proud father.

Ashley stared up at the man of her dreams, no words able to describe how she felt. Watching Austin and C.J.'s relationship grow these last few months meant everything to her. Sure, they bickered, but what two strong-willed, independent people didn't? Though she wasn't privy to all their conversations, she saw respect pass between them whenever they talked, even when they had a war of words. It was all she'd prayed for and more, because she was here witnessing it, something she wasn't sure of months ago when she'd sought out Austin at their reunion.

"Come on, Ashley, let's go congratulate him," Austin said as he extended his hand down to help her to her feet.

She grinned, loving the way he looked in his Wrangler jeans, Ariat boots, and pearl snap shirt. She didn't think he could look any sexier, but cowboy Austin was pretty hot.

With a firm hand, he helped her navigate the steep steps of the bleachers. People congratulated her, left and right, and asked her to pass on their regards to C.J. She loved this community of people. They came from all over the state but treated each other like neighbors. Seeing a few people she'd known for years, she stopped and introduced Austin as her new husband. She loved the expressions on their faces. The men shook his hand and welcomed him to the group, while the women studied Austin like he was a side of beef seeking FDA approval. Ashley had to work hard to hide her grin and not burst out laughing.

When they finally reached the bottom of the bleachers, a circle of men turned their way.

Ashley rolled her eyes and groaned silently. *Not them.*

They were a group of ranch owners from the San Fernando Valley. Unfortunately, most of them were divorced and had asked her out at one time or another. Being an unmarried female ranch owner was an oddity in this crowd, so the fact that she'd had so many pursuers was based more on percentages than attraction. At least that's what she told herself each time she turned one of them down.

"Ashley . . ." Mike Forrester tipped his hat as he took a step forward. "Just the woman to put these nasty rumors to bed." He glanced at Austin, but immediately turned back to her. "Gossip has it, you were on death's door, then you married a complete stranger; some guru who miraculously healed you." He fixed his eyes on Austin and glared. "I guess that's where you come into the picture."

Ashley laughed but could see Austin did not think it was funny.

She squeezed his hand.

He got the message and forced a smile.

"Well, you're half right. I was diagnosed with cancer, had surgery, and underwent radiation treatments. But I was never on death's door. As for marrying a complete stranger, I've known Austin for more than twenty-five years, but he's not a guru; he's a businessman."

"But you *are* married?" Tom Seafort chimed in.

"Yes." She smiled even wider, then introduced Austin to each of them. The men were less than cordial. "Well, we were just on our way to congratulate C.J. Nice talking to you all. I'm glad I could clear up those crazy rumors."

As they walked away, Austin leaned down and whispered against her ear. "I didn't realize I had such competition."

She chuckled. "You *never* had competition."

"I don't know . . . that Forrester guy . . . he's pretty good-looking, and definitely has eyes for you."

"He's also an egomaniac who thinks money can buy anything or anyone. He should have figured out by now that his over-the-top ways only interest a certain kind of woman. That's why he's been divorced three times, is paying thousands a month in alimony, and is on the prowl for number four."

Austin wrapped his arm around Ashley's shoulders and pulled her to his side. "I'm so proud of you."

She looked up at him. "Where did that come from?"

He shrugged. "Just watching you today, in your element, you're a female, in a male dominated world, but you held your own with every one of them. You gave your opinion, and they listened to what you had to say. They respect you."

"Well, it wasn't always that way. When the Andersons died, a few of them teamed up and set their sights on the Circle-R. There are only a few ranches in the valley that board horses, so they wanted to minimize the competition. They planned to buy the ranch, raze the buildings, then resell the land. They were shocked to find out the property had been willed to me. They tried to buy me out, thinking I would be a pushover. When I refused, they tried to intimidate me with idle threats and a few mishaps. I dug in my heels and kept pressing forward. After a while, they stopped challenging me. I would say the rapport we have now is tolerable at best."

"Well, you definitely are the prettiest one in the bunch."

By the time Willow made it down the bleacher and to the arena gate, C.J. had already dismounted and handed the reins to Billy.

She threw herself into his arms, and he swung her around, with a whoop and a holler.

"You did it! You won!"

"Did you doubt my success?" he said when he set her down, his smile not boastful, but proud.

"Not for a minute! I am so proud of you. You worked so hard. You earned it!"

"Then where's my prize?"

Smiling, she reached up and kissed him soundly. C.J. matched her passion, doing his best to take her breath away. When she opened her eyes, and saw others gathered around them, she pulled back, feeling embarrassed. She cleared her throat. "I think there are some people here who want to congratulate you."

Riders walked up to C.J. and congratulated him with a handshake or a pat on the back. Willow was surprised by the camaraderie considering most of the men were his competitors. But just like she had witnessed earlier with Ashley, C.J. had earned the respect of this community.

Willow saw Austin and Ashley walking their way, Austin holding her close. They were the picture of what real love looked like.

"Congratulations, C.J." Austin wrapped him in a bear hug and slapped him on the back. "That was incredible. I thought for sure

Knight was going to slide right out from under you on that last barrel."

Before C.J. could respond, Ashley wrapped her arms around his neck. "I am so proud of you." She hugged him tight, her eyes brimming with tears.

"Come on, Mom, don't cry." He leaned closer and said something Willow couldn't hear. Ashley only smiled then stepped back next to Austin.

"Come on, C.J.," Billy said, "they're ready to announce the winners."

~®~

C.J. and Knight were ready to enter the arena when his title was announced. C.J. looked for Willow and saw her standing next to the rail with his mom and Austin. He smiled at her, and she waved back.

The roar of the crowd signaled C.J. to enter the arena. He did a victory lap, holding his hat high in the air, before stopping at the makeshift stage in the center of the rink. As he climbed the stairs, he glanced at the emcee with a knowing look. The man just tipped his head and smiled.

"Ladies and gentlemen, may I present to you our Barrel Riding State Champion, Christopher John Summers." A round of applause followed as the emcee handed C.J. an impressive gold and silver belt buckle inscribed with his new title.

"Congratulations, C.J.," the emcee said, with a firm handshake. "What could be better than winning a state championship?"

"Actually, now that you mention it, there is one thing I can think of." The crowd quieted, clearly confused, but the emcee continued to play along. "Well, what *could* make you happier than a new state title?"

C.J. looked at Willow, standing outside the arena. "I would be the happiest man in the world if Willow Jenner would agree to be my wife."

Willow looked at him in shock while the crowd roared.

~®~

Did he just say what I think he said? Did he just propose in front of all these people? Willow's eyes locked on C.J.'s. Ashley said something, but Willow couldn't comprehend it. All she could do is stare at C.J. and get lost in his incredible smile.

"Well, I don't know about you folks, but I think we should have the little lady come up here, so we can hear what she has to say."

The crowd erupted, whooping, hollering, and applauding.

"Go on, Willow." Ashley gave her a nudge.

She turned and looked at Ashley's glistening eyes. The eyes of a woman Willow had grown to admire and love.

"Are you okay with this, Ashley?"

"Of course I am. Who do you think encouraged him to do it?" A smile joined her tears.

"He planned this?" It dawned on Willow, what she thought was a spontaneous surprise, C.J. had planned it all along.

"Yep! I've never seen him more determined to win anything in his life."

The crowd was chanting Willow's name, goading her into taking the stage.

"You'd better go, Willow, because it doesn't sound like this crowd is going to let you off the hook."

Ashley squeezed Willow's hand before she slithered through the rails of the fence. Slowly, Willow made her way across the arena to the stage where C.J. stood, the crowd growing louder the closer she got.

C.J. met her at the stairs and extended his hand to her, his smile bigger and brighter than she'd ever seen. Though tears flooded her eyes, she managed to hold them in check. C.J. helped her up the stairs, never taking his eyes off her.

"I'll get you for this, Christopher Summers," she whispered sharply, smiling at him through her tears.

"That's what I am hoping for."

When C.J. dropped onto one knee, the crowd went wild. Holding her hand, he said, "Willow Jenner, would you consent in front of all these witnesses to be my wife?"

The emcee quickly shifted the microphone from C.J. to Willow.

Swallowing back her emotions, she answered, "Yes, C.J., I will."

The crowd was on their feet as C.J. pulled a little, blue velvet pouch from his shirt pocket. When he shook it, a ring dropped into his hand. He shoved the pouch back into his pocket and held the ring to the tip of her finger.

"Willow, please take this token of my affection as a promise that I will do everything in my power to make you the happiest woman in the world."

Willow could not find words to convey what she was feeling.

She just pulled C.J. up to his wonderfully rugged height, threw her arms around his neck, and squeezed like she would never let him go. Sobbing into his chest, she couldn't remember a time when she felt happier.

"Hey, hey . . ." C.J. brought his hands up to frame her face, his thumbs brushing away her tears. "This is supposed to be a happy occasion," he smiled.

"I am happy, C.J., incredibly—head-over-heels happy." Willow looked at the crowd, then dipped her head into C.J.'s chest. "Can we get out of here, please? I'm not a huge fan of public displays of affection."

"I would like nothing better than to ride off into the sunset with you." C.J. winked, then led her to where Knight stood next to the stage. Though C.J. filled the saddle, he pulled her onto the exposed trim of Knight's blanket. With her hands firmly pressed against his chest, she held on tight as they galloped out of the arena to a standing ovation. When they came to a stop, C.J. flipped the reins to Billy and gently lowered her next to Ashley and Austin. When C.J. hit the ground, Austin reached out to shake his hand.

"Hold that thought, Austin, I have some unfinished business to attend to."

C.J. pulled Willow into an embrace and kissed her soundly.

Willow soaked up the feeling of C.J. pressed against her chest.

It was like she was in a dream.

There once was a handsome prince who saved a damsel from a villain. And then he taught her how to love again.

Her life had been no fairytale, but the way she was feeling right now, felt like a happily ever after.

"C.J., let the girl come up for air." Ashley swatted his arm. "You're smothering her."

He pulled back and looked at Willow. "Am I smothering you?"

"Yes, and I'm enjoying every minute of it." She held up her hand, so she could see her ring. She rolled it from side to side, and watched as the sunlight danced off the solitaire, and the string of diamonds that circled her finger. "Wow! It's beautiful."

"Do you like it?"

"I love it, but it's huge. You shouldn't have spent so much money."

"Are you kidding me? I wanted to get the biggest solitaire I could find, but Mom said anything bigger would look out of place on your small hands. Besides, nothing could be big enough to represent how much I love you." C.J. held Willow's hand and inspected the way the ring looked on her finger. "It's called a princess cut. I thought it was perfect." He smiled at Willow with a look that made her melt.

"Okay, enough you two. Knight is beginning to feel left out," Billy teased. "He deserves a little congratulating, too. After all, he is the state champion."

It had been a long day.

One Willow would never forget.

Leaning against the stall door, she watched as C.J. settled Knight in for the evening. "It's like he knows he's a champion," she said. "The way he walked into the stables and whinnied, wanting the other horses to see him. Posturing."

"Well, of course he does." C.J. stroked Knight's neck and rubbed his ears. "Don't you, boy? We were both winners today, in and out of the arena." C.J. winked at her as he draped Knight's blanket over his shoulders. After stroking Knight's nose, and congratulating him one more time, C.J. latched the door behind him, and wrapped his arm around her shoulders.

The walk to the house was chilly, but she wasn't complaining. C.J. stroked her arm, trying to ward off the goose bumps, not realizing he was just creating more.

"So, how soon before we can set a date?" he asked as they neared the backdoor.

"I haven't had time to think about it, yet."

"Well, I want you to have the perfect wedding; just like you always imagined it. So, as long as you don't expect me to wait a year, you can have the wedding anywhere and anytime you want it."

Willow was thinking as C.J. was talking. She had never really thought much about what she wanted her wedding to look like. The few relationships she'd had were disasters, Steven being the worst of them. The thought of marriage had never even entered her mind.

"You're not really thinking of waiting more than a year, are you?" C.J. said as he opened the backdoor and ushered her into the house.

Willow realized she had left C.J. hanging. "No, no, I'm sorry; I didn't mean to give you that impression. I was just thinking. I never was one of those girls who planned her wedding when she was a teenager, so I'm going to have to give it some thought."

Walking in the backdoor, Willow saw Austin hovering over the

459

stove cooking a late dinner, and Ashley perched on a barstool watching him. They both turned and looked at them as they entered.

Ashley laughed. "I'm guessing you're trying to set a date?" she said as she took the bowl of chili Austin offered her.

"How did you know?" Willow asked.

"Because of the panicked look on C.J.'s face and the puzzled look on yours."

Austin ladled up three more bowls of chili. Once everyone had one, they moved to the dining room table where a pan of cornbread rested on a trivet next to a bowl of shredded cheese. C.J. set down his bowl and offered to get drinks for everyone. Once he was done, he asked if Austin would do the honors. Austin accepted with a smile.

"Dear Lord God, what an amazing day this has been. To see Ashley out and about was so great, and then C.J.'s championship and a proposal. I am so proud to be a part of this family. We thank You for this day that You ordained from the beginning of time. As Willow and C.J. plan their wedding, I ask that You would always be at the center of their relationship. I pray they will honor You with their lives as they become one. Thank You again for Ashley's returning strength and thank You for this food. In Your name we pray, Amen."

Willow paused and thought about Austin's words. She too was grateful to be a part of this family. She wanted to live a life that would make them proud and honor the God who had saved her and given her so much more than she could have ever dreamed of.

"So, what's it going to be, Willow: indoor, outdoor, church wedding, private ceremony?"

Willow looked at Ashley and shrugged. "I don't know. I think I'm still a little stunned." She sprinkled some cheese on her chili. "I've never liked big weddings; they're so impersonal. Outside would be nice like yours." She stirred her food. "I don't know. It's almost more than I can take in. It all seems like a fairytale." She gasped. "That's it!" The minute the words were out of her mouth, she knew exactly where she wanted to get married.

"What?" C.J. asked.

"I know where we should get married."

"Where?"

"There's this place up the coast; I came across it last year when I was hiking with some friends. It has incredible views and the ruins of a castle. Well . . . maybe not a castle. But still, it looks amazing.

It has massive arches and some rock walls are still in place. Oh, and we could dress in costumes to match. You know, a themed wedding."

"You, a princess, and C.J. as your Prince Charming; it sounds wonderful." Ashley added.

C.J. dropped his spoon on its way to his mouth, splattering chili down his shirt. When he reached for his napkin to wipe it off, he tipped over his cup, sending water everywhere. He tried to recover, but everyone was laughing as he mopped up the mess on the table and wiped the chili from the front of his shirt

"Maybe a court jester was more what you had in mind?" Ashley laughed.

"Thanks, Mom."

"I'm only kidding. You'll look great in leather boots. A bloused shirt. Tights."

"Oh no you don't. I'm not wearing any tights." He looked at Willow. "Please tell me you're not going to put me in tights?"

"No tights."

"Then what?"

"It's hard to describe. I can see it in my head, but I'll have to see if I can find a costume place that has what I'm looking for. I want it to look authentic and real, and romantic. Not something you would wear to a Halloween party."

"But no tights?" C.J. clarified.

"I promise, C.J, no tights."

Willow tried to explain to Ashley what she had in mind, while C.J. and Austin talked more about the competition earlier that day. The four of them chattered away most of the evening at the dining room table. Then they shifted to the kitchen, cleaned up from dinner, and Ashley and Austin called it a night. Willow and C.J. headed for their favorite place, the porch swing. They snuggled close together as Willow held her hand out in front of her for the umpteenth time.

"It's so beautiful, C.J. I can hardly believe it's on my finger." They shared a kiss filled with longing.

Knowing she still needed to talk to C.J. about something important, she cut their embrace short.

"Are you all right?" he asked, obviously concerned with the quick disconnect.

"Yes. I'm fine. I just wanted to talk to you about something. It bothers me, and I don't want you to be caught off guard."

"Okay," C.J. said, looking even more concerned. "Just tell me."

She stalled for a moment, figuring out the best way to phrase what she had to say. But there was no *best way*. Taking a deep breath, she just blurted it out. "I have scars, C.J.—physical scars."

"I know," he whispered, stroking her arm.

Puzzled, she twisted around so she could look up at him. "How do you know?"

"That first night, after I came and got you. You were changing and I . . . well, I turned around before you were done and . . . well, I saw the scars on your back. Are those the ones you're talking about?"

Willow nodded, then rested her head back against his chest.

"You don't need to worry about things like that, Willow. The past is the past. I love you. Right here, right now. That's what I want you to dwell on, okay?"

"But is there anything else you want to know? Maybe something you were afraid to ask? I don't want any secrets or uncertainties between us, C.J., so if you have anything on your mind, I want you to ask me now."

"Well, there was just one thing . . ."

Willow braced herself, wondering what C.J. had kept bottled up.

"How is it that you were right here, under my nose all these months, and I never did anything about it?"

Willow poked him in the side. "This is serious, C.J. I need to know if you have any doubts about us."

"I am being serious." He tipped her chin up, his beautiful blue eyes staring back at her. "I know you've been through something awful, and it's not going to go away overnight. Just don't close me out. Tell me how you're feeling and let me help you. Promise me, you'll let me hold you through the bad times, not just the good."

"I promise." Willow wiped the tears from her eyes before reaching up to give him a reassuring kiss.

C.J. leaned down, deepening their kiss, nudging her lips apart. Willow twisted around, sat across his lap, and wrapped her arms around his neck. The feel of C.J.'s chest pressed against hers, his hands stroking her back.

It felt so good.

Too good.

Hearing warning bells she wanted to ignore, she held on a little tighter. But C.J. pulled away slightly, just enough for her to know he'd felt the warning as well.

Resting his forehead against hers, he whispered, "We should probably go inside."

She sighed, "You're probably right."

Getting to her feet, she pulled C.J. up next to her. He brushed her hair back over her shoulders and kissed her again. Just a peck.

Arm in arm, they walked into the house. "How about Thanksgiving?"

C.J. turned around to shut and lock the door. "How about Thanksgiving, what?"

"To get married. What better day than the one dedicated to thankfulness?"

"As in next month?"

"Well, yeah, next month. I don't think we have the will power to wait until next year."

He pulled her close and smiled. "You've got that right. But what about your big plans? How will you be able to take care of everything in just a month?"

"It's six weeks," she corrected. "And except for finding the right dress for me and an outfit for you, there isn't going to be a whole lot to do. I don't plan on having anymore guests than Ashley and Austin did, so we don't have to worry about invitations. Instead of a reception, we can have Thanksgiving dinner here following the ceremony. And if Austin's friend, Simon, is available, he can be our photographer. I think the biggest obstacle is going to be my mom. Then again, she probably won't even want to come."

C.J. stood back. "Why wouldn't she come? I thought you said you two were mending fences. That's why you were considering moving back to Colorado.

"No, I said I wanted to *try* and mend fences. Unfortunately, my mom wasn't on the same page. She has a new boyfriend, and he's pretty young. I don't think she will want to admit she has a daughter my age. It might blow her cover."

They took a seat on the couch, C.J. draping his arm around her shoulders.

"Have you told her anything about what happened? About Steven, or me?"

"No. She's not really interested in anyone but herself."

"I'm sorry, Willow. That has to be tough."

"I've come to accept it. We've never really been very close. When she and my father finally broke up, I pretty much was on my own. She had a social life to worry about, and my father disappeared after a few years."

"How is it that you ended up in California?"

"My junior year of high school, two friends and I decided we would move to California after graduation. Hollywood. Malibu. The O.C. It all sounded so glamorous and exciting. So, we saved all year. Well, *I* saved all year. Lindsay and Theresa figured they'd make it on good times and good looks. Before we left Colorado, we made arrangements to share a spacious two-bedroom, beachfront condo with two other girls. It turned out to be an upstairs, two-bedroom shack, six blocks from the beach."

"You're kidding?" C.J. laughed, scooting sideways so he could look at her. "What did you do?"

"We stayed. We were in California. That's all that mattered."

"How did you end up in the Valley?"

"Well, the first few months were exciting. We spend a lot of time at the beach, but things kind of fell apart after that. The two girls we split rent with were only there for the summer, so they were gone by the end of August. Lindsay hooked up with a surf bum who followed the waves, so they split in November and flew to Hawaii. Theresa bounced around from job to job, but she was the kind of girl looking for a man to take care of her. She found him in April. That left me holding the bag. I had lucked out with a decent job as an administrative assistant—a.k.a. gopher for the administrative manager—of a plastic surgeon in Bel Air, but there was no way I was going to be able to pay the rent all on my own, and I really wanted to go to veterinary school. So, I looked for something closer to my field. When I saw your mom's ad in the paper for an office manager, it was perfect. I used the last of my savings to secure a studio apartment, and the rest is history."

"But your mother never offered you help, or asked you to come back home?"

Willow looked down. "Nope. When Theresa left in April, I seriously thought about going home. But my mom had a new boyfriend. I just would've cramped her style." When she glanced up, C.J. looked disheartened and depressed. "Don't feel bad for me, C.J. Remember, if I hadn't come to California, I never would've met you."

"So, do you think she'll come? Your mom, that is?"

She leaned back against the couch. "First, I have to decide if I'm going to invite her or not. I mean I know it's the right thing to do; I just don't want the drama. Our wedding day should be about us, not my mom. I don't think I could handle it if she tried to fuss over me. She hasn't been there for me since my dad left. There's no reason for her to start now."

"How do you think she'll feel if you get married and don't tell her?"

"Oh, I'll tell her. I'll just wait until after the ceremony."

"It's your call, Willow. I want your day to be—"

"Uh-uh," she corrected. "*Our* day."

"Okay," he smiled. "I want *our* day to be exactly what you want. If you think she's going to make it too nerve-racking for you, then maybe it would be best to wait until after we're married. We could even plan a trip to Colorado to visit her."

Crossing her arms against her chest, she frowned. "Even if I ask her, and she decides to come, I know she'll complain about the cost of a plane ticket, and a dress, and missing work. She'll just make me feel like an inconvenience."

"If that's what you're worried about, I'll pay for those things, if you want her here."

"I can't let you do that. It's not your responsibility."

"Oh, but it is. It's my responsibility to keep the bride calm, cool, and collected before the wedding." C.J. sat back and pulled her to his side. "And don't let money interfere with any of your other decisions, either. I want you to have whatever you want in order to make the day perfect."

"Nope. The bride is supposed to pay for the wedding. Besides, I have some hidden assets I can liquidate." Willow was only teasing, but when she turned to C.J., he looked way too serious.

"What assets?" he asked.

"Oh . . . you know. A girl has her little secrets." Willow laughed, but C.J. was clearly agitated."

"Willow, we said no secrets, and I don't want you worrying about money."

"C.J.," she turned into him, resting her hand on his chest. "I was only kidding. I didn't mean to upset you."

He stroked the waves of her hair. "Sorry, I didn't mean to snap. I just don't want you to worry about money or finances. I want to do this for us."

"Aren't you even curious what I'm talking about?"

"Yes."

She looked up at him. "Then I'll show you."

Willow took C.J. by the hand and led him to her room. He sat down at the foot of the bed, while she got her old shabby purse from the closet. Plopping down on the comforter next to him, she pulled the vintage cigar box from inside the purse.

Willow looked at C.J.'s confused expression. "It was my grandfather's."

He watched as she opened the old wooden box and turned it toward him.

His eyes bulged with disbelief. "Are these all rookie cards?"

"Yep. Every one of them. They were my grandfather's prized possession. He gave them to me for two reasons: to pass them down to a great-grandson one day, or to use if I was ever in need of money."

"Have you sold any?"

"Nope. I came close a few times, but I couldn't bring myself to part with any of them."

C.J. shuffled through the cards, dumbfounded. "Do you know what these are worth?"

"Well, yeah, that's why they're in plastic. I'm not sure if they're considered "mint" condition, but if they are, these six cards," she shuffled through the stack, looking for the specific ones, "are worth about five thousand dollars."

"Oh, they're in mint condition, all right." C.J. continued to look in the box seeing less famous players, then returned his attention to the cards on top. "You would've sold these to pay for our wedding?"

"I figured even if it wasn't a rainy day, Grandpa would've understood."

"Well, I'm glad you told me about them before you sold them. And Willow, you should know, money is not a problem. I mean, we can't run off to the South of France for a month, or give up working altogether, but we don't have to pinch pennies or sell family heirlooms." He leaned over to kiss her, just as she started to yawn. He smiled. "Look, it's getting late, and I need to say good night." He pulled her to her feet and gave her a slow, lingering, hug.

"Good night." He walked toward the door. "I'll see you in the morning."

After C.J. closed the door, Willow fell back across the bed. Staring at the ceiling, she closed her eyes.

God, if what they say is true, then I guess I had to go through the crummy stuff in order to end up where I am today. She thought about the abandonment of her dad. Her estranged mom. Steven. Her baby. *I still don't understand why You let Steven do to me the things he did. But even if I deserved it—because of the bad decisions I made—my baby didn't deserve to die. I don't understand that, and I don't know if I ever will. I guess it will be one of the things I ask You when I get to heaven. But I do want to thank You for bringing C.J. into my life. And Ashley, and Austin. Thank You for the family You've surrounded me with. Thank You for being a God that forgives, and a God that redeems. Thank You for showing me Your love through my pain.*

SEVENTY-SIX

Willow was on the phone when C.J. walked into the office. She offered him a quick wave, then turned toward the window, concentrating on the call. He assumed it had to do with the wedding, since that was occupying most of her time.

He chuckled to himself. *So much for not having a lot to do.*

Not wanting to distract her, he grabbed a soda from the mini fridge in his mom's office and was going to leave. But when he heard what sounded like a sniffle, he turned around and waited for Willow to hang up the phone. When she put the receiver back in its cradle, he asked, "What's wrong?"

She quickly brushed away a tear, then looked up. "Well, we don't have to worry about my mom coming to the wedding."

"What? She's really not coming? What did she say?"

"That's just it. I've tried all week to get a hold of her, but the phone just rang and rang. So, I called information and got the number for the apartment building manager. That's who I was just talking with. He told me she moved out last week but didn't leave a forwarding address."

C.J. stood up straighter. "You're kidding? Why would she move and not tell you where she was going?"

"Because she's an inconsiderate person who only thinks about herself," Willow snapped, throwing a pen down on her desk.

"Uh, well, maybe she's just waiting until she's settled somewhere?" he stammered, trying to come up with a logical reason.

"C.J., I just talked to her a few weeks ago. She said nothing about moving. That's why she didn't want me coming home. She had plans, and I would have just gotten in the way."

"But, Willow . . ."

"You know what? I don't care." Willow nervously straightened papers on her desk, acting like the revelation really didn't bother her. But C.J. knew it did, or else she wouldn't have been crying.

"That's okay. I always knew I was extra baggage in her life. At least now I won't feel the need to keep her involved in mine."

Her tough exterior did nothing to disguise the deep hurt she was feeling.

C.J. came around to her side of the desk, bent and placed a kiss on her forehead, then brushed his hand across her cheek. "I'm sorry, Willow."

"Her loss, not mine."

"You're right; it is her loss. Because she has no idea how special you are." He gave her another kiss. "Are you going to be okay?"

"Sure. I don't know why I got so upset; I'm used to this kind of thing from her." Again, Willow busied her hands by straightening the clutter on her desk, then looked up at him and smiled. "I'm fine, C.J., really. Now, get back to work before I tell the boss you're goofing off during work hours."

C.J. headed toward the stables.

He couldn't wait for the day when he would be able to hold Willow all night, never letting her go, loving her the way she deserved to be loved.

SEVENTY-SEVEN

Willow could not believe it.

After two weeks of searching, she was driving home with a backseat full of costumes that would make her fairytale wedding a reality.

"Call Ashley." Willow activated her phone, hoping Ashley was still at the ranch.

"Hey Willow, I was just getting ready to call it a day. What's up?"

"So, you're still at the ranch?"

"Yes. Is something wrong?"

"No. Nothing's wrong. I found them, Ashley. I found the perfect costumes for the wedding."

"That's great. Are you on your way home?"

"Yes."

"Then I think I'll stick around to see them."

"I was hoping you would say that. I'll pick something up for dinner, then we can have a fashion show after we eat."

"Well, I wouldn't call two outfits a *show*, but I'd love to see them."

"Actually, I have four costumes." She waited, to see if it would register.

"Willow, why do you have *four* costumes?"

"Because they're absolutely beautiful, and the moment I saw them, I knew they would be perfect for you and Austin."

"Willow . . ."

"Please, Ashley. I know I didn't ask, but since you and Austin are our witnesses, technically, you are part of the wedding party."

Ashley laughed. "That's a pretty flimsy technicality."

"Do you think you can sell Austin on it?" *Please, please, please.* Willow waited for an answer, the silence killing her.

"Oh, okay. I'll see what I can do. No promises, though."

"Thank you, Ashley; thank you so much. I should be home in an hour."

"An hour? Good. That will give me time to work on Austin."

Once everyone was sitting around the dining room table, a dozen Chinese food containers open between them, Willow explained her amazing day.

"Okay, so it started out horrible," she said, while picking up a dumpling with her chopsticks. "I ended up on the wrong off-ramp and got turned around trying to find my way back to the freeway. Then I got sucked into a detour. So, I pulled into a strip mall to make a U-turn, and there was this little thrift store tucked in the corner. I almost didn't see it. But there was a sign in the window that caught my eye: *Movie props and Costumes.* So, I figured I'd take a quick look around."

She took a swig of her soda and continued.

"Well, I almost walked out the second I walked in. There was a woman standing behind the counter, who looked like she'd just walked off a movie set. Long grey hair. Peasant blouse and skirt in crazy colors. A dozen necklaces, and bracelets. Well . . . she looked like a gypsy, and it kind of gave me the creeps."

C.J. sat up straighter, looking concerned, but Willow quickly assured him. "She was harmless, C.J.; she just made an awkward first impression. Anyway," Willow turned back to Ashley and Austin, "she shows me where the costumes are in the far corner of the store in six huge trunks. So, I get on my knees and start rifling through everything—the whole time, the woman's watching me, but not saying a word. Again . . . creepy."

Willow stabbed a piece of orange chicken with the tip of her chopstick and shoved it in her mouth. After swallowing, she said, "this is really good. I can't remember the last time we had—"

"Hey," C.J. interrupted, "you can't stop there. Creepy store. Creepy woman. My mind is having a field day."

Willow laughed. "Sorry, I didn't eat all day, and this really tastes good."

"Yeah, well, forget your manners then. Eat and talk at the same time if you have to."

Willow hurried, took another bite of chicken, then continued. "So, after digging through five of the six trunks—I don't find a thing, and I'm ready to give up. That's when the woman asks me what I'm looking for. So, I explain. Well, she gets this crazy gleam in her eyes and tells me I can't leave. 'It's destiny,' she said, then mumbled something about the universe clearing a path to her door. Next thing I know, she's running down the aisle toward the front of the store."

Willow looked at everyone. "Again, creepy. So, I casually make my way to the front of the store, planning my escape, when she reaches out her phone and says, 'you need to talk to Abby.'"

"Who is Abby?" Austin asked. "Did I miss something?"

Willow smiled wide. "Abby just so happens to be a costume designer who has worked over sixty years for movie studios, Broadway, television, operas, community theater. You name it, she's done it. In less than half an hour, I am standing inside a storage facility filled with costumes from every imaginable time period and theme. Civil War. Stone Age. Futuristic. Medieval. Abby has kept and cataloged everything she has ever designed and loves sharing her *art* with others."

"That's amazing," Ashley said, then turned to Austin. "See . . . you can't say 'no' after hearing a story like that. Like creepy woman said, 'it's destiny.'"

Willow looked at Austin. "I know it's asking a lot. But it would be so perfect. That way when you address the guests, you'll be dressed like C.J. and—"

"Wait a minute," Ashley interrupted, looking back and forth between Austin and Willow, "why would Austin address the guests?"

Willow looked at C.J., realizing she spoke out of turn, then quickly turned to Ashley. "Well . . . I just figured . . . you both would. I mean, I just assumed you would mingle with everyone before the service started."

"Yeah, Austin," C.J. chimed in, "we're going to put those people skills of yours to work."

Austin rolled his eyes. "You're loving this, aren't you? Because, if I agree, you won't be the only one wearing tights and pointy shoes."

C.J. laughed. "What can I say, there is safety in numbers."

"For the last time," Willow insisted, "there are no tights . . . or pointy shoes. In fact, I think you'll both be surprised. The costumes are really quite masculine."

With Austin finally conceding, and dinner over, the men went upstairs to try on their costumes, while Ashley and Willow cleared the dishes and put the leftovers in the refrigerator.

"So, how do I look?" C.J. asked as he walked into the room.

Willow was speechless. He looked like he'd just traveled through time, embodying that of a Medieval baron. The long sleeve brown tunic, crafted from intricately tooled leather, fit him like a glove. The lace-up placket and cuffs and stand up collar oozed masculinity. Paired with brown suede pants and black knee-high cuffed boots, C.J. looked like a fairytale prince.

Her prince.

Willow watched as he walked back and forth, his hand gliding up his arm, feeling the texture of the soft leather. He shrugged his shoulders and pulled at the flared hem.

"It's a little snug in the shoulders and chest. Are you sure it fits all right?"

"Uh, huh." Willow was mesmerized at the way the leather sculpted to his chest and arms. C.J. was attractive no matter what he wore, but the way he looked, right now . . . Willow felted her pulse accelerate to dizzying proportions. Taking a deep breath—to calm her senses—she noticed Ashley and C.J. staring at her.

"What?" She turned to C.J. *Is he blushing?*

Then she understood. What she thought had been an internal groan of attraction had been audible. Wishing she could melt into the floor, she ducked her head, mortified.

Ashley chuckled, wrapped her arm around Willow's shoulders, and whispered in her ear, "It's okay. I feel the same way every morning when I wake up next to Austin."

Appreciating Ashley's attempt at diffusing the situation, Willow took a few seconds to gather herself, then chanced a look at C.J. where he stood inspecting his outfit in front of the mirror on the living room wall. He winked, mouthed *I love you,* then went upstairs to change.

Draping her costume over her arm, Ashley started up the stairs. "I'll go check on Austin—make sure he's not backing out."

When C.J. walked into the great room and saw they were alone, he took the opportunity to steal a kiss.

"You looked amazing, C.J., just how I pictured you would."

He shrugged. "It's not as bad as I expected. At least it's warm."

"Come on, Austin."

Both C.J. and Willow turned around when Ashley walked into the room, Austin begrudgingly following behind her.

Ashley looked regal in the dress Willow had picked for her. With a cream underskirt, a teal velvet overdress, and bellowing sleeves that fit snugly at the elbow, Ashley looked absolutely stunning.

Austin on the other hand, walked into the room with a frown.

"Why do I have to wear a blouse?" he moaned.

Austin's outfit was similar to C.J.'s with cuffed knee-high boots and suede pants, but he wore a leather vest over a cream-colored shirt.

"It's *not* a blouse," Ashley laughed as she plucked at his full sleeves. "It's made of linen."

"Well, it looks like a blouse to me." He walked over to the mirror and grimaced. "Maybe I could wear one of my own shirts. Something in black. Or at least something more masculine."

"But I chose that shirt because it complements Ashley's dress."

Ashley stood beside Austin, looped her arm through his, and stared at their reflection. "I think you look quite dashing."

"Well, I think you both look amazing," Willow said. "Thank you so much for being willing to do this."

Austin eked out a smile. "Of course. Anything for the bride."

Willow could tell he wasn't thrilled, and only smiled for her benefit, but she appreciated it just the same. When everyone was done trying on their outfits, they gathered in the great room.

"I still don't know why I can't see your dress," C.J. said. "I thought it was the bride the groom wasn't allowed to see? And that's just a wedding day myth."

"It doesn't matter," Willow said, giving him a peck on the cheek. "I don't want you to see my dress until I'm in it."

"Help me out here, Austin," C.J. said as he plopped on the sofa. "It's the bride the groom isn't allowed to see, not the dress, right?"

"You want my help? Well, here it is. The bride is always right. It's her day. Let her do things her way."

Willow sat down next to C.J. and smugly crossed her arms against her chest. "Thanks, Austin."

"No problem. Oh . . . I forgot to tell you, Simon is on board to be your photographer."

"Really? That's great!" Willow squealed with excitement, then stopped abruptly. "But you did tell him it's on Thanksgiving *Day*, right? Not the weekend, but the actual *day*?"

"Yes. I made sure he knew it was on Thanksgiving *Day*. In fact, when I told him where the ceremony was going to be held, and that we would be dressed in period attire, he got pretty excited."

Willow snuggled up next to C.J. "Then, I think that's everything." She looked up into his beautiful blue eyes and smiled. "Okay, Mr. Summers, no backing out now."

SEVENTY-EIGHT

When Austin heard the shower running, he rolled over.

It was barely dawn, and Ashley was already up and out of bed.

He smiled.

She was her old self again.

Although her infection had set back her recovery a few weeks and given them all a scare when she collapsed in the yard, she was growing stronger every day . . . and feistier.

And today would be yet another milestone in their new life together.

Last night, Ashley told him she wanted to start moving her things to his house.

He had left the timing up to her, knowing it would be difficult for her to leave the ranch, but with C.J. and Willow's wedding just a month away, she wanted to be completely moved before they returned home from their honeymoon. After all, it was C.J.'s house now. Ashley had drawn up the paperwork a few weeks ago and presented the deed to the house to C.J. and Willow, her wedding gift to them. C.J. was speechless and Willow erupted in tears, but Ashley beamed. She loved her family so much.

Austin listened as the shower continued to run, then looked at the bedside clock. Ashley was taking longer than normal. Stretching, he got out of bed, and pulled a shirt and a pair of slacks from the closet. Glancing at the clock again, he tossed his clothes on the end of the bed and sat back down, staring at the bathroom door. Combing his fingers through his hair, he tried not to overreact.

She's just taking a long shower, that's all.

But Ashley had a way of hiding when she wasn't feeling well. Her infection—case in point. Not wanting to worry anyone, she had tried treating it herself with a medicated ointment.

Just remembering how he felt when he saw her lying in the yard brought him to his feet. Walking to the bathroom door, he reached for the doorknob. But when the water stopped running, he decided

475

to wait.

A minute later, Ashley stepped from the bathroom—a towel wrapped around her body, her hair twisted in another—looking good as ever. He sighed with relief. "You took so long, I was beginning to get worried. Are you feeling okay?"

"Actually, I feel great." Clutching the towel to her chest, she stretched to her tiptoes and gave him a kiss. "In fact, I can't believe how good I feel."

Seeing the smile on her face and the bounce in her step was such a relief.

She crossed the room, grabbed some things from her dresser drawer, and grinned at him. "In fact, I think I'm going to go for a ride." She sat on the edge of the bed, unwrapped the towel from around her hair, and ruffled it.

"Do you think a ride is a good idea? I mean, it's great you're feeling better, but should you exert all your energy so early in the day when you have packing to do?"

"The doctor said I could return to my normal activities as soon as I felt strong enough. Besides, Dominus is feeling neglected."

"Then why don't you just go brush him, give him a little massage."

Ashley walked over to where he was standing by the bathroom door. With a gleam in her eyes, she dropped her towel and wrapped her arms around his neck. "So, you think I shouldn't overexert myself too early in the day?"

Ashley's overtly seductive attitude stunned Austin.

But he liked it.

Caressing the smooth slope of her back, he smiled. "Well, I guess we could work on building your stamina." Austin scooped her into his arms and gently laid her on the bed, covering her with his body.

"I like your kind of therapy, Mr. Taylor."

SEVENTY-NINE

Willow could not believe how quickly time had passed. If felt like only yesterday when C.J. proposed. But now their wedding was only a few days away.

She walked into the kitchen, and saw C.J. hovering over the stove, creating some kind of omelet concoction. She hugged him from behind and whispered, "Just five more days and I'll be Mrs. Christopher John Summers."

"It can't come soon enough for me. Bunking with Billy is no walk in the park."

She giggled. "It's only for a few more days. Besides, it was your idea." She turned to the refrigerator and grabbed a yogurt, then took a seat at the bar.

"That's because I didn't trust myself. With Mom and Austin gone, I thought it was a necessary precaution. But Billy is driving me crazy." He slid his egg creation onto his plate, set the pan in the sink, then took a seat beside her. "I love the guy to death, but he snores, talks in his sleep, and having to be in bed by ten o'clock . . . I haven't had a ten o'clock curfew since I was sixteen."

Willow laughed but was thankful C.J. had suggested the safeguard. It had kept them from crossing a line on more than one occasion. "Well, it's done wonders for my beauty sleep. I think we should keep the ten o'clock curfew even after were married."

He leaned in close and gave her a kiss. "Oh, believe me, we'll be in bed before ten. We might not be sleeping, but we'll definitely be doing something that adds to our quality of life."

His eyebrows danced with amusement, causing her to blush. She gave his arm a playful shove as she hopped off the barstool. "Well, cowboy, I'll leave you to your eggs. I have to get to work." She put her spoon in the sink, her yogurt cup in the trash, and walked toward the backdoor.

"Willow . . ."

She turned to C.J.

"That beauty sleep you were talking about, you're right. You've never looked more beautiful. I can't wait for you to be my wife."

After giving C.J. a well-deserved kiss, she nearly floated to the office, feeling like the luckiest girl in the world.

EIGHTY

Ashley couldn't believe it.

The day had finally arrived.

The day her son would get married.

She watched the wedding guests make their way up the wooded hillside to the castle ruins. Since there was no place to sit, they roamed around the structure, surveying, exploring, admiring the view and the beauty of the old landmark.

"Oh my gosh, you two look amazing!"

Austin and Ashley turned around.

Jenna hurried over and gave them each a hug, then stepped back to look at their costumes again. "Uncle Austin, you look so handsome."

"Well, you don't have to sound so shocked."

She laughed. "I didn't mean it that way. You just look so different, so . . . exotic."

"Doesn't he though," Ashley teased. "I thought cowboy Austin was pretty sexy, but Lord Austin is kind of hot."

"All right, all right. Very funny." Austin turned to Jenna. "Why are you so late? You said you were going to get here in plenty of time."

"My plane was delayed. I got here as fast as I could."

Austin's brows knit together in a frown.

"And by fast, I mean safely obeying all speed limits and traffic signs."

"Yeah, yeah, good come back. So, how is Chapel Hill?"

She tipped her chin up. "Best business school in the U.S."

"No. Berkeley is the best. You know . . . Berkeley, *California.*"

"Come on, you two, not this again," Ashley scolded playfully.

"Austin," Pastor Stan spoke quietly as he stepped to Austin's right. "I think it's time."

Jenna gave them each one more hug, then hurried over to where the others had gathered. Austin reached for Ashley's hand as they followed Pastor Stan to the far corner of the structure.

Ashley looked at Austin, still amazed by their own journey.

Austin's relationship with God was rock solid when they reunited and had helped Ashley stay strong when her future seemed uncertain. C.J. found his way back to the Lord on the heels of her diagnosis and had helped Willow put her faith in God. Their relationships had been hewn and cultivated by the God who loved them so well. And now the four of them stood as shining examples of God's grace and mercy. Ashley had so much to be thankful for.

It was almost incomprehensible.

When the crowd stirred, she turned and watched C.J. step through the large arched portal, nearly losing her breath. Her little boy was all grown up, and as handsome as any fairytale prince she'd seen in the movies. From his suede boots, to his laced-up tunic, he exuded strength and courage.

A tear slipped down her cheek.

C.J. stepped to her and gave her a firm hug, then turned to Austin and embraced him as well. She marveled at the relationship the two men had built. It was nothing short of remarkable.

She thought back to the night of her high school reunion, when she felt lost in a sea of emotion. Her diagnosis had not been good at the time, and she thought she might be leaving C.J. all by himself. She needed to know there would be someone C.J. could turn to, someone he could lean on. Austin was the only person she thought worthy of that position. And God, in His ultimate mercy and grace, accomplished just that. Austin had become a strong influence in C.J.'s life in such a short amount of time, but the miracle of it all was that Ashley had been allowed to witness it for herself. God had touched her body and allowed the three of them to build a relationship, a relationship that now included Willow. A shiver raced through her body at the realization. She was at her son's wedding, watching him step into a dream, and she was witnessing it from within a dream of her own.

Willow came into view, atop Dominus, her silky white gown laying across the white stallion's back. Dominus looked regal, standing tall, as if he knew the importance of the occasion. He high-stepped toward Ashley, Austin reaching for his bridle to steady him while C.J. gently lifted Willow down from the white blanket cinched to Dominus' back. She slid into his arms as he gazed at her, mesmerized. Ashley watched his eyes well up with tears.

Willow was a vision in her gown. It was long and sleek, and

made her look like a princess. The billowy sleeves were fitted at the elbow and the gold detailing on the forearms matched the gold braiding on the empire waist and bodice. A sheer cape sat atop the waves of her hair and flowed the length of the gown and further. She held no flowers, she simply held onto C.J.

"You look so beautiful, Willow, and this all feels like a dream."

"Then let's do this thing, before we wake up, shall we?"

Ashley smiled, as she listened to C.J. and Willow exchange whispers.

C.J. extended his elbow to Willow and they took a few steps forward, stopping in front of Pastor Stan.

Ashley brushed a tear from her eye and was thankful for the way Austin held her firmly to his side. The service was intimate, much of it being said barely above a whisper. Ashley heard every word spoken, but to keep from crying, she allowed Simon to be her distraction. She watched as he took pictures, seeing the care he took not to disturb the service, even as he flitted from one place to another, exhausting every vantage point and angle. Everything was going beautifully, when C.J. turned to face the small gathering.

"Austin and I have a few things we would like to say before Willow and I recite our vows." C.J. nodded to Austin, and Ashley watched as he stepped forward to join Willow and C.J.

This isn't how we practiced it.

Austin cleared his throat before speaking. "Many of you don't know the long journey it took for me to be here today. I searched for Ashley all my life, and even though I gave up, God—in His infinite mercy—allowed her to find me. Ashley told me in no uncertain terms, her search had more to do with her son than herself. She thought her life was hanging in the balance, and she wanted to make sure C.J. had someone he could turn to if her life was cut short." Austin stopped for a moment and turned to Ashley. She remembered so well the desperation she felt, thinking her life was over. "Thankfully, God had other plans. I am blessed to not only have Ashley as my wife, but C.J. as the son I never had." Austin turned to C.J. and hugged him before stepping back to Ashley's side.

She squeezed his hand and whispered, "What was that all about?"

Austin brought his finger up to her lips and shushed her just as C.J. stepped forward and began to speak.

"I didn't care much for Austin when I first met him. In fact, I had a right hook to prove it."

C.J. and Ashley laughed at the memory while Austin rubbed his chin in acknowledgment.

"I thought I was all the man my mom needed, or so I tried to tell myself." C.J. smiled at her. "But it is through the example Austin has shown me these last few months that I now know how to give love, receive love, and fight for the love God has given me. Austin has been a man of God and the father I never had."

No amount of determination could hold back the flood of emotion that came over Ashley. C.J. had just paid Austin the highest compliment, or so she thought.

"Before Willow and I exchange vows, we've made a slight change in the words. See if you can catch it."

Ashley looked at Austin, then back to C.J. and Willow, still not understanding what was going on.

Pastor Stan turned to C.J. and said, "Christopher, repeat after me. I, Christopher John Taylor . . ."

Ashley gasped as Austin squeezed her hand.

"I, Christopher John Taylor. . ."

C.J.'s taken Austin's name.

She looked at Austin for some sort of explanation. He bent close with red-rimmed eyes and whispered, "I'll explain in a minute." He stood up straight and motioned for Ashley to follow the rest of the service.

C.J. glanced at Ashley and winked, then focused his attention back on Willow.

"Willow, repeat after me. I, Willow Lynn Jenner . . ."

The vows were completed.

The moment sealed with a kiss.

Then C.J. and Willow turned to the small band of people.

"It is my great pleasure to present to you for the first time, Mr. and Mrs. Christopher John Taylor."

A smattering of applause broke out as Christopher kissed Willow for a second time. They looked at each other as if they had just realized what true happiness was all about. Ashley stepped forward and embraced C.J. so hard, she felt lightheaded. She stepped back, looked into his dancing eyes, and waited for an explanation.

"Were you surprised?" he asked, with an ear to ear grin on his face.

"Are you kidding? I thought my ears were playing tricks on me. I couldn't believe what I was hearing."

"I wanted Willow to have the name I should have had all along. It seemed only right. We're one family now."

Ashley felt a wave of sorrow. It was true. C.J. should have had Austin's name all his life. She had prevented that from happening.

C.J. placed his arm around her shoulder. "Mom, don't feel bad or second guess anything. God had a time and a place for all of us to come together." C.J. pulled Willow to his side, while Austin wrapped his arm around Ashley's waist.

Ashley could not believe it. She looked at C.J., Austin, and Willow, unable to remember a time when she was happier. Never, in her wildest dreams, could she have imagined a more perfect day.

EIGHTY-ONE

Ashley closed her journal against her chest and basked in the memory of the last ten years. From her place on the back porch, she watched C.J. in the arena while the sun warmed her face.

She and Austin were living on the ranch again; her time coming to a close. They had moved back months ago so she wouldn't miss a single minute with C.J., Willow, and her precious granddaughter, AshLynn.

The return of the cancer—that had plagued her body years earlier—had been a horrible shock to them all. At first, Austin played the blame game, arguing with Ashley that he should have done something sooner. He had noticed the difference in her behavior, the fatigue, the days she opted to stay home instead of going to the ranch. They were all signs something was wrong. He should have known better. He should have insisted she see a doctor. But she wouldn't allow him to blame himself. In her heart of hearts, she had known something was wrong, too.

She sensed it months before her diagnosis but didn't want to address it. The warnings were there, but she didn't want to acknowledge the "C" word had invaded her life once again. So, she ignored it until after their thirty-five-year high school reunion. They both had been looking forward to it for months, and she didn't want to put a damper on it. Austin was so excited to be able to walk into the ballroom, with her on his arm. And as expected, it was a magical night. They were the hit of the party, the envy of all their high school friends. Their story was what fairy tales were made of, or so she wanted to believe.

A month later, she got the devastating news. By the time she made an appointment to see Dr. Allen, and got the test results back, it was too late. He assured her—with more surgery—they could prolong her life, but the quality of it would be uncertain. He explained different scenarios, and spoke of new drug studies, but she decided against treatment. She did not want her last year to be spent in and out of the hospital or recovering from surgeries that would leave her body weak and her mind fuzzy.

She didn't tell Austin right away because she knew he would try to talk her into some form of treatment. Instead, she enjoyed every day to the fullest without worrying her family. Worry would not extend her life, it would only sadden the time they had left. She decided God would take her home in His time, and she would enjoy every day until then as a precious gift.

She had known for three months when she told Austin. He had come home one evening after work and surprised her with a trip to the Netherlands—something they had talked about for years. Even though it sounded amazing, she didn't want to waste a single day away from C.J., Willow, and AshLynn. That's when she finally told him the truth. He was shocked. Devastated. Angry she didn't tell him sooner. But after the shouting and the tears, he held her close and prayed for a miracle.

A miracle that never came.

Or had it, and they just didn't know it?

One night, after an unusually horrible day, she completely broke down. She yelled and screamed and hollered. She lashed out at God and accused Him of being cruel and unfair. Austin held her tight, absorbing the angry fists meant for God. But when she was composed enough to listen, and he swallowed back the knot in his throat, Austin reminded her what a gift the last ten years had been.

Remember on our honeymoon, I said I would take the three days God gave us, over no days at all. That's where we are, baby. We're looking at this the wrong way. What if God intended on taking you home ten years ago? Maybe that was your appointed time. But because of His great love and compassion, He gave you . . . gave us . . . the last ten years. Ten of the most amazing years of our lives. I know it's hard to comprehend. In our humanity, we feel it's unfair, and we want to be angry, blame someone. But if God had given you a choice—ten years or nothing—wouldn't you have chosen the past ten years? Ten years of adventures as we traveled the world. AshLynn's birth. Witnessing what an amazing father C.J. is. Us. The incredible, passionate love we've shared. I am so thankful for the last ten years, Ashley. I wouldn't trade them in for anything.

She had to recite Austin's challenging words daily. *Ten years or nothing.* It was her rally cry. Ten years of amazing; that's what she had experienced. She had to remind herself over and over when bitterness crept into her heart and mind. But, even though they were thankful for the blessing of one more day, they cried together at night, not knowing how many they had left.

Though she relied on Austin's strength when it was just the two of them, she buoyed her tenacity whenever she spoke with AshLynn. She told her granddaughter she would be going to live with Jesus soon. AshLynn didn't fully understand why her grandma couldn't stay with her, but when Ashley read from the Bible, describing how beautiful heaven was, it made AshLynn happy, knowing her grandma would be in the prettiest place in the world.

Gazing out at the rink, Ashley smiled as she watched AshLynn ride Prince. She was a natural. Ashley had no doubt she would be a champion someday, just like her father. C.J. worked with her with such care, firm but gentle. He treated AshLynn like the precious gift that she was.

While Ashley reminisced about the past, Willow slowly walked up the stairs of the porch and gently lowered herself into the chair next to her. Resting her hand on her protruding belly, Willow groaned. With her due date just days away, Ashley anxiously awaited the arrival of her second grandchild. She felt blessed she'd been given enough time to see this little one come into the world.

She smiled at Willow. "I don't think he's going to wait much longer."

"That suits me just fine. I don't think I can handle this heat and this extra weight another day."

Willow and Ashley sat in companionable silence. Ashley looked at daughter-in-law with a sense of pride. She had survived a devastating past and grown into such a beautiful woman. She and C.J. had experienced moments of difficulties those first few months after they were married. Willow would lapse into periods of depression over her past, but they always came through those times stronger and even more committed to each other. Then, after the birth of AshLynn, it seemed as if Willow was finally able to put the demons from her past to rest.

Though she never did go to veterinary school, she spent plenty of time with C.J. assisting him with the horses. Even though C.J. encouraged her to go to school and get her degree, Willow never did. She was content working side-by-side with C.J. and being a mom. She no longer felt the need to prove her worth by having a degree.

Ashley leaned back and allowed her head to rest on the rim of her favorite chair, in her favorite place. *Thank you, God for one more day.*

When Ashley opened her eyes, she found Willow staring at her. "What?"

Willow cleared her throat, "I was just wondering if you were still convinced this one is going to be a boy?" She stroked her belly and smiled.

"Yep. You're carrying him just like I carried C.J. It's a boy all right." Ashley was sure of it. She prayed she was right. She knew how important it was to C.J. to have a boy carry on the Taylor name.

When she heard the screen door shut, Ashley turned to see Austin climb the back porch stairs. He bent down and pressed a kiss to her forehead and looked into her eyes. "How did we do today?"

"Good." Ashley answered quietly. What else could she say? It wasn't like she had accomplished anything, but neither did she feel any worse than she had all month. The doctors had no real answers regarding how much time she had left. Weeks. Months. They could not say for sure. Nor did they put limitations on her. She was allowed to do whatever she wanted, but her body tired easily, and she did little to challenge herself. Being observant was what was important right now. Being with family. Watching them. Listening to them. Enjoying every bout of laughter and every conversation. She wasn't watching life pass her by. Instead, she chose to think of it as life passing by her, allowing her time to enjoy every minute of it.

Done with her ride, AshLynn climbed the porch stairs and gave her a hug. Her clear blue eyes danced with excitement, her pigtails resting on her shoulders. "How'd I do, Grandma? Do you think I'll win?"

"Absolutely, AshLynn. You are going to be the best rider there."

AshLynn's competition was in two days, same as Willow's due date. For AshLynn's sake, Ashley hoped Willow could hold on until Sunday.

"You'll be there, right, Grandma?"

"I wouldn't miss it for the world, but you'd better pray your little brother takes a nap between now and then. We wouldn't want Mommy and Daddy to miss your first competition."

"I know, but they'll be able to see others. I just want to make sure you see me win at least once."

AshLynn's words were not meant to be hurtful, but Willow gasped all the same. Ashley placed her hand on top of Willow's and gave it a squeeze, assuring her it was okay. AshLynn was only speaking what they had talked openly about with her, that her grandma wouldn't be around much longer.

"Don't worry, missy," Austin chimed in. "Wild horses couldn't keep your grandma and me away from your competition, but remember what I said, "Winning is not always the measure of a true champion. It's the way you complete the task." Austin gave AshLynn a slight bop on the nose, as she smiled at him and climbed up into his lap.

"I know, Grandpa, but is it really that bad that I want to win?"

Austin chuckled as he pulled her into a bear hug, knocking her riding helmet right off her head. He squeezed her like he would never let her go. "Of course not, precious . . . of course not."

AshLynn squirmed out of his lap, picked up her helmet, and started down the steps, then quickly turned around and asked, "You did call Aunt Jenna, right? She told me she would talk to the captain, and make sure their boat was back in time."

"They were on a ship, honey," Austin corrected, then answered, "and yes, she and Uncle Matt will be there."

"I thought they were still on their honeymoon?" Ashley asked.

"They got home yesterday."

"Who got home yesterday?" C.J. asked as he climbed the stairs.

"Jenna and Matt."

As C.J. ascended the steps and AshLynn descended, C.J. stopped her. "Where are you off to, little miss?"

"I'm going to give Prince his rubdown. Uncle Billy's going to help me."

"And what else are you going to do?"

AshLynn sighed, "Clean my tack, and muck Prince's stall."

"That's right. And why are you doing that?"

She stood up straight. "Because a true equestrian takes care of the needs of his horse and his equipment," she recited what C.J. told her was the first rule of owning a horse.

He playfully pulled at one of the pigtails. "That's my girl."

AshLynn skipped across the yard while C.J. took a seat next to Willow, a smile stretched across his face.

"She's gonna blow away the competition," he said, like any proud father would, then gently placed his hand on top of Willow's belly. "Any action yet?"

"No, not yet, and now I have to hope he holds off until after Saturday. AshLynn's going to need you at her competition, and if

I'm in labor, I'm going to want your undivided attention."

"Still think it's a boy, huh?"

"That's what your mom keeps telling me." They both looked at Ashley.

She smiled with confidence.

C.J. had the hardest time looking at his mom without crying. The realization that she could be gone before the end of the year made him want to run to the hills and plead with God to take him instead. He knew in his heart of hearts, his family would be devastated if they knew he felt that way, but his mother had done so much for him; he just wished there was something more he could do for her.

He was still struggling with guilt. He hated himself for not noticing sooner, that her health had started to fail. He'd been so caught up in his own little world, he hadn't paid attention to the signs. She had slowed down and stopped coming to the ranch on a daily basis. He just thought she was enjoying her life with Austin and adopting a slower pace.

He should have known better.

C.J. knew there was nothing to gain by second-guessing what he could not change, but his heart ached when he thought about having to do life without her.

"Hey," Willow patted C.J.'s knee, "why don't we have a barbecue? You can make me one of your killer steaks. Maybe that would be enough incentive for this little guy to get moving."

"Sounds good to me. How about you guys?" C.J. looked at Austin, then his mom.

"Sounds perfect," she said.

"Well, if you're doing the cooking, I'll do the cleaning," Austin volunteered.

Ashley rested on the couch, while C.J. and Austin busied themselves with dinner. Willow worked at the table with AshLynn, helping with her homework. Ashley caught Austin staring at her from across the room, a goofy grin on his face. Even with a "kiss the cook" apron and oven mitts on his hands, he was still the handsomest man in the world.

When C.J. came in from the grill, with a plate loaded with steaks, AshLynn put her homework away and everyone found their place at the table. C.J. was the last to sit down and asked AshLynn to say grace.

"Dear Jesus, thank You for this food that You gave us, and for making Prince such a good horse. Please help mommy at the hospital and please let Grandma stay with us as long as You don't need her. I pray I get a brother, and that he looks just like daddy. I love You, Jesus, amen."

Ashley loved that AshLynn's prayers were always direct and to the point. Just like C.J., when he was a little boy, she talked to God like He was her best friend. Ashley gazed around the table while everyone exchanged conversation. Austin and C.J. debated what was the best cut of beef like they did every time they barbecued, and Willow stroked her tummy while she helped AshLynn butter her baked potato.

Life.

Everyday life.

Ashley wanted to freeze-frame moments like this. Slow down time

God, please tell me this is what heaven will be like? That I will be able to see them from Your side . . . to watch them grow, and see the changes in their lives? I hope so. Because I can't imagine leaving them behind.

Willow looked at Ashley from across the table, admiring the woman who'd been like a mother to her.

When Willow had learned of her mother's death not long after C.J. and she got married, it was Ashley who helped her deal with her loss and fill the void that had been missing from her life all along. Willow could not imagine what life was going to be like without this very special woman. She tried not to think about it, knowing God could perform a miracle if He chose to. He had already done it many times in the lives of those that made up the Circle-R Ranch.

Willow prayed every day for just one more.

With dinner almost over, Willow glanced at Austin. He was staring at Ashley. He watched her like a hawk now, and at the slightest sign of discomfort or exhaustion, he encouraged her to lie down so she wouldn't over exert herself.

"I think it's time for someone to call it a night," Austin said as he took his dishes to the sink, then walked back to stand at Ashley's side.

"I'm fine, Austin, really. I was just enjoying watching and listening to you guys, that's all."

He leaned over and kissed her tenderly on the neck. "How about you take a nice relaxing bath and then maybe you and AshLynn can watch a movie in bed?"

"Willy, Ganpa?" AshLynn mumbled around the food in her mouth. "Cool! Ets watch Eeping Buty."

"AshLynn . . . you and Grandma must have seen *Sleeping Beauty* a hundred times already," Willow said, trying to run interference for Ashley's sake. "I'm sure Grandma would rather watch something else. And don't talk with food in your mouth," she reprimanded.

"*Sleeping Beauty* is just fine with me. I'll have Grandpa come and get you when I'm all settled in, okay?"

AshLynn nodded her head quickly, pointing to her mouth, clearly not wanting to get in trouble for talking with food in her mouth again.

Willow waited for Austin and Ashley to leave, then turned to AshLynn. "What is so special about *Sleeping Beauty*? You've watched it at least ten times in the last two weeks."

AshLynn shrugged. "I just don't want Grandma to be afraid of dying. Sleeping Beauty gets woken up by a handsome prince; like Jesus will do when Grandma gets to heaven," AshLynn said, so matter-of-factly before asking to be excused.

Willow watched as C.J. pushed back from the table, tears in his eyes. "I have some work to do in the stables."

She watched out the picture-window, tears streaming down her face as C.J. walked across the yard with his head hung low. Seeing the torment in his eyes was always her undoing. She tried so hard to be strong for his sake, and for AshLynn's, but knowing Ashley wouldn't be with them much longer was devastating. She stroked her tummy. *Come on, little man, she needs to hold you before she goes.*

Austin walked slowly beside Ashley as she made her way upstairs. She knew he would've rather carried her, but she hated feeling like an invalid.

"I'll go start your bath water," Austin said, as she sat on the edge of the bed, in what used to be C.J.'s room—now their room since returning to the ranch.

She stared at the picture over the dresser—the one Simon had taken on their wedding day. The black-and-white photo of Austin kissing her shoulder. It was her favorite.

Closing her eyes, she remembered every nuance of the day, like it was yesterday. The way Austin held her and lightly placed a kiss on her shoulder. The way he looked in his tuxedo shirt and linen pants. She desperately wanted to go back, back to a time when she and Austin were experiencing love brand new and promising their future to each other. She felt like she had not kept up her end of the bargain. Their future had only consisted of a few years, instead of the many they had planned to spend together.

After starting her water, Austin sat alongside her on the bed. She tried to push away her sadness, but Austin knew her too well.

"What is it, Ashley? What are you thinking?"

"It's getting so hard, Austin. I feel myself getting weaker every day, even though I'm trying to be strong. What am I going to do without you? It makes me ache just thinking about it." Ashley stroked at the tears that ran down his cheeks. He was always so strong when he was around C.J., Willow, and AshLynn, but when they were alone, his true emotions always showed.

"I don't know, Ash, because I'm not sure I'll make it without you. You are the air that I breathe, and without you here, I think I'll forget how."

"Don't say that, Austin. You need to be here, for AshLynn and C.J. He's going to need you now more than ever. You know, I was thinking earlier today about how much I wanted you to be in C.J.'s life. When I went to our reunion to find you, I imagined what a wonderful father you could have been to C.J., if only I had let you. But it's happened. You two are inseparable, and I know he loves you as much as any son could love his father. Please be strong for him, Austin. Don't let him get angry or turn his back on God. I need to know when I leave here, he's going to be okay. Promise me, Austin, promise me everything is going to be okay," she pleaded as she fell into his arms, sobbing, needing his reassurance. He held her to his chest, stroking her hair, his tears mingling with hers.

At the sound of running water, Austin kissed the top of Ashley's head, and whispered, "I need to go check on the tub."

The tub was almost overflowing, so he sat on the edge and pulled the plug. As he watched the water subside, tears continued to run down his cheeks.

He felt as if he was dying a little more each day. Every time he looked at Ashley, he realized there would come a day when she would no longer be there. He wanted to be strong for her, but he barely had the strength to make himself go on.

Austin knew this is not what God wanted from him. God expected him to be strong—to draw on his faith—but Austin wasn't sure he could. *You know my heart, God. I'm trying to be strong, but I'm afraid; if this is a test of my faith, I'm not going to pass.* Sitting on the side of the tub, Austin talked with God, arguing that He was making a mistake, apologizing he wasn't being stronger.

My grace is sufficient for you, for My power is made perfect in weakness. The verse in Corinthians washed over Austin, bathing him with comfort. God reminded him, He understood Austin's weaknesses, and would provide His power when the time came.

Digging deep, Austin changed his thinking. Blowing out a cleansing breath, he thanked God for the last several months, months the doctors didn't think Ashley had. Even though she grew weaker every day, God had given them more time together as a gift, not a sentence. God had extended her life once again.

Austin swiped at his tears and straightened his shoulders.

I will not mourn Ashley's death before it comes.

He would have plenty of time for sorrow after she was gone, but while Ashley was still with him, he vowed to enjoy each day as the gift that it was.

EPILOGUE

Austin Carrington Taylor II came into the world quietly on September 10th, weighing in at a little over eight pounds. To his credit, he'd done the polite thing and waited until after AshLynn had won her first championship. AshLynn was amazed by her baby brother, and Austin Sr. had been reduced to tears when he found out C.J. had given him a namesake.

The arrival of A.J.—Austin Jr.—filled the ranch with joy again and the old house with life. Even so, Ashley could feel herself getting weaker. She barely made it up the stairs at night and found herself wondering what it would be like to wake up in the arms of Jesus.

God had filled her with peace after A.J.'s birth. No longer was she angry with Him or pleading for a miracle. She was ready to go home. God had allowed her enough time to come to terms with her passing. Each day, she thanked Him for the many precious gifts He'd given her over the years. Even the darker periods in her life, she looked back on with thankfulness, for if not for those hard times, she never would've known how rich a life she had led.

Ashley had only one more prayer; that she would make it until Christmas.

Lord, it has been AshLynn's constant prayer, that I be with her and A.J. on Christmas Day. Please give me the strength to celebrate Your birth, and ring in the New Year, just one more time. Be with Austin when I pass. I know I am ready, but I fear he is not. Strengthen him, Lord. Encourage him each day. Be with C.J. as he raises the beautiful family You have blessed him with. I am so proud of the husband, father, and man of God he's become. You gave me an amazing family, a precious gift. I leave them in Your safe care because I know You love them even more than I do.

I find it hard to sleep at night when I have so much I want to say, but I guess I will be with You soon enough, so let me use what strength I have while I am here with my family. I love You, Lord, and I know that You know best. Amen.

Ashley rolled over and put her head on Austin's chest. She fell asleep listening to the beating heart of the man she loved more than life itself.

Christmas was ushered in on the heels of a freak storm that actually brought snow to the foothills of the canyon. Ashley watched, from her place on the porch, the excitement in AshLynn's eyes when she saw the winter wonderland. She was off the porch in seconds, scooping it up—throwing it in the air. Though there wasn't enough snow to make snow angels, there was enough for a snowball fight. AshLynn shrieked and giggled when Grandpa helped her make snowballs and teamed up against her daddy. They were all kids on a day like this, and Ashley loved watching them play together.

The rest of the day was filled with Christmas traditions. Their cinnamon roll breakfast. Reading the Christmas Story. Opening presents. Singing Christmas carols. Then, after dinner, they all curled up in front of the television and watched the traditional showing of *It's a Wonderful Life*.

Willow was busy with A.J., while AshLynn brushed the hair of her first American Girl doll. C.J. was building Willow's Christmas present in the corner, while Ashley snuggled close to Austin.

Ashley listened to the T.V. with her eyes closed as she breathed in the scent of her family. It was intoxicating. She wanted to bask in it as long as she could.

"Mommy, do angels really earn their wings, like Clarence did?" AshLynn asked from her place on the floor.

"I don't know, AshLynn, why?"

"Because I think Grandma deserves the biggest pair of wings, because she is the bestest grandma in the whole wide world."

Ashley looked at Willow, and saw a flood of emotions fill her eyes, as she pressed A.J. to her chest. And when she turned to C.J., she saw him squeeze his eyes shut, trying to force back his emotions. Knowing neither of them had the composure to answer AshLynn, she spoke up.

"I sure hope so, sweetie. In fact, that's how you can find me, when you get to heaven. You can look for the biggest pair of wings and know I will be the one wearing them."

AshLynn got up from her place on the floor and crawled up on the couch next to Ashley. Snuggling her head next to Ashley's heart, she looked up at her with her beautiful blue eyes. "Don't go, Grandma. I know you said Jesus needs your help, but I want you here with me. How is A.J. going to know he had the best grandma in the whole wide world if you're not here?"

"Well, I guess you'll just have to tell him, sweetie. Besides, every time he plays with Grandpa, he'll know he has the best grandparents in the world *and* in heaven."

Ashley was the only one who had been able to control her emotions that night. When she headed off to bed, C.J. held her for a long time. She could feel his struggle. "I love you, Mom."

"I love you, too, Christopher. I'm so proud of you, and the man you've become. Love your family well. And take care of Austin for me."

Austin held her all night, willing her to be with him again in the morning, which she was.

It wasn't until a cold night in January that Ashley felt the breath of God blow across her face. She knew then she would soon be home in the arms of Jesus. She felt the strength in her body return as she walked down a wintery path of white. The only thing that went with her was the scent of her family. It would serve as a reminder of the love they had shared and the incredible life she had led.

She would hold on to it until they were all reunited.

A reunion God had planned before the beginning of time.

ABOUT THE AUTHOR

Tamara Tilley writes from her home at Hume Lake Christian Camps, located in the beautiful Sequoia National Forest. She and her husband, Walter, have been on full-time staff at Hume for over twenty years. Tamara is a retail manager and an active book reviewer. You can read her reviews on her blog at http://tamara-tilley.blogspot.com. Along with reading, spending time with her grandkids, and crafting cards, she loves connecting with readers at www.tamaratilley.com. Or on Facebook at https://facebook.com/tamara.tilley.author.